BRENNA EHRLICH

KILLING TIME

inkyard
PRESS

Recycling programs for this product may not exist in your area.

ISBN-13: 978-1-335-41867-8

Killing Time

For questions and comments about the quality of this book, please contact us at CustomerService@Harlequin.com.

Inkyard Press
22 Adelaide St. West, 41st Floor
Toronto, Ontario M5H 4E3, Canada
www.InkyardPress.com

Printed in U.S.A.

For my family—Ehrlich, Enos, Nedds, and Riggs

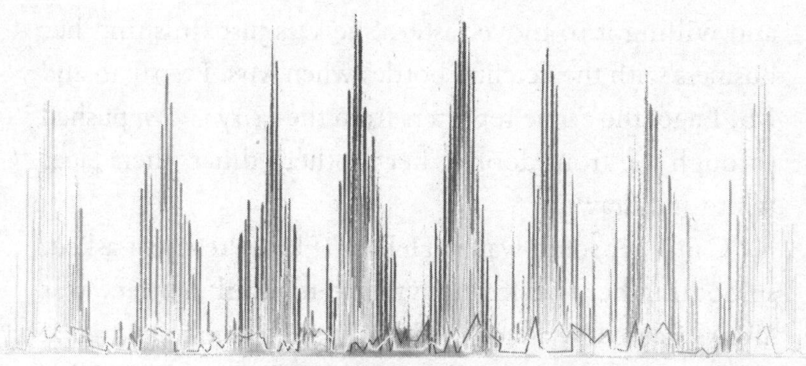

CHAPTER ONE

After that summer, Natalie Temple would forever associate the smell of ketchup with death. Her hometown, Ferry, Connecticut, was in the midst of one of its famous heat waves as Natalie finished up her shift at her mom's diner, marrying half-empty bottles as it got dark out. She had spent the evening sliding ice cubes down her freckled neck and across her collarbones as she served up burgers to sweating summer kids fresh from the sidewalks. They'd play in the shadows until their parents called them home from under the porch lights: packing like sardines into someone's shed, hunting fireflies by the pine trees, slurping rapidly melting ice-cream cones from Sammy's Shack, a roadside spot flanked by the ocean and the graveyard.

Ferry was any neighborhood in summertime, and Natalie was any kid with a summer job, watching the clock and willing it to move faster. She was just finishing her business with the ketchup bottles when Mrs. Pressman and Mr. Lugo, the crime reporters from the *Ferry Caller*, pushed through the front door of her mother's diner, their faces white and drawn.

"Can I get some water, Helen?" Flora Pressman asked, smoothing her frizzled ponytail to no avail; her face was always framed by a halo of flyaways. She plunked down at the counter and guzzled the water Natalie's mother, Helen Temple, placed in front of her. Henry Lugo settled onto his stool and, despite the sweat streaming down his bald head, ordered a hot coffee.

"Long day?" Helen asked, leaning on the counter, fanning herself with a menu. "Did a bird get into the Shop-Rite again?" Ferry wasn't exactly a hotbed of crime, much to Natalie's chagrin: she wasn't entirely sure why the paper needed a crime reporter, let alone two. People kept their hedges trimmed and their noses clean. Parents had jobs in offices that their children didn't understand, and everyone went to the beach on the weekends to turn like rotisserie chickens in the sun. It was more tourist destination than town—its seaport teeming with antique boats, the aquarium boasting daily sea lion shows. The same creatures doing the same tricks year after year as the kids got older, left and then came back to have kids of their own.

Natalie always felt like there was something darker under the soil, though, like a hand struggling to burst from the grave in an old movie. That perfection had to come at a cost. Not that she had experienced firsthand any real darkness in her eighteen years. It was just a hunch—and she was an avid fan of the hunch. Or maybe it was that she just *hoped* her town wasn't as utterly boring as it seemed.

Mrs. Pressman shook her head, draining her glass, and tears started running down her cheeks. Natalie's hands stilled, and her breath froze: an adult crying was distinctly *wrong*, like a pet talking or something. She kept quiet, despite her alarm. It seemed that the adults had forgotten that she stood by the jukebox, surrounded by ketchup bottles, and she didn't want them to remember her—or their manners—and hush up.

When Natalie had started getting interested in true crime a few years back, Helen had hastily put the kibosh on her intrigue. Natalie wasn't entirely sure why her mother was so vehemently against the subject; she figured it was just part of Helen's generalized anxiety about the world at large. She did know, however, that Helen would not like it if she knew her daughter sat up nights poring over books about the Golden State Killer and the Zodiac, or about the hours she spent on true-crime message boards, trading theories with faceless strangers. She would especially hate Natalie's blood-drenched podcast, *Killing Time*—if she knew that it existed, which, thankfully, she did not. Sometimes, when Natalie listened to old episodes, she kind of scared herself. But it was hard not to get carried away in the drama.

"You know I worked in the city before this. Ten years," Mrs. Pressman said, accepting another glass of water. Helen nodded. "Well, this one… It was worse than anything I saw there. Burned into my brain. Will be for a long time.

Found her at the bottom of the stairs. It was...bad," she continued, playing with her wedding ring. "The worst part is? She was John's *teacher.*"

Natalie felt the fine hairs on her arms rise, a chill like a kiss racing up the nape of her neck. Jonathan Pressman was in her class—or had been, before they'd graduated the week before. Natalie and her mom usually had Thanksgiving at the Pressmans' house, and she and John had paid their dues at the kids' table together. He also interned with her at the *Ferry Caller.*

Mr. Lugo nodded. "Yeah, Katie had her, too." Katie Lugo, another Thanksgiving kids'-table regular—also Natalie's best friend and podcast cohost. "She was her favorite. A good woman. Whip-smart."

Pressman wiped her eyes, her hands trembling now. "Who the hell would want to kill Lynn Halsey?"

Natalie's hand seemed to atrophy around the neck of a ketchup bottle, and it plummeted to the floor, red haloing the black-and-white tile, dripping down the front of her shirt. The smell of sugary tomato inundated the air. Bile rose in her throat. Mrs. Halsey taught senior-year English. She had written Natalie's recommendation letter to the University of Pennsylvania. She had helped Natalie get a full scholarship, meeting up for hours after school to go over her essay until it shone. Now she was dead, and the last thing Natalie had said to her had been "You never cared about me."

The shame threatening to choke her, Natalie thought of her cat, Lemons, hit by a car when she was ten. She had found him on their lawn by the mailbox, his head dented and his ribs jutting through his skin where some neighborhood dog had probably gotten to him. She had just stared down at his inside-out body, lying on the lush grass under the spring sun, a bee lazily alighting onto his nose, then moving on in search of something more fragrant. It seemed impossible—the carnage—and how everything around the cat kept going despite it.

Natalie didn't remember sitting down, but she suddenly felt her head resting on the table and the vinyl of the booth stuck to the backs of her legs. Her mother sat next to her, tracing small circles in the center of her back. She took a shuddering breath and sat up, blinking away a tide of dizziness. Her mother's hand went for another rotation before Natalie shook it off, cringing. Helen was the reason she'd left things so poorly with Mrs. Halsey. How dare her mother try to comfort her now? As her eyes cleared, she saw Mr. Lugo and Mrs. Pressman staring at her, sweating. She pushed a hand through her pale blond hair and tried for a shaky smile—for their benefit, not Helen's. They hadn't ruined her life.

"I'm sorry, Helen," Mr. Lugo said, speaking over her head and abandoning his coffee as he rose to his feet. His shoes were shiny, Natalie noticed through her haze, and she wondered how he kept getting up and polishing them when he had to report on things like murder and mayhem. It seemed pointless, somehow. "I didn't see her there..." he continued, muttering another apology as he practically sprinted toward the exit. Mrs. Pressman took a final sip of her water and stood up less hurriedly. She knelt down by Natalie and put a cool hand on her knee, bare and bruised below the hem of her cutoffs from pedaling around on her bike. Helen gave her friend a warning look but didn't interfere.

"We'll find out what happened to her, honey," Mrs. Pressman said, her voice quiet and even, eyes level with Natalie's. "I promise you."

Natalie nodded. Lemons and Mrs. Halsey flitted through her mind again, the unreality of their deaths. The largeness of Mrs. Halsey's, so much *bigger* than a cat's: a human was gone, would never come back, and someone had made her that way. Someone still out there. Someone she might even know.

Mrs. Pressman gave her knee a final squeeze and turned to follow her coworker. The door jangled open, and a blast of hot air eddied into the weakly air-conditioned diner, bringing with it the smell of impending summer storms and the arrival of a single bee. The insect landed on the livid pool of ketchup oozing like tar across the linoleum, and Natalie sat and watched the red spread.

Natalie had first met Mrs. Halsey the second week of her freshman year, not because she had a class with her or anything so mundane. Natalie had been called into the school counselor's office after writing an essay for English class about Ray Bradbury's short story, "The Crowd," which she compared to the 1964 murder of Kitty Genovese. Natalie's thesis: human nature is dark and terrible, and we're all doomed. Her teacher, Mr. Miller, had been less than thrilled with her moody conclusion and had promptly sent her to Mrs. Ketchum, the school shrink.

Sitting in Mrs. Ketchum's office, Natalie studied her

lap and assured the spindly, bored-looking woman, who sipped primly from a mug with a dog dressed as a nobleman on it, that she had no suicidal or homicidal ideations. She was just incredibly realistic about human nature, in her opinion, and also maybe the slightest bit jaded; it wasn't her fault her teacher didn't understand nuance. Natalie had been told that high school sucked, but faced with the bald reality of what she saw as its aversion to critical thinking and creativity, the next four years seemed insurmountable. At least until she met Lynn Halsey.

After Mrs. Ketchum released her with a final promise that she would check out some of the wonderful clubs the school had on offer—except improv, Natalie had her limits—Natalie fumed her way into the hallway, her paper crumpled in her hands. She had gotten a C due to her supposedly *weak thesis*. She didn't get Cs. Tears threatened to overflow the corners of her eyes as she made her way to her locker, but before she could dig in her pocket and text Katie about the indignity of the whole ordeal, someone tapped her on the shoulder. Expecting the counselor to appear with a pamphlet of some sort, Natalie whirled around, a smile plastered on her face that she hoped read as *I'm fine! I'm excited to try new activities!* But instead of Mrs. Ketchum, there was a fine-boned woman with long, dark hair pulled back into a ponytail. Her eyes were bright blue and, Natalie noticed, she was wearing a battered leather jacket that seemed far too cool for a teacher.

"You're Natalie, right?" she asked, gesturing at the paper clenched in the girl's hand. *Natalie Temple* was clearly printed across the top, but that still didn't explain why the woman had stopped her.

Natalie nodded, dumb. The woman didn't look like a teacher—and it wasn't just the jacket. Her eyes still had some light in them. Her mouth had fine lines around it that suggested she laughed more than once a year.

The woman nodded back. "I thought so. Mr. Miller told me about your essay. About Kitty Genovese."

Natalie felt the tears threatening to spill once more. It had gotten around school that she was a freak. Obsessed with murder. Probably in need of a padded cell and restraints. She was pretty sure her mother would let her be home-schooled if she asked. In fact, Helen would love it: mother and daughter living together in quiet solitude until they were eaten by cats—cats they didn't even own.

The teacher seemed to see the terror reflected in Natalie's eyes, because she reached out a tentative hand and touched the girl's shoulder. "Relax. He told me about you because he thought I could help. I'm Mrs. Halsey. I teach senior English, but I also run the True Crime Club here at East Ferry. I thought you might want to join."

Natalie's eyes widened. She knew there were clubs for math and science and football and whatever, but she never imagined anyone else at East Ferry High would be interested in true crime. She and Katie had started their podcast the summer before, but no one really listened to it except for a couple of internet randos.

The teacher held up a hand as if attempting to temper Natalie's excitement. "It's not official yet because there's a dearth of members, but the would-be president, Jessica, has asked me to be the adviser, and I jumped at the chance. We just need two more on the docket to get our picture in the yearbook."

Natalie stared at the trim woman with her bouncing ponytail and soft eyes. "*You're* into true crime?"

Mrs. Halsey laughed. "Well, I'm into a good story. And crime has a lot of them."

"Fuck yeah, it does!" Natalie exclaimed, forgetting she was talking to a teacher for just a second before blushing. Natalie's mom always warned her about swearing too much, about how it made her sound stupid and young—the exact opposite of the poised journalist she longed to be. *Excellent first impression*, she chided herself. *You sound like an idiot.*

Mrs. Halsey only laughed, though; then her face got more serious. "But the *telling* of those stories… Well, that could use a little work. When it comes to both the genre and your essay."

"What do you mean?" Natalie asked.

"Take Kitty there, for instance." The woman gestured at Natalie's essay. "Your piece made some great connections between Bradbury and the original crime—the passivity of the bystander, the complicity of the crowd—"

Natalie snorted. She knew it wasn't a C assignment. Maybe this woman could get her grade fixed. She was an English teacher, after all. "Tell that to Mr. Miller…" she said, half-serious.

"But," the woman interjected, "you're ignoring an important ramification of Kitty's death. One that debunks your theory that the world is some soulless hellscape." She smiled like she had a secret, and Natalie couldn't help but like this strange, little woman. "Because of Kitty's death," she continued, "we have 9-1-1, a direct line to help when someone's in peril. It was directly inspired by Kitty's situation. A great invention, I would say. One worthy of its own story."

"I didn't know that," Natalie murmured, crumpling up her paper further. Maybe she'd deserved that C after all. Maybe just because she was smart in middle school didn't mean she'd cut it in high school. Fantasies of homeschooling once more flitted through her head.

"That's because you were just focusing on the crime," said Mrs. Halsey. "Which is perfectly natural," she added when Natalie's face fell even more. "*It bleeds, it leads*, right? But what makes the salacious the stupendous?"

Natalie frowned, at a loss.

"The story," the woman said, pointing at Natalie. "What happens around the blood. What came before and after. Otherwise, you're just rubbernecking."

The bell rang then, interrupting Natalie as she opened her mouth, eager to find out more, to ask the woman how she knew so much about Kitty and murder and true crime.

"I have to get to class, but it was nice to meet you, Natalie," Mrs. Halsey said, extending a hand. "And I'll see you after school in the library for the first official meeting of the East Ferry High True Crime Club."

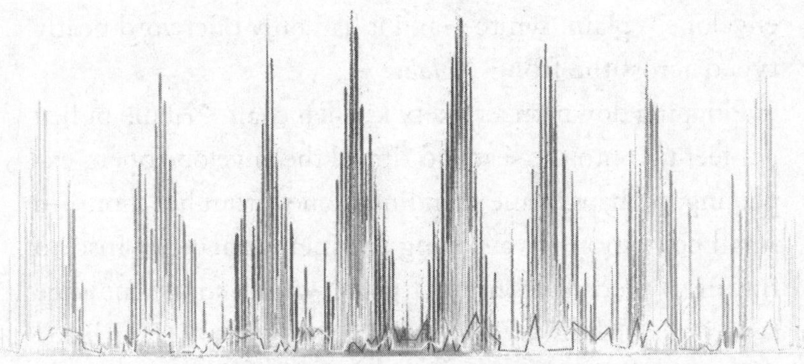

CHAPTER TWO

Natalie didn't ask her mom if she wanted to come to Lynn Halsey's memorial, which was just as well because, apparently, Helen did not want to go. When Natalie came down for breakfast that morning, she found a note under the orange juice saying that Helen was heading to dojo in the next town over to train for a while—which meant she was either stressed, angry, or both. (Helen said a while back she had started doing karate for self-defense, not that Natalie was aware of anything she'd need to defend herself against in Ferry.)

Natalie balled up the note and threw it on the floor, equal parts relieved and pissed off by her mother's absence, but she quickly forgot all about it when she saw the envelope leaning against the box of cinnamon cereal her mom had left sitting out for her. It was your standard business envelope—plain, white—and it had only one word neatly typed across the front: *Natalie.*

Plopping down on a rickety kitchen chair, Natalie pulled her feet up onto the seat and ripped the envelope open, expecting, perhaps, some spending money from her mom—a small contrition for avoiding the memorial—but instead finding a piece of computer paper with a single message typed out on it: *Stay out of it. I'm warning you.* Her heart did a cold, little leap like it always did when the first body was found in one of her books, then confusion set in. She blinked, scanning the words again, flipping the paper over to see if she'd missed something—a name, an address, anything. But that was it. Just those two ominous sentences. She shivered despite the heat of the kitchen, which was barely mitigated by the lazily oscillating ceiling fan. Her mom was too cheap for AC.

Cereal forgotten, Natalie pushed away from the table and scanned the room as if the toaster or the microwave might suddenly fill her in on where, exactly, the letter had come from. The kitchen seemed eerily quiet in the diffuse morning light, the only sound the birds that spent the day gossiping at the feeder in the backyard. Natalie pulled out her phone, typing off a quick message to her mom.

Did you leave me a note?

It seemed the mostly likely scenario, since the envelope had been on their kitchen table, but a vague threat wasn't exactly Helen's style. No, her mom was more direct than all that, much to her daughter's annoyance. And then there was the *it* she was supposed to be staying out of. She could guess what that was: Mrs. Halsey's murder was the only thing that had happened in Ferry for decades, as far as she was concerned. But someone would have to know about her podcast to suggest that she stay out of anything, and no one really knew about that aside from Katie and the internet randos. They had one all the way in Mount Carroll, Illinois (wherever that was). Could one of them have turned stalker? Broken into her house to… What? Warn her not to discuss a very local crime with her audience of roughly three people who had probably clicked on her podcast by mistake?

Three bubbles appeared immediately on her phone screen. Natalie scoffed. Her mom was supposed to be sparring. Did she keep her cell phone tucked into her black belt?

Yes, honey, I'm at the dojo. Be back around 4.

Natalie snorted. Well after the memorial. No, another one, she typed, her fingers shaking slightly. This was all too bizarre. In an envelope?

There was one with the paper that I brought in for you. More dots, as if her mom were trying for casual. Why? Who is it from? Katie?

Natalie rolled her eyes. Helen would have implanted a tracking device in her daughter's neck if she could, like those chips they have for cats and dogs—watched her roam the town on her trusty path from school to Katie's to home, called the cops if she veered off course. It was a wonder she hadn't just opened the envelope herself. There wasn't time to fume, though, now that there was a mysterious, threatening letter with her name on it. Which Natalie was aware sounded like a sentence from a bad teenage soap opera. That didn't negate its existence, though.

She sank back into her chair, staring at the words marching across the page. *Stay out of it. I'm warning you.* It *could* be Katie playing a bad joke, but that didn't seem likely, as Katie could never keep a secret and would have spilled that morning, when they were texting about the memorial. Feeling silly, Natalie sniffed at the paper. Nothing. As if it had just materialized on the table, origin-free. She considered calling the police, but that would mean telling them about her podcast, which would mean telling her mom about her podcast, which would mean never seeing the sun again. Instead, she shoved the note into her backpack—not bothering to put away the juice and cereal—and trundled outside to her bike and Mrs. Halsey's memorial. She would let it all stew, she decided. Maybe an answer would come to her while she was biking to the high school. She always thought better when she was in motion, legs pumping and lungs full of clean air.

It was as hot if not hotter than yesterday, and beads of sweat rolled down Natalie's forehead into her eyes as she crested the hill toward the school that had been her de facto prison for the last four years—the only bright spot being a woman who would no longer walk its halls. The only teacher who didn't hold her eccentricities at arm's length.

The Halsey house wasn't on Natalie's route, but she could feel its presence a few streets over—could imagine the yellow police tape and silence—and a tremor traveled over her neck like phantom fingers.

The True Crime Club had only lasted for one year, officially; after Jessica graduated and her parents effectively bought her way into Columbia, Katie and Natalie were the only members, meaning that the club was no longer valid in the school's eyes. (No yearbook picture, which was good since Natalie didn't relish explaining *that* to her mom. She used to lie and say she was staying after school to study until, well, it all went to hell when she said what she said.) Still, Mrs. Halsey kept up their meetings, critiquing the relative merit of different podcasts, documentaries, and true-crime books through the lens of story. She was a fan of gripping, well-researched accounts of criminal investigations, like Michelle McNamara's inquiry into the Golden State Killer, but felt a decided disdain for podcasts like this really popular one called *My Murder Obsession*, which was basically just two guys discussing their favorite murder mysteries. She thought the name was bad enough, but she couldn't stand the gleeful, error-riddled way the hosts talked about crime. She was a stickler for accuracy—and empathy. "If you can't get the facts straight, you don't deserve the story," she used to say.

As she coasted past Sammy's Shack and the flinty sea, Natalie wondered what Mrs. Halsey would think of the note on her kitchen table: *Stay out of it.* Her legs pumped harder, sweat running down to her eyes as she squinted into the sun, her breath getting ragged. Lynn Halsey was the only person she wanted to talk to right now, and she couldn't because she was dead. The thought brought sudden, angry tears to her eyes. She was dead, and there was nothing Natalie could do about it. Who was the letter writer to tell her *stay out of it*? How to care? Maybe her mom *had* written the note. Maybe she had found out about her podcast somehow and wanted to punish her. Helen hated Lynn Halsey; Natalie knew that. Tears flooded her eyes as she pulled into the school parking lot, dropping the toes of her black shoes to the ground to steady herself as her vision swam.

The last time she had spoken to her teacher was at the diner midway through senior year. She had been crying—or trying not to, rather. Her shift had ended, and she was crammed in a booth where her mother couldn't see her—couldn't send her home and straight to her room. The night before had been bad. The kind of bad that made your stomach heavy and your mouth flood with acid when you thought about it. She and Katie had been celebrating getting into the colleges of their choice by having a clandestine marathon of the worst true-crime movies on offer. Straight-to-streaming shit. Cheesy cable fare. Trash. Helen's rules were pretty clear when it came to her daughter's interests: fine, she could study it in school, but true crime as entertainment was completely off-limits. Sure, she got away with the occasional horror movie or novel, but true stories were, for some untold reason, strictly verboten.

Which was why she and Katie had waited until Helen went to a Garden Club cocktail night to indulge. Helen, not being the biggest drinker, had come home in the middle of a truly terrible early-thousands clunker called *Teacher's Pet*—all about a TA who had an affair with his student, then killed her—and had lost her shit. She'd gone so far as to threaten to move to college with Natalie and live in her dorm room, which seemed like an empty threat if you didn't know Helen, who wouldn't let Natalie sleep over at Katie's until she was thirteen.

"You okay, Natalie?" Mrs. Halsey asked, sliding into the booth across from her, holding a to-go bag of burgers and fries. She was wearing her leather jacket and had her hair up in a blue paisley scarf, her cheeks pink from the early spring chill; she brought with her the smell of the omnipresent daffodils that blanketed Ferry this time of year.

Natalie shook her head mutely, picking at a plate of cold fries she had pilfered from the cook. People in town knew her mother was strict, but she wasn't quite sure she wanted her role model to know that Helen had had a meltdown over a Lifetime Channel movie.

"I dunno," she muttered, chastising herself internally for her lack of eloquence. She always tried to speak as intelligently as possible in front of her favorite teacher, but right now she was too wrung-out to care. Her mother's overprotectiveness was a shroud, stifling and heavy. And what was so ironic was Natalie had gotten into true crime because of her mom in the first place—she'd found a box of old books in the attic when she was twelve about the Manson murders, the Night Stalker, all the big ones. She had read them under the covers until all hours, equal parts scared and thrilled. She loved it when the killers were caught, the intricate work it took to track them down. That is, until her mom found out and burned all the books in the yard with the autumn leaves. She wouldn't even tell Natalie where they'd come from in the first place.

"Did something happen with Katie? A friend?" Mrs. Halsey pressed, her voice so gentle and caring that Natalie caved.

"My mom flipped out on me last night," she choked out, studying the table. "I was watching some stupid true-crime movie, and she just…lost it." Natalie dug her chipped nails into the red vinyl of the booth and let it all spill out. "She's just so controlling. Like, why does she care what I watch? I'm eighteen. I'm an adult, basically. And I'm good!" She raised her eyes to look at her teacher, who was studying Natalie with a furrowed brow. "I don't break curfew. I have, like, no social life. I don't drink. So why can't I just… read and watch and do what I want? Who am I hurting?"

Mrs. Halsey gave a sad smile. "I understand, Natalie. It's hard being eighteen. Almost independent, but not quite. But, I promise, it'll get easier. You might even miss your mom worrying about you."

Natalie grunted and folded her arms. "I doubt it."

Mrs. Halsey laughed, then steepled her hands on the diner table. "I'm confused, though, Natalie. Why would a movie upset your mom so much when you're in a true-crime club at school?"

Natalie swallowed hard. In her fit of rage, she'd forgotten all about forging her mother's signature all those years ago to join Mrs. Halsey's after-school group. She had forgotten the countless lies she'd told. Or maybe she was just subconsciously tired of it all.

"You're in what?" Helen appeared behind her like the ghoul from that horror movie—the one that just slowly wanders after its prey until it wears it down and eats it. Natalie didn't turn around. Instead, she gritted her teeth and dug her nails even deeper into the booth, anchoring herself to the spot. She couldn't even sit with her favorite teacher for five minutes without her mom butting in. Without her ruining everything.

"You didn't know about this?" Mrs. Halsey asked Helen, as if Natalie weren't there, which Natalie found hard to believe, considering anger was radiating off her like a bad aura. Why did everyone treat her like a child? Like she couldn't make her own choices without consulting her mother first? Why didn't they *see* her?

Helen shook her head, her eyes locked on Natalie's teacher, a twin rage coursing through her. The pencil she used to take orders snapped in her hand, but she didn't seem to notice the pieces as they clattered to the floor and rolled to rest under the booth.

"I'm sorry, Helen," Mrs. Halsey sputtered, getting to her feet, looking between mother and daughter, both practically vibrating with indignation. "I thought you knew about the club." She raised a conciliatory hand. "And, really, it's all educational. We talk about story and methodology and..." The words died on her lips as Natalie's mother shook her head again.

"I appreciate all you've done for Natalie, Lynn, but we have rules," Helen said in a voice befitting an android. "This stuff is not entertainment. If she wants to go to school and learn the proper way to engage with it, then fine. But no clubs. No movies. No bullshit."

Mrs. Halsey cut in. "I would hardly call our club bull—" Natalie couldn't help smiling, which didn't make matters any better. Her mom gave a look filled with such pure menace she dropped her eyes to her feet.

"I don't care," Helen snapped, smoothing her apron as if eradicating the wrinkles would fix everything. As if she could control the world with her nervous hands. "My kid, my rules. Now, I think you should leave."

Mrs. Halsey opened her mouth, shooting Natalie an inscrutable look. She took a step toward the door.

"Please, don't go," Natalie asked in a small voice before she knew the words were coming out of her mouth. "You don't have to listen to her. Please."

With her hands tucked into her jacket pockets and her hair coming free from her scarf, the teacher suddenly looked younger than she was. She was probably the same age as her mom, thirty-eight, but Helen's face was much harder. Likely because she'd had Natalie so young, because she'd been worrying for eighteen years. "I'm sorry, Natalie." She glanced at her bag of food but made no move to pick it up. "I think I should go..."

Natalie got to her feet then, leveled her eyes at her teacher, watching her one tether to everything she cared about cut her free, let her go. "You never cared about me," she said finally, seething and holding Mrs. Halsey's eyes for a long moment before retreating to the kitchen so she wouldn't have to see her mentor go, regretting the words as soon as they left her mouth. She turned back to stop her, to apologize, but her teacher was already gone.

Mrs. Halsey deserved more than that. More than her mom's disdain and her own parting words. She deserved to be remembered. To be avenged. And no anonymous note writer could tell Natalie otherwise. An idea that prompted a mix of excitement and shame deep down in her stomach germinated in Natalie's head as she pushed through those familiar swinging doors and entered the bizarre world that is school during summer.

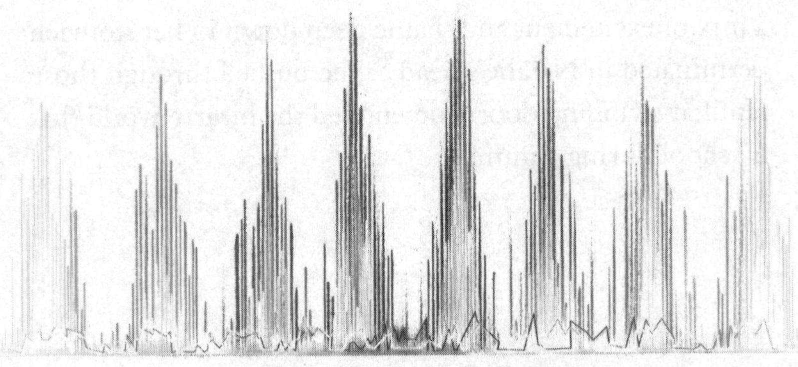

CHAPTER THREE

Being at school after hours always felt especially wrong. Whether it was for parent–teacher meetings or school dances, the worn carpets just seemed sadder outside the context of academic monotony and social terror. It felt even more wrong to Natalie, then, to be sitting in her former high school's gym, a few weeks after graduation, to memorialize her favorite teacher. The gym was the biggest space that Ferry had, though, and a lot of people wanted to honor Mrs. Halsey, from the yoga instructor at the YMCA with his storm-cloud explosion of gray hair to the manager of the grocery store with his bumpy red arms (who also served as a substitute history teacher).

The school's industrial AC was cranked to arctic temperatures, and Natalie felt goose bumps breaking out on her arms, exposed by the sleeveless black dress she'd taken from her mom's closet. She wasn't used to wearing dresses, and she ached to trade it in for her more familiar shorts and T-shirt. Lately it was getting harder not to see a stranger in the mirror, and this morning, in her mother's dress, she barely recognized herself: she looked older, her formerly rounded cheeks higher, her recently cleared skin pale against the black of the dress. She was starting to look like an adult; her overgrown blond hair was the only thing that made her still look like a kid. While everyone else had started experimenting with their hair in middle school—Katie had green hair until she dyed it black for her MIT interview—Natalie's still hung straight down her back, all one length. Her mom was not so secretly pleased that she had never chopped it off.

At least the discomfort distracted her from the sea of grief rippling around the gym. Pretty Miss Grove, the freshman math teacher, wept by the doorway—until Mr. Quirk, the gym teacher, finally led her out into the hallway—and her fellow former seniors leaned on each other for support, summer and sadness dissolving the cliques. Would they all cry today and forget by tomorrow? Probably. Summer was long and held the promise of parties and, after that, college. Would anyone remember Mrs. Halsey when they finally left home? Would they care? Or would she just become a faded photo in a yearbook, an anecdote about small-town life? The thought of Mrs. Halsey being forgotten, being relegated to her classmates' hazy memories, made her furious, somehow. Mrs. Halsey was unforgettable—she was *special*. Natalie resolved then that she wouldn't let them forget. And she certainly wouldn't *stay out of it.* Instead, she would immerse herself in Mrs. Halsey, her life, her death, her impact. And she would start right now—while her classmates actually still seemed to give a damn.

Natalie shot a quick glance to either side of her to make sure no one was paying attention and pulled out her phone, flipping to her recording app. Trying for casual, she held the device out to catch the chatter of the auditorium: the muffled crying, the awkward laughter, the muttering of the low-voiced teachers. She wanted authenticity, and people might not give her that if they knew she was recording.

"What are you doing?" Katie asked, shivering in the chill. She blew on her fingers and stuck them under her arms, her own tight black dress straining as she perched on her painfully quiet boyfriend Simon's lap. (It was fitting Katie was using him as a chair since Natalie always secretly thought he had the magnetism of a piece of furniture. A table, maybe.) Natalie recognized the dress as the one Katie had worn to Grandma Lugo's funeral back in eighth grade—the puffy sleeves, the satin bow. The fact that neither of them even had proper funeral attire made Natalie even more sad. They were so young, on the cusp of their future; death had previously been so far out of reach in their boring little town that hardly anyone her age even thought to prepare for it.

Natalie looked down at the seconds ticking by on her recording app. Would Katie understand what she wanted to do? She'd already decided not to tell her about the note—Katie's dad was a crime reporter, after all, which was like one step away from a cop—but she needed her help if she wanted to do this right. To make a real podcast, not just an unorganized half hour or so during which she and Katie talked about whatever murder or murderer interested them that day. *Killing Time* wasn't supposed to be serious: it was a way to blow off steam in between epic study sessions. Still, she had listened to enough *real* podcasts, had enough lessons from Mrs. Halsey on story. And Katie certainly had the technical know-how. Who was to stop *them* from reporting the facts, as they happened, instead of picking them apart secondhand, decades later?

"Hello, Natalie?" Katie waved a hand in front of her friend's face. "You're zoning out creepily at a memorial service. People are starting to stare."

Natalie blinked back to the present just as Katie shoved her arms even deeper into her armpits. Simon seemed nonplussed; as usual, he was working on a crossword puzzle on his phone, an obsession that made no sense to Natalie, as he was neither elderly nor infirm. He did have the personality and coloring of tapioca pudding, though, a favorite treat among both groups. Natalie was at a loss as to why her brash best friend liked him. Maybe because he didn't get in the way.

"Yeah, well..." Natalie said, kicking one of her mother's black pumps against the already-scuffed bleachers. "And you're touching your pits at a memorial service, so I guess we're even."

"Dude, I'm sorry, but I'm freezing." Katie shivered dramatically. "I loved Mrs. Halsey, you know that, but everyone's turning into Popsicles."

"Get your hands out of there," Natalie retorted, gently

pushing her friend's arms down to her sides. "Here, I'll rub them for you."

She put down her memorial program to grab Katie's hands, catching sight of Mrs. Halsey's smiling face on the cover. How could someone hurt *her*? Natalie wasn't sure if she would ever know the answer to that question, no matter how much digging she did.

Katie sighed as her hands warmed up, and she nodded her thanks. "Anyway." She turned to her friend. "What's up?"

"I have an idea..." Natalie began, a palpable shake inching into her voice. "And it's a really, *really* good one... But I'm not sure this is the place to—"

Simon shot her a rare direct look, his watery blue eyes narrowed, and she realized she was talking way too loudly. She leaned closer, but as she opened her mouth to continue, the lights flickered on and off, giving Natalie unpleasant flashbacks to school assemblies, cheerleaders tumbling, and a cappella groups tuning up for stirring renditions of whatever pop songs were on the radio. Luckily, the cheerleaders seemed to have decided a memorial service was not the ideal place for pom-poms, but that didn't stop the Ferry Fantasias from bleating out a semihungover version of "Amazing Grace." It was summer, after all, and most of the kids in town had pregamed the night before in the woods at an old, decaying Victorian house on Sycamore Street, passing around warm bottles of beer. Despite the less-than-stellar quality of the vocals, Natalie reached her phone toward their source. The quavering music would make for amazing color in her podcast. She could even start off the first episode with that clip.

"Hey, you okay?" Natalie felt a hand alight on her shoulder, and when she turned toward the arm it belonged to, she saw a concerned-looking Jonathan Pressman, dressed neatly in his black suit from prom. He knew how close she had been with Mrs. Halsey. He even came to a True Crime Club meeting with her and Katie once but left halfway through, claiming that his mother wanted him home. Natalie knew it was really because Jonathan was not the type to sit around obsessing over horrors.

With his neat haircut and blue eyes, Mrs. Pressman's son was attractive in the dull way that all so-called all-American boys were, but he also had that natural kindness that very few popular kids seemed blessed with. He wouldn't go on to do anything all that special, but he would live a nice life.

She nodded, wondering herself whether she were okay or not. Was it weird that she was so excited about doing this podcast? Shouldn't she be home in bed, weeping? Would Mrs. Halsey have wanted that? Or would she have wanted Natalie to press on? To do her justice?

"Lucy is doing great," Natalie said, gesturing to Jonathan's girlfriend, straight and prim in the front row of the Fantasias, a similarly friendly and unextraordinary sophomore with pretty blond hair cropped in a close pixie cut. She didn't really care about Lucy's singing, but Jonathan was looking at her expectantly, and she didn't think blurting out her concerns about her mental state would go over that well.

"Thanks. She's been working really hard on her high notes," Jonathan said, stroking his stubble and watching his girlfriend clasp her hands and warble. He frowned. "Hey, there's Mr. Halsey." He pointed to a man standing by the gym door, his wrinkled white dress shirt stretched across his broad chest, tie as askew as his usual pristine black hair. Even his brown loafers looked wilted, somehow.

He looked a stark contrast to the grinning man the town knew and loved, idling down the country roads in his midnight-blue vintage convertible with Mrs. Halsey beside him, reclining against the creamy leather seat, her hair blowing back in a smart kerchief. They were a mainstay in Ferry, as much a part of the town as the Fourth of July parade and the Christmas-tree lighting down by the water, the one capped off every year by a visit from Santa, puttering up to the dock in a tugboat. Mr. Halsey was also the history teacher at the high school and the town's Little League coach. Natalie had heard that he had his own club at school for history buffs, during which they watched big-budget war movies and critiqued their accuracy.

Jonathan leaned toward Natalie's ear. His breath smelled like milk. It was oddly comforting. "I heard my mom say they're looking into what he was doing that night. Like, if he had an alibi. I hope he does." His voice hitched. "To think that he could do something like that…" He trailed off, tears glinting in his eyes.

Natalie's eyes flicked down to her recorder briefly, simultaneously hoping that it had picked up Jonathan's whisper through the din of the auditorium and fighting off the guilt that accompanied that hope. She would have to ask for his permission to use the recording later on, but she'd think about that when the time came to release the whole thing. She leaned forward, close to his ear, as the Fantasias tapered off and the principal moved to the podium with a Bible in his hands. Apparently, the separation between church and state didn't apply in the summertime.

"I don't know... It's always the husband," Natalie said with the confidence of someone who had her own not-so-modest library of true-crime novels (albeit hidden in her closet)—then cringed at the blithe way she was discussing Mrs. Halsey's death. She was a little scared of herself, how quickly she had switched into true-crime mode. She couldn't let herself do that with Mrs. Halsey. Luckily, Jonathan didn't seem to notice: he was too busy gawking at Mr. Halsey.

"Maybe not in this case," Jonathan said as he gestured at the newly minted widower, who leaned against the science teacher, Mr. Sprouse, tears rolling down his stubbly cheeks. "He looks pretty broken up to me." Again, that bland kindness that would make Jonathan an excellent Little League coach one day. The kind of niceness that something in Natalie distrusted out of principle. And the kind of niceness that made for golden quotes if one wanted a balanced story, which she most certainly did.

"Can you let me know what your mom says, do you think? About the alibi?" Natalie asked, wondering how far she could push Jonathan before he thought she was being weird. "I just... I just want to know what happened." Tears pricked her eyes as she realized how much she meant it.

Jonathan sat back, his eyes wide, nervous as most boys are when a girl starts crying. He rubbed her arm awkwardly. "I mean, sure, Nat. If I can." Jonathan smiled blandly again, then stared off into the middle distance as if not looking at her tears would make them go away.

"What did the golden retriever want?" Katie asked, using

their old nickname for Jonathan. Katie had extricated herself from Simon's lap, and he was watching her balefully, his crossword half-finished on his phone screen. How he was going to survive when Katie left for MIT and he went to Yale was a mystery. The crowd was getting restless in the cold, shuffling their feet and coughing. Everyone loved Mrs. Halsey, sure, but listening to Mr. Kaufman read the King James seemed not all that fitting, when you considered that Mrs. Halsey was not even remotely religious. While everyone else went all out for Christmas, she loved Halloween and threw yearly parties for practically the whole town at her house.

Natalie picked at a dark blue fingernail. "He said people are looking at the husband." *Her husband*, a voice whispered in her brain. *Hers*.

Katie pushed her glasses farther up her nose, cocked her head to the side. "Yeah, makes sense. It's always the husband," she said, echoing Natalie's theory.

After Mr. Kaufman finally called the memorial to a close, they both watched as Mr. Halsey stood listlessly at the gym door, accepting hugs and handshakes as the Ferry residents trickled by. More than a few seemed to share their suspicions, though; about a third of the people who left the gym gave him a wide berth. Natalie caught the eye of one such boy, a tall blond in all black, as he made his way toward the exit. She didn't recognize him, which was weird, considering how small Ferry was, but he could easily be an ex-student come back to pay his respects.

"Wanna come over?" Katie asked, standing up and dusting off the seat of her dress. "All these people and their performative crying is bumming me out." Glitter rained onto the bleachers from her skirt, left over from the senior prom. Natalie stood up with her; when she looked back toward the door, the boy was gone.

Although both of them were probably a little too obsessed with darkness, Katie could be more callous about it all than Natalie—likely because her dad was a crime reporter. She was a super-tech whiz and had gotten into MIT on the strength of LegalAid, an app that allowed people to easily connect with free lawyers if they were arrested during a protest or otherwise unjustly. She was the technical brain of *Killing Time*. Natalie was the heart—or she tried to be. When they recorded episodes, she found herself steering the conversation more toward the facts of the case than the grisly details, even though she understood their sick appeal. It's like how people go on roller coasters to get a glimpse of what real danger is: researching murder lets you get close to death without experiencing it firsthand—and everyone's curious about that.

Natalie groaned. "I wish, but Mom will be waiting for me. The diner'll be packed after everyone gets out of here. But later, for sure." Although the town had been wandering into modernity of late, with a swank wine bar opening downtown and even a fancy cheese shop, people still preferred congregating en masse to down fries and shakes in the wake of social events in Ferry. That's what kept the diner afloat. Nostalgia and a fondness for grease.

"Crying does make people hungry," Katie agreed as the two filed out of the gym and into the parking lot. Then she stopped at the door and looked back over her shoulder into the darkness of the school. For a moment, Natalie thought

Katie might cry herself. She had loved Mrs. Halsey, too—not as much as Natalie did, but a whole lot. Still, Katie had developed her own defense mechanisms when it came to pain, mainly humor and salty snacks. So Natalie wasn't all that surprised when Katie fist-bumped her and slid into her black Jeep Wrangler, hand already plunging wrist-deep into a bag of Doritos. Simon had somehow materialized in the passenger seat like a sad ghost with glasses.

"Sure you don't want a ride?" Katie asked, revving the engine and wiping her hand on her black dress. The orange dust gave it a distinctly Halloweeny effect. "I can make Si sit in the back." He cringed—just barely.

Natalie smiled and shook her head. "You know how Mom feels about me driving with anyone who isn't her."

She waved goodbye to Katie as her friend sped off, then threw a leg over her bike, the faded basket covered in pink flowers still affixed to the handlebars. Her mother wouldn't let her take it off, wouldn't let her ride with a backpack on her back or a purse banging around her side. And a helmet was an absolute nonnegotiable.

Natalie would never completely get over Helen's overprotectiveness—and it rankled even more after what had had happened with Mrs. Halsey. The way her mother always watched out the window when she left for school or arrived home. The way she hung over her while saying good-night, standing just a bit too long as if making sure that Natalie was still breathing. Helen had had her young, when she nineteen. One would have thought she'd be cool, then—a young mom who was more like a sister than a parent. One would be wrong. She wouldn't even tell Natalie who her dad was. All she would say was that it had been a mistake with an old boyfriend that had made a miracle—before shoving condoms at her daughter that the perpetually single Natalie did *not* need.

Those were the thoughts spinning through her as she pedaled up to the diner, already packed with hungry mourners, and as the summer breeze kissed her sweaty forehead and the smell of the nearby sea skunked the air with rotting seaweed and fish. The thoughts sputtered and stilled as a cop car pulled into the parking lot, the siren silent, yet still somehow screaming in the depths of Natalie's mind. Mrs. Pressman and Mr. Lugo hung in the background, dark silhouettes in the daytime, pads held aloft.

Drawn by the sight of the prowling cops, the crowd inside the diner started spilling into the street almost immediately, their voices chattering like the seagulls circling above them, calling for scraps. First and foremost was Sandy Tarver, town gossip and Garden Club president. She clutched her cell to her ear. But the cops just kept soldiering forward, parting the crowd until they stood in front of a blue car—a gleaming convertible.

Natalie stood up on her bike as the first cop, a man with a beer gut and thinning hair, approached Mr. Halsey, still behind the wheel, squinting into the sun, as if the scene before him were simply a mirage. Sweat stained his armpits in wide circles, and his tie hung loose around his neck. On his handsome face Natalie could read shock and something else. A grim resignation? Fatigue?

Mr. Halsey got out of the car as the detectives reached the driver's-side door, conferring with them in low whispers that Natalie still strained to hear above the screaming of the gulls. They didn't appear to be reading him his rights, and no handcuffs were in sight, but their faces were stern and hard. Mr. Halsey nodded finally, then slid back into his car. He waited behind the wheel until the cops got into their Vic, then followed them out of the parking lot. Not arrested then, but definitely under suspicion.

Natalie wondered if he knew all along he was going to be brought in, if he was on his way to the diner to have his last meal. Did that mean he'd done it? The idea sent anger shooting through her, and her hand itched for her iPhone. She wanted to get down all the details of his perp walk. Every bead of sweat on Halsey's brow. Every kid with skinned knees watching, openmouthed, as the police led their neighbor away.

"You need to get inside. *Now.*" Natalie's mom spoke into her ear, grabbing her daughter's shoulder and wheeling her toward the diner.

"But I want to see—"

"I know you do," Helen said, fuming. "And that's the goddamn problem." Her fingers dug into Natalie's shoulders as she slunk toward the diner, shoving the phone back into the safety of her pocket in case her mom wanted to confiscate it. "Now, show a little respect. These are real people, not characters in some horrible book."

But that, Natalie thought, *is exactly the point.*

CHAPTER FOUR: THEN

If Helen had known that the first person she met on her first day of college would go missing, she wouldn't have introduced herself at all. Let's face it: if she had known that introducing yourself to someone in a crowded lecture hall was so thoroughly uncool—*she had also gone in for the handshake!*—she would have abstained. But the past cannot be changed, and so here we are.

"Hey," Helen said, plastering a smile on her face and swallowing down a lump of fear, "I'm Helen." Her extended hand shook and the sparkly nail polish that had looked so cool this morning when she put it on just seemed so very middle school now.

The girl in the seat next to her blinked at her desk, and Helen wondered if perhaps she were sleepwalking or something. She was wearing sweatpants and a hoodie and big, plush shoes that looked like slippers—a stark contrast to Helen's tan slacks and red blouse. She had been proud of her outfit this morning—she thought she looked like the journalist she aimed to become when all four years were through—but now she realized that the majority in the hundred-plus-person lecture hall also appeared to be dressed in glorified pajamas. And, perhaps, she shouldn't be trying to shake hands with people in a hundred-person lecture hall.

Finally, the girl looked Helen's way and, perhaps taking pity on the her—or maybe because Helen was now fully shaking—she grabbed her hand and gave it a firm squeeze, her messy topknot vibrating as she flashed a truly blinding smile. "Hey, I'm Jenny." She narrowed her eyes, not unkindly. "You're a freshman, huh?"

Helen felt herself deflating. "Is it that obvious?" She flashed back to the night before, when all the kids on her hall headed to downtown Evanston to get ice cream. Starting college—an institution where people actually wanted to learn!—had felt like the chance to show everyone the person she knew she was on the inside: smart, funny, someone people *wanted* to hang out with. She had been all set to dazzle everyone with her wit and verve but had frozen up on the walk to the creamery. Instead of talking to the girl in the Bikini Kill shirt with the clove cigarette clamped between her teeth, she had fallen to the back of the group, walking in fearful silence with a greasy girl who kept talking about cadavers. (She was a med student, but still.) The night did not bode well for the rest of her college career.

Now, Jenny was smiling at her, though. And she seemed far cooler than the clove girl, who had also been wearing a fedora. "Well, this is Journalism 101," she said, rolling her eyes. "And I'm guessing not everyone here failed last year." She pointed at her head, then mock-shot herself with a chipped red nail. "The grammar tests are basically sadism, and they, like, expect you to memorize the newspaper every day."

Helen rolled her eyes and smiled, like she knew she was supposed to, even though she had committed the *AP Style Guide* to memory that summer and had subscribed to the *New York Times* since she was eight. "Wow, that sucks," she replied and was rewarded with a toothy white smile from Jenny.

"At least we have the hot TA again," Jenny said, her eyes going to the front of the room where a boy—man?—with floppy blond hair sat at a desk next to the podium, his legs akimbo, his eyes scanning the room. When they reached Jenny and Helen, he stopped scanning and shot them a slow smile. Helen's hands started buzzing, and she looked at the desk. She had a boyfriend, Tom, who had stayed back home in Connecticut to go to state school while she had traveled to the exotic Midwest to go to Northwestern's prestigious Medill School of Journalism. Staring at the TA somehow felt like cheating. When she looked up again, though, he was busy gazing at Jenny. Naturally. She internally sighed. Jenny looked sleepy and rumpled, unworried, cool. Helen, now that she thought about it, looked like a missionary. Slowly, she untucked her shirt.

"Fuck, here comes Lucifer," Jenny muttered as the class stopped talking abruptly. Helen's back stiffened as a man in all black strode into the room, his face rigid behind black-framed glasses. Silence descended somehow more deeply as he positioned himself behind the looming podium, and even the hot TA froze, as if he were a woodland creature in the presence of a mighty predator. The professor scanned the room as his assistant had done but without a trace of a smile. Helen's heartbeat accelerated, and somehow, she suspected that memorizing the *AP Style Guide* wasn't going to save her.

The silence now was so complete that Helen realized she had stopped breathing, so when the loud burst of classical music erupted from beside her, she jumped in her seat, her legs banging against the built-in desk. Next to her, Jenny swore softly, seemingly unaware that all eyes were on her as she dragged a tiny, gray cell phone from her sweatpants. "Sorry!" she called out to the dozens of faces that were turned her way. Helen swore she heard someone in the vicinity of the TA chuckle softly.

So unbothered that it was enviable, Jenny flipped open her phone, her eyes immediately widening. "Aw, shit!" she shouted. "My sister had a boy!" Her face broke into an enormous grin, and slowly, someone started to clap. Soon, all one hundred previously stony faces gave into Jenny's infectious joy, and the clap erupted into a joyful roar. When Helen looked to the front, the professor, too, had started applauding, albeit impatiently. Jenny was just that kind of person. You couldn't not smile when she smiled, cheer when she cheered. Which is why when she disappeared a few weeks later, it was like the sun had gone down.

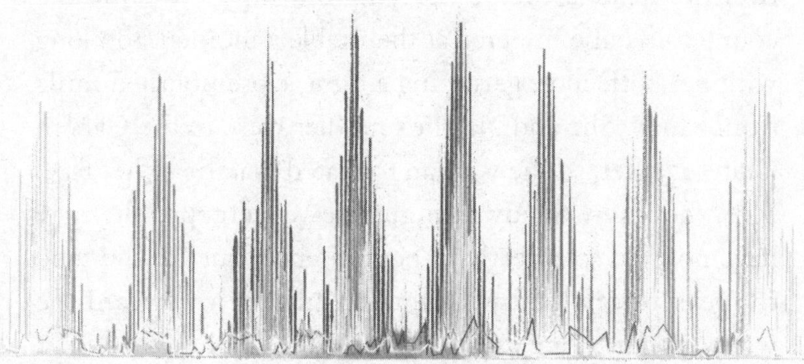

CHAPTER FIVE

Natalie hadn't been able to make it to Katie's the night before, as it turned out. Her mother had kept the diner open late into the evening; Mr. Halsey's public humiliation had made people even hungrier than their grief did. Until roughly midnight, Natalie stood on throbbing feet, slinging omelets and burgers, but there was an upshot: people were talking about the Halseys. A lot. And there was nothing her mom could do to keep her away from it—unless she wanted to force Natalie to wear noise-canceling headphones like a baby at a concert. Sandy Tarver in particular—oh she of the loosest lips—had heard that Mr. Halsey had a mistress, a bartender over in West Ferry. Some woman named Eliza Minnow.

"If that's not motive right there, I don't know what is,"

she insisted to her sun-flushed husband Carl, who nodded over her head at the Sox playing on the TV behind the counter. Natalie lingered at their table a moment too long with her coffeepot, garnering a tight, closemouthed smile from Sandy. She and Natalie's mother were in the Garden Club together, so the woman tolerated Natalie to her face. Still, she knew Sandy thought she was creepy. She may have not said so directly in her presence, but she did tend to speak pretty loudly. One time, Natalie overheard the woman refer to her as *pale and weird*.

Natalie returned the tight smile and stood her ground in the hopes that Sandy would forget she was there and continue gossiping, but no such luck.

Sandy's thin, drawn-on eyebrows lifted briefly, then she recovered with another frosty smile. "Your mommy looks a little harried over there, kiddo," she said in a voice that suggested Natalie was six years old. "Maybe you should go…fry something."

Natalie shrugged off Sandy's condescension and turned away. She had heard enough: she had Eliza Minnow, the mistress—another possible source. Sandy herself was just secondary—like *Wikipedia*, you probably wouldn't quote her without double-checking the facts.

Natalie mulled over this new information the next morning as she and her mother did their daily workout in the backyard, her bare feet awkward and damp in the dewy grass, her head fuzzy from too little sleep.

"One, two, three, four, five," Helen Temple counted off as they both threw punches into the humid summer air, scented pink with Helen's climbing roses. Her dark ponytail swung behind her like a whip as she punched. When in motion, Natalie's mom looked like a character in a video game, all sharp edges and precision.

Beside her, Natalie puffed, red-faced and sweating, her own hair sticking to the back of her neck as it escaped from its heavy braid. She stopped punching for a moment to wipe the sweat from her brow and watched a butterfly drift by on its kite-thin wings, drawn toward the bursting, bright garden. She hated karate, and right now she really, really hated her mother. It was summer, and she was supposed to be sleeping in, not sweating and punching imaginary enemies.

"Come on, Nat! Faster! Harder!" Helen shouted. "It'd be tragic if those evil robots won!"

Natalie huffed and rolled her eyes, pulling her feet back into fighting stance. When she was younger, after a long day in the diner, her mother would come home and drag an old CD player into the kitchen so that the two could have dance parties, prancing wildly around the table and over the chairs to Helen's not-so-modest music collection. Their favorite song was an old Flaming Lips track about a girl named Yoshimi who was a black belt in karate, tasked with defending the world from evil pink robots. Natalie had loved that when she was five or six, but as she grew older, the so-called dance parties morphed into pretty rigorous martial-arts workouts that she had been forced to participate in every morning. She couldn't help suspecting that she had been tricked.

"You need to learn how to protect yourself," her mother

told her the first morning she shook her daughter awake before the sun rose to kick and punch on the dawn-dappled lawn. To add insult to injury, they didn't even practice flashy karate like the people in movies and on TV. Theirs was all about self-defense—no flying jump kicks and spins, just solid punches and blocks.

"You'll thank me for this when you're in college," Helen said, finally dropping her arms to her sides—only to start immediately bouncing on the soles of her feet and framing up a solid roundhouse kick. "All the other girls will be walking around with their whistles and their mace, but you—" she shot her daughter a grin over her shoulder "—you'll have your whole body at the ready!"

Natalie kicked the air half-heartedly, then stopped, panting, hands on her knees. "Why can't I just get some mace like a normal person? Or," she brightened, "a Taser."

Helen's face clouded, and she grabbed her daughter's arm in a fist like steel. "Or you could just *try harder.*" She squeezed. "Now, get out of this hold."

Natalie glared at her mom with sleepy, red eyes. She tried plenty hard when it came to things she actually cared about, not that she could discuss any of that with Helen, unless she wanted to be grounded for the rest of her life. It didn't matter that these morning workouts weren't her thing: the first time she'd tried to opt out of them, her mother just told her that they weren't *quitters* and dragged her out of bed.

Helen looked down at her vise grip and gave Natalie a shake. "Come on, Nat. You know how to get out of this. Twist your arm and pull!"

"If I twist and pull, can we be done?" she whined, her

eyes wandering to her bike, propped against the side of the house. She had yet to talk to Katie about the podcast, but she wanted to get started either way, do some reconnaissance: pedal past the Halsey's house, or even Eliza Minnow's bar. She was still figuring out how she could get an interview with the woman without pissing her off, but she wanted to see what she was dealing with first. If Eliza worked in West Ferry, she was likely a bit different from the women she and her mom knew.

"No, you can't be 'done,'" Helen spat, dropping her daughter's arm and pulling her hands across her flushed face. She took a deep breath like she was asking for strength from some sort of deity and leveled her eyes at Natalie. "You're leaving soon, and I—"

Her voice caught briefly, and Natalie softened, just a little. It's not that she wouldn't miss her mother. She would. She'd miss pancakes at their little kitchen table and movie marathons and her mother's hands in her hair. She'd miss how she always smelled like hyacinth and how she sang along (poorly) to the radio in the morning when she thought Natalie was asleep. She just wouldn't miss the pressure, the expectations, the endless worry.

Natalie swallowed, opened her mouth to say… Well, she wasn't entirely sure, but she stopped when Helen shook herself, clearing her throat and pointing to the grass. "Now, give me twenty push-ups," she barked. "And none of those idiotic *half-assed* ones they let you do in gym class."

After thirty more push-ups (her mom always lied), Natalie finally slumped into the kitchen to grab a bottle of water, her face red and legs shaky. Once she heard Helen start the shower, she stood on top of a kitchen chair to grab a Pop-Tart from her hidden stash in the back of the top cupboard—behind a giant bag of rice that her mom had bought and forgotten. Helen's opinions about processed sugar were pretty similar to her thoughts on biking without a helmet: the result was death, instant or slow, it made no difference. You were heading straight into its cold embrace either way.

Natalie was just about to climb down from the chair when she spotted something in the trash under a pile of coffee grinds from her mom's a.m. pot—the newspaper. She frowned. Her mom usually grudgingly left it out for Natalie to flip through during breakfast; she knew her daughter would look up the crime logs online, anyway. Judging by the liberal application of the coffee grounds, it seemed like her mom was trying to hide today's issue.

Hopping to the floor, Natalie pulled the paper out of the trash by the corner and shook off the muck, revealing Mrs. Halsey's smiling face over Mrs. Pressman's byline. It was a photo from that year's yearbook; her teeth were white and even, freckles scattered across her nose. She was wearing her favorite sweater, a red and yellow and green color-block like some kind of modern art. "Local Teacher Found Dead," the headline blared.

Natalie sank onto her chair and dropped the Pop-Tarts on the table, her eyes caught on the words. They were so stark, so...clinical. Her eyes skipped down to the text below Mrs. Halsey's photo, taking in words that were similarly dry: *Local and state police have termed Halsey's death suspicious.*

She had no known medical problems, according to her husband. Police say that they will know more after the state Office of the Chief Medical Examiner performs an autopsy.

Natalie shivered and shoved the paper back in the trash, stopped by that last sentence: they were doing an autopsy. She had read countless autopsies online on cold-case forums, lingering over details of mysterious bruises and ligature marks, trying to crack the code of a broken body. But when she thought of Mrs. Halsey on a metal table and strangers cutting into her flesh, her mind just…refused to go any further. That made it real. It made her dead. Her body wouldn't be whole again; pieces would be taken out and weighed and examined, then stitched back together.

A wave of dizziness swept through Natalie, and she chugged at her water, almost choking as it poured down her throat. Her hands shook, and her eyes burned; she felt tears coming and was momentarily almost relieved. This is how normal people reacted when someone they loved died, right? They cried. They felt ill. They mourned, and then they moved on. Memories brought back the pain, but each time it dulled a little until it was just a scar, faint and almost forgotten. Life went on.

Her hands stilled; the tears retreated. Did she really want to do that? Move on? Forget? Or did she want to do something bigger, more important? She thought of her podcast then and clenched her fingers into fists on her thighs. She had to get a hold of herself. If she wanted to do this, really do this, she would have to deal with stuff like this all the time. She couldn't just let grief run its course, distract her. And if she wanted to tell Mrs. Halsey's story—the real story beyond the clinical words in the newspaper—she would have to look things like this in the face. The realities of the crime. The bodily facts of death. She owed Mrs. Halsey that.

Her hands still shaking a little, she reached back into the trash and smoothed out the paper again, staring into Mrs. Halsey's newsprint eyes for a long moment before turning back to the words below.

CHAPTER SIX: THEN

The day Helen heard that Jenny was missing started poorly, to put it mildly. Tom had come for a visit, and after they effectively sexiled Helen's roommate—Amanda, the cadaver queen—he announced that he thought they should have an open relationship.

"What does that even mean?" Helen sputtered, clutching her flowered sheets to her chest as Tom reclined against the wall, his head resting against the Klimt poster her father had bought her at the college bookstore. Half her dorm had the same one, and Helen wasn't a huge Klimt fan, but she had kept it up, anyway—a reminder of her dad and home. Now, it seemed the kissing couple in their flowery bower was laughing at her.

Tom studied the ceiling, which was dappled with an amber morning light that seemed to momentarily awe him. Helen clucked impatiently until he finally tore his eyes away from the sunbeam and twisted the quilt in his big hands. "It's just… Helen, it's like…" He squinted as if doing math in his head. "It's like I'm in a room in a house, and there's all these other rooms."

"What?" Helen said flatly. Tom was studying philosophy, was always blissfully staring at flowers and talking about the mighty hand of nature, but this was loopy—even for him.

"It's just…" Tom turned toward her, not quite looking her in the eye. "I think I need to be able to visit other rooms, you know? Maybe…even leave the house?"

Helen blinked. "Are you comparing our relationship to being stuck in a room? Like…jail?"

"Not exactly," Tom said, sighing. "But…kind of… But hey." He reached out to awkwardly touch her shoulder. "We can still hang, though…"

By the time Helen had reached the student center where the school paper met in one of its myriad conference rooms, she was fuming. At her worst moments, Helen worried that she was boring. That she was too safe. That she was, apparently, a room to be escaped. Sure, she went to movies with her dad on Saturday nights and woke up at seven in the morning to study for her AP tests, but that's what you *did* in high school. (Maybe not the movie part; that was actually kind of sad.) You did well, you got out, and you ended up somewhere better. Unfortunately, it seemed that Tom's *somewhere better* was outside whatever metaphorical house arrest he had been prattling about in her bed before she kicked him out—much to roommate Amanda's delight. Not that she smiled when she shuffled back into the room and burrowed under the covers; she *had* had to sleep in the lounge, after all. Still, Amanda regularly stayed up all night, studying, swearing, and studying some more, so Helen thought she was owed a break.

Fighting tears and shaking with rage wasn't the best look for her first college-paper meeting, but Helen slunk into the conference room anyway, slinking to the end of a long table packed with neatly dressed students clutching notebooks. Her shoulders relaxed a bit under her blue button-up. These were her people: polished, alert, more than slightly high-strung. A quick scan confirmed, too, that no one was wearing pajamas. She had wondered if Jenny would be there, but the other girl's laissez-faire attitude about the class screamed *requirement* rather than *passion*.

"Okay, people, settle down," a boy-man in a full suit barked as he barreled into the room—despite the fact that no one was talking. His red tie hung loosely around his neck like he had just finished a long shift hounding sources and breaking news, and his hair was thinning, despite the fact that he was probably only twenty or so. "I know this is the first meeting and we should all be learning each other's names and doing trust falls or whatever, but I believe we have our first scoop." His finger shot into the air, seemingly of its own accord. Helen noticed he was sweating.

The girl next to Helen—a petite redhead with the smoothest, perkiest ponytail she had ever seen—rolled her eyes and mouthed *scoop*.

The boy slammed his hands on the table. "What else would you call a missing student, *Carla*?" Carla blinked, her smile—and her ponytail—drooping.

All around Helen, heads started swiveling, whispers swirling around the room like bats. In the midst of the commotion, though, her eyes were locked on a photo that the boy had pulled from his briefcase (?!). It was a glossy class picture of a blonde girl smiling with bright white teeth—grinning so hard it looked like she was about to start laughing. Even without her messy topknot, Helen recognized the smile.

"Jennifer Roberts. Sophomore. Communications major. Who knows her?" the boy barked again.

Helen's tablemates hushed, squinting at the photo, but no one made any noises of recognition or raised their hands, which seemed weird to her. Jenny seemed like the kind of person that others noticed, that they angled to be friends with. But the boy-man had said she was a communications major, and this lot seemed pretty insular. Maybe, despite their intention to be journalists—professional curious people—they stuck to their own. With a final glance behind her to make sure no one had made any revelations about Jenny, Helen raised her hand slowly, then cringed slightly as everyone spun around to stare at her.

"You, yes." The boy punched a finger through the air toward Helen, then frowned. "Who are you?"

Helen swallowed, thinking back to Tom and all his bullshit about houses and rooms. About watching movies with her dad and never going to parties in high school because she had to study. This is what she had spent all high school preparing for. It was time to open the goddamn door of her own goddamn room. "I'm Helen, sir." Undeterred by the giggles that erupted at the word *sir*, Helen sallied forth. "Jenny is in my Journalism 101 class. I believe her sister just had a baby." The latter half of the statement didn't seem super relevant to the task at hand, but Helen knew it made her seem like she had insider knowledge—despite the fact that Jenny had said as much to a lecture hall of a hundred.

"Journalism 101?" The boy frowned even more, so that he resembled the apple-head doll Helen had made in third grade, then left in her locker for two months. "Who let a freshman in here?" He glared around accusatorily. No one laughed this time. "Don't we usually haze them or something before they get to come to meetings?"

Helen started to panic—she was a legendary rule-follower—then summoned her own disapproving frown. "Yes, I'm a freshman, but I'm the only one in this room who knows Jenny," she said, jutting her chin out and leveling her eyes at the suited boy. "So do I have the assignment or not?"

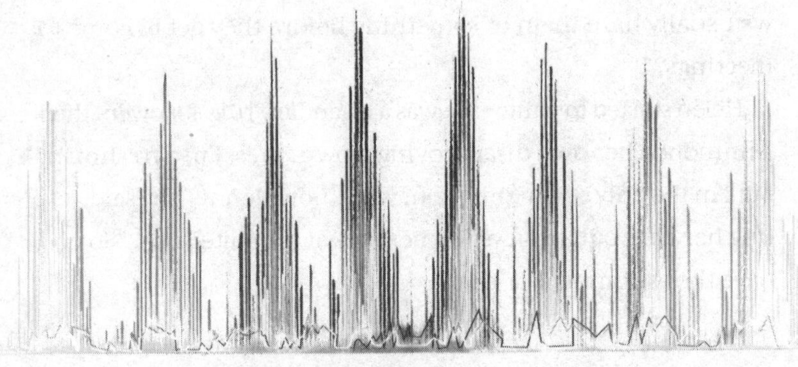

CHAPTER SEVEN

Katie shoved a handful of cereal into her mouth and glowered. "Dude, did you have to come over so early?" She yawned, giving Natalie a prime-time view of the contents of her mouth. "You want to launch a full-scale investigative podcast, and I'm not even wearing a bra yet."

After her near breakdown in the kitchen, Natalie had read the article about Mrs. Halsey until she could recite it almost by heart, then pedaled over to Katie's. She needed some of her friend's levity, her humor, and Katie was delivering—as usual.

Katie sprawled across her mess of a bed in a bizarre bedtime outfit of neon-yellow bike shorts and a shrunken T-shirt her mom had bought her at age ten emblazoned with the words I Don't Need a Prince, I Have Dad. (They would have to discuss *that* later.) Her thin form was dwarfed by the sea of pictures and posters plastered to her walls: K-pop bands, all. Hundreds of photos of K-pop bands—half of them were of BTS's Kim Taehyung, who Katie had said multiple times she would trade Simon in for in an instant. Natalie had tried to mock her about them once, but Katie just shook her head, her eyes full of stern warning, and Natalie dropped it.

"Are you *ever* wearing a bra?" Natalie shot back, eyeing Katie's flat chest under the creepy T-shirt.

"Says the weirdo who wears hers to bed," Katie sneered.

"Whatever!" Natalie protested, snapping at one of her straps as jauntily as she could, which was hard since she was wearing a plain, black sports bra. "It's just an added layer of protection from the outside world. Like a bulletproof vest for your boobs."

Natalie and Katie had initially bonded in middle school over their complete inability to be subtle. East Ferry, Connecticut, was all about tennis and boating and being polite. Natalie and Katie were decidedly not into any of those things—perhaps because Natalie's mom was much more concerned with teaching her daughter how to do karate than how to wear makeup, and Katie grew up the daddy's girl of a crime reporter. While everyone was whispering in eighth grade about finally getting their periods, the duo loudly called it their *monthly massacre* and shrieked like they were being murdered as they passed each other tampons in the halls.

"Okay, enough about underwear," Natalie said, snagging some Lucky Charms. "Let's talk about the new podcast.

As I see it, we have a few leads we need to follow: Eliza Minnow and Mr. Halsey. Of course, with Halsey we have to be strategic about getting an interview with him. The cops are on him already, and I'm not sure he'll be too into talking to anyone yet."

Discussing the facts of the case was comforting; Natalie could feel her usual equilibrium returning as she hashed out their battle plan. She felt in control, like she was blazing through her high-school math homework: every problem had a solution; she just had to find it.

"So you wanna go all *Serial* on this?" Katie asked, pulling the bowl out of reach and shoving more hearts, stars, and rainbows into her mouth. "I admire your can-do attitude, Nat, but… How should I put this? That seems like a fuck-ton of work. I leave for MIT in less than two months. I'm not sure we can pull this off."

Natalie looked around Katie's bedroom, the massive video-game console that presided over the mess like some kind of holy monument, the discarded cereal bowls littering the floor, mold forming along their edges. "I mean, it's not like you're busy…" she ventured.

"Oh, but I am," Katie nodded, her face grave. "I'm busy doing absolutely nothing after busting my ass for four years." She flopped back into bed as if to demonstrate. "I need—no, *deserve*—a break. Plus, Simon is on me to hang out more before college, and I don't think this is his thing."

Natalie scoffed. Simon's sole *things* seemed to be following Katie around and word puzzles. Perhaps he could buy a book of the latter and call it a day. "Okay, but—" Natalie bounced on her knees next to her friend, who closed her eyes with a groan "—you won't *really* have to do anything but the editing. I'll do all the reporting and researching."

Katie snorted. "Except that what you're talking about doing requires, in fact, much more work." She attempted to chew a handful of cereal while lying on her back and immediately commenced choking. She sat up.

A flutter of panic started up in Natalie's belly. She couldn't do this without Katie. Forget all the technological know-how—she needed her best friend, someone who understood her and what she wanted to do. How much she cared about Mrs. Halsey. She thought back to how that story in the newspaper had affected her, how it had rendered her immobile. She needed Katie to move forward.

"Please, Katie?" Natalie pleaded. "This isn't just some summer project. I want to do this for Mrs. Halsey. I want to make sure… I don't know… That's she's not forgotten. That if someone tells her story, they'll get it right."

Katie stopped chewing, leveling her eyes with Natalie's. "And you think that that someone is us? You really think we're qualified to do this?"

There was a rare note of seriousness in Katie's voice that stopped Natalie in her tracks. This was a big undertaking. This was Mrs. Halsey's whole life. But then a voice spoke up in her head that sounded a lot like her teacher's, a rerun of one of her lessons. *The best crime stories are the ones in which you can feel the teller's hesitation to tell—their humanity. Their horror at the act. If you approach something horrific with sympathy for the victim, your story will have more layers. It will be truer.*

Natalie nodded, both in response to the voice and to Katie. "Yes. I do."

The K-pop bands on the wall looked on like a silent Greek chorus as Katie mulled it over, but after only one slightly lengthy, wistful glance at her game console, she gave a tight nod. "Yeah, sure. I don't really have anything else to do. Simon'll live."

Natalie leaped up from the bed and punched the air, a contrast to that morning's lackluster sleepwalk through her karate routine. She felt more awake than she had in days—that was the only way to describe it. It was as if she had been dozing like a cat in a beam of lazy sunlight only to see a mouse scamper by. The chase was on.

"So what do we do first?" Katie said, still not getting up from her nest of blankets. "Go to the library or something? Look up shit online?"

"There'll be plenty of that, sure," Natalie said. "But first, I wanna go a little gonzo." She grinned so hard her cheeks hurt.

"What does that mean?" Katie frowned. "You're smiling a lot, and it's scaring me."

"Does your cousin still make fake IDs?" Natalie asked.

"Yes…" Katie replied, drawing out the word, and layering it thick with suspicion.

"Well," Natalie replied, "we're going to take a little trip to the other side of town. Then…we're going out."

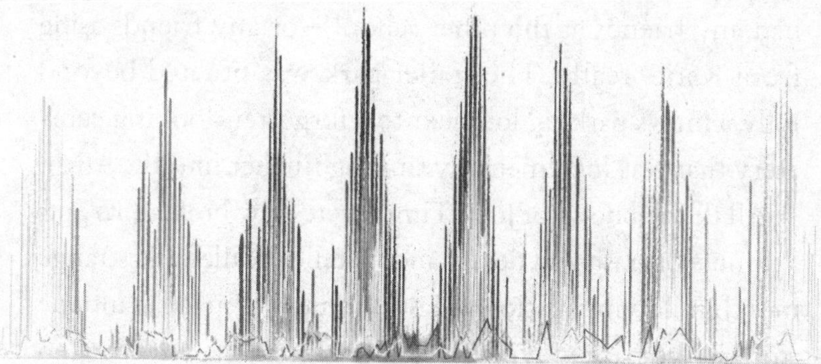

CHAPTER EIGHT

Katie's cousin Jack lived in a trailer park at the edge of Ferry, known as West Ferry, as it was on the other side of the Ferry River. To the Sandy Tarvers of the world, West Ferry was *the bad side of town*, but Natalie's mother had told her on many occasions that there were just a few mortgage payments' difference between them and the denizens of the other side of the river.

The kids went to another high school, sure, and some areas were a little dicey, but it was, overall, a well-scrubbed working-class neighborhood. Even the trailer park was pretty nice. As Helen frequently griped, house prices were on the rise, and you made do with what you could afford.

Natalie hadn't had much reason to visit that side of the

river since she was a child, though—when she used to frequent Jolly Times Entertainment Center. It's not like she had any friends at the other school—or any friends aside from Katie, really. The trailer park was situated beyond Jolly Times's parking lot, next to a forgotten-looking cemetery that was incrementally sinking further into the earth.

All the windows of Jolly Times were now broken, its guts a jumble of trash and decay, and Natalie recalled the strange month following its closure last summer when local antique stores were packed with bits and pieces of the old wooden carousel and carnival games. Her mother had turned her down flat when she begged her to purchase the ominous-looking clockwork clown that manned the dunk tank for her bedroom.

Although the trailer park was in significantly better repair than Jolly Times, it was not without a little trepidation that Natalie approached the door to Jack's trailer, hanging back as Katie knocked. She hadn't seen Jack in a while, and Katie was definitely a more seasoned traveler across the river, if only because she had to go there to buy weed.

For a long while there was no sound but the clicking of the cicadas and the constant hum of the nearby highway, which sounded oddly like the waves she could hear from her own bedroom window. She didn't live right next to the beach—that was high-dollar real estate—but she could still make out the ebb and flow of the ocean.

"Maybe we should come back later?" Katie suggested. She was still not sold on the idea of purchasing fake IDs to sneak into a bar, and still less sold on purchasing fake

IDs from Jack. Natalie didn't blame her. He was, quite famously, a dick.

Natalie cursed and knocked on the door herself—hard.

"Chill," Katie sighed. "He might not be awake yet."

Natalie snuck a peek at her phone. "It's three in the afternoon."

"Yeah, but sleep is goood," Katie replied with a shrug, then started pounding on the rickety door again. "Jack! Get your ass out of bed, and help your little cousin out!" she bellowed, drumming out an erratic beat with her fists.

The door banged open, and Jack lurched into the sunlight, his greasy black hair standing on end. He was wearing nothing but a pair of long, camouflage board shorts and a scowl.

"What in the actual fuck, Katie? Stop banging!" he yelled as if in agony. Judging by his red eyes, he probably was.

Katie smirked. "You going swimming, Jack? Finally get one of those cute little turtle pools?"

"Huh?" Jack snarled, then looked down at his half-naked body. "Laundry day." He shrugged. "What do you need, Assface?"

"Be nice, Dickhead. We have a little project for you."

"You guys really love each other, huh?" Natalie interjected with a wry smile. "Anyway, Jack," She turned to the sweaty boy in the bathing suit, his sunken chest covered in zits. "We need some fake IDs. We'll give you two hundred dollars."

Jack folded his arms and jutted out his bottom lip. "Each?"

Katie pushed past him into the trailer. "Total. Family discount."

Jack threw his scrawny arms into the air and followed his cousin. "Fine! But I want it all in twenties. None of those hundred-dollar bills like the last time you bought weed. Those things are fucking impossible to break."

The door slammed in Natalie's face, and she rolled her eyes as she pushed it open again. She wasn't entirely sure how Jack could have turned out so differently from his MIT-bound cousin. It probably had something to do with the fact that Katie's dad was a writer and Jack's dad sold weed. It was like *Breaking Bad*, but Frank Lugo wasn't a chemistry genius. Jack, however crass and strange, was pretty damn smart, though. He'd won pretty much every regional science fair in middle school—until he dropped out at age sixteen to make criminal activities his full-time gig. So far he'd been at it for three years with no sign of going on the straight and narrow.

As Natalie shimmied into the trailer, she steeled herself for the onslaught of smells and textures that had caked Jack's home the last time she reluctantly visited with Katie a few years back, but when she emerged into the little kitchen/living-room area, she was surprised to smell Palo Santo and evergreens. The kitchen appliances shone bright and clean, and the floor was vacuumed down to its original color, which was actually a pleasant blue. The cracked-leather couch was obscured by a soft-looking blue blanket of a similar hue, and a Tibetan tapestry fluttered over the window. There was even a bamboo plant on the milk crate that served as the coffee table.

"Did you get a girlfriend or something?" Natalie asked, spinning around the small space to take in her surroundings.

Katie apparently didn't notice any difference—or didn't care. She was counting out twenties with her tongue between her lips.

"Why? You jealous?" Jack replied, running a hand down his chest and raising his eyebrows with a leer.

Natalie just glowered at him and folded her arms.

"Nope, no such luck." Jack relented, dropping his hand and his eyebrows. "This is all Kurt, my roommate—Craigslist random. Been living with me for about a year now. He owes me a shit-ton of rent, but I tolerate him because he cooks and cleans." Jack smirked. "You would probably like him, actually. He's reading that huge-ass book about sewer clowns you love so much."

"You mean *It*?" Natalie asked, perching on the edge of the couch, which actually smelled nice now. Like lavender. "By Stephen King?"

Jack shrugged. He was pretending, Natalie knew. He and Natalie and Katie had practically gorged themselves on King in middle school.

"Sure, whatever," Jack said, watching Katie count the money, eyes shiny. "He reads big, weird books, too, is my point."

"And he also cleans up after your sorry ass." A boy emerged from one of the back bedrooms, loping across the trailer and draping himself across the couch next to Natalie. "Since Jack has no manners: hey, I'm Kurt Bachman."

"Natalie Temple," she responded. "And that's Katie Lugo."

"Oh, I've met Katie. She likes weed." Kurt rolled his eyes and stuck out a hand. When Natalie took it, she noticed how clean his nails were; everything about Kurt was clean, really. His curling blond hair, his black jeans, his black T-shirt, the bulky metal wristwatch that looked incongruous with his otherwise utilitarian outfit. He was skinny, like Jack, but where the other boy's chest was sunken, Kurt's was broad. The frame was there; he just wasn't done growing into it yet.

"Hey, man," Jack said, tucking the money into his bathing suit pocket. "Can you do your ID magic for these weirdos? And before you ask, I'm keeping the full commission until you pay up for your room."

Kurt waved a hand. "I'll get you your money, dude. Don't worry about it."

"You're the one who should be worried," Jack shot back, throwing a laptop plastered with hardcore stickers into Kurt's lap, and crashing back into what was presumably his bedroom. He started snoring shockingly fast.

"So fake IDs! Wild!" Kurt drawled, his thin fingers dancing across the keyboard. Natalie tried to lean over to see what was on the screen, but Kurt not so subtly angled the laptop away. "You guys going clubbing or something? That's what all the rich kids on your side of the river are into, right?" He smiled, but there was something sarcastic about that smile. Something more than a little superior.

"Asks the dude who's reading the most overrated King book of all time," Natalie snarled back. She did not like when boys acted superior to her, as they were so often wrong. Natalie wasn't one to raise her hand in class or brag about her grades, but she had graduated with top honors. The more outspoken smart kids had seemed shocked when she walked away with prizes in nearly every subject at the end-of-year awards ceremony. She'd come a long way from that embarrassing C in freshman year. There'd even been an article about her in the paper at the end of last year after she'd won a regional essay contest, Mrs. Halsey beaming beside her.

Kurt shrugged. "So? I'm a completionist. I was putting this one off, but once I got through the one about the sentient train, I figured I should just get it over with." He cringed slightly as he delicately pecked at the keyboard; as it was festooned with Insane Clown Posse stickers, this was clearly Jack's laptop, which meant it was likely caked in all sorts of…things.

Natalie snorted. "*Train?* Don't you mean *car*? Like *Christine*?"

Kurt smiled, sarcastic again. "No, I mean *train*. Like *The Dark Tower* series. Someone needs to brush up on their overwhelmingly prolific Maine-based authors."

Katie looked up from her phone. "You guys don't *need* to talk, you know? We could just sit here and wait for our IDs in blissful silence."

"Which brings me back to my question." Kurt gave Natalie's shoulder a poke. "What do you all need the IDs for? Katie's wearing a *Fangoria* T-shirt—" he jutted a thumb at Natalie's friend "—so maybe I was wrong about the clubbing thing."

Natalie rolled her eyes. Katie was right, she didn't have to talk to Kurt, but she couldn't help it. She was used to holding her own against arrogant trolls in true-crime forums. Plus, it was kind of fun.

"Not really your business, but it's a professional thing…"

Natalie replied. "Anyway, do they even have clubbing around here? Aside from, like, the 4H?"

Kurt stopped smirking, a real smile ghosting across his face. "I don't know, to be honest. I'm not a party kind of guy, if you can possibly believe it." He poked a few more keys, and Natalie heard the sound of a printer starting up in Jack's room—accompanied by an almost prehistoric moan. Jack hath risen.

"That makes two of us." Natalie leaned back a bit, relaxing. "Unless by *party* you mean *steal red wine from my mom and binge* Forensic Files, then, yeah, sure, I party *hard*."

It was true. Natalie was, unsurprisingly, not the most social of people. She had tried to go to parties when she was younger, something to do to pass the time until graduation, but eventually she gave up after the third time someone accidentally spilled beer on her head in a crowded living room. Why waste your life doing something you actively dislike for the sake of appearances, when you could just do what you actually enjoy—even if that meant being alone? That was also what initially had drawn her to Katie. Her willingness to not only shirk the trappings of school but to disconnect from them entirely.

"Give us our IDs, Jack!" Katie yelled abruptly, banging on Jack's door. She had been fiddling with a beta version of her app while Natalie and Kurt talked and was getting frustrated, if the figurative storm cloud above her head was any indication. She looked between Natalie and Kurt with a furrow between her dark brows, digging a candy bar from her pocket that Natalie had not noticed previously. Katie tore the candy wrapper open with her teeth and took a bite, speaking the rest through a whirlpool of chocolate and caramel. "We need to go get lunch. My blood sugar is crashing."

Natalie looked away from Katie's snack and noticed that Kurt was staring at her, his gaze unfocused and somewhat confused. A piece of his light blond hair had fallen across his eyes, and his mouth was just a little open. It was weirding her out.

Jack banged back into the kitchen. "Jesus, calm the fuck down!" He threw the IDs into Katie's lap. "Don't get too wasted, little cuz!"

Katie tossed an ID at Natalie and missed: it landed in Kurt's lap. He looked down at the piece of plastic, then shot Natalie a crooked smile. "Would you like me to hand this to you, princess?"

Natalie glared at him until he tossed the ID over, and she made a big show of wiping it off on her shirt before she raised it to her eyes for a close study. It was good, really good. Her senior photo in the upper right-hand corner, a slightly adjusted birthdate, and her name and address printed over a subtle hologram. Or half her name, really. "Natalie Baker?" she muttered.

"Can't put your real name," Kurt spoke suddenly from over her shoulder, jabbing a finger at the faux last name. "Guessing people know your mom and whatever around here."

Natalie blinked, still staring at the ID. "How did you get all this info? My birthday and my address?"

When she looked up, Kurt was grinning full on. "I'm

kind of good with the internet. I even found your cell number, if you'd like me to use it? I have a car and everything."

Natalie rolled her eyes and looked back down at the little piece of plastic. And, all of a sudden, she felt nervous about what she and Katie had planned. She hoped to god that she was up for a *real* criminal investigation, especially without the necessary training she would get in college. But she had read enough books, watched enough movies and shows—she had to have absorbed *something*, she reasoned. At least enough to have a friendly chat with the mistress of an alleged murderer. All she needed for that was a mouth and a brain.

"Nice!" Katie swallowed the last bite of her candy bar and shoved the ID in her back pocket. "Let's go, Natalie! I hate everything about it here."

"You still never told me what you needed them for," Kurt said, his eyes fixed on Natalie. "Maybe I can help." He reached into his pocket for his phone and tapped at it a second. Instantly, Natalie's own cell vibrated in her pocket.

Before she could reach for it, though, Katie grabbed Natalie's arm and hauled her toward the door, crowing over her shoulder, "None of your fucking business, dude!"

As she exited the trailer, Natalie saw Kurt smile at her again, but she didn't have time to figure out whether or not it was sarcastic. When she finally pulled out her phone later that day, she had a new text from a local number.

This is me. If you ever need a ride.

CHAPTER NINE: THEN

As it turned out, the boy-man from the newspaper meeting was named Sam Gleeson and, as the editor in chief, had access to the student database. Which is how Helen came to find herself standing outside the Robertses' massive stone Evanston house. As it also turned out, Jenny lived locally with her parents, who Sam had told Helen to interview in order to add *color* to her story. When she had asked for a little more guidance than that, he had thrown a stack of old newspapers at her and slammed out of the room.

Now, Helen cowered, stock-still, at 45 Elmwood Street, studying the cheerful red of the door on which she very much did not want to knock. What was she supposed to say when they answered? *Hey, I met your daughter once, and I'm writing a story about her going missing. Want to tell me everything, even though I'm a stranger and have zero reporting experience?* That didn't seem all that smart. The absurdly early jack-o'-lanterns next to the door seemed in agreement, sneering in her direction as she stood there, lost.

Sighing, Helen smoothed her red cardigan over the top of her pencil skirt and took a big breath of fall air, preparing to bite the bullet and let her fist fly. Illinois was a lot like Connecticut in September: crisp, chilly, full of red leaves, it made her just a little bit less homesick for her dad. So did the potted herbs on the Robertses' porch. Her dad loved his vegetable garden, the herbs on his windowsills. He had had to learn to cook when Helen's mom died—when she was six—and he embraced the practice with gusto. Helen always loved watching her dad, with his surgeon's hands, deftly cutting away old growth to let through the new.

She was still gazing dreamily at the rosemary, her fist aloft, when the red door burst open, followed by a woman in a plush blue robe, her blond hair lank around her face. "What? What do you want?" she raked her hands over her cheeks. "I've told you people over and over, no interviews." The woman pressed her pale, shaking hands over her eyes and drew in a shuttering breath.

Helen froze, hands clutching the straps on her backpack. The urge to run flooded through her like cold water, but her legs refused to listen to her brain. She vaguely remembered what her dad had been like when her mom died—he had stayed in bed for days, so long that she finally curled up with him in the dirty sheets and cried and cried until he pulled himself together enough to get them both of out bed. Mrs. Roberts's grief was rawer, more feral—maybe because Jenny wasn't gone entirely. Maybe because she still *needed* to fight. So there Helen stood, roasting in the woman's rage, the rosemary, and the rank scent of her own sweaty shame in the air.

Finally, the woman dropped her hands and, as she took in Helen quivering before her, her face softened. "Oh, you're a kid," she said as waking from a nightmare. Helen tried not to bristle at the word; she knew she looked younger than her eighteen years. "I thought you were a reporter. They've been circling since Jenny..." Mrs. Roberts trailed off, her eyes filling.

Helen opened her mouth to correct the mistake, but she had seen the blind fury in the woman's eyes when she had opened the door. She didn't want to be on the receiving end of that anguished stare again, so instead, a whole new series of words came spilling out of her mouth: "Um, I—I'm in her class..." she stuttered. "Journalism 101?" It was technically not a lie. It didn't really mean anything, either, though.

Mrs. Roberts smiled, the expression shaky, like she wasn't used to it anymore. "Oh, you're one of her friends, then? She never lets me meet anyone from school." Her face hardened. "She's always going to parties, so I know she has them, but god forbid someone come for dinner." She paused—putting her hand to her mouth as if horrified at herself for sounding bitter—then gave Helen an appraising look, taking in her neat outfit and straight posture. "You seem like a good person for her to know, though. I mean, I don't know you, but you don't have any tattoos or piercings so..." She laughed, a manic thing that was too loud in the autumnal afternoon air.

The two stared at each other—Mrs. Roberts tugging at the neck of her robe, Helen unsure what exactly to say following the initial lie. The interview was obviously shot. Mrs. Roberts was looking at her like the last known link to her missing daughter, and she couldn't bring herself to sever it. "Uh," she said finally and coughed. "Congratulations." At Mrs. Roberts's blank expression, she added, "Jenny told me about the baby?"

Mrs. Roberts smiled again, less shaky this time, then cocked her head to the side. She nodded, as if Helen had passed some sort of unknown test. "Do you want to come in?" she asked, stepping to the side so that Helen could see a velvety blue couch covered in flowered pillows and a nest of blankets, like someone had been sleeping there—as close to the door as possible, in case Jenny came home. "I have some pictures of Jenny if you want to see?" She frowned. "Is that weird? It would just be nice to sit with you for a while...someone who knows her."

Helen swallowed hard, guilt sitting in the pit of her stomach like an anchor. She was getting first-rate access to Jenny's life, the perfect background for her story. But was it ethical to do so under false pretenses? Something told her that the answer was an emphatic *no*, but with Jenny's mom staring at her like Helen had her daughter somewhere on her person, it was hard to say to say anything else by *yes*. In the end, she settled for a mute nod and followed Mrs. Roberts into the dark cave of Jenny's home.

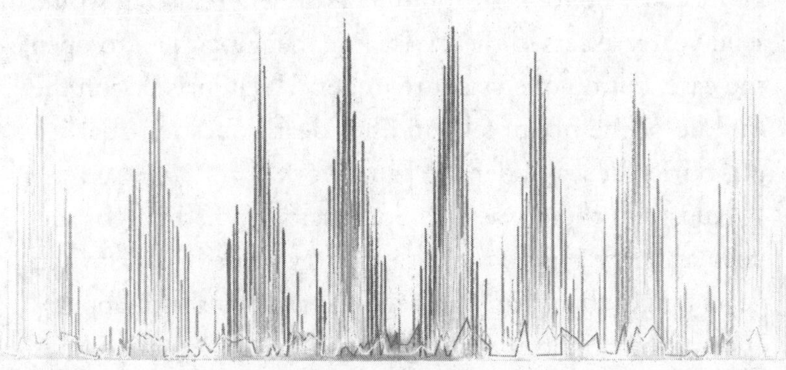

CHAPTER TEN

Natalie knew, on some level, that no town was really perfect—not even Ferry. But most of the mayhem that had befallen her town had happened before she was born; therefore, it took on the feel of folklore. Ghost stories told around campfires and whispers exchanged at sleepovers that kept you awake long past your friends drifting off to sleep.

She had heard Dan Petras, the yoga teacher at the local YMCA, tell the tale of his cousin Arlene on a date one night at the diner after too many whiskeys. How she'd taken a cruise to Jamaica to celebrate her high-school graduation and was found dead in her cabin two days into the trip. The coroners said she tripped and fell and hit her head on the nightstand, but Dan heard from a friend of Arlene's that her ex-boyfriend Charles was also on the cruise. An ex-boyfriend who took great umbrage at being *ex*. Dan would send yearly letters to the cruise line, begging them to open the case, but no one was sure under which jurisdiction the middle of the ocean fell, and her death question-marked on, buried at sea under the paperwork.

And then there was Mr. Sprouse, who had taught science at Ferry High for the last thirty years—and, for ten years longer than that, had been haunted by the disappearance of the bright-cheeked girl who used to cut his hair as a child. Sprouse told Natalie's mother all about it one evening when he was the only one left at the diner before close. Natalie had hidden low behind the counter so her mother wouldn't see that she was listening. Claire Hastings went missing the day after her twenty-sixth birthday without a trace—except for a single white Keds that was found on the periphery of the great forest that wove its way through Ferry, bringing whiffs of the wild into manicured backyards, and driving house cats mad. Teddy Sprouse used to wander through those woods as a young teen, convinced that he would find her there. In his more optimistic moments, he imagined that she had treaded, Walden-like, into the abyss to live off the land—away from shrieking toddlers suffering through their first haircuts and the sting of bottle-blond bleach. In his darkest, most feverishly excited reveries, he pictured her rotting away under the forest floor, her face stretched in an eternal, skinless scream. Natalie might have taken some poetic license when imagining how that particular story played out.

From town whispers and all those hours logged watching documentaries and trolling forums, Natalie knew that everyone knows *someone* who has been murdered, who has been lost, who almost took that final ride with some infamous highway killer. And everyone, each one, holds that story somewhere in the bad part of their heart that thrills at being a breath away from tragedy, yet safe in their beds, free from the stink of death. Now, as she pedaled up to Eliza Minnow's bar, she supposed she could count herself among their lucky and equally unfortunate ranks.

When Katie and Natalie approached the big plate-glass window of O'Riley's, the only real dive bar to speak of in Ferry—West Ferry, to be specific—it looked relatively empty. There were just a few clusters of patrons in the shadows of the room.

"This seems like a bad idea," Katie said, pulling out her ID for a closer look, a muscle ticking near her eye. "They're going to know this is fake."

Her eyes widened, and she spun around to face Natalie. "What if they call MIT? Can they change their minds at this point? Fuck, I don't want to go to trade school." She groaned, examining the interior of the bar again. "Plus, I don't even see Eliza."

There was a young redheaded man they didn't recognize standing behind the bar, cleaning glasses in a lazy way as he stared at the baseball game on the wall-mounted TV.

Natalie snorted, trying to pretend she wasn't worried about all the same things. "She could be in the back. Let's go."

Natalie had expected that there would be a bouncer checking IDs at the door, someone big and round-bellied and dressed in black; she was almost disappointed when she walked into O'Riley's without any issue. Most of the patrons clustered at tables back in the dim recesses of the bar: a woman and man on what seemed like their first date sitting awkwardly on the same side of the table; a pack of women in sparkling tops laughing like gulls; and the occasional loner skulking over a drink and their phone. Natalie strode to the bar and plopped down on a stool, trying to look like she belonged, which was hard considering that she and Katie were the youngest people there—by far. This dive bar was decidedly the haven of the older, hard-living set.

"I need a drink," she said, trying for a seasoned growl. "Maybe whiskey."

Katie scooted onto the stool next to hers. "Me, too. But I want a Sex on the Beach. Do you think they make them here?" They gave the room another scan and erupted into stifled giggles.

"Quiet." Natalie composed herself. "We're going get thrown out," she cautioned, spinning slightly on her seat. Her feet didn't reach the ground, which was good, because it looked sticky. They had to focus. This wasn't about sneaking into a bar and drinking—they weren't boring teenagers in a raunchy coming-of-age comedy: they had a mission.

Natalie eyed the man behind the bar again, trying to figure out what to say. She couldn't just ask for Eliza, could she? He would want to know why. They had to act natural, like they went to bars for drinks all the time. Like this was no big deal.

"Excuse me," she called out in a weak voice.

The man kept cleaning glasses, his eyes on the TV screen;

he hadn't heard her—or pretended not to. She shook her shoulders. She had to be authoritative. She had to act like she belonged. She cleared her throat. "Excuse me," she said again, her voice coming out extra loud. The man turned around.

"Can I have a whiskey," she announced more than asked, then breathed out shakily.

The man squinted at her, and suddenly Natalie imagined what he probably saw: two girls sliding across their seats, their shoulders sharp in faded T-shirts. Two girls who stuck out like those proverbial sore thumbs among the weathered crowd. He scoffed, putting a semiclean glass behind the bar. "I can't serve you," he sneered. His nose was a spray of freckles, and he didn't look much older than them.

Natalie's heart plummeted, and she fumbled in her pocket for an impotent moment or two, finally extracting her wallet and phony ID. "Why not?" she tried for a laugh, and it came out shaky, like a lamb bleating. "I have an ID, see?" She shoved the piece of plastic toward the man, and he just stared at her.

"No, hon," he said, leaning back against the wall, tucking his thumbs into the front pockets of his tight jeans. "I can't serve you because I'm a *barback*. You have to order from Eliza, the *bartender*. She'll be back in a few."

"Oh..." Natalie said, reaching for the ID, her cheeks flaming.

The man snatched it up before she could nab it and examined the piece of laminated cardstock in the gloom of the bar. "Jeez. Jack do this? He's getting good."

"No! No one made it. I mean the DMV did, of course,

but… I don't know what…" Natalie stalled, her heart sinking. They were going to get thrown out for sure now—all because of her. Because she couldn't get it together enough to order a drink in a bar without having a nervous breakdown. How was she supposed to be a serious journalist—go undercover, talk to criminals—if she couldn't handle one small-town barback?

The man tossed the ID toward Natalie and interrupted with a gruff laugh. "I don't give a fuck if you drink, kid. I dunno if Eliza will feel the same, though."

"And just what am I feeling something about, Jimmy?" A sweet voice emerged from behind the barback as a woman pushed her way through a set of low swinging doors.

Jimmy cocked a thumb at the girls on their stools and snorted at the new arrival.

Natalie's eyes widened. Eliza Minnow. The mistress, in the flesh. The woman who, possibly, had impelled Mr. Halsey to kill his wife in cold blood. Or, was Mr. Halsey a fall guy? Did Eliza actually do it? Had jealousy turned to bloodshed? Natalie just stared, slack-jawed, as the woman slid behind the bar and poured herself a scotch. It was like seeing a character from a movie step off the screen, but not at all. This woman could have been partially responsible for her favorite teacher's death—and here she was, slinging drinks, living, breathing. Dislike started to uncurl in Natalie's chest like a snake and, with it, an anger that burned away the previous shame over botching it with the barback.

Eliza doesn't look like a mistress is supposed to, Natalie thought grudgingly. All leopard-print and spandex and loud jewelry. She was trim. Small. Light. She wore tailored black pants and a crisp white shirt, and her dark hair was pulled back in a low ponytail. She was pretty, undeniably, but not in a way that shouted. Her face was clear, makeup-free, and more than a little lost around the eyes.

"Hey there, kids," Eliza said, leaning close to the girls. "What is it you hope I won't give a fuck about?"

Natalie and Katie froze, staring at Eliza's ski-slope nose, her clear-ice eyes. Natalie tried not to glare. *The sanctity of marriage?* she thought. *Mrs. Halsey's life?*

When the silence didn't show any signs of breaking, Jimmy piped up. "They wanted some drinks. Not sure I trust those IDs, though."

Eliza tilted her head to the side. "There's lots of places to get drinks in Ferry that aren't so…public. Larry at Gas 'N' Go is pretty lenient, as I'm sure you know. I got a kid. I'm not totally out of the loop."

The girls just stared, and Natalie racked her brain for something, anything, that she could say to Eliza. She wanted to ask if it were true. If she had ever met Mrs. Halsey. And, if so, how she could have ruined her life like that. More than anything, she wanted someone to blame for what had happened to her teacher, and Eliza was there, convenient. She clenched her fists, trying to quell her rage, reminding herself of another of Mrs. Halsey's lessons, the one on villains. *In all fiction*, Mrs. Halsey had said, *you have to have empathy for the bad guy. If you paint them as one hundred percent black-and-white bad, you're making your story less believable—and less interesting. Find out why they do the things they do, and try to understand.*

"I…have a podcast," she began, mustering some kernel

of strength from the center of herself. She was aware that she sounded shaky, less than professional, but she soldiered on. For Mrs. Halsey. For the story. "And I came here to get your side. To let you speak for yourself about Mr. Halsey and your relationship with him. With your involvement in everything that's been going on." The words rushed out of her mouth but, thankfully, tumbled out in order. She folded her hands in front of her and silently congratulated herself on not letting any trace of the anger burning in her belly leak into her voice.

Eliza's eyes locked on Natalie's phone, which was open to a recording app. "And what is this podcast about, might I ask?"

Katie leaned across the bar, her *Fangoria* T-shirt immediately getting soaked with spilled beer. "Usually we just bullshit about serial killers and murders—"

"But—" Natalie cut in, casting her friend a dirty look "—we've recently gone more journalistic. We're looking to tell the stories behind tragedies. We just want to be true—to be fair."

Eliza studied Natalie's eager face for a moment or two, then gave a humorless smile. "What I think we have here, Jimmy, is a couple of lookie-loos. Rubberneckers. Emotional vampires."

"Seems like," Jimmy replied, leaning in for a close look at Natalie. He smelled like tobacco and something else. *Man.* That was all she could think to call it. It was dark and somewhat wild and warm. "Already had a few wander in from the newspaper and whatnot, but seems like they're making 'em younger every day. What are you guys, like, thirteen? Are you even allowed to have a podcast?" Jimmy tapped Natalie's ID and leered.

Natalie sat back on her stool but tried for a straight back, tall and proud. She felt just the opposite, though, like she wanted to vacate her seat so fast it spun. Like she wanted to pedal home as quickly as she could and hide in bed. She wondered if any of her podcasting heroes ever felt as uncomfortable as this—like someone had read her diary in front of her and laughed. She swallowed, though, determined to fight to the last.

Sliding her phone further along the bar and flicking on the recording app, she looked away from Jimmy and locked eyes with Eliza once more. "I promise I'm not a rubbernecker. I'm a journalist. I just want to capture the truth." The word felt hollow in her mouth. *Journalist.* But she ached for it to be true. She willed it to be so. She couldn't pretend to be an of-age drinker, but she could be this. She had been practicing all her life.

Eliza leaned forward, her pink nails drumming the bar, her face impassive. "You want to know what I have to say about Mr. Halsey—Bill?" she asked, looking down at Natalie's phone, the Record button glowing red.

Natalie nodded, her hand gripping the device. It was working. She had been direct, and now she was going to get a quote—her first. And from a prime source that not even the papers had managed to snag yet.

Eliza looked at the phone for a long moment, like it was a thing that might bite. Then she looked at Natalie, looked her in the eyes. Locked in on them with her cold blue ones.

"Anything I like? Anything I want to say? You'll put in your podcast?"

Natalie nodded. Her neck felt stiff.

Eliza cleared her throat. "Okay." She leaned toward the phone, cocked an eyebrow at Natalie. "That thing's on, right?"

Mutely, Natalie nodded, leaning forward on her stool as close as she could get to the bartender.

Eliza coughed softly, bringing her coral mouth almost timidly toward the mic. "Hello, my name is Eliza Minnow, and I have just one thing to say to you all about this whole, sad mess. Fuck…off."

"Oh, man, dude, your face," Katie chortled, pedaling fast across the bridge that spanned the Ferry River. "It looked like she told you Santa didn't exist all over again."

Natalie's hands gripped her handlebars until they hurt. She hadn't said a word to Katie since they left the bar. She was too embarrassed and, now, pissed off. At least the night air was cool on her face. Small favors.

"Come on." Katie pulled even with Natalie, shooting her an imploring look. Their bikes bumped over the last of the bridge and hit the more smoothly paved streets of East Ferry. Up ahead, the church speared the shadows, and the neat lines of houses marched toward the horizon like building blocks. "I'm sorry," Katie said. "I shouldn't joke about it. I know you were stoked to talk to her."

Natalie kept her eyes on the road. "Maybe she wouldn't have reacted that way if you hadn't told her our podcast is basically just bullshitting about murder."

"Nah," Katie mused, not taking the bait. "I think she would have. I mean, what do you expect? She was having an affair with this guy, and now his wife's dead, and all of a sudden everyone's asking her all these questions. She must be freaked. I wouldn't want to talk to us, either."

"Then, why did you even come," Natalie huffed, "if you thought it was doomed from the start?" Her house came into view ahead, and a sense of relief flooded her bones. It looked snug in the dark night. A little blue-trimmed haven against that evening's shaming.

"Because I love you, you idiot," Katie said, pulling her bike to a stop outside the Temples' house. "And you wanted me to." She slung her arm around Natalie and pulled her toward the door, and despite her earlier rage, Natalie leaned into her friend, grateful. Plus, the house was filled with the smell of warm butter and popcorn, and the geranium candles her mother liked to light on summer evenings, the lights low. She could almost forget that she had utterly failed at being a proper journalist. Almost.

"My children!" Helen yelled from the plush red couch, raising her glass of wine in a joyful toast. "Come watch my stories with me!"

Katie and Natalie flopped on either side of Helen, kicking off their shoes. Katie reached for a handful of popcorn and turned to the TV. "I love that your stories are *Buffy the Vampire Slayer*, Mrs. T."

Buffy was the one remotely violent show that Helen watched with her daughter—especially after the entire series had started streaming on Netflix. Natalie always assumed it was because her mom hoped the slayer's karate skills would transmit to her daughter while she watched, like osmosis.

Helen took a sip of wine and shrugged. "What can I say? I like Giles."

Katie frowned. "The librarian? He's old."

"And so, my dear, am I." Helen threw an arm around Natalie. "When you get older you'll learn the value of a man who is steady and true. Cautious. Informed."

Natalie rolled her eyes at Katie. "She's only saying that because I made the mistake of admitting that I have a crush on Spike."

"Excuse me for being worried that my daughter has a propensity for soulless vampires with bad dye jobs!" Helen squeezed Natalie hard. "Bad boys are fun on the silver screen, kid, but in real life they're just that. Bad."

"On that note, we're going to my room to watch something that's not twenty years old." Natalie got to her feet, nudging Katie with her sneaker. Her friend was halfway through the popcorn now, eyes glued to Buffy as she staked down a rapid succession of vampires.

"I can see why you like this show, Mrs. T," Katie said, rapt. "Buffy is fucking incredible."

Helen looked up from the couch and shot Natalie a smile. "Listen to Katie, Nat. She is wise."

"Hell yes, I am," Katie replied, as Natalie sank bank down on the couch with her mother and her best friend, the evening's failures forgotten. At least for now.

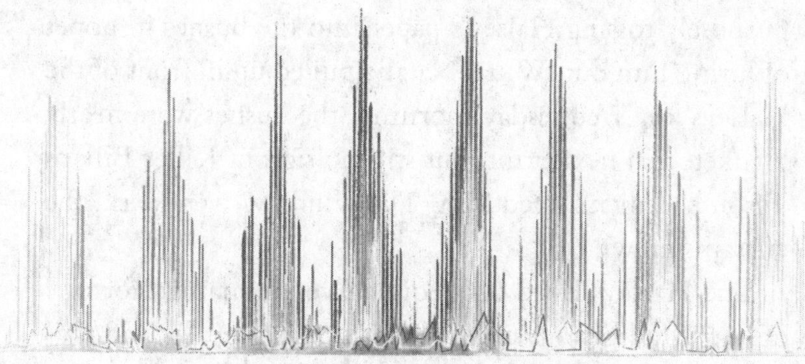

CHAPTER ELEVEN

The diner was absolutely chaotic for the next few days, which was good because Natalie's ego was still stinging after her failed interview with Eliza. It was hard to contemplate abject professional failure when everyone was yelling at you about burgers and fries and kids were constantly spilling stuff all over themselves and everyone else. The mop got a good workout—and so did Natalie.

When Wednesday rolled around, though, she was more than ready to take a break from fryer grease and get back to investigating: luckily, she had her internship at the *Ferry Caller.* She planned to make a pass by the Halseys' house on the way to work, maybe see if she could see Bill Halsey in the flesh. No one had laid eyes on him since that day at the diner, and Natalie had heard Tyson DeGraw, the newspaper man, bragging to his friends that he had started purposely tossing Halsey's paper into the bushes in hopes of luring him out. When Natalie pulled up in front of the Halseys' on Wednesday morning, the bushes were nearly blanketed in newsprint, but still no sign of Killer Bill, as Tyson had nicknamed him. The windows were dark, the curtains drawn.

The Halseys lived on Pequot Avenue, named for one of many Indigenous peoples that English settlers had ravaged when they ostensibly discovered Connecticut. Their stately white colonial was nestled right in the bosom of the East Ferry; it faced Sandy Tarver's saltbox house, which she had painted a sickly light pink. The Ferry Historical Society would have definitely complained if Sandy weren't the president. As she slid off her bike, Natalie shot a glance at the Tarver home, just in case Sandy loomed in the window, as she so often did. Thankfully, the frilly curtains were drawn, and neither of the family's mint-green PT Cruisers were parked in the driveway. It looked like Mr. Halsey's convertible was in the garage; Natalie could see a glimpse of blue through the windows. He was probably still holed up inside.

Still, the Halseys' house looked just as deserted as the rest of the block, and despite the sunshine, it looked haunted. Natalie wondered if it was because she knew that Mrs. Halsey had died there, likely afraid, or if something fundamental had changed about the structure. If tragedy had leached into it like smoke. She stood for a while, staring at it without understanding what she was waiting for.

Answers? Mr. Halsey to come bursting through the front door, confessing to the crime?

The blank eyes of the house froze her to the spot, terrifying her and thrilling her all at once, until a man emerged from around the back of the house, toting a spade and a burlap bag. He stilled when he saw Natalie, and she froze as well. She knew pretty much everyone in East Ferry, but she didn't know him. Anyone wandering around the Halseys' house was fair game when it came to suspects, as far as Natalie was concerned. Her hands got cold as she imagined that maybe this man was the killer, that he had come back to the scene of the crime to collect some kind of sick trophy. He was carrying *a shovel and a bag*, after all.

She straightened her back and fought the urge to run, which is what any sane person would do when face-to-face with a possible murderer. But this is what she wanted to do: investigate the dark, stare evil in the eye. She may have struck out at the dive bar, but she was on her home turf now. She was within her rights to ask questions, and it wasn't like the guy would attack her in the middle of a sunny street, she reasoned. She *hoped*.

"Hey!" she called, taking a few tentative steps toward the Halseys' lawn. "Are you a friend of Mr. Halsey's?"

She was pleased to find that her voice didn't shake. She sounded confident, poised—although some sort of residual anger about what had happened to Mrs. Halsey must have leaked through, because the man looked up with shock painted across his face—and not a small amount of indignation. There were deep-cut lines etched around his mouth, and his dark brow furrowed under the brim of his ball cap.

Natalie swallowed, taking a step back. The stranger wasn't a small man. He had a strong back and wide shoulders that tapered down into a waspish waist—a sharp contrast to most of the men of Ferry, who had long ago gone soft in both the stomach and the hands.

"Hey!" Natalie said again, her voice wavering. She cursed herself for her lack of composure, forcing her feet to stay in place—then changed her plan of attack. If he didn't respond to directness, maybe she should go softer—nonthreatening, innocent. She was glad her hair was down today, that she was wearing a loose T-shirt and shorts that made her look younger.

"I'm doing a project for school," she said, praying that this guy didn't have kids. That he had no idea when summer vacation started. He wasn't wearing a ring, so it was possible. "Do you have a minute to talk? I just want to ask a few questions."

Her hand fumbled for her phone, and as she extracted it from her pocket, the man's eyes widened. That's when Natalie saw it: fear. He was afraid of *her.*

Natalie and the man stared at each other like a deer and a hunter—it was unclear which was which. Finally, the man forfeited the staring contest and tossed the spade into his bag, ducking his head and dashing across the lawn to the street. Natalie flinched back, expecting him to run toward her, to strike her, but he veered to the right and threw open the door of a rusted, red pickup and climbed inside, gunning the engine. The vehicle tore off, but not before Natalie could sort out that the back of the truck was filled with lawn-care gear—lawn mower, rakes, and the like—and, of course, snap a photo.

She watched until the last of his bumper disappeared, then studied the photo, where she had clearly captured his license plate. He could have just been a gardener who didn't get the memo about the murder, Natalie reasoned. But that seemed highly unlikely in a town where the front-page news more often than not dealt with the prowess of the Ferry High football team, the Falcons. And if that were the case, why run?

The police could keep investigating Mr. Halsey, and she would, too, but anyone hanging around the Halsey residence was fair game, as far as Natalie was concerned. Especially ones who carried spades and bags and ran from questioning. And, as luck would have it, she was on her way to the one place in town where she could launch an investigation of her own.

Natalie's mother hadn't been all that thrilled at first when Natalie had posited interning at the *Ferry Caller*—especially since she knew her daughter would spend most of her time sniffing around the crime department. But when she found out that Natalie's job mostly comprised scanning old editions in the paper's unending quest to create a digital archive, she loosened up. It was a thankless job, and Natalie had almost quit more than once, but it did look good on her college applications, even if all she did was sit in a cramped copy room for eight hours per week collecting paper cuts. Which was exactly what she was doing mere minutes after jetting away from the Halseys', stranger's license-plate number in hand.

Usually, she popped in her headphones and disappeared into a podcast as she got down to the mindless task, but today she needed to keep her ears open if she wanted to seize the opportunity to do a little digging on the mystery man. She knew that Mrs. Pressman had access to the DMV database—she'd once made a crack about checking up on all of Jonathan's dates—so locating the man's ID was as good as done. She also knew that all the computers were password-protected, so she'd have to get to her computer while it was unattended just long enough that it didn't lock again. Easier said than done, but not impossible. She kept an eye on the main floor, waiting for the crew to start to trickle out for lunch.

"Hey, Nat!" Jonathan appeared at the door to the copy room, looking fresh and scrubbed in a Red Sox T-shirt and jeans—and effectively obscuring her view. "How many paper cuts you got so far?"

Natalie smiled and held up her hands, all the while craning to keep an eye on the room over his shoulder. "Only two," she said, pointing to the webbing between her right thumb and pointer. "The older papers are much softer than the new ones." She sniffed her palm and cringed. "They smell a lot worse, though."

"I keep telling you to wear gloves, Nat," Jonathan chided, giving her a smile that caused cheerleaders to spontaneously combust and, thankfully, moving into the room and out of the doorway.

"And I keep forgetting." She groaned. "Next week, for sure." She fed a sports page from 1976 into the scanner and wrinkled her nose when she saw that it was smeared with what looked like mustard. A stain older than her mother.

"Here, you can have mine," Jonathan said, tossing a pair of latex gloves into her lap. "I don't need 'em anymore. I got a promotion." He raised his hand for a high five, and Natalie just stared at it, momentarily forgetting her mission.

She had been interning at the paper for two years now. Jonathan had just started last year when he needed to beef up his college applications. He wanted to be a social worker or something. Natalie hadn't been listening. How had he secured a promotion over her? She frowned. Nepotism truly was the scourge of small towns, but this was ridiculous.

Jonathan's face crumpled as he took in her frown and Natalie inwardly rolled her eyes. He really was a golden retriever. She forced a smile. "Congrats. Do I need to be too jealous?" Maybe his job wasn't all that exciting after all, she mused. Maybe they had just put him on coffee duty or something. Anything was better than the scanner. It haunted her dreams. Literally. Last night it had been chasing her, snapping its lid like teeth.

"Depends," Jonathan said, looking relieved that she wasn't frowning anymore. "How do you feel about talking to super-intense people for eight hours a day?"

"Fine, I guess. I'm friends with Katie." Natalie paused to feed another page of 1976 into the machine. "Can you be a little more specific?"

"Well," Jonathan said, his sunny face dimming a bit, "I guess Mr. Halsey is offering a reward for any information about what..." his voice shook "...what happened, you know. Twenty thousand dollars."

Natalie nodded. It was a good move, she thought. It made Halsey look far less guilty if he was reaching out to the community for help. But it also looked like he was trying too hard, if the dollar amount was any indication. The US Marshals offered rewards like that for info on high-profile fugitives.

"Where do the intense people come in?" she asked.

"I'm helping with the tip line. He teamed up with the *Caller* on one," Jonathan said. "Basically, I field the calls and listen to the messages and turn in anything that sounds interesting to my mom. Most of the calls have been pretty bogus, though. Someone suggested it was the Zodiac Killer."

"Nah, pretty sure he died in a men's prison in California," Natalie replied. "Or at least, I've heard."

Jealousy was back. Working the tip line was mostly futile, sure, but it would be a major help when it came to her investigation. Natalie looked at the unending pile of ancient newspapers on the floor and sighed.

"I can ask my mom if she needs another volunteer?" Jonathan ventured.

Natalie jumped out of her chair, flinging her arms around Jonathan's neck, surprising both him and, mostly, herself. "That would be amazing, Jonathan! Thank you!"

He hugged her, then stepped back with another cheerleader-igniting smile. "No sweat." He rubbed the back of his neck. It could have been her imagination or the terrible copy-room fluorescents, but Natalie thought he was blushing. "Anyway, Mom and me are going to lunch, if you want to join?"

Natalie's heart banged into her rib cage. "You mean, like, she's leaving her office?"

"Yeah..." Jonathan raised a quizzical eyebrow. "Unless they installed a hamburger grill in there that I don't know about."

Natalie didn't even need to force a laugh. She was feeling giddy with possibility. "I'm brown-bagging it today, but I'd like to drop by and say hi, if that's cool?"

"Knock yourself out..." Jonathan shrugged.

The copy room didn't have any windows, so Natalie blinked like a mole as they emerged into the rest of the office; even though the lights were fluorescent and everyone was permahunched over their laptops, it was a bright day outside, so it felt borderline cheerful in the big, open workspace with its chorus of clacking keyboards. Mrs. Pressman had one of the only private offices on the floor—the perks of being one of the most senior staff members at a very small paper.

Jonathan knocked just to the right of Mrs. Pressman's nameplate but opened the door nearly immediately after. "Hey, Mom!" he cried, then bounded into the room.

His mother looked up, blinking, as if she wasn't sure who Jonathan was or how he came to find himself in her office. Her desk was a mess of half-filled coffee cups, plus papers and files that Natalie valiantly fought the urge to snatch up and clutch to her chest. Instead, she pillaged the papers with her eyes, lighting on a glossy photo half-covered by a folder: it showed a woman's leg, bent at an unnatural angle, her red pump hanging from her toe. Natalie stared at it, blinking. She knew that shoe. It was from the pair

Mrs. Halsey had been wearing when they first met. The woman had the biggest shoe collection Natalie had ever seen. One pair of pumps for every color of the rainbow. The red were her favorite.

Natalie couldn't stop looking at the shoe in the photo. Couldn't stop herself from picturing the rest. Mrs. Halsey's blank eyes. The blood. Was she wearing her leather jacket, too? Was it bagged up in evidence somewhere now?

Noticing Natalie's eyes on her papers, Flora Pressman hurriedly bundled everything together and shoved it into a drawer, turning the lock and pocketing the key. Then she smiled, turning toward her son and his friend. "Hey, Johnny, Nat! What can I do for you two?"

"We have lunch plans, remember?" Jonathan said, gently.

"Is it lunchtime already?" Mrs. Pressman said, looking at her watch. "So, it is… Time flies when you're…"

"I can come back later if you like?" Jonathan put a hand on his mother's shoulder. "If you need to keep working?"

She rubbed at her eyes behind her glasses. "No, no. I should get out of the office for a bit." She dropped her hands and looked at her son fondly. "Spend some time with my boy before he leaves me forever."

"Mom, I'm just going to Pennsylvania." Jonathan frowned. "We've talked about this. I'll probably be home every weekend with my laundry, anyway, so you'll hardly know I'm gone." He grinned, giving her shoulder a shake.

"In that case, remind me to never teach you about darks and lights," his mother replied, tears thick in her voice. She glanced at Natalie and sniffed. "Are you coming with us, hon?"

Natalie shook her head, feeling more than a little bit

awkward. If she bristled against her own mother's overprotectiveness, Jonathan seemed to bask in his. It bothered her in a way she couldn't articulate. Perhaps because she felt like this was the time when they should all be growing up, not going backward. Or maybe it was just because she had been doing her own laundry since fourth grade. Sure, her mother wanted to keep her safe from the ills of the world, but those ills certainly did not include learning how to be a self-sufficient human with an ample supply of clean clothing.

"Just wanted to come say hi," she said, her eyes wandering to Mrs. Pressman's computer, which was still logged in. Jackpot. "Also, um, mind if I raid your stash of…women's things?" She shot a faux embarrassed glance at Jonathan, who looked at his feet as every boy did when faced with the reality of women's bodies. Mrs. Pressman famously had a drawer full of tampons for all the women on staff, her mothering extending even beyond the home.

Mrs. Pressman gave her a knowing smile, collecting her purse from the back of her chair. "Be my guest. Bottom drawer on the left." She grabbed her son by the elbow. "Come on, then, John-John. I'll buy you a burger."

After the Pressmans left the office, Natalie counted to ten before closing the door and sliding into Mrs. Pressman's desk chair, her phone already in hand. It took her a minute or two to locate the right database but, then, after only a few strokes on the keyboard, she sat there in shock for a moment or two. It seemed almost too easy, the way the information showed up. Like magic or a lightning bolt or something else clichéd. When she got over the initial disbelief, she fought the urge to smile. This was her first break—but it was also a terrifying one. The man with the sack was named Ron K. Stackman, 121 South 68th Place, West Ferry, Connecticut—and he was listed on the sex-offender registry.

CHAPTER TWELVE: THEN

Screams erupted outside Helen's window—guttural, wrenching, throat-wrecking. She jumped, her knees thwacking the underside of her desk, heart racing until she remembered it was Primal Scream Night: everyone was supposed to blow their lungs out together come ten o'clock as a sort of release from the constant academic grind.

"That's not annoying at all," grumbled Helen, who was decidedly more into inwardly seething than having big displays of overly dramatic emotion. Lumped in bed with her laptop and a half-eaten pizza, Amanda just grunted into her hoodie. Helen was beginning to suspect that Amanda's workload was far more intense than hers.

Woozy from the scent of festering pepperoni and Amandaness,

Helen turned back to her laptop, where the cursor was blinking at the end of her article. She scrubbed at her face and cracked open one of Amanda's Red Bulls as she read it over for the hundredth time, the words ceasing to make sense as they sieved their way through her brain.

Northwestern University Communications student Jennifer Roberts, 19, was last seen leaving a party off campus on Saturday, September 30th, before a dormmate reported her missing to campus police early Monday morning.

Campus police declined to comment further, as Roberts's disappearance is now an open and ongoing investigation under the jurisdiction of the Evanston Police Department. Evanston PD did not immediately respond to the *Daily Northwestern*'s request for comment.

"All we want is for Jenny to come home," Roberts's mother Stella told the *Daily*. "She's always been a sweet, trusting girl, and I love her very much."

English major Paul Marshall, 19, said that he saw Roberts at a party Saturday night on Noyes Street. "She didn't seem drunk or anything," Marshall said. "She left around eleven p.m. with her friend Tara." Communications major Tara Phillips, 18, told the *Daily* she last saw Roberts about three blocks from her friend's off-campus apartment on Elgin Road. "It was probably around eleven thirty," Phillips said. "I remember she was on the phone when she left, but she was always calling her sister, so I assumed that was the case. I wish I had made sure she got home okay."

Roberts's sister, Constance, did not immediately respond to the *Daily*'s request for comment.

She had thought it was a pretty solid piece—the reporting was there, all the facts were in order—but across the top Sam had written in big, red letters, *This is fucking boring.* In a smaller, no-less caustic note at the bottom of the piece he wrote, *I thought you interviewed the mom?!!! Is that cut-and-paste bullshit all you got?! Just make it fucking better.*

"Make it better," Helen muttered, dropping her head to her desk as the screams started petering out in the courtyard. "How?" It was getting cold outside, but the breeze felt nice on the back of her sweating neck, so she left the window open, wrapping herself up in her comforter from home, which still smelled like the detergent her dad used, practical and clean. She missed him then, almost too much. It was like a piece of her heart was gone, and the hole there ached.

It was late, and her dad worked early hours, but she knew he'd answer if she called, so she wandered out into the hallway to sit in the echoing concrete stairwell that all freshman used as a phone booth to make teary calls home. Luckily, tonight she was on her own, likely because everyone was screaming, studying, or both.

Her dad answered on the second ring, his voice groggy. "Champ?" he asked, yawning, and Helen pictured him sitting up in bed, having fallen asleep under one of his myriad mystery books. Nero Wolfe—the portly detective who solved exclusively from behind his desk—was his favorite. He'd taken to reading the pulpy novels in medical school to take his mind off the gory work at hand—in between stretching out on the cold, metal tables in the morgue for naps—and Helen had started stealing them when she turned ten. You could probably trace her interest in investigative journalism to those early days of gorging on pilfered paperbacks.

"Dad?" she said. "Did I wake you up?" The stairwell was cold and echoing, and Helen pitched her voice down so no one could hear her voice shake.

"No, nope," her dad said, and she smiled. He was clearly lying. "What's wrong? It's late."

For a moment Helen's whole body seemed to ache with nostalgia; she missed her twin bed, her view of the woods behind the house, and the deer that grazed there. She even missed the pockmarked dining-room table where she'd spent endless hours doing homework with her father. Maybe she wasn't cut out for college. Maybe she should just go home, work in her dad's office and grow old in her childhood bedroom, acquiring gray hair and wrinkles under the watchful eyes of her Leonardo DiCaprio posters. She opened her mouth to suggest as much, but her dad cut her off.

"You know how proud of you I am, right?" he said softly. Helen could picture him propped in bed, his reading glasses askew, wearing the soft flannel pajamas she'd gotten him for Christmas. "Just for getting out there, for taking the plunge. You're so brave, Champ," he said, and Helen thought back to the first day of college, when he'd skipped through the hallway to make her laugh when he saw her looking into all the open dorm rooms—at all the new students chatting and laughing—terrified. She'd acted appropriately mortified at the time, but she had been grateful for him. For his brashness, for how he never really seemed to care what anyone else thought of him. She owed him for that—at the very least, to try.

Helen nodded, tears dripping onto her cell phone. "Yeah, thanks, Daddy. I just wanted to call and say good-night…and that I love you."

"I love you, too, kid," he said, yawning. "Call me tomorrow, okay? Maybe when it's light out?"

Helen sat for a moment in the stairwell, in the cold, thinking of her house, her bed, her books. For a second, she could smell the woodsmoke that always wreathed the neighborhood when everyone burned their leaves in their yards, could hear the wind sighing in the evergreen outside her window—her first Christmas tree, planted by her father after the holiday. She thought then of the Robertses' house—the smell of Jenny's home (like pine and bread) and the family photos climbing the stairs to the second floor, where the girl's bed was made, as if waiting for her.

Yes, she had quotes from Mrs. Roberts—three hours' worth. She basically had Jenny's life history. Mrs. Roberts had shown her photos of Jenny dressed as Charlie Chaplin for Halloween at age eight, when she was obsessed with slapstick comedy and was always getting hurt trying out Three Stooges stunts. She had watched a so-called newsreel Jenny had made when we she twelve and decided she wanted to be a broadcast journalist; she'd set up a lemonade stand at the end of her driveway and interviewed customers in a neat little blazer her mom got her for Christmas. She'd heard all about the terrible boys Jenny started dating at sixteen—the goths and skaters and potheads—and how her sunny blonde girl had dyed her hair black and pierced her eyebrow. And, finally, how Jenny had returned to her broadcasting dreams and applied to Northwestern; she wanted to be on a sports channel, like ESPN. She loved football. She'd talk to anyone about anything. She was friends with the mailman and the people at the corner store and even their cranky, old neighbor, who had six cats and liked smoking cigars on the stoop.

Those things didn't seem relevant to the story, though. Or, rather, they didn't seem like anyone's business. Helen still felt guilty about that visit: she hadn't exactly lied about knowing

Jenny, but Mrs. Roberts certainly wouldn't have spilled her guts like that if she had known Helen was a reporter—even a boring one. Still, Sam's words spun before her eyes, and her head hurt from staring at the computer and from all the screaming. Pulling her comforter over her head like a hoodie and hunching her shoulders, Helen started to type.

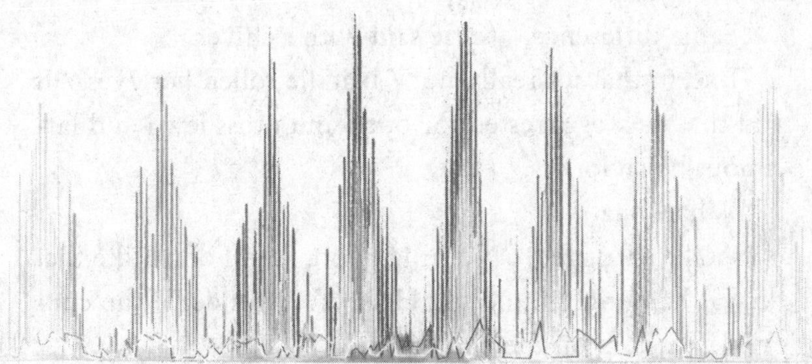

CHAPTER THIRTEEN

"Oh, fuck..." Katie abandoned her milkshake, her perpetually cheerful face falling. "So...he's a rapist?"

Natalie had told her friend that she wanted to meet and talk at the diner first thing the next day, which, for Katie, translated to well after noon. Katie had practically frothed with excitement when Natalie told her about seeing Ron Stackman in the Halseys' yard, but her morbid curiosity had its limits. Natalie didn't blame her. A possible murder was one thing. A rapist-murderer was a lot more cinematically splashy—and a lot more frightening. Still, Natalie felt excitement churning in her stomach. Stackman was a suspect now, through and through. And she had his address.

Natalie shook her head, her blond hair flying. "Not necessarily," she mused. "He was just on the sex-offender registry."

"Same difference," Katie said with a shiver.

"Except that it's really not." Natalie rolled her eyes. "It said that he was arrested for open and gross lewd and lascivious behavior."

"What's that?"

Natalie shrugged. "Nothing good. And I don't like that he was hanging around the Halseys'. I wonder if the cops even have him on their radar yet."

Katie pushed the rest of her shake to the edge of her table, appetite lost, which was a first. "You should tell my dad. Or Mrs. Pressman."

Natalie shook her head. "I want to check him out first. Try to talk to him for the podcast and see what he knows about everything. If we set the paper on the guy, we'll never get a minute alone with him."

"So…" Katie pursed her lips, looking uneasy. "What now, then?"

That was the question Natalie had been asking herself for about twelve hours now. She could just show up at Ron K. Stackman's door, phone in hand…but that hadn't worked out all that well with Eliza. Plus, the last time she had seen Stackman he had literally *run* away from her. *Plus*, he could very well be a sexually depraved murderer.

"I have no idea." Natalie sighed, dragging a fry through her ketchup, looking around to make sure her mom wasn't in the vicinity. Luckily, she was posted up at the register, dealing with the lunch rush. Natalie would have to join her in about ten minutes, though, when her break was over.

"I was thinking a stakeout?" she suggested. "Watch him for a while and see where he goes, find an opportunity to get him alone in a nonthreatening environment. You up for it?"

"Ohhh, look at you with the lingo." Katie waggled her eyebrows, but she still sounded subdued. "A *stakeout*, Nat? Really? For a *sex offender*? Isn't that a bit much?" She looked down at the table and dawdled her finger through a pile of spilled salt.

Natalie knew she was losing Katie, so she plunged her hand into her backpack and pulled out the yearbook she'd stolen from the newspaper office after she'd gone digging to see if Stackman was a new resident or if he had history with the town—and, maybe, the Halseys. And, well, bingo.

"He's known Mrs. Halsey for years, Katie." Natalie plopped the yearbook on the table, stabbing it with her finger. "They were in the same class at East Ferry High. If they've known each other that long, there could be a *motive* somewhere in there."

Katie reached out to lazily flip through the pages of the book. "Of course they went to high school together. We live in the smallest town in the entire fu—" She paused, pulling a crumpled piece of paper from between the pages where it had lodged itself in the depths of Natalie's bag. When Natalie saw the typewritten letters dancing across the page, she made to grab it back, but it was too late. Katie had obviously seen what was written there: *Stay out of it. I'm warning you.* Natalie had totally forgotten she'd shoved the note in her bag all those days ago.

"What the frick is this?" Katie gaped.

Natalie snatched the paper back, checking to make sure

her mom was still busy behind the register. "Nothing," she whispered fiercely. "Stop freaking out, or my mom will see."

"Bullshit. Where did that come from, Nat?" Katie asked, eyes wide, stabbing a finger at the paper. "Tell me now, or I'm showing it to her myself."

Natalie pressed on her temples hard. She had almost forgotten about the note, the reason she had decided to start the podcast in the first place. She still had no clue where it had come from, and there hadn't been any others, so she was kind of hoping it would all just go away, which now she realized was pretty stupid. "It was in my mailbox," she said, finally. Katie's eyes looked like they were about to pop out of her head behind her glasses. "The day of the memorial."

"And you didn't tell me?" Katie asked. "Nat, this is seriously messed up. You get a threatening note and just decide to keep it to yourself?" Realization dawned on her face, and she looked even more pissed. "And the podcast? Natalie." She banged her head lightly on the table, knocking her glasses askew and getting salt in her black hair. "In what universe was this stupid podcast a good idea?"

All words fled Natalie's mind, leaving it an utter blank. She didn't know how to convey to Katie why she needed this. What she had done. What she had said to Mrs. Halsey. She'd never told her friend about their falling out; she was too ashamed. She balled her fists on the tabletop, searching for something, anything, to tell Katie, who was looking at her like she was one phone call away from having her committed.

"Nat," her mother interrupted them, appearing by the

booth like an aproned ninja. "Break's over, back to work. You can talk to Katie later."

Katie kept her eyes locked on Natalie, the salt still dusting her hair like early snowfall. "I'm coming over tonight," she said, her voice ominous.

Helen blinked, apparently confused by Katie's doomy tone. "That'll be nice, honey. You're welcome anytime, you know."

Natalie just glared back. "Don't you have to hang out with Simon, Katie?"

Katie shook her head slowly, warningly. "Nope, tonight I'm all yours. We have a *lot* to talk about."

Natalie watched as her friend shoved a few more fries into her mouth, chewing furiously as she got to her feet. Katie shot her one more warning look as she stomped out of the diner into the parking lot to her Jeep—a.k.a. Natalie's one and only ride. Disappointment flooded her limbs as she stood up, picking up her order pad and heading toward a couple who had just sat down near the front of the diner. She had a lead—a real, solid lead—and no car. No help. No Katie.

She zoned out twice while taking the couple's order and excused herself to the bathroom, where she splashed water on her face with shaking hands. Stackman lived in West Ferry beyond Jack's and the bar—way too far to get to on her bike, unless she wanted to pedal along the highway. She would never be able to check him out now. She supposed she could wait around the Halseys' for him to show up again, but judging by the way he'd run earlier, he wouldn't be back. A cab or an Uber was out of the question, too. Her mom would see the charges on her card.

What she needed was someone with a car. Someone who wouldn't ask questions. Someone with very few morals in the first place. Someone, it dawned on her slowly, who had given her his number just the other day. Water still dripping from her flushed face, Natalie dug into her pocket, and before she could think about it too much, she typed out a message to Kurt Bachman.

I'll take that ride now.

The diner was starting to empty out a bit, but there were still plenty of tables needing bills and top-ups, so Natalie worked head down until nearly the end of her shift, the hours becoming a blur of receipts, scattered coins, and spilled ketchup. By six thirty, she was starting to feel more than a little bone-tired, and she was almost relieved that Kurt hadn't texted her back. Almost. Why guys got girls' numbers with no intention of calling them was a mystery even her favorite podcasters couldn't solve.

"Excuse me, miss, I want to buy someone a coffee," a voice called out from booth two, which was decidedly not in her section.

She heaved a huge sigh and pasted on a smile, turning toward the source of the inquiry. Kurt was leaning against the shiny red vinyl of the booth, his arm draped over the back. He was dressed in black once again, but this time he wore a nautical woven belt, pink whales cavorting around the small circumference of his waist.

"You're here," Natalie said, startled.

Kurt put down a tattered copy of *Pet Sematary* and folded his hands over the cover. "I'm here," he parroted.

They stared at each for a second. "I texted you," Natalie said simply, inwardly cursing her lack of poise. Apparently, all she could do at present was state facts.

"You did." Kurt nodded. "And I came."

"But you don't even know why I texted you yet." She put the coffeepot down on his table and a hand on her hip. "Plus, I never told you where I worked." She thanked whatever deity was currently on duty that her mom was out doing a supply run. This was not a conversation she needed to be having around Helen.

"I assumed you texted because you wanted to see me and maybe have coffee or something," Kurt said with a small smile. "But it seems like you're well-stocked here, so maybe ice cream instead?"

Natalie's mouth fell open. Kurt thought she was *hitting* on him? *Of course he did*, the rational part of her brain said. *You texted him asking for a ride with no explanation. He can't read your mind.* She'd obviously been single for far too long. Unsurprisingly, Natalie hadn't really dated in high school; and she didn't count making out with Ireland during a Model UN trip to Tampa sophomore year as much of a romantic interlude, either. It wasn't that she didn't like boys, just that most of the ones at her school were just that: boys. They were more interested in getting drunk or high or touching boobs than listening to her talk about herself—and it didn't help that most of her tried-and-true topics of conversation (murder, kidnapping, and the like) were not all that amorous. So she was a little more than confused that

Kurt was seemingly interested in her, despite her being, well, *her.* Not that she didn't like herself—most guys were just too stupid to appreciate her many beguiling qualities.

"As for where you work," Kurt said, fiddling with the book, "I may have asked Jack—" he thumbed the cover, looking down at the table "—and showed up yesterday and sat here for hours until I realized you weren't working that day." He looked up at her through his lashes and gave her a crooked smile. "So I'm pretty glad you finally texted me so I'd have an actual excuse to be here."

"I have an internship at the paper on Wednesdays," Natalie said, basically so she wasn't just gawking at him. There was a lot going on in Natalie's head at the moment, and none if it made much sense, which was profoundly annoying.

Kurt's face darkened, then he smirked. "Are you some sort of junior reporter?" The way he said *reporter* suggested he didn't think that highly of the profession.

She scowled. Did the guy like her or hate her? It was hard to tell, and she was not a fan of ambiguity. If a podcast didn't end with the mystery being solved, she was not a happy listener. "No. At least not yet," she replied, starting to turn away from his table. He had wasted enough of her time. She'd walk to West Ferry if she had to.

"But you *are* reporting. You have that podcast—about murder. And it sounds like you've been pretty busy," he shot back before she could make a run for it. He sounded genuinely interested, despite the attitude. But the attitude was hard to overlook.

"How do you know about that?" Natalie asked, flustered. No one listened to their podcast—okay, like, three people did, but in online parlance those were practically negative numbers.

"Jack told me," Kurt said with a shrug. "Plus, your Twitter account said something about you all investigating a local crime, and since literally nothing happens here, I can guess which one."

"We don't have Twitter," Natalie replied, before silently cursing Katie. Of course they had Twitter. She just hoped they didn't have TikTok. Seemed highly unlikely, since neither of them could dance.

"Social media aside, *you* texted *me*. So why don't you come over here and tell me why." Kurt leaned back in his booth, motioning with his head for Natalie to join him.

Natalie fought back the urge to tell him to suck it. But he did have a car and apparently plenty of time to follow her around. She reluctantly slid into the seat across from him, putting the coffeepot back down. She was so close to him she could smell him: clean laundry and cigarettes. "I told you," she said. "I need a ride."

Kurt leveled his eyes with hers. "So I'm guessing that this isn't a date, huh?"

"No," Natalie tried to inject a healthy dose of disgust into her voice, lest he get the wrong idea. "I want you to help me follow a guy." She was aware that it was a bizarre request, but it's not like she really cared what Kurt thought. Or had to see him again.

Kurt blinked. "Excuse me?"

Natalie sighed, frustrated. This was obviously a bad idea. Involving Katie had been a bad enough idea, and she was her friend. Kurt was a stranger. "Never mind… Forget I asked," she muttered.

"No, wait." Kurt reached out, stilling her hand with his. A tiny little sizzle went through her that wasn't entirely unpleasant. "Is this for that podcast? Some sort of…investigation?"

Natalie shifted slightly under his gaze; it was far too intense. As if realizing he was staring, Kurt grinned, flashing her his white teeth. "The show is cute. Real twisted. Not sure why you need my help, though. Seems like it's just you and Katie talking about dark shit."

Natalie simultaneously bristled at the word *cute* and inwardly blushed at Kurt's interest—and the fact that he liked her podcast. "It was, until now…" She trailed off, trying to figure out how to explain to Kurt what she wanted to do. That she actually wanted to investigate a crime instead of just talk about it—that what he'd heard of their podcast was just the tip of the proverbial iceberg. Finally, she decided to just say it. If he wasn't interested, if he thought she was crazy, she could just ghost him. Not like her mom, not like Katie. She looked up. "My teacher, like you probably read…she was killed. And I want to find out why, how." Natalie was horrified at the way her voice started to shake. She took a deep breath, trying to focus on the facts. "I think I have a new lead, but it's in West Ferry—he is. And I don't have a car…"

"And I do," Kurt said quietly, as if disappointed.

"Yes."

It was so quiet for a few seconds that Natalie could hear a woman across the diner biting into her pickle, someone crunching on chips. "Okay," Kurt said finally. "I'll do it. I'll help you."

"You will?" Natalie looked up, shocked. She hadn't really thought he'd say yes, especially if he'd been expecting a date. "Why?"

Kurt laughed, studying the table for a few moments. "Not everyone lives in East Ferry and owns their own diner," he replied.

"What's that supposed to mean?"

"It means…" Kurt folded his hands and looked up, his eyes flinty "…I know the case you're talking about, and some of us could use that twenty-thousand-dollar reward money. For rent. And just life in general." Natalie flashed back to the trailer, how Jack kept asking about rent, and Kurt kept putting him off.

"And I was thinking," Kurt continued, "if I'm gonna help you, maybe if we find something, we can split that money."

In truth, Natalie hadn't thought about the reward. Not because she didn't need it—she and her mother weren't at the top of the East Ferry food chain by any means—but because she wasn't sure she would feel right about accepting the money. Mrs. Halsey was dead. Money was the last thing on her mind. And it bothered her that this boy she barely knew saw this whole tragedy as a payday. But she didn't really have any other options.

"I'm not interested in the reward," Natalie replied, starting to slide out of the booth. "Sorry to waste your time."

"Wait." Kurt reached out and grabbed her arm. Natalie twisted and pulled it away, years of karate training kicking in. *Thank you, Mom.*

"Please, just wait," Kurt said, holding his hands in front of him as if he realized touching her was not the right move.

"I gotta get back to work," she spat.

Kurt half stood in the booth. "How's it been working out for you? The investigation? Talking to people from the other side of the river? The dreaded *other* Ferry?"

Natalie stilled, thinking of Eliza's last words to her: *Fuck off.*

"I can help you with that, you know," Kurt said, fully standing now. He was close to her again, so close she could feel the heat of him through his T-shirt. "I live there. Been living there for about a year now. I know who to talk to."

Natalie thought of Brian Reed of *S-Town* then, the host of one of her favorite podcasts. He had had an in when he went to investigate the goings-on in Woodstock, Alabama: John B. McLemore, who invited him there in the first place and eventually became the subject of the whole podcast. Mrs. Halsey loved *S-Town*—the tragic tale of a man too smart for his own good who, nevertheless, stayed tethered to his shit town. She said the telling did story justice—and stressed to Natalie just how much a journalist needed a gatekeeper to the world they were investigating, how that person gave the story authenticity and life.

Natalie had Stackman's address in West Ferry. She knew what side of the river he lived on—and she really did need someone to help ford it. Plus, having backup when talking to a possible murderer wasn't the worst idea in the world.

She turned toward the boy, looking up into his strangely pretty face. "If that's the case, why even help me? Why not just do this on your own and take the whole pot?"

"Maybe I want to keep an eye on the competition?" Kurt raised a golden eyebrow. "Maybe I think it's smarter to take half than nothing at all?" His eyes wandered to her lips. "Or maybe I just want to have ice cream with a real-life girl who likes horror novels as much as I do?"

Natalie rolled her eyes. He couldn't just give a compliment without ruining it, could he? "Tons of girls read horror novels, dude. In fact, women are by far the biggest market for true crime out there."

Kurt grinned. "You *are* smart."

"That was never really in question."

"Will you get ice cream with me, then?" Kurt reached out to touch her arm, then dropped his hand when she glared at the appendage.

Then she rolled her eyes. "Fine, sure. But after that we're going on a stakeout."

The seats in Kurt's car were tattered and worn, but it was as clean as the trailer, and he was a good driver. He kept his hands on ten and two and looked fixedly ahead as they tooled through Ferry proper, past the downtown knickknack-boasting shops and homey cafés. They left East Ferry High in their taillights and crested a sloping hill at the top of which crouched a gracefully decaying Victorian house, an ever-present *For Sale* slightly askew in the summer breeze. Seemingly forever abandoned, it was a popular spot for high-school kids to have parties. Classical music lilted from the car stereo, and Natalie felt herself uncoiling a bit. She still wasn't sure about Kurt, but he had promised to help her check out Ron K. Stackman—and he had wheels. But first, at Kurt's request, they would stop for ice cream.

When they pulled into Sammy's Shack, it was unusually

deserted for a Thursday night in the summer, but maybe that was because it was just after seven and all the little kids had gotten their fill of sweets for the night. Like the diner, the Shack was a slice of fifties nostalgia, boasting a faded sign featuring a couple doing the twist while clutching ice-cream cones. Needless to say, no one she knew hung out there anymore. Not since they'd graduated to drinking in the woods.

"I haven't been here in years," Natalie said, sliding out of the car. Sammy's was snug against the river that separated East and West Ferry and, incongruously, abutted a massive graveyard to the right. As Natalie looked across the sea of white markers, which made shadows in the night, she realized she had yet to visit Mrs. Halsey's grave and felt a dark pang of shame. She vowed to do so tomorrow after her morning workout with her mother, before she had to be at the diner. She would bring some flowers from her mother's garden, she decided. Mrs. Halsey always liked roses.

"Have you ever been before?" Natalie asked as Kurt got in line behind a couple of portly tourists wearing *Ferry, CT* T-shirts. He hadn't said much in the car, and she was starting to feel a little awkward.

He shook his head. "Nah. Haven't had much reason to come to this side of the river. But I hear their chocolate vanilla swirl is something special." He gave her a lopsided smile.

Natalie nodded. "I went when I was a kid, but only when I had a babysitter, which was rare. My mom is kind of overprotective, so she didn't leave me alone that much."

"What about your dad?" Kurt asked, maneuvering to the side so that the tourists could get by with their heaping waffle cones.

"Don't know him," Natalie said, stepping up to the window to order. She wasn't a big fan of sweets, so she just asked for a vanilla cone, while cutting her eyes to the side to see Kurt's reaction. Usually at this point in the conversation people apologized or got red in the face, assuming that her father had died or left; she wondered what this strange boy would do.

Kurt didn't apologize or stutter, though, which was actually sort of a relief. He just paid for their ice cream and headed toward one of the empty picnic tables by the edge of the river. "What do you mean you don't know him?" he asked as they took a seat on the splintered wood, stained with decades of sugary spills.

"I mean I've never met him," Natalie said, scuffing a sneaker in the gravel. "He wasn't in the picture when I grew up."

Kurt's ice cream had started dripping on his big hands, but he didn't seem to notice. "Wait, so you mean you literally have no idea who your dad is? You seem kind of like a nuclear-family girl."

Natalie scoffed. "Well, I'm not. I guess." She bit into her cone awkwardly. "Whatever that is, nowadays."

"Hey, I'm not trying to offend you, I promise." Kurt took a lick of his ice cream to stop it from dripping all over his hands and leveled his eyes with hers. "I'm just surprised, that's all. I figured you'd have, like, a dossier on the guy. You don't seem the type to let anything go."

Natalie snorted. "Don't think I didn't ask, because I did. All the time when I was little. I used to write him letters and put them in our mailbox. I'd just address them to *Dad*. No state or city or anything. They were always gone when

I went to look, but I'm guessing that was my mom and not the mail carrier."

"That sucks," Kurt said, his voice heavy. When Natalie looked up, he looked sad and, perhaps, a little angry. "My dad left like an asshole when I was a kid, but at least I know where to send my hate mail."

Natalie smiled slightly. Maybe they weren't so different after all. Sucky parents were universal. "Yeah, well, my mom basically controls my life, so maybe I'm lucky not to have someone else hovering over me." She trailed off, realizing that she had said more about her dad to a total stranger than she ever had to Katie. It was hard to talk about that kind of thing with Katie, who had a mom and a dad and seemed to resent their existence. She knew most kids had divorced parents these days, but most of her classmates at least *knew* their dads.

"Anyway." She got to her feet, blushing. "This is real pretty and all, but maybe we can eat ice cream *while* we stake out the sex offender."

"Whatever you say." Kurt got to his feet, dusting off the seat of his jeans. They started back toward the car, but Kurt paused before he opened the driver's-side door. "For what it's worth?" he said, catching Natalie's eye. "You're probably better off not knowing him—your dad. One less person to disappoint you." Kurt held her gaze for a second or two before breaking away with a bitter chuckle. "Everyone does in the end. Trust me," he muttered to himself as he got into the car.

Natalie had been to West Ferry more in one week than she had during her entire eighteen years, and now she was heading into the heart of it. As Kurt followed the GPS directions to Ron K. Stackman's house, she took the opportunity to gaze out the window at the passing streets. There was a compact downtown by the Amtrak station replete with cute little brick buildings, but it seemed there were more for rent signs than open businesses. And those few businesses were well-worn: a comic-book shop, a women's clothing store with a few dated dresses fading in the window, an electronics store hawking hulking TVs. It wasn't as scary as the East Ferriers like Sandy Tarver made it out to be, though; everyone out on the streets was smiling, it seemed, hustling home with shopping bags and small children. There were no trendy wine bars or souvenir stores slinging ceramic lighthouses and taffy, like in East Ferry; it was just a neighborhood where everyone was living and breathing and doing their thing. Instead of the big shiny ShopRite, there was a little market with a fruits-and-veggies stand outside and a gaggle of stooped ladies with string shopping bags and overly tan knee-highs gossiping and squeezing tomatoes.

"I think we're here," Kurt said, pulling into a residential street and turning off the headlights. A row of neat brick houses marched toward the distant low-slung hills. "What now?" He turned to Natalie. In the darkness his face was a pale moon. She'd filled him in on the ride over, recounting how she'd seen Stackman in the Halseys' yard, how he'd gone to school with her teacher.

Natalie squinted through the windshield. "It's that house there." She pointed. "The one with the truck out in front." Like the rest of the houses on the street, the Stackman abode was compact and brick, and through the gloom,

Natalie could make out neatly trimmed bushes flanking the door. As they watched the facade of the house, the taillights of Ron K. Stackman's truck flickered to life.

"Guess he's on his way out," Kurt said, peering over the wheel as the truck backed out of its parking place. "What now?" he asked, whipping his head around to face Natalie.

"I guess…follow him?" Natalie said, her hands knotting in her lap. She hadn't expected tonight to turn into a chase. At most, she was hoping to *case the joint*, as they said in old movies, and come back another day when it was light outside and follow him to the grocery store or something. She had just been so excited by the prospect of driving by that she hadn't thought that far ahead.

Kurt didn't seem all that bothered by the situation, though. "Whatever you say, miss." He gave an ironic little salute and took off behind Stackman's truck.

The truck hit the downtown, belching smoke, and then rolled across the bridge straddling the river heading, it seemed, for East Ferry.

"Maybe he's going back to the Halseys'?" Kurt said, his hands tight on the wheel, excitement edging into his voice.

"What would he be doing there?" Natalie mused, her eyes on Stackman's taillights as they signaled a right turn.

"Aren't murderers always returning to the scene of the crime?" Kurt signaled and kept on Stackman's tail. "Maybe he's going back to get a trophy or something?"

Natalie was impressed; she had had the same thought when she had first seen Stackman in the Halseys' yard. Maybe, in addition to not being totally annoying, Kurt was more useful than she'd thought.

"I mean, maybe..." she replied, watching as the car turned off at the exit for Downtown East Ferry. "But he's going the wrong way. Toward the library and the..." She trailed off as Stackman turned right again and pulled into the parking lot of the church.

Kurt hung back as the man eased out the truck dressed in slacks and a clean white shirt. Stackman headed toward the arched doors of the church.

"He could be...repenting?" Kurt suggested, drumming his hands on the wheel.

Natalie inspected the front of the church with pleasure. This was perfect. Churches were safe; they were public. If she was going to interview a possible murderer and definite sex offender, she couldn't have picked a better spot if she tried. She just needed Kurt to help her figure out what to say first, to get the man to trust her.

"So." She turned to Kurt. "You ready to do this?" She reached for the door handle but froze when she saw the expression on Kurt's face: he looked nervous. Scared.

"I'm going to stay here, if you don't mind... Me and churches don't really mix."

"What?" Natalie's mouth hung open. Maybe she had been wrong about him, after all. Was he a coward? Worse, was he really planning on letting her go interview a possible *violent criminal* all by herself? Sure, she could protect herself to some degree (thanks, Mom), but even cops needed backup.

"I thought you were going to teach me how to talk to people from the other side of the river?" Natalie protested, not even bothering to keep the anger out of her voice. Let him squirm. "Dude could be a maniac for all we know, and you want me to go in there *alone*?"

"Pssh." Kurt flapped a hand. "Ron wouldn't hurt a cockroach. You'll be fine."

"Wait, you know this guy?" Natalie froze.

"I know a lot of people in West Ferry," Kurt said, drumming at the steering wheel again, this time a bit more erratically.

"Then, why did we follow him here, if you know him?" Natalie said, seething. "Couldn't you have called him or something? And if you think he 'wouldn't hurt a cockroach,' why are we even bothering to investigate him?" Anger seared through Natalie's chest. "You better tell me if you're messing with me. Right now. Seriously."

She hoped she sounded threatening but feared she just came off as hurt, and she didn't want this boy, this stranger, to know that he had hurt her. Didn't he understand that this was important—the story she was trying to tell? Didn't he get that this was about more than a reward—that it was about her life? Hers and Mrs. Halsey's. Tears formed in the corners of her eyes, and she hated herself for them.

"Hey." Kurt unbuckled his seat belt and turned toward her. She pressed her back against the door. "First of all, we followed him because you seemed so intent on a stakeout, which was kind of adorable."

Natalie snorted. "That's fucking infantilizing, dude."

"It's not my fault," Kurt cried, fighting a smile. "I'm a sucker for Veronica Mars, so sue me! But okay, hey." His voice took on a more serious tone as she crossed her arms and glowered. "I would have taken you to Ron directly if we were friends. But we're not, okay? He would have turned you down flat for an interview with me in tow, and that's a stone-cold fact."

"Why?" Natalie unfolded her arms, some of her previous anger leaching away. But only some. He was still being an infuriating asshole. "What did you do to him?"

"Why do you assume I did something to *him*?" He looked up, hurt. "And does it matter? We're just not… friends, okay?"

"Yes, it matters," Natalie snapped.

"Fine." Kurt stared up at the steeple of the church. "He dated my mom, okay? When we first got to town. And it didn't end well."

"Your mom dated a sex offender?"

"She didn't know about that."

"And he still holds a grudge?"

"It's a small town." Kurt gestured across the river. "You know how it is."

Natalie thought of her own mom, how long it had taken her to become part of the community as a single mother. "Unfortunately, yes. I do."

"Okay, then!" Kurt slapped the wheel. "If you're done interrogating me, maybe you can go interrogate Ron, God help him."

"Didn't you say he was harmless?" Natalie still wasn't sold on that. He had a record. He was lurking around the Halseys' with a bag and a shovel. All those things didn't really scream *solid guy*.

Kurt busted out a wry smile. "That's what they always say about killers, though, right?"

Natalie let out a shuddering sigh and shook out her shoulders. She didn't want to go in there alone, but was she really going to let this opportunity pass her by? Who knew how long Stackman was planning to hang around a church this late at night? She had to do this. She had to swallow all her fears and worries and just go.

Without another word to Kurt—he was proving to be utterly useless, regardless of her initial impression—Natalie climbed out of the car and headed toward the church, a chill rattling up her bones. She closed her eyes and pulled in a deep breath, trying to steady her rapidly beating heart, then reached out and pulled open the heavy door to the church, the smell of candles and floor polish immediately flooding her nose.

She and her mother were not all that religious, but she had been to this church a few times with Katie when they were younger and the Lugos went more regularly. The little entryway was the same as it ever was, plush red carpet and dark wooden benches, as was the main worship area, with its rows of pre-America pews. It didn't seem like there was a service that night, but there were a few people scattered among the seating, reading from the Bible or just praying. Ron was sitting near the back, his head bent so low over his hands that his forelock brushed the back of the pew in front of him. She watched him motionless on the hard, wooden seat, his lips silently moving, the muttering of the scattering of people ebbing and flowing like a tide. Natalie wondered what they were praying for. Selfish things, like money and fame? Or more expected prayers for friends, family, and those who had passed? She had never prayed, so she could only guess.

After what seemed like hours but was probably only fifteen minutes, Ron's lips stopped moving. By then, Natalie was lulled into a meditative state by the smells and sounds of the church, and when the man turned toward her, his eyes widening with recognition, she looked back calmly. She held her ground as Ron walked toward her, his baseball hat clutched in his hands.

"You're the girl from before. At the house," he said, plainly. He wasn't accusing, he was just stating a fact. He had a nice voice, a voice made to be recorded. It almost made Natalie jealous; she always thought hers was too high and squeaky for a podcast host.

"Yes," Natalie said, nodding. "I wanted to talk to you."

"So you followed me to church?" Again, there was no trace of accusation. He just seemed curious.

"I didn't mean to follow you," Natalie lied, her cheeks growing warm. "I just didn't know how to…reach out. I'm doing a project on Mrs. Halsey, and I just wanted to talk to the people who knew her. I saw you at the house the other day, and then I saw you headed in here, and I just figured…maybe you might have something to say?" The words tumbled out of her mouth like they had done at Eliza's bar, and as they did Natalie's stomach dropped. She had done it again. She had flubbed it. Ron would tell her to fuck off, just like Eliza had, and she would be left with nothing.

He didn't look angry, though. He just peered into her eyes with his dark brown ones and then nodded, once.

"I'll talk to you for your project. Sure. Lynn was...a good woman."

He gestured toward the bench in the little entryway, and Natalie sat down. Then Ron lowered himself next to her, bringing with him the smell of leaves. He waited as Natalie took out her phone, putting it on Airplane mode and flipping to the recorder app.

Ron looked down at the blinking red light on Natalie's cell. "How do I do this, then? Just talk into your phone?"

Natalie nodded, mulling over what to ask first. Mrs. Halsey had always said you should ask the hardest questions last when you were doing an interview. That way, if the subject got mad and left, you'd still have enough to work with. Still, the question came out of her mouth, anyway. She had to know. "Why don't you start by telling me what you were doing that day at the house. Why you ran when I tried to talk to you."

Ron nodded, then rubbed at his whiskered cheeks. She was relieved when he didn't storm off. "Yeah, sorry for scaring you there. I've been working for the Halseys' for years now, doing yardwork. I came back that day out of habit, I guess? I was worried her garden would get overgrown if no one else came to tend it. And that made me sad."

"But why did you run away?" Natalie asked, any fear she had felt when she'd first entered the church leaking away. She knew it was a cliché, but this man didn't seem like he could do something so brutal. So violent and wrong. You never knew, though. And if he had been friends with the Halseys for so long, maybe he had some insight Natalie lacked.

"Well, I wasn't supposed to be there, was I?" Ron shrugged. "The cops told everyone to keep away. It just made me so sad to think of her yard going to seed. Lynn, she hired me when no one else would. She didn't deserve that. She didn't deserve any of it."

"Why would no one else hire you? If you don't mind me asking." It felt like a dicey question, but Natalie asked anyway, making sure to keep her voice gentle and low to match his.

Ron looked down at the recorder. "I'll tell you, if you don't mind turning off your recorder there. I'd rather keep this about Lynn if we can."

Reluctantly, Natalie turned off the recorder. She wanted to know what he had to say, even if she couldn't include it in her podcast. If it was worth it, she could get a second source on record after the fact.

"All right, then." Ron settled back in his seat. "You see that I'm at church on a Thursday night." He gestured at the pews, which were mostly empty now.

Natalie nodded.

"Well, I've been at church every night for ten years now. Fact is, I had a drinking problem for a long time that got me into all kinds of trouble. Got me arrested a few times and got me labeled a few things that make it hard to get a job."

The gears clicked in Natalie's head. "Open and gross lewd and lascivious behavior?" The words came out of her mouth before she could stop them.

Ron dragged a hand over his face. "Can't hide anything in a small town, huh? Yup, that was the charge. It sounds so terrible when you put it like that." He shuddered. "All

I did was…relieve myself in a parking lot once when I was wasted out of my mind. I quit drinking after that."

"And Mrs. Halsey hired you, anyway?" Natalie asked, fondness for her teacher flooding her, along with guilt. She had judged this man based on words—labels, as he said. Mrs. Halsey always said you should gather together all the facts before writing the story, but Natalie had started constructing Stackman's narrative before she even knew his name. She felt bad she had judged him, sure, but she felt even worse for letting Mrs. Halsey down.

Ron nodded. "We went to school together when we were younger. She was always nice to me. She even invited me to all those Halloween parties she and her husband had every year. Even though she knew people would talk. And I came, every year. Wore a mask so no one would flap their jaws, but I came. For her." He gestured toward Natalie's phone. "Turn that on now. I want you to get this." Natalie obliged, and Ron leaned forward, aiming his mouth at the recorder. "Lynn Halsey was just a top-notch person, through and through. From the time she was a teen to the time she was teaching them. She didn't deserve to die. And she certainly didn't deserve to die like that."

By the time Natalie was done talking with Ron, he was in tears. They hugged each other, briefly, and Natalie watched as the man she had been partially convinced had something to do with her teacher's death waved to her from the church doors. She waited a moment or two for him to disappear into the night before exiting the place of worship herself. When she finally made it back to the car, Kurt was behind the wheel, paging through *Pet Sematary.*

"I always liked Church, even after he became a zombie cat," Natalie said as she climbed into the car.

Kurt startled and dropped the book in his lap. "Jesus, creeper, wear a bell next time," he cried, flustered.

Natalie poked him in the arm just a little too hard. She was still pissed that he had bailed. "A bell like Church wears? The cute little decaying kitty? Stephen freaking you out there, Mr. Completionist?"

"This is like the tenth time I've read this one," Kurt scoffed, tossing the book in the back and starting up the engine. He pulled out of the church parking lot. "So what did you find out in there? Did Ron go from meek to murderer or what?"

Natalie shook her head, then leaned her forehead against the cool car window, thinking back to the handyman and his almost Zen persona. "Nah, I think he's in the clear." Ron had told her that he had been at church the night Mrs. Halsey died, and she had believed him.

"He did give me some wonderful quotes about Mrs. Halsey, though," she added, gazing down at her recorder. She shot him a look. "No thanks to you."

"I know, I know," Kurt said, groaning. "I promise to help next time. Providing you're not interviewing any more of my mother's exes."

Natalie didn't respond. She wasn't sure yet if there would be a next time. If this was all Kurt was good for—wheels—she would ride her bike. "Did you know Mrs. Halsey?" she asked, hoping for an answer in the affirmative. Perhaps there was a more noble reason for his interest in the case beyond money.

"I didn't go to East Ferry High," he answered, his eyes suddenly distant, his lips downturned. Natalie wondered if he was lying. Her teacher's name was certainly having an effect on him. Maybe he was like Ron, someone she had helped—and maybe he was ashamed for needing that help.

Kurt passed the library on the left and headed downtown. "Hey," he tossed his phone in her lap, "Where am I taking you? Mind punching your address into the GPS?"

Natalie picked up the phone and obliged, then turned her eyes back to the boy next to her—his fine nose and blond, blond hair. "Are you okay?" she asked, taking in his spaced-out eyes. Maybe she could get him to talk, like Ron.

Kurt shrugged as the diner flickered by on the right. By the rules of dinerdom, Helen's was not considered a real *diner* since it wasn't open twenty-four hours a day. But Helen Temple was okay with that. "Work to live," she always told Natalie, "don't live to work."

"I'm fine," Kurt said, then turned onto Natalie's street. "Would have been nice to just the solve the mystery tonight, though, right? Collect the cash prize, and blow this town?" He shot Natalie a crooked smile. "Guess we're stuck with each other for a little longer."

So that was it, then. It was all about the money for Kurt. She probably imagined that sad look on his face—the humanity. She suddenly wanted out of this boy's car. And fast. "Can you stop here?" she interjected when they were a few houses down. "I don't need my mom interrogating me about you right now."

"Better wait 'til the second date." Kurt nodded sagely.

"This is not a date." Natalie froze, turning toward Kurt.

"You know that, right? Just because I got ice cream with you doesn't mean—"

"Yeah, yeah," Kurt cut in. "I'm just kidding. We do have to figure out our next steps, though." His face got serious.

Natalie nodded, even though she wasn't entirely sure Kurt would be present at the next stage of her plan. Obviously, Ron was out, so who did that leave? Mr. Halsey? Some as-yet-undiscovered person harboring a grudge?

"The cops are heavy into Halsey, right?" Kurt said, as if reading her mind. "Think any of the reporters you work for have any more info?"

Natalie pursed her lips, remembering the other day in Mrs. Pressman's office. "I saw some folders at the paper, information one of the crime reporters was pretty interested in," she said. "But she keeps it in a locked drawer."

Kurt turned to her, incredulity painted across his handsome face. "And you're going to let that stop you?"

Before she could say anything further he held up a hand. "I have an idea. But I'll text you tomorrow."

"You're not going to give me a hint?" Natalie asked. She couldn't remember the last time she had texted a guy this much—at least for something else other than a school project. Not that this was anything other than basically that: a project. And not that she was actually going to answer him. Unless his idea was really, really good.

"Nah," Kurt said, shoving her shoulder. "This way you'll have to answer when I text. Now, get out of here, Veronica Mars. You're gonna need your rest."

Natalie was exhausted when she unlocked her front door. She could hear the sound of the TV in the living room; her mother was apparently watching *Buffy* again. "Hey, Mom," she called out, yawning. "I think I'm just going to—"

"Natalie, you're home!" a voice called out that was distinctly not her mother.

Natalie froze in the entryway, then peered over the back of the couch. Her mother and Katie smiled up at her, but Katie's grin seemed forced and almost manic.

It all came flooding back. Katie finding the note. Her threat that she was coming over. Natalie had ditched her—*and* put her phone on Airplane. Katie was going to murder her. Her *mother* was going to murder her. Murder was catching, it seemed.

"Did you have a fun time with Jonathan, Natalie?" Katie said, overemphasizing each word. Helen peeked over the red couch and gave her daughter a soft smile.

"Umm," Natalie said, her brain made sluggish by anxiety. "Yes?"

"I'm so glad you two are hanging out more!" Helen exclaimed, slopping a little wine on the couch as she did. "With both of you going to college in Pennsylvania and all, it'll be nice to have someone you know nearby. And you know I always thought you two would make a sweet couple."

Natalie scrunched up her face. "Mom. No." Jonathan was cute, but she had known him since they were kids. He was basically sexless in her eyes, like a teddy bear your mom gave you on Valentine's Day out of pity.

Katie saved her by leaping to her feet and grabbing Natalie's arm. "Nat and I need to go talk now, Mrs. Temple. Don't we, Nat?" She glared into her friend's face. Perhaps *saved* was not the right word in this case.

Natalie swallowed, hard. "Or we could hang out with Mom and watch some more *Buffy*?"

"I'll save you some time," Katie said through gritted teeth. "She saves the world. Again. Now, come *on*."

As soon as Natalie's bedroom door clicked closed behind them, Katie whirled around, eyes burning like laser beams through Natalie's skull. "Where. Were. You?" she growled, the periods between the words evident in her voice.

Natalie flopped on her bed, avoiding Katie's stare. She and Katie had never fought before. At least not about anything that mattered. Unless if you counted whether the dude in *Serial* was guilty or not. And she had never blown Katie off before.

"Would it help if I told you that I love you very, very much?" Natalie asked, cringing.

"No." Katie plopped next to her, her arms folded. "Because you lied to me, and then you ditched me. I was planning on yelling at you and then forcing you to do a synchronized dance to BTS to make it up to me. I even bought one of those movies on Amazon about the kids with cancer who fall in love! I thought we could mock it while we cried."

"I know, you're right." Natalie nodded. "I'm sorry. But something came up and... I..." The lie came far too easily. "I was kind of on a date." At least Kurt could be useful for something: evading Katie's ire.

Katie leaped up so quickly her glasses fell off. "A date? You don't go on those."

An odd eddy of hurt sidled through Natalie then. She could date if she wanted to. She wasn't utterly repugnant.

And it's not like Katie had cornered the market on romance with Simon the Puzzle Master. She jutted out her chin. "Yes, a date. I'm not an android, Katie."

"Were you actually with the golden retriever?" Katie asked, her voice rising with excitement. "I hate lying to your mom. It would be cool if I were I actually telling the truth."

Reluctantly, she shook her head. If only it were that easy. Jonathan was far safer than the truth. "No, it was actually… Remember that kid, Kurt, from Jack's trailer?"

Katie blinked. "That guy you practically boned? But, like, with words?" She paused. "Makes sense. He seemed super into you."

"Excuse me? What?" Natalie sprang up from her place on the bed, suddenly jittery. Yes, Kurt had said she was pretty, and yes, he kept talking about dates, but he didn't like her *that* way, did he? He just wanted the money. Was he actually being serious when he said all those flirty things? And what was wrong with her that she apparently didn't know the difference?

Natalie started pacing around the modest perimeter of her room—past her library of true-crime novels disguised as schoolbooks, her little desk with her laptop and gooseneck lamp, the Klimt poster her mom had hung there when she was a baby. "That's stupid," she sputtered. "You're being stupid. It was just a casual thing. Ice cream. I'll probably never hear from him again."

"Dude." Katie rolled her eyes. "The guy was all about you. And you weren't hating the attention, either." She leaned forward. "I'm not psyched that he's friends with Jack, but at least he seems to know how the shower works. How did this happen?"

Natalie stopped pacing and collapsed on the bed. *Did* she like the attention? That sizzle she'd felt back at the diner hadn't sucked. Still, she'd been alternately pissed off and amused by Kurt all night—plus, she really didn't have time to think about dating right now. Not that she ever did. She probably never would. She'd likely carry on her grand family tradition of spawning her own new best friend and leaving the dude in the dust.

Realizing that Katie was still staring at her, waiting for some sort of answer, Natalie cobbled together a lie about how Kurt had texted her about getting ice cream and she'd accepted. She left out the part about her texting him first—and the whole stakeout thing, of course.

"Wow," Katie said when Natalie was done. She had found a bag of salt and vinegar chips somewhere and had been munching all the way through. The acrid smell of fake flavor laced the air. "My little Natalie has her first real suitor."

Natalie paused, thinking over the events of the night. Katie could be right. He could be into her. But what did that mean? Was he trying to hang out with her—or was he just out to get paid? *Or* did he consider her a bonus prize—an extra perk in addition to the ten thousand dollars he was so hell-bent on collecting?

That all seemed a little too much to sort out in one night, so she threw a pillow at Katie and grabbed her laptop. "Whatever. Can we still watch the cancer-kids movie?"

"Hell yes, we can." Katie pumped a fist in the air. "And it's not even the famous one. It's a knock-off, so you just know it'll be good."

"Fire it up," Natalie said, leaning back in bed. "I could use a good laugh."

CHAPTER FOURTEEN: THEN

"Helen of Troy!" Sam yelled so loudly that Helen had to hold her phone away from her ear. "Congratu-fucking-lations!"

"I have a nickname now?" Helen stopped, baffled, outside her Journalism 101 class and leaned against a marble pillar, her cell phone under her chin. Northwestern was just lousy with marble pillars. The classroom was still empty. Helen had a bad (good?) habit of getting everywhere fifteen minutes early.

"I'll call you whatever the fuck you want, Scoop," Sam said and chortled. Helen didn't know that people could actually chortle, but that was exactly what Sam did. "That story you wrote? Fucking brilliant. I swear I almost cried at that part where Jenny and her dad won the potato-sack race at Spirit Day after her first boyfriend dumped her. Actual gold."

Helen grinned, biting her lip and shifting her book bag to her other shoulder. She hadn't heard from Sam for days after turning in her story, so she had been worried she had been unceremoniously fired. Believing herself doomed, she had actually joined Amanda in eating an entire pizza in one evening while listening to the Shins on repeat. She wasn't entirely sure if Amanda knew she was there, though.

"Awesome," she chirped, relieved. "When's the story out?"

"Is there a rack of *Daily*s in whatever echoing hallway you're standing in?" Sam asked. "Look at the front page."

There was just such a rack outside her classroom door, and when she rushed over to grab a copy, Jenny's face stared back at her from the cover—along with the headline "Missing Co-Ed—The Inside Story"...and her byline. Her actual name, right there on the front page. She squeaked into the phone, and Sam laughed.

"And you will not believe this, Scooper." Helen liked that nickname a lot less. "You're getting *syndicated*."

"What?" Helen choked, the hand holding the paper starting to shake.

"Syndicated," Sam said, his voice slipping back into his usual pedantic tone. She could hear his bow tie through the phone. "Like, it will be in the local papers—the *real* papers that *real* people read. Not just the kind that idiot college students spit their gum into."

Helen blinked. She knew what *syndicated* meant, of course, she just never imagined that her words would be out there for people to see. And so soon. Most people didn't get published in a real paper until they were in grad school or whatever, and she was just a freshman. This was a major coup. She'd just had to lie to a grieving mother to get it. Her heart twinged with guilt when she thought back to Jenny's mom in her bathrobe, her eyes wide and lost. Had it been worth it? To trick someone into trusting her? Into telling her things they never would have otherwise? Helen wasn't sure; it was hard to look away from her name on the front of the paper, though. The *front.*

"Okay, now get to work," Sam was saying.

Helen realized she had zoned out—and that her hands had sweated through the entire paper. She snatched up a few more copies to send home to her dad. "What was that?" she asked.

"Jesus Christ, Helen, pay attention," Sam groaned. "We got an anonymous tip this morning. Roberts was apparently sleeping with her sister's husband, which sounds like motive to me. So you're going to interview her. See what she says."

Helen scooted to the side to let a widening stream of kids into the classroom. "Her sister?" she asked, her voice young and dumb-sounding to her own ears. "How do I do that?"

"Jesus fucking almighty Christ. Don't make me break my phone," Sam growled. "There's a vigil tonight, kid. Go there. Find her. Talk to her. Find me another story. A thousand words. By Thursday. Bye." He hung up before she could reply.

Still stunned and mulling over how she could possibly approach Jenny's sister—a prospect that was equal parts terrifying and thrilling—Helen shuffled into her classroom, where she noticed that she wasn't the only one with the copy of the *Daily* in her hands. Jenny's face smiled back at her from a sea of papers, and Helen swore she could hear more than a few sobs. Fighting a smile, Helen moved toward her seat—and was almost barreled over by someone booking it toward the door. The hot TA. He muttered a vague apology at her, and for the second that he looked her way Helen could see that his eyes were wet—and that a copy of her story was clenched in his hands. She watched, baffled, as he burst into the hallway, as the click of his heels echoed through the marble halls.

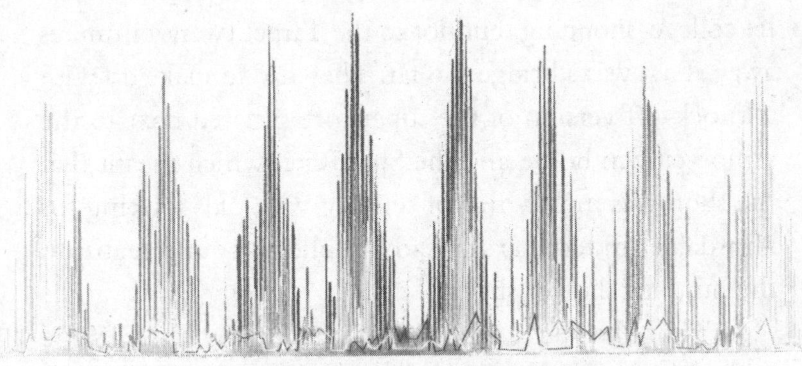

CHAPTER FIFTEEN

"I don't think you'll need a neon fanny pack in college," Natalie said, eyeing the object with undisguised disdain as Katie deposited it into her shopping cart. "What exactly is that for again?"

"For carrying all the mace that I'm apparently going to need since I suck at karate," Katie huffed. "Which reminds me, where's the mace?"

Natalie scanned the aisles of Lot for Less dubiously. "I don't think they have that here. But holler if you're looking for an enormous sports bra."

Since Katie had stayed the night (the third in a row), she was subjected the next morning to Helen Temple's daily workout, and if Natalie thought she was unfit to protect herself, Katie couldn't defend an egg from a brisk wind. As a consolation prize, Helen had allowed Katie to take Natalie college-shopping, but not to the Target twenty minutes away. That was a bridge too far. They had to make do with a knock-off version of the superstore situated next to the senior-citizen home and the ShopRite, which meant that the shop was mostly full of seventy-year-olds looking for affordable underwear instead of college-bound teens on the hunt for shower shoes.

"It's not like you're shopping 'til you drop, either," Katie said, gesturing toward Natalie's cart, which held exactly three packages of pens. "According to the handy checklist that MIT sent me, we're going to need shower caddies, extra-long sheets, a laundry basket, an alarm clock, and, like, four hundred other things that all need to fit into a room the size of my closet. So pick up the pace!"

Natalie paused, perusing a shelf packed with dishes and plates. She plucked a bowl from the melee and placed it in her cart. "There, now I have something to eat my cereal in. Can we go now? This place is depressing." She scanned the shop, which was filled with the aforementioned elderly people, as well as a middle-aged housewife or two, screaming children in tow. She was excited about college, sure, but she was a little more than distracted with the here and now lately. Plus, she didn't want to outfit her dorm room with the off-brand wares of Lot for Less. She wanted to start fresh.

"Sure, I think I'm all set." Katie shrugged, dumping her haul onto the counter. "I don't know about you, but I feel *ready* for college now."

Natalie paid for her purchases, and as the two dragged

their bags out into the parking lot, her phone chimed in her pocket. Then chimed again. And again. She paused, then rooted out the device and held it up to her face. It was Kurt. She was frankly surprised to see his name on her phone screen. When she hadn't heard from him over the last few days, she figured he had decided to go after the reward alone. That seemed about right. Katie was wrong; he didn't like her that way. It was all about the cash. Now, though, her phone was practically exploding with texts.

Meet me at Jolly Times!

Jack is gonna teach us how to pick locks!

Now now now

Katie leaned over to look at Natalie's phone, but Natalie pulled it away just in time. "Privacy, Katie," she snapped playfully.

"Was that Kurt?" Katie asked, a scowl spreading across her lips. "Is this the first time he's texted you since the other night?"

Natalie grunted. Did Kurt really think he could ignore her and then demand her presence? At a deserted fun center, no less. She didn't need him, she decided. She had a bike—and her brain.

The phone chimed again.

Sorry I didn't text you earlier. My phone service got shut off. Just one of the many joys of having the spaciest mom in the world.

Natalie stilled, reading over the words a few times. She didn't remember him saying much about his mother besides the fact that she'd dated Ron, but he was living in a trailer with Jack, so life couldn't be that great. A stab of sympathy went through her heart—as well as appreciation for her own mom. Still, the guy couldn't even be trusted to keep his cell in service. *Yeah*, a far corner of her brain protested, *maybe that's why he's so eager for that reward money. Because he needs it. You're lucky you don't.*

Katie poked her arm. "Is he sexting you?" She leaned over to look at Natalie's phone, and Natalie snatched it away. "Show me. No, don't show me." Katie covered her eyes, then peeked out between two fingers.

Natalie ignored her, eyes locked on the screen. Three little bubbles danced across the screen; he was still typing.

> I have a surprise for you, in addition to the lock-picking. Please say you'll come.

Her rigid shoulders softened. Would it really be that bad if she saw him again? If she found out what surprise he had in store? It was either that or continue talking about dick pics with Katie. She slid her phone into her pocket.

"Kurt wants me to meet him at the trailer," Natalie said, not looking her friend directly in the eye. "Would it seem desperate if I went?"

"I dunno, Nat," Katie said, sliding into the Jeep. "If I were you, I'd make him wait. Show him who's boss."

Natalie shrugged. That would have been fine advice if she were actually dating the guy, but she had the investigation to think of. And she didn't know how much longer she could leave it. "Nah, I'll go," she said finally, avoiding Katie's eyes.

Katie started the car and leaned back in her seat, staring out the window as all the moms and old people shuffled out of Lot for Less, their arms laden with bags. She rubbed at her face and sighed. "Okay… I'll drop you off. But someday you're going to have to start listening to me. I know a lot more than you about a lot of things, you know."

Before Natalie could throw her arms around her friend, Katie raised a finger. "Only thing is, I'm not lying to your mom again. No way. If she asks where you were, you come up with something that has nothing to do with me. Not only do I love the shit out of Helen, but that woman could kill a man with her little toe, and I do not need that kind of stress in my life." She paused, cocking an eyebrow at Natalie. "Understood?"

Natalie grinned. "Understood."

Stepping into Jolly Times, Natalie was flooded with memories of afternoons wasted in the best possible way. Still, it was like looking at a picture of the *Titanic* pre-iceberg—majestic and bright—then seeing a photo of the ship rotting at the bottom of the sea. There was the dunk tank, sans scary clown, now a massive, cloudy glass container filled with leaves instead of water and shrieking kids. Eerily, Big Bertha of the titular Big Bertha game still loomed in the shadow of her booth, her livid, red mouth forever open, hungering for the baseballs that children once lobbed down her gullet for trinkets. And then there was the carousel, horseless, now just a series of broken poles ringing around a column of broken mirrors. For a moment that was strangely long and aching and sweet, Natalie missed being a kid. Missed riding around on the carousel, trying to snag the brass ring. Things had been easier back then, when her only goal had been bringing home the biggest bear Jolly Times had to offer.

"I haven't been here since I was eight years old," Natalie mused, taking in the dusty interior of the fun center. "It was my friend Jonathan's birthday, and the clown was clearly drunk, and then Sadie Mathers threw up in the ball pit. This is very creepy." She bopped Big Bertha on the nose. "I approve."

"Good," Kurt said and grinned. "I mostly chose this place because there's tons of old locks to pick, but it does have a certain charm, does it not?"

"Can you two stop flirting and pay attention, please?" Jack said from the floor, where he was demonstrating picking the lock to a storage closet with a bent paper clip. "Do you want to learn or not?"

Natalie watched Jack work with a bemused expression on her face. He really knew what he was doing, and it was kind of impressive—despite the fact that Jack was, by and large, a creep. "I keep forgetting you were a smart kid, Jack," she said, leaning forward to watch him maneuvering the bent piece of metal. "Too bad you gave it all up for a life of crime."

Jack just grunted, working the lock until it finally gave. The door swung inward, revealing nothing but a quietly moldering mouse carcass. "Do you guys have it or what? If so, can I have my twenty bucks, please?" He swung around to face Kurt, his face smudged with rust and dirt.

Kurt turned toward Natalie. "You wanna give it a go first? Make sure you have it down?" He was dressed in all black once again, but today he wore a pair of slightly too-large loafers. Regardless, Kurt looked angular and, Natalie was loath to think it, pretty cute.

She nodded and stooped to pluck the paper clip from Jack's grimed fingers, then relocked the door. It took a few moments, but after digging with the bent clip for a bit, the door clicked open once more. She leaped to her feet and pumped her fist. It was surprisingly and terrifyingly easy to make the lock bend to her will. She made a mental note to ask her mom if they had enough of a security system in place at home. Knowing Helen, though, they had trip wires and silent alarms.

Kurt reached out and gave her a high five, his hand lingering a bit too long palm to palm against hers. He caught her eye and smiled.

"Congrats, Nat." Jack doled out his own slightly grimy high five. "Remind me why I'm teaching you this again?"

Before Natalie could speak, Kurt piped up. "Life skills, man. Gotta have 'em." He slapped a twenty in Jack's hand. "Go buy yourself something pretty." Natalie eyed the money, wondering where it had come from. Wasn't he just complaining about his phone bill?

"Whatever, dude." Jack slipped the money in his pocket. "I have a date. See you guys later."

Once Jack had exited Jolly Times, Natalie turned toward Kurt and put a hand on her hip. "We'll get to who in the hell would date Jack in a second. First, I have to state the obvious. You didn't tell him. Followed by the query: Why didn't you tell him?"

Kurt shook his head. "Of course I didn't tell him! You want to split the money three ways? I don't think so. It's just you and me."

Alone with Kurt, Natalie felt somewhat shy. The other night it had been dark, and they had been on a possible killer's trail. Now, they were standing in stark daylight, alone in a dusty relic from her youth. She wasn't sure how to proceed with that. So she did what journalists always did when face-to-face with someone she didn't know. She asked questions.

"Are you a criminal mind, like Jack?" she asked, wandering toward the broken carousel. The spokes looked lethal, almost: they were broken off like jagged fence posts. She hoped she sounded casual instead of worried.

"God no," Kurt said and laughed, trailing behind her. "I don't have a record or anything. Scout's honor. I haven't known Jack that long. He's not actually that bad. Aside from his attitude. I guess weird kids just find each other."

Natalie thought of Katie and their screeching tampon trade-offs in the hallways. "You're right about that." She paused, looking back at the boy behind her with his high cheekbones and uniform of black. "I feel weird. Working on this with you when I don't know you at all..."

Kurt stuck his hands in his pockets. "You're going to like my surprise, then." He grinned.

"Surprises are things I do not enjoy," Natalie replied. "But...proceed."

Kurt nodded and dashed behind the broken carousel, emerging with a bag of neon-yellow tennis balls. Helen had had a brief country-club phase during which she forced her daughter to play tennis and *socialize*, as she called it. Belonging to the country club meant that you belonged in Ferry, and it took Helen nearly ten years of living there to even get an invite to join. The tennis classes were filled with unsmiling girls who only drank plain seltzer and hated Natalie, so after the sixth lesson she'd spent hiding in the clubhouse, her mother had finally let her quit.

"What's with the balls?" Natalie asked, finally shaking off the ice-cold grip of nostalgia.

Kurt hefted a ball. "Glad you asked. We're going to throw these in Big Bertha's mouth!"

Natalie blinked. "And..."

"And have fun?" Kurt replied. "With balls?" He winked.

"Excuse me while I spontaneously combust from excitement," Natalie deadpanned. Was this the surprise he'd been talking about? If she had known it involved physical exertion, she would have stayed home. Still, if she were honest with herself, she was intrigued. Kurt was kind of cute when he was excited.

"But that's not all!" Kurt cried like a carnival barker. "If a player successfully sates Bertha's hunger, they get to ask the other player: truth...or dare? It's a getting-to-know-you game I thought up especially for you and me."

Natalie considered the offer for a second or two. She did want to know more about Kurt. And it wasn't like she had anything else to do. It was the weekend, so she wouldn't be back at the paper for a few days.

“Sure,” she said, shrugging. “I’m game. Only I get to go first.”

Kurt offered her a tennis ball with a little flourish, and Natalie planted her feet for the throw. Luckily, her mother had also forced her to play softball until she was ten, at which point Natalie had decided that the sun was bad and other people sucked, so when she threw, she threw true. She whirled on Kurt and crowed, “Truth…or dare!”

Kurt crossed his arms and cocked his head to the side. “All right. Truth.”

Natalie mirrored him and crossed her arms, narrowing her eyes, searching for a question to ask this boy who was basically a mystery.

“Why do you want to know if the reporters at the paper think Mr. Halsey is guilty?” she asked, the words coming out of her mouth as she realized that she had been wondering about this very question all along. “How does that help you get the reward money?”

Kurt’s face relaxed. “That’s your first question? Really? Don’t you want to know how many people I’ve slept with or something?”

Natalie raised an eyebrow and grimaced. “Nah, I think just this.”

Kurt gave her an indulgent smile. “Because if he’s guilty, there’s no reward money of course. I want to know if I’m wasting my time. Also…” his eyes lingered on her lips “…I figured it would probably make good fodder for your podcast, so I thought I’d be generous.”

Natalie picked up a ball to hide her blush and lobbed it at Kurt. He caught it against his chest, his eyes widening as if surprised by the force of impact. He turned and threw it toward Bertha, missing her mouth by a mile and letting out an epic groan.

"Looks like it's my turn again," Natalie said, scooping up another ball and deftly tossing it into Bertha's mouth. "Truth or dare."

Kurt raised his eyebrows. "Looks like we have ringer, ladies and gents."

"Truth or dare," Natalie repeated.

Kurt rolled his shoulders and cracked his neck. "Uh, truth again. Why not?"

Natalie looked at his brown loafers, thinking back to the whale belt, the massive watch. "What's with the getup?"

Kurt looked down at his black jeans and T-shirt. "Getup?"

Natalie nodded. "Yeah. The whale belt. The old-man shoes. What's the deal?"

Kurt tipped his head back and looked at her through his eyelashes, smiling. "You're really observant. You'd make a good journalist."

She tilted her head to the side, a silent signal to continue.

"They were my dad's. The only kind he ever wore," Kurt said, his voice shedding its almost-constant bemusement and taking on a bitter tenseness. "I don't see him anymore, so I wear something of his every day. To remember him and everything he gave me. He made me who I am." His face betrayed a battery of emotions—sadness, anger, and longing.

Natalie's eyes softened, and the competitive force that had driven her before started to slacken. "You called him an asshole before—at Sammy's," she said quietly. "But you still miss him, don't you? He's still your dad." For a long second Natalie wished she knew her father well enough—or at all—to have such conflicting feelings. Silence stretched out between them; it was peaceful in the abandoned fun center, almost too peaceful. All they could hear was the highway and its white-noise buzz, and the humming of lazy flies bobbing in the sunlight.

Kurt stood for a second or two in a shaft of light that streamed through one of the broken windows, then shook his head. "That's more than one question," he said, his voice bright once more. "And it's my turn."

He stooped and grabbed a ball, aimed with one eye closed, and tossed it as hard as he could toward Bertha's mouth. This time it sailed through her painted lips and slammed against the back wall, making the old wood reverberate with the force of it. He leaped into the air, pumping his fists and cheering, then wheeled on Natalie.

"Truth or dare?" His lips parted into a smile that made his whole face beautiful.

Natalie watched the ball as it rolled across the floor. She tried not to think about his lips and failed. "Dare?" she said.

Kurt raised his eyebrows and took in Natalie from her sneakers to her ponytail. "If you don't mind," Kurt said and smiled a crooked smile, "I'm going to save that one for later. But I promise I'll make it good."

CHAPTER SIXTEEN: THEN

Helen had never purposely followed anyone before, but she'd also never been to a vigil for a missing girl. Now, she was trailing Jenny's sister, Constance, past the wrought iron gates of Northwestern University, where the vigil had been held midcampus in front of a hulking piece of stone known simply as the Rock. Rival clubs apparently camped out all night to paint the Rock with slogans and applicable colors, but tonight it was all white for Jenny. Constance had come with her mother and husband, a tall blond man with a pleasant face, but split off from them when it had all drawn to a close. Helen wondered where her baby was as she followed Constance down Evanston's main shopping and dining strip, Sherman Avenue. Should she tap the woman on the shoulder? Shout her name? None of these seemed like particularly subtle ideas. For a moment, Helen almost turned around and went back to her dorm room. Was she really following a young mother whose sister had just gone missing? Was this *really* who she was now? Before she could mull that over too much, Jenny's sister stopped abruptly and pushed open the door to a café boasting a red awning stamped with the words *the Unicorn Café*, a sparsely populated coffee shop Helen herself had visited on lonely nights to get a tea when she couldn't spend another moment in her room.

It was too late now; Helen found herself following the other woman into the café. The setting eased her a bit; the cozy spot seemed like the ideal place to approach Constance—perhaps tell her, like she had her mother, that she was a friend of Jenny's. Ask if she had been to the vigil and go from there. Helen pulled off her heavy pea coat as the heat of the place hit her, the smell of coffee sure to linger on her hair and clothes far into the night. She queued up behind Constance as Iron & Wine wafted from the stereo, watching as the other woman blinked glassily at the tattooed man behind the counter and ordered a mint tea. Helen was just pulling out her wallet to order the same thing when Constance spun around, her dark brows drawn together, her lips pinched.

"Are you seriously following me right now?" she snapped, sloshing hot tea on her hand. She didn't flinch, even though it must have burned. The man behind the counter widened his eyes and turned to tinker with the espresso machine. Working at a coffee shop near a college campus, he'd probably seen his share of late-night drama—two girls yelling at each other likely didn't warrant an intervention.

"Uh," Helen replied, her wallet gaping open, forgotten in her hand, "I just wanted some, uh, tea?" She gestured lamely at Constance's cup.

Constance slammed her drink down on the counter, slopping it all over the crackly lacquered wood, and crossed her arms in front of her chest. Iron & Wine changed over to Gogol Bordello, perhaps to drown out any discussion that might disturb the rest of the patrons of the Unicorn, which was unlikely since about seventy-five percent of them sported giant headphones. "So you stood next to me, *staring*, during my *missing* sister's vigil, then followed me here—the one time I've found in *days* to be alone—for *tea*?"

Helen felt a tide of mortification, so intense she felt like crying, crash through her as she stared at Jenny's sister. The woman was pretty, young, with rosy cheeks and dark hair like a fairy-tale character. Her stomach still swelled slightly under her denim jacket where the baby had once been. "I'm sorry, I just, um, write for the school paper and..." Before Helen could continue, Constance snatched her wallet out of her hand and flipped to Helen's student ID.

"Oh, Christ, it's you," she said with a moan. "Do you know how much grief you've caused my family, *Helen*? Do you know how angry my mother is that you wormed your way into our house, lied to her?" The barista had given up all pretense of making coffee and was now watching the women, casting Helen a glance of hearty disgust at Constance's words. She would never be able to come back here. She'd have to make her tea in the dorm bathroom like a shut-in. That was the least of her concerns, though. First and foremost was that humiliation, that guilt, that sense of intense failure.

"Look," Constance said, tossing Helen's wallet on the counter, vibrating with rage. She poked a finger at her and growled, "Stay away from me, stay away from my mom, stay away from my family, you heartless, talentless *bitch.*" Constance stood for a moment, shaking, barely registering that the entirety of the coffee shop had erupted into cheers on her behalf—headphones be damned—before crashing her way out the door.

Helen forced herself to wait a second before running out of the coffee shop herself—so it wouldn't look like she was following the other woman yet again—marinating in the worst moment of her entire life. Outside, she leaned against the brick storefront, pinching her arms and shuddering, willing herself to wake up. In her haste to get out of there, she had left her coat behind and her thin sweater was doing little to battle the Midwestern cold. Luckily, she had had the presence of mind to hold onto her wallet. It had to be a nightmare. It was all just too terrible. Slowly, she slid to the ground, not caring that she was sitting in a pile of cigarettes butts and spilled coffee. Maybe if she sat there long enough, she would melt into the concrete and disappear. That's what she deserved. To not exist. Constance was right: she was talentless and, now, it seemed, a bitch. She'd never been called that word before. She'd always been *nice, sweet.* But all that had gone out the window when she'd tricked Mrs. Roberts, when she'd gone against her principles. Her dad would be so disappointed.

Her hands were starting to go numb when something soft and warm dropped around her shoulders—her jacket. Natalie looked up to see a handsome man crouching down, his hands loose between his knees. Her TA.

"I saw everything that happened in there," he said. Helen started to cringe, but he didn't sound angry. He sounded almost… regretful. "I get it. It happens to everyone eventually in this game." The TA gave her a lopsided smile and reached into his jacket, pulling out a silvery flask. "Wanna talk about it?"

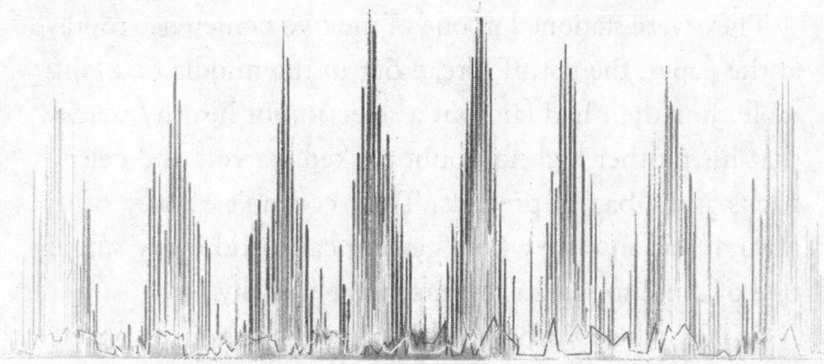

CHAPTER SEVENTEEN

Jonathan was good at talking to people, and Natalie was impressed. It only took her two rambling calls—one with an elderly woman who said Mrs. Halsey came to her in her dreams, the next from a man who seemed pretty sold on the existence of aliens—before Natalie wanted to unplug the phone from the wall and go back to scanning food-stained metro sections. Paper cuts be damned. Plus, Kurt kept texting her, asking if she had had the chance to break into Mrs. Pressman's drawer yet. She didn't see how she'd be able to get away at this rate with the tip line ringing nonstop.

Meanwhile, Jonathan answered phones like a seasoned telemarketer, nodding and smiling along with whatever nonsense the person on the other end spewed. He was even taking notes. Frankly, Natalie felt like a slacker.

They were stationed in one of the two conference rooms at the paper, their stuff spread out in the middle of a long table. Jonathan had laid out a selection of healthy snacks that his mother had no doubt packed: carrots and celery sticks and a bag of pretzels. They couldn't eat any of it, though, because they kept getting calls, and every single one of those foods was distractingly crunchy.

Finally, there came a lull in the marathon of phone calls—perhaps because it was lunch and people were too distracted by their stomachs to hatch any asinine theories. When Jonathan put down his phone at long last, Natalie looked at him with raised eyebrows.

"What?" Jonathan asked, crunching into a carrot.

"I'm just surprised you're finding anything to take notes on." Natalie nodded toward his notebook. "I feel like an underachiever."

Jonathan laughed, putting his half-eaten carrot stick on a napkin. He pushed his notebook toward her. "I'm not taking notes. I'm playing tip-line bingo. See?" He pointed at the grid on his notepad. "You get a space if someone mentions a suspicious neighbor. A space if the word *ghost* comes up. Then, of course, there's aliens..."

Natalie laughed, a bit taken aback. She and Jonathan rarely spent any time one-on-one; Katie was always there, and she and Natalie pretty much dominated the conversation—and the jokes. The bingo card seemed a little edgy for a boy who'd refused to dissect the fetal pig in science last year.

"Jonathan Pressman, this is hilarious," she said with an

appreciative smile. "Why didn't I know you were hilarious?" She snagged a carrot and tapped the notebook. "Can you make me one of these?"

"Of course." Jonathan turned to a new page in his notebook and started sketching. "And as for the other thing... I dunno. Maybe you weren't paying attention? I got jokes, my friend."

Jonathan was intent on the notebook, but Natalie didn't miss the slight hurt in his voice. "What are you talking about?" she asked, trying to force some levity into her voice. "We spend every Thanksgiving together. We've known each other since we were, like, five. Of course I've been paying attention."

Jonathan's pencil stopped moving for a second, then he carried on, his lips curving into a sad smile. "Nah, I get it. You and Katie were always close. It makes sense, since you're into the same stuff. I know you guys think I'm boring."

"We don't think that—"

"You call me *the golden retriever*, Nat." Jonathan looked up, his eyes crinkling with false mirth. "I have ears. And apparently they're floppy and canine."

Natalie felt the rest of her carrot stick in her throat. She hadn't thought Jonathan noticed much of what she and Katie did. He was popular. They were...weird. So, yeah, they poked fun at their golden-boy friend. She just never imagined that he knew. Or cared.

"I'm sorry," Natalie said, after finally swallowing the carrot. "We only called you that because you're so...*nice*. Which is not a bad thing!" she rushed to add when she saw Jonathan's face fall. "Look, Katie and I are obsessed with murder and monsters and bad things. We just figured that you were above all that."

Jonathan nodded, playing with a piece of celery. "Yeah, I'm not into all that dark stuff, sure. But I can listen. And I can talk to you guys about why you are." He looked at her with his big blue all-American eyes, which seemed now far deeper than she had given them credit for. "So tell me. Why are you? Into—" he gestured vaguely "—all that?"

Natalie looked around at the walls of the paper. They were just cinderblocks painted a sad mustard yellow. The floors covered with ugly nubby brown carpets. And everyone out there were just people—people who drank their bad office coffee and showed up to work and logged into their computers and typed. To anyone else, it would all seem mundane. Oppressive, even. To Natalie, this room was full of possibilities. Questions to be answered. And if—*when*—she became a journalist, she would be reporting on it all. The everyday tragedies and dramas that, when held under a loving magnifying glass, when given *words*, became epic stories. Stories that could change and save lives. Or, in Mrs. Halsey's case, shine a light on those lives even after they'd ended.

She didn't know how to articulate that to Jonathan, though, so she shrugged and said it as simply as she could. "I want to tell stories. Real ones. That's all I've ever wanted to do."

Jonathan nodded, turning his pencil between his fingers. "That makes sense. I get that. But will you promise me one thing?"

"Sure," Natalie said. "Unless it's my firstborn child or something."

He shook his head as if indulging her. "Nah, nothing like that. Just…when you start telling these stories, when they start getting out in the world, send them to me? I'd like to read them."

A blush crept across Natalie's cheeks, and she smiled, feeling awkward. She nodded, though, and when the phones started ringing again, she and Jonathan set about filling out their bingo grids in pleasant solidarity.

After about an hour, Natalie started feeling antsy again. It was already halfway through her shift, and she didn't see how she was going to be able to sneak away to Mrs. Pressman's office, especially with Jonathan next to her. Kurt had texted her three times in a row in the last thirty minutes. Apparently, he was getting antsy, too.

"Is your mom in her office?" Natalie asked at last, taking her phone off the hook after Jonathan put his back in the cradle.

"I don't think so." Jonathan shrugged. "She usually gets lunch around now. Why?"

Natalie searched her brain for some other excuse aside from her period but kept coming up cold. She couldn't have been bleeding for more than a week. It made no scientific sense. But did Jonathan know that? Likely not. "I'm just going to go by and grab…something, if you don't mind covering the phones for me?"

Jonathan shot her a grin, and he looked so content to be here, hanging out with her, that she felt bad. That didn't stop her from walking as confidently as she could toward Mrs. Pressman's office. She often found that if you acted as if you were supposed to be somewhere, people rarely questioned you. When she reached the office, she knocked on the door, praying that Jonathan was right and his mother was out for lunch. No one answered, and the door was unlocked.

Once inside, Natalie's heart immediately started trying to claw its way out of her chest. She was doing this. Picking a lock like a criminal. Breaking into newspaper property. Taking a deep breath, she knelt by Mrs. Pressman's desk, pulling a paper clip from her pocket. Her hands were shaking, but she still managed to insert it into the lock. She took a few deep inhales and then started to move the piece of bent metal like Jack had taught her. Her heart started beating like a jackhammer as she twisted, the lock holding firm. Desperate, she pushed the paper clip in farther, less expertly, wiggling the metal from side to side. It occurred to her then that ancient locks in abandoned fun centers and locks on desks might not be equally pickable. When the clip snapped in half and clattered to the floor, she swore and banged on the drawer, forgetting for a moment where she was.

"What are you doing?"

Natalie leaped to her feet and spun toward the door, where Jonathan was standing half in and half out of the office. She blinked at him, her head entirely emptied out. There was no way to explain this that didn't look bad. She was trying to steal information from his mom. Jonathan was nice, but not nice enough to let that go. She was going to get fired, her journalism career over before it even started.

"I was just coming to see if you wanted to get some coffee..." Jonathan trailed off. "But...what are you doing?" he repeated.

"I…" Natalie's mind went immediately blank. "I was looking for a tampon."

Instead of flushing with embarrassment and backing out of the room as she had expected Jonathan to do at the mention of her monthly massacre, he closed the door behind him and crossed his arms. "I'm not stupid, Natalie. I know you know that's the wrong drawer. And I'm pretty sure you're not so desperate for a tampon that you'd try to pick a lock."

Natalie collapsed into Mrs. Pressman's desk chair, her cheeks hot. Jonathan was disappointed in her, which felt somehow worse than being caught. She had never seen him look so serious. Maybe when his dog Kipper died in third grade, but there had been a lot more tears and snot involved then. Now he just looked like kind of…lost.

"I'm sorry, Jonathan." She looked at her lap. "I was just trying to find out what the paper has on Mr. Halsey. I saw that your mom had a file on him, and I just—"

"Decided to break into her desk and steal information?"

Natalie cringed. "It sounds bad when you put it like that."

Jonathan looked down at her, slumped in the desk chair, her face a mask of misery. "You really loved her, didn't you? Mrs. Halsey?"

Natalie nodded, feeling a little guilty for going behind Jonathan's back, for not being straight with him after that honest moment they'd just had.

"And you're not going to use this information to, like, get yourself hurt in some way? You just want to know, that's it?" He opened the door and peeked out at the floor, then closed it again, apparently satisfied that no one was there.

"Are you saying you'll help me?" Natalie asked, getting to her feet, her guilt, for the moment, forgotten. Her legs shook with leftover adrenaline. "You'll help me get into the drawer?"

Jonathan shook his head, and Natalie's heart pooled in her sneakers. Then he sighed and dragged his hand across his face. "You don't need to break into my mother's desk, Nat. You think I don't pay attention to what she's working on? You think I don't take a peek or two of my own when she brings her work home?"

Natalie's spine straightened. "You know what the police have on Mr. Halsey? Why they're looking at him so closely?" She had always assumed Jonathan just floated through life, filtering out any negativity he came in contact with like a sieve. She never would have guessed he would be interested in his mother's work; that was more her domain.

"I do," Jonathan said, nodding. "But I gotta hear you say it. Tell me you won't get yourself hurt with this. That you won't go...writing about it somewhere. Promise me."

She certainly wasn't going to get herself hurt. She wasn't sure how she could even do so in this case. And the writing thing... Well, she wasn't going to *write* about it. And the podcast would come out much later. She just needed some insight into where to focus her attention right now. That was all. Finally, she nodded. "I promise."

"Okay," Jonathan said. He looked a lot less bright-eyed than usual. A little tired. A little dimmed. Natalie never stopped to think what it was like having a mother like his. Someone who brought that horror home.

"Here's the deal. They don't have much. Not enough to

arrest him on yet, anyway. But they do have a footprint at the top of the stairs where Mrs. Halsey..." Jonathan swallowed, his face cast in green. "It matches a pair of shoes that Mr. Halsey owns."

Natalie frowned. "Well, that's normal, right? The guy left footprints in his own home."

"That's what I thought." Jonathan nodded. "But they didn't find any other footprints upstairs. Aside from his and Mrs. Halsey's, so..."

"No one else was in the house." Natalie finished his sentence.

"Yeah."

She nodded grimly. It certainly didn't look good for Mr. Halsey. She wasn't sure why she was so disappointed. She wanted her teacher's murderer found. But could it be that simple? That cruel? A man so tired of his wife, so eager to move on to greener pastures that he killed her? Bashed her on the head and let her tumble to her death? She felt cold all of a sudden, and it wasn't due to the overly aggressive air-conditioning in Mrs. Pressman's office. It was all so human. So *sad*.

"Are you okay?" Jonathan said, coming forward to put a hand on Natalie's shoulder. She realized then that she was shivering.

"Yeah," she croaked. She had to get it together. This was going to be her job someday. She would have to deal with stuff like this constantly. Stuff that was much worse. "Let's just go back to the phones, okay?"

Jonathan squeezed her shoulder and led them both back to the conference room where, indeed, the phones were ringing once more. Natalie slid back into her chair and lifted the phone to her mouth. "Hello, you've reached the *Ferry Caller* Tip Line. How can I help you?" she recited.

"There you are!" a familiar voice said down the line.

"Kurt?" she said, looking to the side to see if Jonathan had noticed. He was busy crossing another square off his bingo board. "Why are you calling me here?"

"You weren't answering my texts," he said, his voice tinged with annoyance. "Come on, don't leave me hanging here. You find anything out?"

Natalie sighed. "Yeah, but—" she turned away from Jonathan and lowered her voice "—I can't really talk right now. Can we meet up later?"

"Sure. I wanted to collect on my dare, anyway." She could hear the crooked grin in his voice.

"Okay, where? When?" she asked. Jonathan had hung up and was watching her from the corner of his eye now.

"The big, abandoned place on Sycamore. Nine," Kurt said rather than asked, then hung up.

"Thank you so much for your time," Natalie said to the dial tone, then hung up herself.

Jonathan was studying her, his pencil tapping his chin. "Anything good?"

Natalie looked down at her bingo board, then drew a decisive line through *ghosts*. She tapped at the paper and screwed up her face. "Good for my game, yeah! Only two more spots till bingo."

The house on Sycamore had been abandoned for more than ten years now, ever since the family who owned it, the Parkers, had lost their savings to some Ponzi scheme.

For a while, no one wanted to live there because it just seemed wreathed in bad energy. And then it came out that the place was built on swampland, and no one could sell it, anyway. At one point, a big theme-park developer had proposed building one of his sites there, but Sandy Tarver and all the other town ladies soon put the kibosh on that. They said it was because of some kind of endangered duck that lived in the swamp, but everyone knew they just didn't want to deal with any more tourists.

It was silent at the Victorian when she arrived—not even an errant, rare-duck call. In the quiet, Natalie could hear the house groaning around her, the scarpering of something exploring the basement for food. She watched her blurred reflection in the face of an old TV crouching in the corner, on the top of which, mysteriously, was perched a jar of ancient pickles. She wondered if they were from the last party that was thrown in the house—or if they belonged to the previous residents.

"Kurt?" she called out in a half whisper, flicking on her phone light. "Are you there?" She jumped as he emerged from the shadows in the adjoining room.

"This place is wild," he said, running his hand over the moldering wallpaper—dusky roses and fat angels. "There's used condoms in every room. Every room! Who the hell would want to have sex here?"

Natalie wrapped her arms around herself. "Yeah, no kidding. Even I'm not that creepy."

"I don't think you're creepy at all." Kurt stepped into the light. He was wearing black again, shocker, but this time he had topped it all with a battered Yankees cap.

"Didn't take you for a baseball fan." She pointed at the cap.

Kurt chuckled and flicked the brim. "My dad's. I hate baseball." His face fell and then snapped back into a smile so fast that Natalie almost missed it. He clapped. "Okay, enough small talk. What did you find out?"

Natalie flinched. She was decidedly not the bearer of good news, and he looked so excited. "Well," she started, watching Kurt's face, "they have a footprint. One of Mr. Halsey's. And that's the only print upstairs in the house, aside from Mrs. Halsey's."

Kurt's face remained blank, then he slammed a fist into the wall. "Fuck!" he growled, then winced and shook his hand when the pain set in.

Natalie shrank away, for the first time feeling more than a little frightened of the pretty boy in front of her. Something about Kurt seemed erratic, like a jack-in-the-box that could burst out at any minute. Natalie loved horror movies, sure, but she was less keen on real-life jump scares. She took a step back, eyeing Kurt's red face. "But that's it," she sputtered. "That's all they have."

"Well, it's not *good*, is it?" Kurt asked, almost pleading. The burst of anger that had made him punch the wall disappeared as quickly as it had come, and he looked at his hand as if he couldn't understand why it suddenly hurt. "He looks guilty as hell, doesn't he?"

Natalie raised her shoulders helplessly. "I guess? But that still doesn't mean he did it. We can still investigate."

Kurt grabbed the back of his neck. "God, I was hoping I wouldn't have to do this." He gave the crumbling wall a weak kick, and loose plaster rained down behind the wallpaper. "This is the absolute last thing I want to do right now."

"What is?" Natalie asked, eyeing the door. She could still leave. Keep working on her podcast by herself and leave Kurt out of it from now on. The thought was more than a little tempting.

"Okay." He turned toward her, his eyes ticking back and forth. "I have a source. Someone I didn't want to get mixed up in this because he's definitely going to want a cut."

"And you're just telling me this now?" Natalie said, anger and disbelief warring in her belly.

"Well, I didn't want to split the money three ways, okay?" Kurt cried. "Anyway, Eliza Minnow, the mistress, she has a son."

"Yeah, she mentioned him that time we tried to interview her."

Kurt flapped a hand. "Yeah, real weirdo. David Minnow Jr. He went to school with Jack, I think. Fact is, he's not the biggest fan of his mom. I'm willing to bet he'd do some digging for us if we asked nicely enough. And offered a cut, of course. I always liked her for a suspect. She's not all that stable."

Natalie frowned at the memory of Eliza's words at the bar. How angry she had seemed. Kurt wasn't wrong: she was a good suspect. "You think he'd give up his own mom? For money?" she asked.

"You met Eliza," Kurt said. "Does she seem like the nicest lady in the world? Not everyone loves their mothers, you know."

Natalie winced. Her feelings about her mom were complicated, but she loved Helen. What about Eliza was so bad? She really couldn't imagine—at least in her own experience with her mom. With a quiet pang of guilt, she realized how sheltered she was, how lucky. Despite the early-morning workouts and overprotective streak, she and Helen were pretty tight. Even if she thought her mother had done something wrong, she wasn't sure if she would be able to rat her out. Even for money. Especially not for money. And she could never hate her—even after Helen had ruined everything with Mrs. Halsey. Even then. Eliza's son had to have a pretty good excuse.

"Okay," she replied, shaking off thoughts of bad moms and scheming sons. She had to focus on the story, the facts. And this was certainly a lead. "That sounds promising, if not sad. How soon do you think you can ask him?"

Kurt pulled out his phone. "I'll text him right now. He's an indoors guy. I bet he's not doing anything."

She watched as he fiddled with his phone, listening to the universe of small sounds in the abandoned house. The tiny footsteps of mice. The drone of a trapped fly throwing itself against what remained of one of the windows. It felt like a haunted place. A place she wasn't supposed to be. And as much as she loved places just like that, she was aching to go home and lie in her clean sheets, letting the fan stir the air in her familiar-smelling room.

"Is that…all, then?" she asked. She still had to sneak back in. Her mother most certainly did not know that she was meeting a strange boy at a gutted house on a swamp.

Kurt pocketed his phone. "One more thing." He

grinned and took a step forward. "I want to collect on my dare."

Natalie felt a surge of something undefined hurtle through her bloodstream. Fear, excitement, and some combination of the two. What was he doing—and why was he getting so close to her? Everything was moving too fast and too slow all at once. "The dare wasn't meeting you in a haunted house after dark?" she squeaked.

Kurt shook his head, his eyes locked on hers. "Nah, you're a brave girl. You're not afraid of a house. Or the dark. I'm hoping you're not afraid of my dare, either, because I'm pretty excited about it myself."

Before Natalie could open her mouth, Kurt closed the distance between them and sealed it with his own. His arms locked around her, and his tongue slid into her mouth, and it was a second or two before she responded, kissing him back tentatively. When he pulled away, Kurt was panting.

"Whoa," he gasped.

Natalie wiped her lips distractedly, trying to process what had just happened. She had only kissed that one boy at Model UN. And it hadn't been like that: it was sweet and messy with Ireland, and this was electric and fast. Harder, somehow.

"I know," she said, looking past Kurt's left ear. He was grinning again, and Natalie was not.

She wasn't sure why she wasn't. It's not like she didn't like kissing him. He was handsome and definitely knew what he was doing. She just wasn't sure if she had *wanted* to. It felt like he had taken something that she wasn't sure she had wanted to give.

The feeling lingered even after she snuck home and tucked herself into those sheets she had been lusting after at the Victorian. And lingered into her dreams, which were tangled and strange.

CHAPTER EIGHTEEN: THEN

Helen stared out at the rippling surface of Lake Michigan, squinting against the smoke of the joint that Matt, a.k.a. the hot TA, held pinched between his fingers. She had waved off his offer of a hit, but the secondhand smoke seemed to be doing its work, because she felt more than a little hazy. She'd gotten caught in a loop of wondering just how it would actually feel to kill someone—to feel their breath cease and see their eyes glaze over—and she was kind of terrifying herself. It wasn't that she hadn't read her share of murder mysteries, she just realized she'd never really stopped to wonder what it was like to *be* the killer. What it would take for someone to make that final step into depravity.

"So you knew Jenny?" Matt was saying; the tone of his voice suggested that it wasn't the first time he'd asked. They'd both made short work of the flask, and Helen wasn't really used to whiskey. After she started feeling a little dizzy, she suggested they sit on one of the many boulders abutting the lake, scrawled with increasingly more graffiti the closer you got to the water. It was quiet here and, miraculously, free of students. Helen realized she'd never really been alone for months. Matt was here, of course, but that felt okay.

"Not really," Helen said, shaking her head, and immediately feeling dizzier. "I'm in that class with her that you TA, but that's kind of it."

Matt took another drag and gave her a curious look. His eyes were as blue as the lake during the daytime. He was, indeed, very hot, and Helen felt a little light-headed just looking at him—smoke and alcohol aside. "From the way you wrote about her, I thought you were friends or something." They hadn't yet discussed what had happened at the Unicorn, Matt perhaps sensing that Helen needed to shrug off some of the residual shame before rehashing it all—or at least dull it with whiskey. For some reason, though, Helen felt like she could talk to him—maybe because she didn't really know him, maybe because she was a little inebriated, or maybe just because people stupidly trusted attractive people.

"I told her mom I was Jenny's friend…or rather, she kind of assumed, and I didn't correct her," Helen said, watching the moon dance on the surface of the lake. It was bright and full and lent the lakefront an eerie glow.

"And her sister?" Matt prodded. "Why were you following her?"

Helen put her face in her hands at his choice of words, but when she looked up at him he didn't look angry or disgusted, just curious. "My editor told me to interview her," she said, deciding to just tell him the whole truth. He was a teacher, after all; maybe he could help. "I guess the paper got a tip that Jenny was hooking up with her sister's husband and that could be a motive." Now that she thought about it, it didn't seem that farfetched. Constance had been so angry, so volatile. Could she be capable of the unthinkable? The whole thing got her thinking, once more, of how it would feel to kill someone, and her head spun. She grabbed Matt's arm as if she were about to fall over, and unexpectedly, he reached out to pull her closer to him.

"Whoa there." He laughed slightly. He snuffed out his joint on the rock they were sitting on and rubbed her shoulders. "Sorry, you're overwhelmed, and this probably isn't helping. Do you want me to walk you back to the dorms? Get you some water?" The concern in his voice made her heart hitch a little. She realized she hadn't felt anyone's arms around her since she got to college—not hugs, not anything. Tom didn't really count. His embraces had been about something selfish, not comfort.

She leaned in to Matt's side, not really caring that she was likely going to be sorely embarrassed next time she saw him in Journalism 101. "No, I'm fine," she said, gingerly sitting up as her vision cleared. "Sorry I freaked out there for a second."

Matt laughed, giving her shoulder a squeeze. "We've all been there, Helen." When he said her name, a little thrill went down her spine. "The first time I tried to cold-call a source I was so scared that when they answered I pretended I was trying to get them to change cell providers. The person screamed at me and hung up." He laughed again. "It gets easier…and it doesn't. You're dealing with people, and people are unpredictable." He looked out at the waves and frowned. "Sometimes they don't even understand their own motivations for what they do."

"Are you okay?" Helen asked after Matt fell into a sad kind of silence, his eyes drifting across the lake and growing glassy.

"Yeah." He shook his head as though clearing it and nodded. "Sorry, I was just thinking about Jenny."

Helen reached out to touch his hand, remembering how Matt rushed out of the classroom with her article. "Were you all close?"

Matt nodded. "We were friendly, yeah. She *did* end up taking my class twice." He gave a wry little smile. "Nice girl, truly. She had spirit." He turned to look at Helen, brushing a piece of dark hair off her face. "You remind me of her, really."

Helen pulled a face. "Yeah, right. Jenny is like…bright, sunny. Beautiful." She looked down at her hands, realizing belatedly that she was envying a missing girl, a girl who might no longer be alive.

Matt tipped her chin up, his blue eyes studying her. "So are you," he said quietly, and then his lips were on hers.

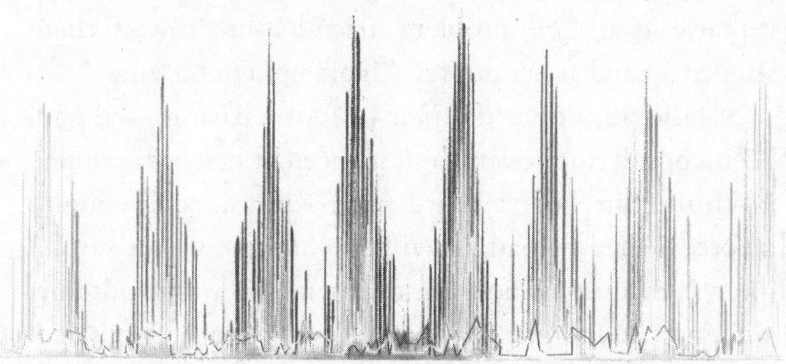

CHAPTER NINETEEN

Natalie was busy cleaning up her room the next day while Katie generally got in the way, balling up old math assignments and tossing them into the trash, cheering each time she *did a goal*, as she called it, and more often than not booing when the paper hit the floor. She still had about a month until college, but Helen was adamant Natalie start getting the place in some semblance of order, and that necessitated a massive purge.

"I really want to thank you for all your help, Katie," Natalie said, examining a thong she had purchased on the sly junior year and then never worn. It had rhinestones on the straps, and it went into the trash with the math assignments. "You're really making this boring task fly by."

Katie lobbed another paper at the trash and missed, the pile of garbage next to the can growing taller than the receptacle itself. "No problem, friend," she crowed, then slapped a hand at her pocket. "Hold up. I'm buzzing."

Natalie put down the pair of footie pajamas she had been considering tossing and glanced at her own phone. Nothing. She hadn't heard from Kurt since the night before—when he had kissed her—and she wasn't sure if she was relieved or not. On one hand, he was handsome and smart and funny. On the other, he punched walls and made their first kiss into a prize—a game that she wasn't sure she wanted to play. She didn't even want to tell Katie about the whole thing, and that seemed like a bad sign.

Still, she was starting to get anxious. She wanted to know if David Minnow Jr. had any information he'd be willing to trade, because if not, they were at an impasse with the investigation. She could start all the background work of interviewing her teachers and classmates about Mrs. Halsey, but that wasn't nearly as fun as tracking down a murderer. And it was much sadder.

"Oh, fuck no," Katie hooted, interrupting Natalie's musings. "Bitch did *not* just text me."

Natalie looked up, putting the pajamas in the Maybe pile. "Who is 'bitch,' and why are they texting?"

Katie's lips curved into a bitter smile. "You will never guess. Not in a million years."

Natalie blinked at her until Katie rolled her eyes.

"Fine, I'll give you a hint. Her name rhymes with… Hessica Mitestone. Which is not a thing. Forget I said that. Jessica Whitestone. She texted me."

Natalie frowned. "Jessica Whitestone texted you? What does she want?"

Jessica Whitestone had been a senior when Natalie was a freshman, the president of the short-lived True Crime Club that Mrs. Halsey had recruited Natalie for on their first meeting. Natalie and Katie joined eagerly when they started high school but soon came to strongly dislike Jessica with her unwashed hair and oversize metal T-shirts.

It wasn't Jessica's appearance that bothered Natalie, though, it was the level to which she thoroughly enjoyed talking about serial killers and murder. Sure, Katie and Natalie were into true crime, but they were more into the process of hunting killers than the killers themselves. Jessica was just kind of obsessed with murderers and their dark deeds. She claimed she was interested in their psychology, but she drooled over them like Katie drooled over BTS, to be honest. She had Charles Manson's entire discography on her iPhone. She had a not-so-secret crush on Richard Ramirez, the Night Stalker. And Natalie always suspected her look was more homage to Aileen Wuornos than sheer laziness. Plus, she took credit for everything the club did, even if she hadn't contributed anything.

The thought of Jessica sent a flicker of hot fire pulsing through Natalie's veins. *"Jessica Whitestone,"* she growled, effectively putting a one-eyed teddy bear into a death grip from which it would not soon recover. "Remember that time we got *Paul Holes* to come talk to the class during assembly, and she took all the credit?" She pounded her fists on her thighs. "That was so shitty."

It had taken her *months* to convince the lead investigator

on the Golden State Killer case to speak at their high school. Luckily, he was an extremely nice guy, because it made no sense for him to interrupt his vacation to scenic Mystic, Connecticut, to talk about murder in front of a bunch of dead-eyed hormone factories.

Katie shrugged. "She was just asking what's up with Mrs. Halsey. I'm guessing she's heard the news." She tossed another ball of paper at the trash—and missed. "I just remembered why I hate sports," she mumbled.

"What a vulture," Natalie scoffed, abandoning the job of packing up her bedroom and instead getting to her feet for a good pace. "I bet she wants all the gory details."

Natalie had never understood why Mrs. Halsey had taken someone like Jessica under her wing: she was pretty unpleasant. Also, Jessica's blatant interest in other people's misery always made her feel guilty. Like she was looking into an unfortunate mirror. It was a fine line between interest and obsession—she knew that—and Jessica had crossed over long ago. Sometimes Natalie felt herself teetering on the edge, like when she pored over accounts of cold cases online, looking for evidence. She had to keep reminding herself that these stories weren't fiction—that these bad things had happened to real people. She couldn't let herself forget that, otherwise she'd become everything Mrs. Halsey warned against.

Katie got to her feet, stepping into Natalie's warpath. "Chill, dude." She turned her phone screen toward Natalie. "All it says, literally, is *I heard about Mrs. Halsey. Does anyone know what happened?*"

Natalie stilled, staring at the screen until it went black.

"Well, what are you going to tell your best friend forever Hessica Mitestone?" she snarled.

Katie pretended to think long and hard, then pulled up the text again. "I think I'm going to employ a method beloved by fuckbois the world over." Her finger hovered over the text, then slid over the words until the option to delete popped up. She stabbed at the red button, lifted her eyebrows and grinned at Natalie. "Annnd ghosted."

Natalie nodded her thanks, and the two tried to pick up where they had left off, but the thought of Jessica Whitestone reentering their lives haunted her well into the evening ahead.

Since Katie was no help when it came to packing, the next few days were an endless cycle of coffeepots and bubble tape as Natalie juggled the diner and college prep. She barely had time to be mad at Kurt, who had yet to text her. So she was more than happy when she got home from work Tuesday evening to find her mother firing up the grill.

"I thought we could just hang out tonight," Helen said. She was wearing the apron Natalie got her last Christmas, screen-printed with the cast of *Buffy*'s smiling faces. "Watch a movie, eat burgers."

Natalie collapsed at the kitchen table. Her mom hadn't done anything to annoy her in a few days, so she mentally decided on a cease-fire for the evening. She was even feeling a little warm toward Helen after hearing about Kurt's mom; she was lucky, she knew that. "Can you mash up my burger like a smoothie? Too tired to chew."

Helen laughed and headed out to the backyard, which

was studded with fireflies and thick with the smell of charcoal. Natalie was just getting up to pour a glass of water from the Brita when there was a tapping at the front door. She changed course toward the front of the house expecting, perhaps, a surprise visit from Katie. Instead, she opened the door to find Jonathan peering through the little stained-glass window at the top of the door, jogging shorts low on his hips and sweat on his brow.

"Hey, Nat!" He broke into a blindingly white grin as he popped his AirPods out of his ears. "I was just out for a jog."

Natalie cocked her head to the side. "That's cool, John. But I will not be joining you." The only sneakers she owned were Vans, and those definitely didn't have the kind of arch support for...whatever he was doing. Also, running sucked.

Jonathan was still jogging in place, jouncing from foot to foot like a kid anxious for the bathroom. He laughed. "No, no, I just wanted to drop by because, well, I heard something else. From my mom." He stopped bouncing and drew an arm across his forehead, flicking off a few drops of sweat like a boy in an ad for bottled water.

Natalie stepped out onto the porch and grabbed Jonathan's arm, despite the ample sweat. "What? What did you find out?" she asked, looking over her shoulder to make sure her mom was nowhere in sight.

Jonathan looked down at her hand, and his cheeks got even redder than before. She let go, and he cleared his throat. "It's not much, really, but I knew you would want to know."

Natalie shut the door behind her, mindful of her mother's supersonic hearing. All mothers had it, it seemed. She stepped closer to Jonathan, who was still blushing and sweating in the summer evening. She punched his arm as if she could shake his words loose. She needed to hear what he had to say, and she needed to hear him say it now. "Just say it, dude!"

"Okay," Jonathan said. He held up his hands in surrender and then leaned down toward Natalie, so close she could smell clean sweat and cleaner laundry. "Apparently, they're thinking Mrs. Halsey was pushed by someone taller than her. Someone stronger."

Natalie widened her eyes, staring up into his. "And?"

"And…that's it?" Jonathan laughed, then looked down at his feet. "Now that I'm here, saying this out loud, it kind of seems like a big *duh*, huh?"

Jonathan looked so sad then that Natalie felt an overwhelming urge to hug him, anything to get that crestfallen look off his face. Instead, she shook her head.

"Not at all. Mr. Halsey is taller and bigger than her," she said, aiming for reassurance. Jonathan was even more of a novice investigator than she was. Everyone deserved their own tiny victories. "If the killer was bigger than Mrs. Halsey, that definitely looks bad for Mr. Halsey."

Or the killer could just be anyone bigger than Mrs. Halsey, a thin woman who barely topped five feet. Still, a picture started to form in her head: a raging Mr. Halsey, in love with another woman and looking for a way out. And Mrs. Halsey, standing in his way. It all seemed too lurid, too soapy, for a quiet night on a suburban street. Too sad.

"Are you, okay, Nat?" Jonathan asked, dropping a light hand on her shoulder.

Natalie looked up into his tan face, blinking. "Yeah. I guess so."

Jonathan nodded. "I know. I don't like thinking about it, either. I didn't know her as well as you and Katie did, but I always liked Mrs. Halsey. And I can't imagine something like that happening to anyone I care about. It just…sucks." He laughed without humor, then drew a hand across his face. "Obviously, I am not a writer like you."

"Obviously not." Natalie hadn't noticed Kurt coming down the street, but now he was at the bottom of her steps, sneering at Jonathan's back. He was also holding a bouquet of flowers. Daisies. She frowned; he hadn't texted for days, and now he was just…showing up?

Jonathan looked back and forth between Kurt and Natalie, but when no one said anything, he shrugged, smiling. "Hey." He raised an affable hand, eyes locked on the flowers. "I'm Jonathan."

Kurt walked past the other boy with a gruff nod and put his arm around Natalie, pressing the blooms into her hands. When his skin touched hers, Natalie was startled to feel a crackle of electricity. She was equally startled to realize that she was happy to see him there, on her porch. Had she missed him? Judging by the mixture of annoyance and pleasure jolting through her, she'd venture a *yes*.

"Wasn't sure what kind of flowers you like," Kurt said, taking a tentative sniff of the bouquet. "You don't seem like a roses type of person, and sunflowers seem like the kind of thing girls who wear rompers and make their own jewelry are into. Hence…daisies."

Natalie smiled hesitantly and took the flowers. No one

had ever given her flowers before—except for her mother. The gesture seemed kind of old-fashioned. Kurt kept surprising her; he could be bitter, he could be dark, but he had an inner sweetness that softened all that. Made him someone she wanted to be around.

"Thank you," Natalie said, looking down at the daisies, then back at Jonathan, who was shuffling his big white sneakers and looking down at the porch. If she hadn't known him for her whole life, she'd think he was jealous, which made no sense. They were practically siblings. "And thank you, Jonathan, for coming over."

Jonathan shrugged with a sad smile, pulling his AirPods from his pocket. "No problem, Nat. I'll see you tomorrow at the paper, okay?" He shot a wary glance at Kurt, then turned his full bright smile on Natalie again. "I want a rematch on tip-line bingo." He stuck his AirPods into his ears and jumped off the porch, throwing a final wave over his shoulder as he went.

Natalie and Kurt watched him round the corner toward downtown, until Kurt turned toward her with a slightly dimmed expression. "Who was that?"

Natalie raised her eyebrows. Jonathan wasn't the only one who seemed jealous. "Just Jonathan. He works with me at the paper. I've known him since I was, like, three."

Kurt looked to where the other boy had disappeared into the distance, then turned back to Natalie with a smile that seemed slightly forced. "So he's like a brother to you," he said, almost to himself.

Natalie nodded, then pushed Kurt's shoulder, trying for playful and failing; he stumbled back a step. "I haven't heard from you in a while," she said with forced joviality. The jealousy had been cute, but now it was getting annoying. "I was wondering if you had bailed or something."

"Aw." Kurt put a hand to his chest. "Did you miss me?"

Natalie blushed. "Um, sure. I was also wondering if you got anything from Minnow's son."

"Hell yes, I did." Kurt grabbed her hand. "And it's *good*. Hence the flowers."

Natalie's heart leaped like it had when Kurt had touched her hand. "Well, tell me!" Jonathan's info had been interesting, but it hardly seemed revelatory.

Kurt looked to either side of him, even though they were alone in Natalie's front yard. "Eliza sent Mrs. Halsey emails. A lot of them. And they were not very nice."

Natalie clutched at his fingers unconsciously. This was it. They finally had something. They were so close to uncovering the truth that she suppressed the urge to squirm like a kid on a sugar high. "So it was her? Or it could have been?"

Kurt squeezed back. "It looks like. Only thing is, Dave doesn't want to go to the cops. I guess he doesn't completely hate his mom after all. And he doesn't want to talk to you for your podcast—for a similar reason."

Natalie dropped his hand. What was the use in knowing who killed Mrs. Halsey if they couldn't reveal it? "Aw, shit..."

Kurt grabbed her fingers again. "*But* he is willing to call tomorrow when you're at the tip line and leave an anonymous tip. At which point the cops and the paper—and you—can do whatever you want with that information."

Before she knew what she was doing, Natalie threw her arms around Kurt's neck and squeezed. "Good job,

Kurt," she said into his ear. He turned his head toward hers and stole another kiss—but this time she kissed him back without hesitation. Maybe it was the excitement shooting through both of them that made it feel right this time; it bonded them. Maybe she was just getting used to him.

"Um, Natalie..."

The two flew apart, and Natalie whirled to face her mother. Kurt ran his hands through his hair as a mixture of almost unreadable emotions passed over his face. He finally settled on a slightly manic smile. Natalie just gaped at Helen in her *Buffy* apron.

"You didn't tell me you were seeing someone." To anyone else, Helen Temple would have sounded teasing, but Natalie heard the tension beneath the surface. The anger. She bristled at her mom's tone. Why should Helen be mad that Natalie had a social life (finally)? Shouldn't she be happy for her?

"We just started seeing each other, actually," Kurt broke in, extending a hand. "I'm Kurt. It's Mrs. Temple, right?"

"Miss." Helen shook his hand, then gestured at the flowers. "Do you two have a date Natalie failed to mention?"

Kurt shook his head. "I just wanted to drop by and say hi. Give my girl some flowers, you know."

Natalie noticed her mother's lips visibly tightening on the phrase *my girl*. Ever the polite hostess, though, Helen gestured into the kitchen with her spatula. "You should join us for dinner. It's just burgers, but I'm an expert at them by now."

"I would love that," Kurt said, beaming, and followed Helen inside. "I've been dying to see Nat's house."

★★★

"I don't know why I pictured you living in the diner—or, like, above it. Pretty lucky to own that spot *and* a house," Kurt said, seated on a crooked stool that Helen Temple had pulled from the basement. Their kitchen table had two chairs; there was only enough room for mother and daughter.

Helen paused at the door to the back patio, a plate of burgers from their little grill balanced in her hands. In the glare of the porch light, her eyes looked sunken, her brown hair limp around her face. She gave Kurt a weak smile. "Although we do spend a lot of time there, we don't live at the diner, no. We did live above it for a while, though, when Natalie was very little, but I think we both got a little sick of always smelling like fries."

She placed the burgers on the table and turned to their red fridge to fetch ketchup and mustard. There was already a plate of freshly sliced tomatoes from their window-box garden on the table, along with basil picked from the same source. Helen loved to make things grow; ferns bloomed from hanging baskets in almost every room of their house, and their patio was an explosion of flowers.

"Now, how did you two meet again?" Helen asked, sitting down with a glass of wine while Kurt hoisted his tumbler of lemonade. "Since my daughter completely failed to inform me of your existence until tonight." She shot Natalie a look that clearly said *We'll discuss this later*, and Natalie said goodbye to the silent truce she'd promised her mom tonight. No way was she getting in trouble for dating a guy like a normal teenager—even if she was also investigating a murder with him. Helen didn't need to know that.

"He's a friend of Katie's cousin," Natalie cut in before Kurt could speak. She had made it pretty clear that her mother was not to know about their investigation, but you never could be too careful.

Helen leaned forward, putting her glass down on their crowded table. "Jack? The kid who's always getting arrested?"

Natalie opened her mouth to respond but filled it with lemonade instead. There wasn't much excuse for Jack's existence. Plus, her mouth was suddenly very dry.

Kurt nodded, but he was distracted, looking around the cozy kitchen, eyes roving to the living room where Helen had lit a few of the fancy sea-salt candles she ordered in bulk from Amazon. That was her mom's one indulgence, really—that and all the plants. Their living room could smell like the beach even if they couldn't see it from their house, Helen always said. "This is a really nice place, Mrs. Temple," he mused, taking a beef patty from the plate. He started building his burger methodically, taking his time choosing the perfect round of tomato. "If you don't mind me asking, did you always run the diner, or did you do something else before?"

Helen reached for her own patty, smothering it with so much hot sauce Natalie's teeth ached in sympathy. "Not really, no. I started out working there when I was in my twenties, and when the old owners were ready to retire, I bought them out."

Natalie nodded, allowing herself a stirring of pride for her mother. It was a story she had heard before—how her mother dropped out of college to take care of her sick father and started working at the diner. How she built a life for herself despite the tragedy of her father's death—her mother's passing having happened years before.

"You bought them out? Whoa..." Kurt took a bite of his burger, chewing slowly. "Your parents must have been *rich*."

Both Helen and Natalie stilled at Kurt's words. In a town like Ferry, no one would have called the Temples rich—so, naturally, people seemed surprised when a one-time waitress bought the diner. Helen didn't really think the truth was anyone's business—that, when her dad died, she had been left with a tidy windfall of insurance money. Enough to buy the diner and put a down payment on a house just big enough for two. Not much, but enough. Natalie shot Kurt a questioning look: he sounded slightly angry. Maybe seeing Jonathan on her doorstep had upset him more that he had let on. The golden boy with his expensive sneakers and Apple products coming face-to-face with a boy who was struggling to pay his rent. Still, it wasn't like Natalie had AirPods. Her headphones were held together with duct tape.

Helen blinked slowly, then shook her head as if clearing it. "Did you go to school with Jack, then?" she asked, ignoring Kurt's commentary on their bank account. "You look kind of familiar, but I know you weren't in Natalie's class."

"No," Kurt said, putting his burger down, his voice tight. "I suppose it's obvious I'm not East Ferry High material. Not sure they even let people like me past the front doors without a police escort. I might make off with all the pens or something, right?"

Natalie looked between Kurt and her mom, head throbbing. Why was he taking everything so personally? And why was her mother's face so expressionless and cold? Was it the fact that she'd been seeing Kurt, or just seeing someone in general, without Helen's knowledge?

Kurt laughed suddenly, abruptly. "I'm kidding, of course." He gave Helen a strained smile. "How about you, Helen? Have you always lived in Ferry?"

"You know my daughter is going to college soon?" Helen snapped, ignoring Kurt's question. She pushed her plate away, the hot sauce pooling around the edges like blood.

Kurt nodded, taking a sip of lemonade. "Sure. She's brilliant. I hear she got a full scholarship, too."

"So she's going to be pretty busy." Helen leveled her eyes at Kurt. "And she barely has time as it is, what with working at the diner and her internship at the paper."

Natalie tensed. "Mom, chill," she snapped. Yes, Kurt was being touchy, but her mom had no right to police her social life like this—to embarrass the one boy who had shown any interest in her in eighteen years. It wasn't fair. Hadn't she spent years working hard to get into college, to make her mom proud? And now she couldn't even trust her to go on a date.

Kurt stared at Helen, his eyes narrowing. Animosity crackled between him and Natalie's mother like heat lightning. He took a deep breath and forced a lopsided smile. "This is a good burger, Mrs. Temple. Thank you for having me." He pushed away from the table, the chair legs scraping loudly on the floor. Natalie shot her mother a final glare before following Kurt to the porch, where the fireflies looped and blinked in the lush darkness.

"I'm sorry," she started, body thrumming with embarrassment and anger. "My mom is crazy. She doesn't..."

The trees sighed in the breeze as Kurt spun around,

grabbing her hand and smiling at her. A real smile, if not a little haunted. "*I'm* sorry," he said finally, looking down at their intertwined fingers. "I'm bad...with parents. I say things..." He trailed off, squeezing her fingers. "I like you, Natalie," he said softly. "I really do."

She gripped his hand, feeling lost, confused—by Kurt's needling at her mother and her mom's haughtiness. She knew Helen was proud of her for getting into college, but she always said that higher education wasn't some magical elixir that ensured a good future. She would have been proud of Natalie, she said, if she wanted to be a plumber—as long as she was happy. Why did she feel the need to shove her daughter's accomplishments in this boy's face? And why did Kurt seem so concerned with their finances? Still, there were a few things she did know: that he was the kind of guy who picked *dare*, who read for fun, and who brought her flowers. She knew, at his core, that he seemed kind. And that was what was important at that moment.

Natalie met his eyes. "I like you, too," she said, squeezing his hand, dreading going back inside, hearing her mom's protestations. "Can you take me somewhere? Just...anywhere that's not here?" She knew her mom would be there when she got back—that she'd be even angrier that she'd left with Kurt—but, frankly, at that moment she didn't care.

"Are we allowed to be here?" Natalie asked as she followed Kurt over the wooden fence surrounding West Ferry Lavender Farm, even though she knew the answer.

Kurt shot her a smirk over his shoulder. "I can't believe

you've never been here before. The river between the two sides of Ferry is not actually made of lava, you know."

Natalie ignored the jab and landed lightly in a fragrant field of knee-high flowers rendered shadows in the dark, which was somehow still redolent of sunshine. The fields stretched from the road to the whispering woods, the border between which was demarcated by a low-slung barn that sold lavender pillows and honeys and all sorts of things she would not have associated with Kurt. He grabbed her hand and guided her through the varieties of flowers until they reached the dead center of the field, where he pulled her down to lie between a row of plants.

"I found this place when I moved here last summer," he murmured, breathing in deep. "I wouldn't be caught dead here during the day. There's, like, an infestation of Instagram influencers here taking photos in floaty dresses. But at night, it's nice." He reached out to hold her hand. "It calms me down, and nothing really does that."

Natalie breathed in, too, and let herself sink into the dirt, not really caring that it was getting all over her T-shirt. "Yeah, I can see its appeal. Especially after tonight." She felt Kurt drawing lazy circles on the back of her hand, and something inside of her unlocked. The dark, the lavender, the boy, all chipping away at the armor she constructed every day just to exist in the world as daughter, student, friend. "I love her, I do, but I can't be here anymore. It's suffocating." Her eyes filled with tears, and she let them roll down her cheeks to water the dirt. The weight of everything pushed down on her chest—her mom, Mrs. Halsey, what she'd said to her teacher—until she couldn't bear to exist under it anymore. Something told her Kurt would understand, so she told him: she whispered in the dark what had happened with her mom and Mrs. Halsey, how she'd thrown her teacher's love away, how she hadn't spoken with her in the months before she died.

Kurt was quiet for a long moment, and all Natalie could hear was the distant chorus of crickets, the wind moving through the trees, their boughs creaking and groaning as it intensified. The tears came faster, thicker now. He was horrified, clearly, and she didn't blame him. She was pretty damn horrified with herself. Natalie started to get up, to run away, but Kurt reached out and put his arms around her. "You did nothing wrong," he whispered fiercely into her ear. "Nothing. You are *good*, Natalie. The only good person I think I've ever met."

Natalie started to shake her head, but Kurt stilled her with a kiss—pressed her down into the field of flowers with the warm weight of his body, breathed her in and held her. When he pulled away he was breathing shallowly, his eyes starry and distant. They cleared as they met hers. "I have been alone my whole life, Nat," he said. "My dad left. My mom…she's there, but not really. It's always been her and me against the world, but I'm the one who's had to do the fighting." He pressed a kiss to her temple. "And now there's you…and you are *good*."

Natalie shivered, pulling his body to hers, needing warmth, needing something. She had never been this close to a boy before, and she felt out of her depth, but she didn't move away. She didn't want to. "But Mrs. Halsey… What I said."

Kurt pulled away, studying her face, pulling a tear-wet strand of hair from her cheek. "That was your mom, Natalie," he whispered. "That was her and her alone and..." He trailed off, sitting back on his heels and breathing in a deep, pained breath.

Natalie pulled herself up onto her knees. "What?" The plants around them whipped in a sudden breath, a whiff of a summer storm in the air. The sky had gone as purple as the darkest kind of lavender, and the air smelled of ozone.

Kurt took another heavy breath, then looked at her, his eyes dark in the night. "She'd do anything to protect you. You said it yourself."

"What are you saying?" Natalie gasped as the first raindrop splashed onto her cheek.

"I'm saying..." Kurt grabbed her hands, pulling her to her feet as the sky cracked open above them. "Do you know where your mom was the night your teacher died?"

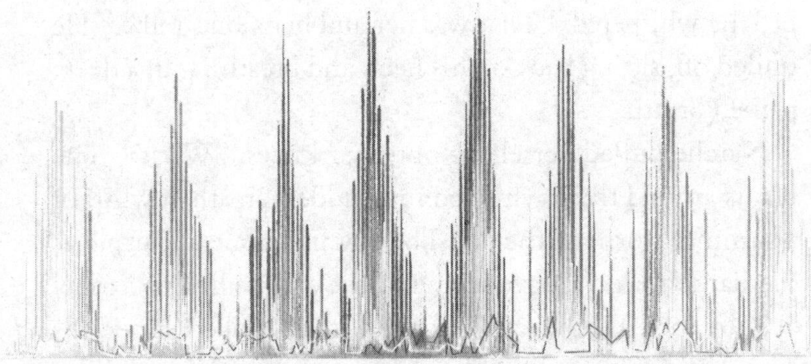

CHAPTER TWENTY

When Natalie got home, drenched, Helen was sitting at the kitchen table, drinking coffee despite the hour. Natalie steeled herself for the inevitable yelling, the chastising, the grounding. She was a little surprised when her mom merely took a sip of coffee and leaned back in her chair, asking wearily, "I don't suppose you'll listen to me if I tell you to stop seeing him, will you?"

Natalie just stared, wet hair hanging in her eyes. She and Kurt hadn't talked anymore about her mother—about his question—but it had hung between them in the car, as they kissed in the driveway, as he squeezed her hand once more as she dashed out into the rain. Most of her railed against the suggestion that her mother could have possibly been involved. But Kurt had planted a seed: just *how* far would her mom go to protect her? How far was too far? And had she already overstepped that line?

"I won't," her mom continued, taking her silence for permission to continue. "But only because you're leaving soon. You're going to school, and you'll forget all about him," Helen said to her mug. "I've spent years protecting you, and I think I've done a good job. You have all your limbs." She looked up, smiled sadly. "But I know I can't protect you from decisions you'll regret. Ones that, I know, won't kill you but will hurt you. And I can tell you—" she stood, coming toward her daughter "—that boy will hurt you. He's a lost kid. He is. And lost kids aren't ready to take care of other people."

All thoughts of her mom and murder fled her head. It might be incomprehensible that Helen had killed someone, but this pressure, this *hovering*, had to stop, or Natalie would explode and take their little family down with them. "None of this is your business," she snapped.

Helen sighed, turning toward her bedroom door. "Everything you do is my business, honey. And I was just calling them like I see them."

"Then, let me find that out for myself," Natalie said, rage working its way through her tired-out body. She was eighteen; she was going to college. Wasn't she old enough to decide who to date? "You can't just follow me around all the time, making sure I don't mess up. I'm not a toddler."

"I know you're not, but you'll always be three years old to me. You'll always be breakable." Helen's hand stilled on her doorknob. "But in this case, I wish you'd listen to me. You'll be happier without him in the end. You'll be happier when you're doing what you want to do, even if you have to do it alone."

"Like you've been happier? All alone?" Natalie spat, anger finally cracking through the shock of her mother's words, the years of coddling and anxiety reaching a crescendo in her brain.

Helen only smiled. "I've never been alone, honey. I've had you. And that's all I've ever needed. I'm sorry if you don't believe that."

"Is that why you took her away, then?" Natalie's voice broke, and for the second time that evening tears started pouring down her cheeks. She wanted to hurt her mother then. Break down those stoic smiles, snap her into a fury to match her own, finally have the showdown they'd been approaching since Natalie started thinking for herself instead of following so closely in her mother's footsteps that she lived in shadow. "Mrs. Halsey, the only person who ever cared about the *real* me? Is that why you did it?"

Helen's face fell, and Natalie felt a sick sort of satisfaction. She took a step forward as her mom opened and closed her mouth, impotently. "You just couldn't stand it, could you? That I cared about someone other than *you*? It wasn't enough to get rid of everything I like, everything I cared about. You had to get rid of her, too?"

"Natalie, I—" her mom said, coming toward her with her hands outstretched.

"No!" Natalie stamped her foot. "I'm sick of your explanations. I'm sick of your excuses, Mom. Just..." Her shoulders dropped, energy gone, depleted. "Leave me alone." And, for once, Helen didn't follow Natalie when she disappeared into her room.

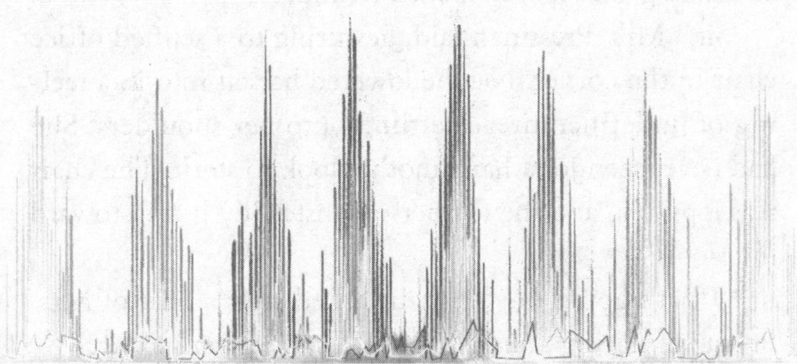

CHAPTER TWENTY-ONE

When Natalie woke up for her internship the next morning, her mom seemed to have taken her words to heart: she was gone by the time Natalie descended the stairs, hadn't even left a note to inform her that she'd left for the diner. Natalie tried not to think about her as she answered phones, though. After all, David Minnow Jr. was set to call any minute, and then she and Kurt could move forward with the investigation. Before she could get too settled in at the phones, though, Mrs. Pressman called her into her office.

All thoughts of her mom and the Minnows retreated when she closed Mrs. Pressman's office door and turned to face the woman, seated at her desk, her legs crossed and her eyes flat. Her lips were set in a thin line that failed to resolve itself into a smile, even when Natalie shot her a tentative, awkward grin. Her suit looked wrinkled and her eyes tired.

"Sit," Mrs. Pressman said, gesturing to a scuffed office chair in the corner. Natalie lowered herself into it, a feeling of undefined dread settling onto her shoulders. She had never seen Jonathan's mother look so stern. The chair was lopsided, and she felt herself unsteadily listing toward the floor.

"What's going on?" Natalie asked after a beat of Mrs. Pressman staring at her. "Did I do something wrong?"

The woman laughed without humor and put her fingers to her temples. "Did you do something wrong?" She dropped her hands to her lap and leaned forward. "Natalie, I fought for you to get this internship. Your mother didn't want you to work here, and I pushed back. I knew how enriching this could be for you, how much you wanted to be here. And then you go and do this… Honestly…"

The center of Natalie's chest went cold, her gut twisting. Mrs. Pressman knew about the paper clip, the lock-picking. The unsuccessful attempt to break into her drawer.

"Did Jonathan…say something?" she almost whispered.

He had told his mom about the drawer and files. Even after he'd promised not to. He lived and died by her word and let her do his laundry. For a moment Natalie hated Jonathan. Hated that he didn't know how to wash his darks and lights.

"No, Jonathan didn't tell me anything, but now I'm loath to discover what my son might be keeping from me." Flora Pressman gripped the arms of her chair and took a deep breath, composing her face into a blank mask. Her reporter face. "You know a lot about newspapers, right, Natalie? About true crime? You've worked here for two years, and I know you're always reading about it, watching documentaries."

Natalie nodded, not exactly sure what she was meant to say. Mrs. Pressman was certainly not about to praise her for her knowledge of the criminal justice system. This was not how one acted prepraise.

"Then, you might know," the crime reporter continued, "that we audit what our search systems are used for. You might also know that if someone uses a database for an unauthorized search, they are subject to reprimand. Or worse. So imagine my surprise when I get a call asking why I looked up the license plate of a man named Ronald K. Stackman."

Natalie's face got hot, and the back of her neck started to itch. She looked down at her hands and willed herself to disappear. She didn't know that they kept such strict tabs on newspaper computers. It made sense now. It was too easy to look up information for personal gain. She realized, much too late, that Mrs. Pressman had probably been joking about checking up on Jonathan's girlfriends via the database.

"Except I didn't. Look up Stackman. Don't even know the man," Mrs. Pressman continued. "So who did?"

Natalie tore at her cuticles and writhed in her seat like a child. "I did," she said.

Mrs. Pressman's shoulders sunk, and her stern reporter face morphed into her mom face. All soft lines and disappointment. "Oh, Natalie, I was hoping I was wrong. Why? Why did you do it?"

"Because I saw him on the Halseys' lawn, and he was acting weird," Natalie cried, panic edging into her voice. She couldn't lose this internship. She couldn't lose access to the inside track on the case. That would mean going back to rehashing old murders and wasting her time watching Netflix. That would mean giving up on Mrs. Halsey.

"Then, why didn't you tell me that?" Mrs. Pressman asked, bafflement painted across her face. "My lord, Natalie. Why would you keep that kind of information from me? From the police?"

"You don't have to worry about him," Natalie said, distracted by the prospect of losing her job. "I talked to him, and he's harmless."

Mrs. Pressman was on her feet before Natalie could register her movement and her hands on Natalie's shoulders. Her nails were bitten down to the quick, and she gripped hard. "Are you trying to get yourself killed? You suspected someone of murder, and you just decided to talk to him? On your own?"

She didn't think it would help to tell Mrs. Pressman about Kurt, so she just nodded.

Mrs. Pressman dropped her face into her hands. "Your mother is going to murder me. Seriously. She's going to bake me into one of those apple pies of hers."

"We don't have to tell her, do we?" Natalie asked, a whole other fear taking a solid grip on her spine.

"Of course we do." Mrs. Pressman looked up. "She and I are mothers. It's our code. Besides, Nat, actions have consequences, and you really messed up this time."

"What if I told you I have something else?" Natalie

pressed, her skin starting to feel clammy and cold with panic. "Something that could help you?"

Mrs. Pressman sighed. "Did you get this information illegally?"

"No, someone just called the tip line." David had yet to call, but that didn't matter. She knew what he was going to say. "Apparently Eliza Minnow sent threatening emails to Mrs. Halsey."

Mrs. Pressman looked up. "That is interesting," she said reluctantly. "But, of course, it could be a hoax."

"Or it could be real," Natalie pressed. She needed to keep Mrs. Pressman talking, keep her distracted from telling her mom, taking away her job. Also, if Eliza really had been threatening Mrs. Halsey, if she had done something to her favorite teacher, she wanted the woman behind bars.

"The cops couldn't get into her computer without a warrant, and an anonymous tip isn't enough to secure that... And it's not like we could just *ask* her..." Mrs. Pressman trailed off.

"Then, you can just go to Mr. Halsey and ask to see Mrs. Halsey's computer," Natalie broke in, the idea just occurring to her. "If what the tipster says is true, I don't see why he would object."

Mrs. Pressman got to her feet, her eyes already on the door. She stood for a beat, and Natalie could almost see her working it out. At last, she turned toward Natalie. "This is good work, Natalie."

"Does that mean I'm not fired?" Natalie asked tentatively, as if speaking might break the spell. Still, she had to know.

Mrs. Pressman paused, looking down at Natalie as frustration and excitement fought their way across her face. She exhaled. "Let's just look at this as your first and second warnings… But next time—"

"No next time," Natalie interrupted, putting her hand on her chest. "Promise."

"Okay, then," Mrs. Pressman said, opening her office door. "Back to the phones with you."

Natalie grinned, relief washing through her like a salve. She paused at the door. "Are you going now? To ask Mr. Halsey about the emails?"

Mrs. Pressman nodded, gesturing toward the room where Jonathan was busy with his phone and his bingo grid.

"Can I come?"

Mrs. Pressman's face answered that question more effectively than any words, and Natalie slunk back to the phone room, relieved but also sparking with excitement. She had to see what went down at the Halsey house. She had to hear what Eliza had to say in the emails. It's not like Mrs. Pressman would tell her. This was integral to the podcast, to the investigation. She had just promised to stay out of trouble, but this was too good. Instead of heading back into the phone room to join Jonathan in his quest to talk to every person in the tristate area, Natalie dashed out to the parking lot and mounted her bike.

CHAPTER TWENTY-TWO: THEN

Sam's text had been simple—maddeningly so.

My office. Now…

Nothing good could come from that many periods in a text message. Helen had been picking at her lunch at the dining hall across from her dorm when he messaged, missing her dad and her home and feeling ill as she inspected the cold fleshy chicken she had slopped on her salad. For some reason it was all that had looked appetizing today, and now it just made her think of the underside of toadstools—slimy and certainly poisonous. Swallowing down a retch—related to her lunch or Sam's text, she wasn't sure—she tossed her tray and shouldered her backpack, heading toward the student center, the paper, and, perhaps, her doom.

She was sweating by the time she made it to the paper—it was fall, sure, but it felt like summer, and everyone had jumped at the opportunity to flash their limbs in shorts and T-shirts one more time before Chicago winter locked everything into a painful permafreeze. Helen, on the other hand, was wearing cords. Cords she was seriously considering burning.

Sam, apparently, had his own office, even though everyone else on the paper seemed to be stationed outside it, queued up on long tables with their laptops and lunches in front of them. A couple of kids even seemed to be sleeping, but the rest followed Helen with their eyes as she made her way to Sam's door which, for some reason, sported a nameplate she suspected he had had made himself. She knocked slowly, and Carla, the girl with the perfect ponytail from the first meeting, gave Helen a sad little salute.

"Yeah," a beleaguered voice called from inside Sam's office. She winced, and Carla gave her a sympathetic smile as Helen pushed the door open to meet her fate. She wasn't scared of Sam, exactly; she just didn't like yelling. And he did. Still, she walked into the office, back straight, chin high, even as he glowered at her under a poster of Hunter S. Thompson she had definitely seen for sale in the student center store.

"Sit down," he grunted, gesturing toward a folding chair propped in front of his desk. The poster was the only adornment—the lack of windows signaled that perhaps he had commandeered a janitor's closet—that and a pile of books by the likes of Thompson, Tom Wolfe, and Charles Bukowski. Helen cringed at the last one, but Sam didn't seem to notice her critiquing his reading material. He steepled his hands in some sad parody of a much older man and leaned forward as she sat on the edge of the rickety chair. His tie had jaunty little alligators on it today. "Do you know why you're here?" he intoned.

Helen nodded, her stomach swooping. "I know I haven't talked to Constance yet. I tried after the vigil, but she kind of freaked out on me." *And then I made out with my TA down by the lakefront,* an inane part of her brain piped up. *And he hasn't texted me since.*

"Oh, really," Sam broke in sarcastically. Sarcasm was not becoming on him; he sounded somewhat like a haunted doll with a pull-string. "Maybe because you pretended to be her sister's friend and interviewed her mom without her knowledge?"

Helen blinked, her hands going cold and panic gripping her in a tight vise. She didn't know why she was so shocked. The story had been syndicated. Did she really think Mrs. Roberts wouldn't see it? Did she really think Constance wouldn't have told her about that night at the Unicorn?

"That's how you got all that juicy info, right?" Sam plowed on, shattering all Helen's hopes that maybe, just maybe, Mrs. Roberts had been happy with her story. "Showed up at her house and pretended to be someone you're not?" Sam dragged his hands down his cheeks until the whites of his eyes showed, amplifying the creepy living-doll effect. "Look, kid, I admire your gonzo spirit," he said, gesturing to Hunter, "but you just can't *do* that. We're not a tabloid. We're not some shitty blog. We're an *institution.*"

Helen nodded, swallowing. She had disappointed Sam. She figured he was always disappointed, but right now he was looking at her with a face filled with far less bluster and far more sorrow. She felt bad. She felt bad for him and for herself.

"Thankfully, Mrs. Roberts isn't going to sue or anything, but she's…she's not happy, Helen." Sam sighed, loosening his alligator tie.

Helen stilled then. For some reason she hadn't thought of how the article would affect Jenny's mom—really. She flashed back to that day in Mrs. Roberts's living room, the videos and pictures and ephemera of her daughter's life. She had been in a living hell of memories. Helen had lost her mother, sure, but at least she knew what had happened to her. A stroke. Simple. Not the gaping unknown. "Was she mad?" she asked in a small voice, studying the top of Sam's desk. Bukowski frowned at her, but he was always frowning.

Sam snorted. "What do you think? You invaded her privacy. You took advantage. That's not what real journalists do—" He slammed his hands on the desk and closed his eyes, taking a deep breath as though struggling to contain himself. "Plus, Constance was taken in for questioning last night, which is a real story, and we've blown any chance of a quote. That family isn't talking to us ever again."

"Do they think she did it, then?" Helen shuddered. "Constance?"

Sam frowned. "That's none of your concern, Scooper. Needless to say, you're off the story. Off the paper." A look of sympathy flickered across his face briefly before he tossed a rubber eraser at her and flapped a hand. "Now, I have work to do. Fuck off, please."

Helen's eyes were blurring when she closed Sam's office door behind her. She wasn't sure why, and maybe there wasn't just one reason. She had messed up. She had upset Mrs. Roberts. Constance was in police custody. And, less important but still annoying, Matt had apparently forgotten about her. She felt utterly depleted, worthless, low. Like a failure. And just a little bit angry. Wasn't college supposed to be fun?

As if reading her mind, Carla put her hand on Helen's shoulder. "Sam is a mouth-breathing shit weasel," she whispered. Helen snorted with surprised laughter. "Wanna go to a party tonight?"

Helen was surprised to find herself nodding. "Yeah," she said slowly. Then, trying it out, "Why the fuck not?"

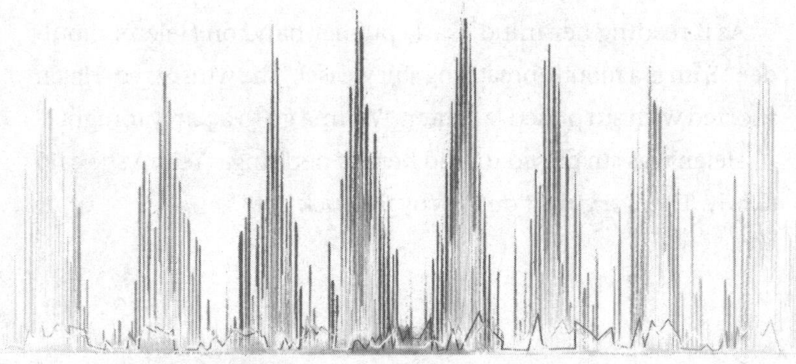

CHAPTER TWENTY-THREE

Crammed behind one of the overgrown hedges flanking the Halseys' front door, Natalie held her breath, waiting for Mrs. Pressman's car to arrive in the driveway. The newspapers now outnumbered the bushes, and there was a pile of boxes from a food-delivery service arrayed in a small barricade around the front door.

It was eerily still behind the bushes, and as she watched an earthworm undulate across her sneaker, she held her breath, straining to hear what might be going on inside. It was quiet on the sunbaked suburban street, and the house held its secrets close. Finally, Mrs. Pressman's car pulled up in front of the Halseys', and Natalie watched through the bush as the reporter exited her vehicle, mopping at her brow with a handkerchief. The sun stood high and sweltering, and ten-year-old Molly Tarver had just toddled outside in her ruffled bathing suit and begun running through the sprinklers at the house across the street. Natalie watched as she shrieked and danced through the spray, rainbows studding the cool water.

Meanwhile, Mrs. Pressman strode down the walk with a purpose and grace that Natalie envied. When the woman knocked on the front door, Natalie saw that it swung partly open. That seemed odd considering the circumstances; there were a few threatening notes papering the bushes along with the newspapers—scraps of paper reading *Killer Bill* and *Murderer Burn in Hell*. It didn't seem prudent to leave the door unlocked.

Mrs. Pressman seemed a bit spooked, too. She paused in the entryway and tentatively called out, "Mr. Halsey? It's Flora Pressman. We have some new information, and I just came by—" Her voice died, and what came out next were not words but a strangled shriek.

Natalie edged out of the hedges as far as she could without being seen and craned her neck toward the door; she hadn't seen Mrs. Pressman look this upset since Mrs. Halsey died. What was going on inside that house? She still couldn't see anything, so she leaned out even farther. The reporter didn't seem to notice. Whatever was in the house was all-consuming. At last Natalie could see through the open doorway, see the long shadow cast across the entryway floor—swinging. She slammed her eyes closed and scarpered back before the rest of the image could resolve itself.

Sunbursts exploded behind her lids as she sunk to the

concrete beside Mrs. Pressman, but she could still see that shadow in her head. It couldn't be real. It was a scarecrow of some sort. A prank, a joke. She couldn't be seeing what she was seeing. It was too impossible, too horrible.

"Natalie." Mrs. Pressman was shaking her, but Natalie couldn't see anything. It was like her vision had given out. Her limbs felt like jelly, and even though it was probably impossible, she felt like she could smell it. Death. It smelled like dirt and overly sweet fruits and the formaldehyde they used to preserve the fetal pigs in science class. She smelled it in a way that would never leave her. She tasted it.

"Natalie, don't look," Mrs. Pressman was saying, in between asking why she was there and asking if she wanted to call her mother.

When Natalie's vision finally cleared, Molly wasn't dancing in the sprinklers any longer. She was standing at the edge of her property like a dog inside an invisible fence, sunburned shoulders glistening, watching Natalie and Mrs. Pressman with her head cocked to the side. She turned toward her front door, no doubt to go tell her mom that the creepy girl had fainted in front of the killer's house.

Natalie clambered to her feet, ducking out of Mrs. Pressman's arms. She had to go. She had to get out of there. She didn't know where, and it didn't matter. Her ears weren't working right—everything sounded slowed-down and wrong—but Natalie jogged down the block to her bike and threw herself onto the seat. The whole thing wobbled precariously. Sandy Tarver had just opened the door to her house when Natalie pedaled off, almost falling as she stood high on her bike pedals, tears blurring her eyes.

The familiar downtown of Ferry looked too bright, too shiny, as Natalie sped past, bunting left over from the Fourth of July fluttering cheery and patriotic in a rare and blessed breeze from the front of Dixon's Creamery, the library squatting high and semigothic on its hill next to the church. To her right, the old Victorian flickered by, and finally, the trailer park swam into view in all its spackled and vinyl-sided glory. Natalie let her bike drop in the grass outside Jack's trailer and banged on the door with both fists, tears streaming down her red cheeks.

She would break down the door if someone didn't show up soon; she wanted to be as far away from the Halseys' as possible. From death. She ached to be in another dimension where the Halseys were still alive and things were simple. West Ferry would have to do.

When her fists were beginning to sting, Kurt opened the door, rubbing at his hair. He was wearing a pair of flannel pajama bottoms that looked several sizes too big and one of his black T-shirts. "Nat, what's going on?" He squinted, taking in her tears, her scarlet face.

Natalie shook her head, unable to say the words. Unable to say anything that might bring back the image of the shadow. She started to feel faint again and let herself be folded into Kurt's eager arms, which relaxed around her as she leaned in to his chest.

"Let's…let's not talk here," Kurt said, looking over his shoulder into the dim trailer. "Jack's sleeping, and he'll get pissed if we wake him up. If we haven't already." He gave her a squeeze. "Lemme just…" Kurt dashed back inside, and for a moment Natalie just stood on the patchy grass, holding herself and feeling utterly and strangely cold.

Kurt emerged with a blanket and a bottle of water. He wrapped the blanket around Natalie's shoulders and ushered her toward Jolly Times, leading her through the door and into the musty interior. It had been cleaned up a bit since Natalie had last been there, presumably by Kurt, and now there was an old couch pulled into the center of the room, under the watchful eyes of Bertha. Kurt guided Natalie to sit and tucked the blanket around her gently, handing over the water. She took a grateful slug and leaned back.

Kurt sat next to her and pulled her against his shoulder. "Do you want to tell me what happened?"

Natalie shook her head, her tears soaking through Kurt's T-shirt. It was impossible to speak. The words refused to form in her brain, to be shaped on her tongue. All she could do was nod or shake her head.

"Did something happen with your mom? Natalie? Give me something here."

She tried, she did. She even thought the words: *Mr. Halsey is dead. He hanged himself.* But in the end, all she could do was shake her head. Again.

He sighed and leaned his head against Natalie's. "Maybe we can talk about something else, then? Like…what do you want to be? To do? Now that school is over. Tell me about your plans to be a crime reporter. Why you want to do that so badly." He kissed her cheek, tasting her tears.

Natalie stared into the jumbled weirdness of the abandoned fun zone, then laughed, wildly, abruptly. The words finally came out, but they were cold and flat. "You spend years wanting something without knowing what it is, and then... Can I even do it? Can I even handle it when the time comes? I don't know if I can." She took a deep, shuddering breath. "But no, I can't... I don't want to talk about that right now. Tell me what you want to be instead."

Kurt gripped her hand. "Something. I want to be something."

Natalie nodded dumbly, finally looking at his face—or his chin at least. She could handle a chin.

"I mean... Most people go through life just being there, right?" Kurt carried on. "And they're okay with that. They're okay with being born and watching TV and having some kids and then dying. They may say they have hopes and dreams and whatever, but most of them are just happy to exist and make money. That's not enough for me." He gripped Natalie's hand so hard she almost yelped. She thought then of how he had bashed his fists against the crumbling walls at the Victorian house and tensed. "I need more. I need to *be* more. I need to *matter*."

Natalie extracted her hand carefully and moved a little farther away from him on the couch, rubbing at her fingers. Did he know how hard he had squeezed her hand? She looked toward the door to Jolly Times. She could just go home—perhaps that was wise.

Kurt frowned, reaching toward her hand. She eyed his warily. "Sorry, I just get overwhelmed sometimes. I didn't mean to squeeze so hard." He stroked her knuckles, and she watched, frozen, as he lifted her hand to his lips. "I just want to matter, you know? When I die, I don't want to be nothing."

Natalie nodded. She understood; that's what this whole dream of hers was all about, too. That's what most dreams were about: leaving something behind. She looked down at his fingers tracing hers and moved toward him again, putting her head on his shoulder slowly. She didn't make first moves, but this didn't feel like one. It felt like giving in. She felt his lips brush her hair and relaxed, content to be quiet. Content to be touched. With his long fingers running softly through her tangled hair, she fell asleep.

When Natalie woke it was pitch-dark in Jolly Times, and Kurt was sleeping curled around her, his spine pressed against the back of the couch. For a second or two, she wasn't sure exactly what day it was, and then Mr. Halsey's face appeared in her mind with a cold jolt—along with the realization that it must be late and her mother was likely worried. Without that adrenaline that had been searing through her a few hours ago, she felt awkward here with Kurt in this nest of decay: all she wanted to do was leave. Go home to her own bed where she had slept before seeing the shadow of death, before a boy knew what she looked like when she was asleep and vulnerable. She extricated herself from Kurt's sleeping arms.

Her bike was still where she had left it by the trailer, and the summer felt close on her skin as she climbed astride it and kicked off toward home. All of Ferry, it seemed, was sound asleep: the shops downtown were shuttered, and even the church was dark. As she rode up to her house, though, Natalie saw that at least one Ferry resident wasn't tucked in her bed, enjoying the weak chill of her ancient fan. The light was on in the kitchen, and Natalie could make out the shape of her mother slumped over the table.

As she walked her bike up the driveway, she considered sleeping in the yard, delaying the onslaught of rage and anxiety that would inevitably rain down on her the moment she entered the house. Mrs. Pressman would have called Helen. It was certain. She would have told her about the license-plate search, about finding Natalie in the bushes outside the Halseys'. But there was no escape from the wrath of Helen Temple, so Natalie just walked into it. She almost felt like she deserved the fire.

"Stop." Helen barked from the kitchen table. "Stop with whatever explanation you have ready, and sit your ass down. Now."

Natalie obeyed, pulling out her chair—the one she had inhabited every school night and many weekends, diligently doing her homework, for as long as she could remember.

"I'm guessing that you know by now that Mrs. Pressman called me. That she told me about what you did on her computer. How you followed her to the Halsey house when she specifically told you no," Helen said to the table, her face white and drawn.

Natalie nodded. It seemed that she had been nodding all night. In the silence that followed Helen's declaration, the fiddling of the crickets outside sounded ominously loud.

"That was bad enough," Helen continued. "But then, you don't come home. You don't come home for *hours.*" Her voice hitched. "So I called Katie, who hasn't seen you for days."

Natalie looked up, the fog she had been inhabiting for

the last few hours starting to burn off. What had Katie told her mother? What had her best friend said to get her mom even more worked up?

"And then Katie tells me that not only do you have some grotesque podcast where you gleefully rehash other people's misfortunes, but that you've taken it upon yourself to supposedly *investigate* your teacher's death for a new podcast. The death of someone you loved and respected. Someone who cared about you."

Anger shot through Natalie's brain, cold and steely, replacing the resignation she'd felt just a few moments before. Katie had sold her out. And why? Because of the time she had been spending with Kurt? Because she wanted to actually investigate a murder instead of being a spectator? And then the anger swiveled its head toward her mother, who felt the undying need to keep her insulated against the only thing she had ever been interested in.

"Mom...you knew I wanted to do this," she started, going for a reasonable tone and failing. She sounded like a whiny toddler even to her own ears. "To be a reporter—"

"And I was never happy about it!" Helen exploded. "But I let you apply to that school under the impression that you would learn the proper way to do things. That you would learn *empathy* for other people's losses. And now I find out that not only are you glorying in people's misfortunes, you're fucking with Mrs. Pressman's job."

Natalie flinched. She had never heard her mom swear as much as she had been these last few weeks.

Helen's eyes were rimmed with red, and they looked more punched-in than ever before. "Jesus Christ, Natalie, you broke into someone's computer. You think that's how real reporters conduct themselves? You think that's something you can actually mention on this podcast of yours? You'd be slapped with so many lawsuits your goddamn head would spin."

"I was going to figure that out later," Natalie said to their old friend the table. Her mom was right. Sure, people pulled stunts like this on TV, but did she really think it would fly in real life? She marveled at her own idiocy.

Helen pulled a laptop from under her chair, a device covered in NPR decals and horror-movie stickers. Natalie's computer. "Well, let me save you the trouble." She opened the computer and clicked over to the *Killing Time* page. "There is no podcast now. You're going to delete every single episode of this trash. Now. While I watch."

Natalie's breath left her. "What? That's years of work." She had been dumb, of course she'd been dumb, but did that mean she had to wipe the slate entirely clean?

"It's years of macabre bullshit is what it is. Delete it. Before you get yourself and Katie in even more trouble." Helen leaned back in her chair. "And I don't think I have to tell you at this point that you're grounded until school starts. If you still want to go to school, that is."

Shaking, Natalie reached toward the computer, almost one hundred episodes of *Killing Time* staring her down. "Mom, you don't understand, though…"

"That's the old refrain, isn't it?" Helen said with a bitter laugh. *"Mom doesn't understand. Mom is just so paranoid."* She narrowed her eyes, and for a second all Natalie could see was rage. Rage, pain, and someone she didn't recognize. Her mom, but her mom broken.

"But, see, you don't get to play that game with me," Helen continued, her voice like a stranger's. "Because I understand all this. Everything you're so fascinated with. I understand it more than you will ever know. It all lives in my nightmares, even now."

Natalie opened her mouth to ask what she was saying. Lived it? She worked in a diner. Always had. Her mom didn't let her take a breath, though. She bulldozed on. "But it seems like I've been too lenient. Apparently, I've given you too much rope. Because God help me, Natalie, I really didn't want my daughter to get that close to a corpse."

Mr. Halsey appeared in Natalie's brain once more, a dark phantom. She shuddered, and the tears started coming again. Pouring thick and hard down her face like a sudden summer downpour. Death was real now—she wished she could go back to before when all it had been was a phantom.

Helen's unfamiliar face melted into her mom's face again, and she was crying now, too, her shoulders shaking, but her voice was even. "This is over. This *investigation* is done. No more, Natalie. No more."

CHAPTER TWENTY-FOUR: THEN

Helen was wearing a glittering tank top emblazoned with a tiger's face, and she was cold. Carla looped her arm through Helen's and swayed. "That looks good on you," she slurred. "You should keep it. Burn the cords!"

"Burn the cords!" Helen parroted, pumping her fist and laughing just a little too hard as she remembered how she had thought just that, earlier today—before Sam and Mrs. Roberts and the two shots of vodka Carla had poured into her. Now, she was wearing borrowed clothes—the sparkly tank and pair of painted-on jeans—heading toward her first college party. She couldn't help but think of Jenny then—the house they were stumbling toward wasn't that far from that fateful party the other girl had attended. Through her vodka haze, Helen worried, again, about what had happened to Jenny, but she also wanted to forget about her for one night. Be a normal college girl. Hence she had accepted the vodka shots instead of being a bummer, which Tom had called her more than once when they hung out at friends' houses back home.

Carla passed her a clove cigarette, and despite having never smoked in her life, Helen took a long drag, tasting Christmas and tar. She coughed, watching the smoke spiral up into the crisp fall night, seeming to loop around the moon and back again. Helen shivered once more—the wind was coming in cold off Lake Michigan—but Carla had refused to let her wear a jacket ("You'll just lose it, anyway. Or someone will throw up on it.") "Whose party is this, again?" Helen asked, dismayed to find her words had become liquid, sliding. She cleared her throat and tried to speak more clearly. "Friend of yours?" She overcorrected, though, and ended up sounding like a robot.

Carla shrugged. "Some grad student in the new media program. I dunno his name. Someone just told me the address and that they have beer."

Helen nodded and smiled as if the mere prospect of beer explained going to a stranger's house and, like a film skipping, the pair found themselves in front of a two-story condo, vibrating with lights and music. Everyone seemed to be streaming in through a side gate onto a concrete patio, which was festooned in Christmas lights. A throng of slightly older-looking students surrounded a card table laden with red Solo cups, and someone whooped long and hard as a petite girl in a short dress landed a Ping-Pong ball neatly in one of the few cups left standing in front of her burly opponent. He winced and chugged down the foamy beer, leaving a faint mustache above his wide mouth. Her friends—all wearing either sparkly tops like Helen's or skimpy dresses—stood on a concrete planter cheering. Helen noticed that the planter had a sign neatly taped to its side: *Do Not Touch, Fresh Concrete*, it read in bold red letters. She stifled a drunken giggle. Despite being grammatically correct, the sign was not working.

"I'm getting a beer," Carla yelled in her ear and wheeled toward a keg in the corner of the yard. Helen nodded and started to follow her through the masses of students but stopped as her stomach rushed up her throat. She paused, blinking her eyes and swallowing. She didn't really drink much in high school—if you counted half a glass of wine on holidays, which most people wouldn't. She obviously needed to sober up or she'd wind up passed out like that guy over there on the deck—and everyone was drawing dicks on him.

A quick scan of the outdoor area did not reveal any water, so she turned toward the open sliding door to the kitchen, which was populated with far fewer revelers. Grabbing what she hoped was a clean Solo cup, she filled it at the sink and took three long gulps—then refilled it and drank some more. Her head cleared somewhat, but her stomach roiled in response. She didn't think she was going to throw up, but she definitely needed some space—and, maybe, a cold towel on her neck. She laughed at herself a little: five minutes into her first college party, and she was already about to crash. What a lightweight. At least she didn't have a dick on her forehead. She giggled.

Wandering through the first floor of the house, which was dark and populated with figures making out on practically every soft surface, she located the bathroom, which appeared to be locked. She could hear someone laughing inside, though—two someones, rather. She rolled her eyes and started up the stairs, ignoring a neat sign reading *Off Limits* in the same red scrawl as the one on the planter. Yeah, she usually followed the rules, but she just needed the bathroom—it wasn't like she was going to have sex in someone's bedroom. She laughed again at the mere idea of her having sex with a stranger, then cocked her head as she stumbled up the steps. "Tom's got all the rooms now," she slurred, realizing, suddenly, just how drunk she was. "I can go find a room, too."

Mercifully, there was a door at the top of the steps, and when she flicked on the light she saw an immaculately clean bathroom with fluffy blue towels on the rods and a big, deep bathtub. Closing the door behind her, she surveyed the scene with a weird kind of nostalgia. She hated the dorm bathrooms. How she had to shower one flimsy curtain away from all the other girls; how she had to wear shoes in the shower and drag all her toiletries back and forth. Slowly, she grabbed one of the hand towels and soaked it in cold water, pressing it to her forehead. She looked in the mirror at her thin, young-looking face above the tiger top, which she now saw was hanging off her in all the wrong places. She looked ridiculous, and she felt ridiculous for even being here. Maybe she wasn't cut out for college. She had messed up at the paper, messed up at going to a party. And she missed home. Tears were just starting to drip down her face when the door flung open. "Hey!" a voice growled. "Can't you read?"

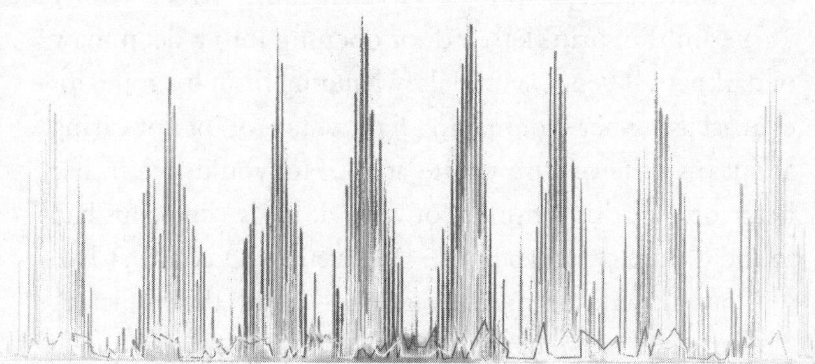

CHAPTER TWENTY-FIVE

Natalie's mother could keep her away from the Halsey case, but she couldn't keep the case away from her daughter. During her near-constant shifts at the diner, Natalie watched Sandy Tarver lord over a table of fellow Garden Club members, rehashing in gory detail the discovery of Bill Halsey's body, as she fluffed her dyed-red bob—even though, as far as Natalie knew, the woman hadn't actually seen anything. She heard her share of rumblings about Eliza Minnow, too, but the police had yet to arrest her. And without her internship at the paper, she would probably find out with the rest of the plebs if they did.

And then there were the nights. The horrible, sleepless nights during which she rolled in sweat-soaked sheets and dreaded unconsciousness. And when she finally dropped off, exhausted, she returned to that sunny street: Molly Tarver in the sprinklers, a door opening into a deep maw of darkness. Then… Mr. Halsey hanging from his rope, his eyes accusing her—of making light of horror, of not caring about his wife or him or life at all. He would live in her head forever, this reminder of what death is. The cops had found a note. It was suicide. Apparently he couldn't live without his wife anymore, couldn't live with the suspicion.

And as she suffered, she suffered alone. Her mother barely spoke to her, unless it was to tell her to refill the creamers, and Katie appeared to have gone into hiding since ratting her out. And then there was Kurt. After that night at Jolly Times, he had gone silent. He hadn't answered any of her texts, and when she snuck out on her lunch hour to see if she could catch him at his trailer, Jack answered. He didn't know where Kurt was, he said. Then he congratulated her on finally getting boobs. Kurt must have heard about Mr. Halsey. The reward was now null and void: he didn't need her. Natalie was fooling herself that he cared. He had probably left town in search of some other scam.

That afternoon, however, her luck turned when Katie came swinging into the diner in a pair of faded cutoffs and a Mickey Mouse T-shirt, her neon-yellow fanny pack burning a hole in Natalie's retinas. It took Natalie a second to register that Katie wasn't alone; she was frog-marching a very sullen Simon in front of her, his glasses askew and dark hair mussed. Her lips started to instinctively tug into a smile at the sight of her long-lost friend when she remembered what Katie had done. She had exposed *Killing Time*. And now she was acting like it was any other summer day—hostage aside. Swiftly, Natalie turned away, hustling across the diner with a coffeepot, topping up people who had barely taken their first sips.

"Hey," Katie said, tapping her on the shoulder. Natalie froze for a beat, then turned around, gripping the pot of piping-hot coffee by the handle until her knuckles turned white.

"Simon has something he wants to tell you," Katie pronounced, pushing her vibrating boyfriend toward Natalie. Simon stared at his shoes, then yelped when Katie poked him the back.

"I'm sorry," he muttered.

Katie poked him again. "For what are you sorry, Si?"

Simon gave a giant sigh. "For that note in your mailbox. Sorry." He finally looked up at Natalie, then scampered a few feet backward when her eyes narrowed.

"That was you?" Natalie growled. She was already pissed at Katie, and now she had two targets. "Why would you do that? What in the hell were you thinking? You get tired of your little puzzles?"

Katie stepped between them. "First of all, Simon is the youngest cruciverbalist at the *New York Times*," she snapped.

"*Cruci*-what?"

"He's a professional puzzle master, Natalie," Katie said, sighing. "I have told you this myriad times, but you keep forgetting. Or not listening to me or whatever." She took a deep breath. "Secondly, he wrote the note. And, yes, it was a bad idea—" she held up a hand, anticipating Natalie's response "—but I guess he was worried that you'd get obsessed and then I'd get obsessed and the whole summer would be shot."

Simon had somehow made his way several feet back in seconds, as if he had teleported. For a moment, Natalie felt sorry for the guy, but that didn't last long. She wasn't sure who she was angrier at: Simon for being a jealous coward, or Katie for not caring that her boyfriend would do something so bizarre and creepy to her best friend.

"Now." Katie clapped. "That's all settled. We—" she shot a look over her shoulder at Simon, who gave a weak smile at his girlfriend "—came here to ask you and Kurt to Jonathan's big send-off party tonight at the abandoned Victorian place. I guess he's going to college early or something?" Katie shrugged. "I can't blame him. This town *sucks*."

Natalie put the coffeepot down on an empty table, taking a moment to gather her thoughts. First of all, Kurt wasn't even texting her; no way he was going to a party. Second, the one time she'd mentioned hanging with Katie and him together, he'd shrugged and said he didn't really like crowds. Thirdly, *what the fuck?*

"Is that all you came to say?" Natalie growled, placing her hands on her hips.

"Yeah…" Katie said. "I mean, I think *you* owe me an apology, too, to be honest." She crossed her arms and shot Natalie a glare. "You deleted *Killing Time* without asking me? I went on our server the other day, and it was all gone. What the fuck? I mean, I obviously have it backed up, but that was super shitty, Nat."

Natalie gave a harsh bark of laughter, and Sandy Tarver

looked up from her gloomy coffee klatch, freckled nose scenting for still-more scandal. Simon had long disappeared.

"What did you think was going to happen when you told my mom? That she would hit Subscribe and pass it on to the Garden Club?" Natalie laughed helplessly. "Of course she hated it, Katie."

Katie's face fell. "I guess I knew she wouldn't like it..." She rallied, setting her lips into a thin line. "But I was worried about you. Showing up at the Halseys' and all that. I swear, I didn't think she would actually delete the podcast. Plus, you said you were done with all that. You lied."

"Are you serious?" Natalie laughed again, wild and long. Everything was falling apart. Couldn't Katie see that? Everything was ruined, and her friend had helped ruin it. "You know my mom, Katie. You know what she's like. And now, thanks to you, I'm stuck waiting tables for the rest of the summer. My mom won't let me work on Mrs. Halsey's story anymore, I got fired from my internship, and Kurt won't answer any of my texts."

Katie gave an enormous, world-weary sigh, as if her friend was being overly dramatic. "Look, Natalie, I'm sorry about the podcast and the internship and everything. But Kurt?" She rolled her eyes. "I mean, honestly, good riddance to rubbish and all that, right? Should have dumped him weeks ago. He was never good enough for you."

Flashes of red light washed across Natalie's field of vision. Katie was missing the point entirely, and Natalie was apoplectic that she didn't realize that. Plus, who the hell was Katie to criticize Kurt when her own boyfriend was a spineless worm who wrote threatening notes because he couldn't stand to share his girlfriend with her own best friend?

"This isn't about Kurt, Katie," Natalie spat. "This is about the podcast. Don't you understand that? About me actually doing what I've been saying I would do for the last ten years. And you ruined it. You ruined everything." As she said it, she knew she was being unfair. She had ruined it herself by not being careful. But it didn't help that her best friend seemed to be enjoying her downfall.

Katie frowned, then reached toward Natalie's shoulder. "I'm sorry, Nat, but—"

"Don't touch me!" Natalie yelled, pulling her shoulder away. Sandy was leaning forward in her booth now, the Garden Club turned fully around to face their fighting. "And don't tell me what to do! Everyone needs to just stop telling me what to do!" She gasped, leaning against a booth, wrung-out and depleted. She would feel embarrassed about her outburst if she weren't so exhausted.

Katie gave the diner a slow scan as all heads turned in their direction. Natalie's face was red and twisted, and her hands were curled into claws. "I think we should take some time…apart." Katie's voice shook lightly. "I think I just need some time. Some… Yeah." She looked toward the exit, swallowed.

Natalie sank into a booth, all righteous anger leaching away at Katie's words. She had lost her job, her mom's respect, and now her best friend. All that was left now was bitterness and a sadness that made her sick to her stomach. "Sure," she whispered to her lap. "High-school friendships don't last, right? Better cut the tie now."

"I didn't mean that..." Katie started.

Natalie looked up, wiping at the tears streaming down her face with shaking hands. She was out of words, out of excuses. All she wanted to do was sleep for a million years and wake up when no one was mad at her anymore. "Please...just go. I have tables to wait, and everyone's staring at us."

Katie stood for a moment, her ridiculous fanny pack perched on her hip like an exotic bird, and for a second Natalie felt that sense of complete loneliness mounting. She missed Katie, even though she was standing in front of her. But she remained silent as Katie stared—and remained silent, still, as Katie finally turned around and jingled through the diner door.

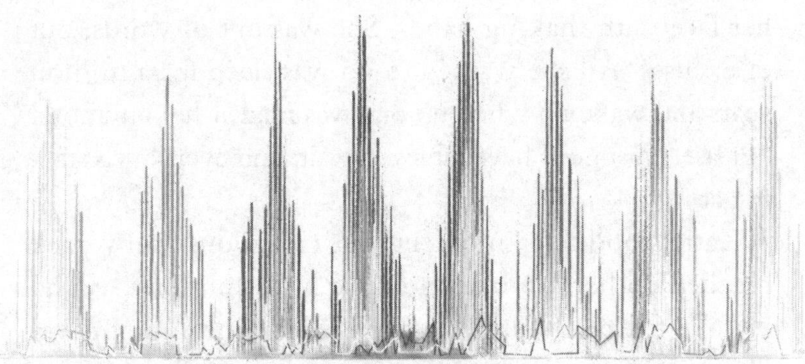

CHAPTER TWENTY-SIX

The recent graduates of Ferry High spilled onto the dead and dying lawn of the old Victorian, their arms slung around each other, their breath sodden with beer and cheap liquor. Soon, they would all head off to college and their respective futures. Natalie envied them, their simple dreams, their straightforward goals. She used to be like them; she used to know exactly where she was headed and why. But now, wandering alone through the throngs of laughing friends, her future was a blank, and so was she, her mind going misty as she poured another double-splash of vodka into a plastic cup and slumped to the floor. She texted Kurt in her haze, telling him to come to the party. To answer her. Please.

It had been almost too easy to sneak out: her mother had been going to bed earlier and earlier every night as business picked up during the summer rush. She was usually stone-cold asleep by nine. Around ten, to be safe, Natalie slipped out the door and onto her bike, no longer able to stand the silence of the house and the noise in her brain. She wanted bodies around her. She wanted oblivion. And now she was well on her way to getting there. She had been at the party for about an hour before Jonathan finally made his way through the well-wishers to her corner of the ruin.

"Hey, Nat," he said, sliding to the floor next to her, a UPenn T-shirt tight across his chest. He tapped her cup with his beer and took a deep drink. "Ready to get out of here?"

Judging by his joviality, Natalie guessed his mother hadn't yet told him she had been fired. Small favors. She snorted, then covered her mouth to stanch the spray of vodka that threatened to escape. "That's the understatement of the year. How come you get to leave so early?"

Jonathan smiled the smile of someone who had only bright days to look forward to and linked his arms around his knees. "Penn has a great outdoors program for freshman before the semester starts. You go camping with other students and get to know each other. Marshmallows, hiking, all that."

Natalie laughed, her head lightly knocking against the wall. "That sounds terrible." The room was swinging around her.

"Come on." Jonathan nudged her. "You can't hate marshmallows."

"I can if they're attached to sticks held by people who enjoy camping," Natalie grumped.

Jonathan put a hand to his chest, a look of mock hurt on his face. "Does that include me?"

Natalie pushed his shoulder. "You are the one exception to this rule. As long as you never, ever try to make me sleep outside when God has blessed us with houses and beds."

Jonathan extended a hand for Natalie to shake. "Deal."

Natalie fit her palm into his, but he didn't let go right away. Instead, sadness stole into his eyes, and he squeezed. "I'm really going to miss you, Nat. I wish we had been better friends sooner. It sucks that we weren't."

Natalie squeezed back. His hand felt nice, warm and safe. "Yeah, it really does."

"Everything's changing, though, isn't it?" Jonathan asked, looking out at their classmates swaying to the R & B crackling from someone's Bluetooth speaker. He was still holding her hand, and Natalie felt all of her nerve endings informing her of that fact. "Like, I'm excited to go, to do new things, but I'm also sad, you know?"

Natalie nodded. She understood being sad. It was the excited part that she was having a harder time grasping lately. College was there, firmly in the realm of things that were happening, but she just couldn't picture herself there yet. Especially since her mother had put her on lockdown.

"You know Lucy dumped me?" Jonathan leaned in to her slightly, looking down at their linked hands. "Didn't want to do long distance. I don't blame her, but damn... Things just really don't stay the same, do they?" He leaned in to her more.

"No, they really don't," she said, an inch or two from his lips, and then he closed the gap and kissed her. His lips were soft and minty and feather-light, as if he was making sure he didn't hurt her. He kissed differently than Kurt; he was want more than need. She was just leaning in to him when Jonathan was wrenched away from her; the wall behind her cracked as he slammed into the plaster and his head thudded against the wallpaper. His eyes rolled back in his head, and someone screamed.

She jumped to her feet, head spinning as she took in the scene: a boy in a black hoodie holding her friend aloft, slamming his head against the wall with sickening force. The people nearest them started to scramble, and as the person in black continued his assault on Ferry's golden boy, phones came out—both to film and to call for help. The old house was filled with glowing lights and screams.

"Stop," Natalie yelled, finally coming back to her body. But the boy didn't stop; if anything, he hit harder. Jonathan slumped in the guy's arms, out cold, and Natalie felt like vomiting. Instead, she sprang forward and grabbed the unknown boy by the arm, twisting him toward her and bringing her knee to his groin all in one fluid move. Her lips pulled back toward her teeth as she raised her fists, poised for another attack if need be. But the boy groaned and sank to his knees, down for the count. Natalie wrenched back his hood and blinked, confused: blond hair, high cheekbones, Kurt.

She took a step back and watched as the boy who had kissed her a week ago writhed on the floor. "What did you do?" she cried, dashing toward Jonathan. The floor was speckled with his blood, and the spatter made Natalie even more ill. It all did.

Kurt grunted and got to his feet. "What did *I* do? You invited me." He coughed, staggering. "And you were kissing *him*." Kurt pointed at Jonathan, anger and hurt radiating off of him like something alive.

Natalie wasn't paying attention to him anymore, though—she was too busy making sure that Jonathan was breathing. Thankfully, he was. He needed an ambulance, however. And soon. As if thinking made it so, sirens rang out in the distance, and even though Natalie knew it was because someone had called the police, just then it seemed like magic. She sat on the floor and cradled Jonathan's head in her lap, murmuring to him that it would be okay. Blood soaked her denim shorts and dripped warm down her thighs.

When she looked up at last, Kurt was gone. Along with most of the party guests. One of the only people who remained, curiously, was Jack. He stood awkwardly in the corner, his hands in his pockets, darting furtive glances toward the exit.

"What are you doing here?" Natalie asked, checking Jonathan's pulse for the tenth time. It was steady, thank god.

Jack coughed. "Kurt said he was going to a party with you. I knew Katie was worried about you hanging with him, so I said I would go along."

Natalie blinked. "You were worried about me?" Maybe she had misjudged this messy boy. Perhaps he had some of his extended family's spark and kindness after all.

"Don't get too excited," he snorted. "There was also free beer. Anyway, you're okay, right? I can go?"

The sirens sounded closer now, and that was good because Jonathan's head was bleeding fast. His eyelids fluttered, and Natalie squeezed his hand.

"Because, you know," Jack said, looking toward the door, "I gotta get out of here before the cops show up. They don't like me much."

Natalie didn't look up at Jack, just flapped a hand. "Yeah, go ahead. No need for you to get in trouble just because Kurt's an asshole."

Jack nodded and made for the door, then turned back toward Natalie. "You're going to tell the cops it was him, right?" His face went unusually soft. "I know you're a thing or whatever, but that dude is not all there, you know?"

Natalie looked up from Jonathan's increasingly pale face and frowned. "I guess, I mean..." She looked down at what Kurt had done to her friend and shuddered. "Yeah, yeah, I am."

Jack paused halfway through the door, his thick eyebrows reaching for his spiky hair. "If you do see him, though, tell him he's done. I'm kicking him out. I don't need that kind of drama in my life." He riffled in his pocket for a moment, then tossed something toward Natalie. "Anyway, I stole his wallet earlier. He owed me a shit-ton of rent. I took all the money, naturally, but you can give him his IDs or whatever. Or not. I don't care."

Natalie reached for the wallet, flipping it open to Kurt's license, a younger version of the boy she knew smirked up at her from the tiny picture, but the name under the photo wasn't his. *David Kurt Minnow Jr.* the license read. Her hand tightened around the fake-leather wallet, and her vision narrowed; dizziness overwhelmed her. None of this made sense. Unless Kurt was lying—unless he had been lying about everything.

"He said his name was Bachman," she sputtered, more to herself than Jack. "That first day I met him. Kurt Bachman. Is that not true?"

"Dunno," Jack said, turning toward the door again. "Only ever told me his first name, and I didn't really care until he stopped paying rent. Wouldn't surprise me, though." He stopped for a second, taking in her white face, her shaking hands. He sighed. "He's a loser, Nat. Really. You know you can do way better."

Natalie nodded silently, lost for words. She felt Jack staring at her for a long moment before he finally left, crashing through the door into the night. She didn't look up from the picture, though, from the name. The pieces were slowly coming together in her muddled mind. Bachman. That was Stephen King's pen name for his early books. That first day in the trailer, Kurt had clearly been messing with her. And he hadn't stopped. He wasn't just some random boy interested in scoring a reward—or with her—he was Eliza Minnow's son. And what exactly he wanted with her, she had no clue.

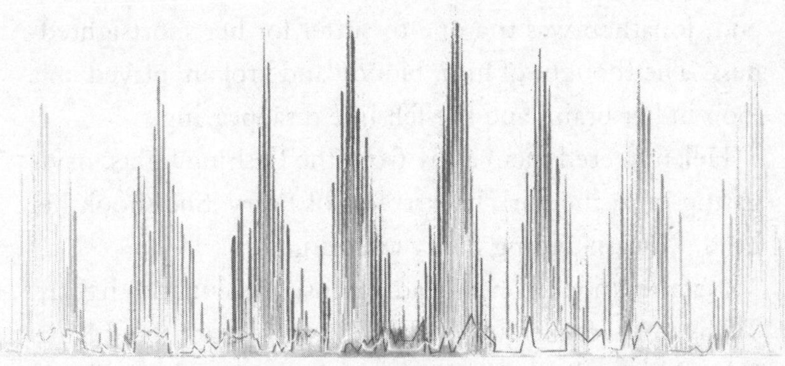

CHAPTER TWENTY-SEVEN

Mrs. Pressman hadn't let Natalie go to the hospital with her and Jonathan after the police took Natalie's statement—even though she begged. Instead, she passed her off to Helen when her mother pulled up past one a.m.

"Please don't say *I told you so,*" Natalie said as she slid into the car beside her mother. Helen was still in pajamas and a bathrobe, pillow creases on her cheek. "I know you're just dying to tell me how stupid I am. How you were right about Kurt all along."

Natalie leaned her forehead against the cold car window, her cheeks hot with shame and alcohol. Why hadn't she questioned Kurt's motives sooner? He had obviously been using her—all the kissing and talking and flowers, it was all a lie. A way to…what? Collect on a reward without selling his mother out himself? It was a mess, and in the end, Jonathan was the one to suffer for her shortsightedness. The thought of him, bloody and broken, played on a loop in her brain, and she felt like disappearing.

Helen steered them away from the flashing lights, navigating onto the dark backstreets of Ferry. She shook her head. "I wasn't going to say anything."

Natalie knocked her head against the window lightly. "Why not? I fucked up. Badly. You were right about Kurt. I should have listened to you. And now Jonathan—" Her voice broke, and a ragged sob ripped through her, sharp and rattling.

Helen pulled over and cut the engine. She reached toward Natalie and grabbed her shoulder, forcing her daughter to look at her. "Yes, I was right about Kurt, and, yes, you have made some pretty big mistakes, but don't you *dare* blame yourself for what that kid did to Jonathan." Her eyes glittered bright in the darkness.

Natalie started to open her mouth to protest, but her mother held up her hand. "Kurt made his own choices here. He made the choice to lie to you. He made the choice to take the violent route. I can't begin to understand why he did what he did, but who he is has nothing to do with you."

Helen tore her eyes away from her daughter, looking instead through the dark windshield. "I've seen a lot, Nat. Too much. And some people…they'll use any excuse they can get to do evil. Bad childhoods, cheating spouses, mean bosses… In the end, though, that's all it is. An excuse. The real impetus isn't some outside force, it's something inside certain people that just…makes them bad. I know that's simplistic. I know it's not scientific. But there it is."

Natalie stared at her mom's face, pale in the darkness, eyes fixed on the dim horizon. "But…" she started, and Helen looked at her, her eyes tired, "he didn't seem…bad. At least not all the time. I don't understand how he could be both. How he could be so sweet and so…scary."

Helen shook her head. "If you can figure out the answer to that, you'll dethrone Dr. Phil. In the end, though, it doesn't matter how nice someone is. It matters what they do. And what Kurt did tonight shows who he really is."

Natalie thought of how Kurt squeezed her hand, how he bashed his fists against the wall—the same wall he pummeled Jonathan into. There were signs, but she'd chosen to ignore them. Or at least she'd tried to.

"But what do we do when we realize someone's a bad person?" she asked, feeling like she was four years old. Shouldn't she know by now? It seemed like a simple question, but all her teacher's lessons about good and evil were now playing on loop in her head. "Mrs. Halsey always taught us to have empathy for villains. To not just dismiss them as evil."

Helen nodded. "And she was right. A villain isn't a very good villain if they do evil for no reason. But just because they have a reason doesn't mean we have to agree with them."

"What do you mean?" Natalie asked, wiping away her tears. Of course she didn't agree with what Kurt did to Jonathan.

Helen took her hand, squeezing hard so that Natalie

would listen. “You can understand that Kurt attacked John because John kissed you. You can have empathy. But you don’t have to agree with that reaction. You don’t have to sympathize with him. You can see his actions for what they are. A bad response. A bad action.”

Natalie nodded, then leaned her head on her mom’s shoulder, the tears starting to dry. “Thanks, Mom,” she said softly, as the two stared into the wooded darkness of Ferry. “Thanks.”

CHAPTER TWENTY-EIGHT: THEN

"I'm sorry..." Helen started as the ceiling spun above her like the blades of a fan. She steadied herself on the sink and cringed as a familiar blond man swam into view. It took her a few seconds of rapid blinking to clear her eyes—and to place him. Matt. It took another few seconds to put it all together. Carla had said the party was at a TA's house. Her TA's. She groaned. He had ghosted her, and now here she was, standing in his bathroom. Real smooth.

Cheeks hot, she mumbled another apology and headed toward the door—trying to extricate herself from any further embarrassments—but before she could get too far, her legs gave out under her, and she crashed to the linoleum, confused. She had never been so drunk before, and she decided she did not like it. She willed herself to stand up but instead slumped forward, her head resting on the cool marble of the counter as if she could hide from Matt by averting her eyes.

"Whoa, are you okay?" Matt crouched and put his hand on her shoulder. "I'm sorry, Helen, I didn't realize it was you. Jamie insisted on throwing this stupid party, and I was just trying to stay away from all the craziness, and when I heard someone in the bathroom, I..." He trailed off. "How much have you had to drink?"

Through her haze, Helen guessed that Jamie was the guy throwing the party—probably Matt's roommate. And Matt, likely, was the maker of all the chiding signs. "Not that much, really," she slurred. "Just...like, two vodkas. But I didn't have dinner." She tried to lurch to her feet again, but Matt gently guided her to the floor and handed her a glass of water he'd magically conjured from somewhere. "I swear I'm not stalking you," she babbled. "This girl brought me to this party, and then there were people having sex in the downstairs bathroom and I—"

Matt groaned. "I'm going to kill Jamie."

"I'm sorry," Helen said in a small voice. "I'll go in a second, I promise."

Matt put his hands on her shoulders. "No, no, no, Helen. I'm not mad at you, I promise. I've just..." He dragged a hand through his hair. "I've been dealing with a lot lately, and I'm not really in a party mood, you know?"

Helen closed her eyes, and the world lurched to the side. She wanted to go to sleep. Very badly. She also wanted Burger King. "Me, neither," she said with a hiccup. "But I'm drunk at a party, and I don't have Carla's number, and Amanda's probably asleep with her pizza." Matt frowned, confused, but Helen barreled on. "And I don't have a boyfriend anymore, and my dad is so far away."

Tears started to leak through her lashes, and when she blinked them away, she saw Matt looking at her, his face inscrutable.

"I guess...you can stay here?" he said hesitantly, like he wasn't really sure it was the best idea. "I'll sleep on the floor if you like, and you can take the bed."

Helen was so tired at this point that she could only nod gratefully and let Matt half lead, half carry her to his bedroom.

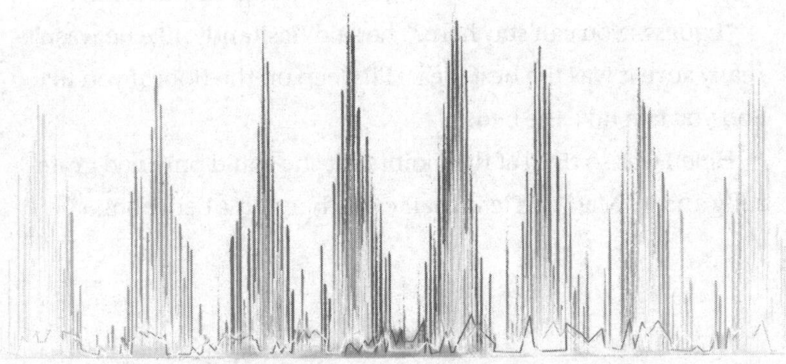

CHAPTER TWENTY-NINE

The smell of bacon and coffee wrenched open Natalie's swollen eyelids the next morning, and as soon as she regained consciousness, the headache settled in. It pounded at her skull from the inside and made it nearly impossible to fall asleep again. It didn't help that the sun was streaming across her face in all its glory and NPR was blaring from the kitchen right below her room. She lay for a few moments, counting her overly loud heartbeats, then struggled into an old robe and shuffled down toward to the coffee.

"Morning, Nat," her mom chirped from the stove. A plate of bacon soaking grease into paper towels stood at her elbow, along with a pot of coffee. Helen cracked a few eggs into a skillet and gestured toward the table. “Sit, eat. We’re taking a day off. We need it.”

Natalie collapsed into her chair and stared at the food arrayed on the table. Her stomach roiled at the sight of it, then growled. She wasn’t used to so much alcohol, so after last night’s party her body wasn’t her biggest fan. And the feeling was mutual.

“Have you heard from Mrs. Pressman? Is Jonathan okay?” Natalie asked in a small voice, her eyes unfocusing and refocusing as she fought the urge to lie down on the table and go back to sleep. If she hadn’t had so much to drink last night, she probably wouldn’t have slept at all. And now that she was conscious again, the worry tore at her belly.

Helen sat down across from her, placing a cup of coffee in front of her daughter. Natalie sipped at it gratefully. “He’s going to be okay, yeah.” Helen nodded. “He’s got a pretty bad concussion, but they say he can come home in a day or two. Luckily, you kids are made of rubber.”

Natalie nodded, sagging with relief. She tentatively grabbed a piece of bacon from the plate and bit into it. The salt and fat worked their way through her body, doing their part to stop the pounding in her head.

“And Kurt?” she asked after she finished chewing. She put the bacon down. “Is he…”

Helen stood up and busied herself with the pan of eggs as if Natalie hadn’t spoken.

She tutted and shoved a plate in front of her daughter. “Have some protein with that grease, please.”

“Mom, what happened with Kurt?” Natalie asked again,

pushing the eggs slightly away. Apparently, her stomach wasn't ready for protein yet.

Helen sighed, fiddling with her fork. "The cops are looking for him. And that's about all I'll say on that. Now..." she said, depositing a small white box in front of Natalie. It was festooned with a sleek pink bow, like the kind that Natalie imagined would come on a fancy jewelry box.

Natalie blinked at the gift. She had snuck out, got drunk, and watched Kurt beat up her childhood friend. And now her mother was giving her a present? It didn't add up, but Helen could be a mystery at times.

"Open it." Her mom pushed the box closer. "I got it on Etsy. For college."

Natalie wiped her greasy fingers on her robe and picked up the box, undoing the little pink ribbon and lifting the lid. Inside was a silver necklace with a cylindrical pendant, like a whistle without the holes. It was engraved with her full name, Natalie Dana Temple. As she turned it over in her hands, she noticed that the top detached and that there was a little pump underneath the cap. "Is this perfume?" Natalie asked, her finger on the pump, lowering her head for a sniff.

"No!" Helen yelled, grabbing for the necklace. "It's mace. Be careful."

Natalie blinked. "You bought me a mace necklace? On Etsy?"

Her mom replaced the cap with care and handed the necklace back. "You mentioned wanting mace the other day, when we were doing karate. I want you to be safe on campus by yourself, so here you go. Besides, I thought it was cute. I just love miniature things."

Natalie laughed, and it felt good, considering what a shambles the rest of her life was. She slipped the necklace over her head and for the first time in a while she felt grateful for her mother, for the fact that she had someone who would love her no matter how much she strayed. No matter how severely she fucked up. "You're so weird," she murmured fondly.

"No, I'm not!" Helen protested. "I'm just giving you the tools to protect yourself."

"Like that time you took me to the gun range?" Natalie said around a sip of scalding coffee; her appetite was returning. When she was thirteen, Helen decided that Natalie needed to learn how to use a gun. Just in case, she said.

They'd had to drive more than an hour outside of Ferry to find a gun range, and even then, it was just skeet shooting, not handguns. Natalie was too small for even the smallest gun, and as she shot at the flying clay pigeons, the butt of the weapon banged against her shoulder. The next day her shoulder was black-and-blue and stiff, and she didn't feel any more confident about handling a gun than before—especially since it wasn't likely any clay pigeons would be involved in the future.

Helen leaned back in her chair and nursed her coffee. "You were a lousy shot. But it's pretty hard to miss with mace."

"You should stitch that into a pillow, Mom." Natalie tossed a piece of bacon at Helen, and she caught it, laughing. For a moment that made her ache, Natalie could almost pretend the rest of the summer hadn't happened. That she hadn't tried her hand at true-crime reporting. That she hadn't seen Mr. Halsey's shadow twisting above his parlor floor. That Jonathan was unmarked and smiling.

"Why don't you go see Katie today, honey? I bet she misses you," Helen said, shoveling the last bit of eggs into her mouth. She swallowed and smiled expectantly at Natalie.

And just like that, Natalie was back to the present—right in the middle of the muddle. The good humor fled from her mind, and she hid behind her coffee cup. She had been trying not to think about Katie since the run-in at the diner yesterday, how she had dumped her, essentially. She had her mother back, sure. She would always come back. But Katie was another story. A much less predictable one. Natalie gave her mom a tight smile and forked some eggs into her mouth, but she was even less hungry than before.

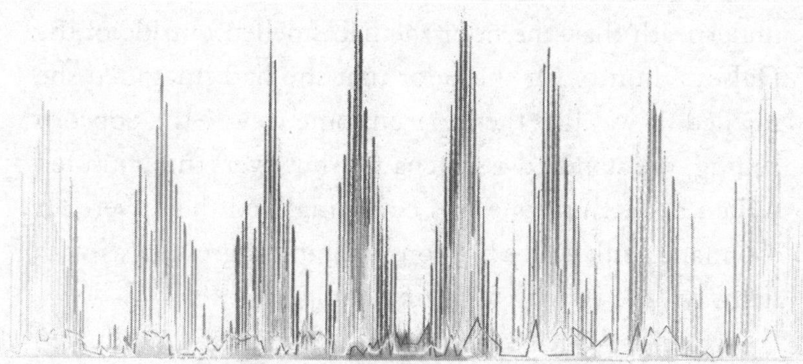

CHAPTER THIRTY

Jonathan was ready for visitors the next day. And, despite the sourness in her stomach over who had put him in the hospital, Natalie let her mother drive her there. Helen poked her head in to say hi and then retreated back to the waiting room with her burned hospital coffee, leaving Natalie standing at the door, shifting from foot to foot. Jonathan's eyes were ringed with bruises, and he had a massive bandage on the back of his head, but he was still smiling, his teeth even and white and thankfully all accounted for.

"Nat! You came to see me!" Jonathan cried, then winced and sat back in bed. He was wearing another UPenn T-shirt that his mother had likely brought him. "Come over here and look at my newest game: hospital bingo."

Natalie inched into the room, her sneakers squeaking on the linoleum. Everything smelled like disinfectant and, underneath that, the odor she had smelled outside of the Halseys' house. Or the odor that she had imagined she smelled. It was like the paper in some ways—the popcorn ceiling, the standard-issue chairs—but everything just felt wilted here. Everyone was coughing, and there were far too many smiley-face balloons bobbing aggressively in the hallways like ridiculous roving emoji.

"Jonathan." She swallowed, taking another squeaky step forward. "I am so, so sorry." As the words came out, so did the tears, and soon Natalie was weeping all over the sterile hospital floors. She hadn't expected the tears. She hadn't expected the crushing shame. But seeing her childhood friend with his black eyes and resilient smile broke her.

She cried for ever calling Jonathan a golden retriever. For ever thinking his niceness made him bland and less-than.

That kindness made him resilient. It made him strong.

His eyes were filled with that strength as he blinked up at her, eyebrows drawn and mouth downturned. "Hey, Nat, everything's okay. Why are you sorry?"

Natalie wiped her eyes on her T-shirt and gripped her elbows. He didn't know. No one had told him how he had ended up here in the first place. She briefly considered just letting it go, living with the lie, but that's not what Jonathan would do. He would tell the truth.

"The guy who beat you up, he was the one you saw on my porch the other day. I was…hanging out with him? I'm not really sure what to call it." She looked at her shoes. "I am so sorry," she repeated, the words feeling flimsy and not enough. She waited for the onslaught. It never came. She should have known.

"Hey, Nat, look at me," Jonathan said, pushing himself up on his pillows with another wince. "This is not your fault. You didn't beat me up. Actually, I heard you kind of busted out the karate on the other guy."

Natalie looked up, her cheeks getting hot. She didn't deserve praise. She opened her mouth to say as much, but Jonathan shook his head.

"Look, my mom told me what went down. How that kid didn't even tell you his real name."

Natalie blushed. She had told Mrs. Pressman and the cops about Kurt's deception, and even though the woman didn't show any outward signs of disdain for Natalie's ignorance, shame flooded in all the same.

"We're both victims here, if you think about it," Jonathan continued, trying to catch her eye. "I just ended up with visible bruises to show for it."

Natalie raised her eyebrows. She hadn't known Jonathan to be all that poetic before. But maybe she wasn't paying attention. She never had. "So…you're not mad at me?" she asked. She still felt like she deserved his ire. Or at least his annoyance.

Jonathan shook his head. "No. Not at all." He paused. "But I gotta ask… Why *did* he lie in the first place? I mean, I know his mom was arrested for murder and all. Was he just ashamed?"

Natalie shrugged. "Probably because he wanted the reward, and it looks pretty shitty to turn in your own mom."

The rest of what Jonathan had said sank in seconds later. "Wait. Did you say she was arrested?"

"Aw, shit." Jonathan winced. "Is that not something people know yet? I feel so out of touch with the outside world. My mom mentioned it was happening. It's probably in the paper today."

"Do you know why? What do they have on her?" The words shot out of Natalie's mouth before she could think them over, and she, too, winced. Had she learned nothing? Her meddling had landed Jonathan in this hospital bed with its scratchy sheets and paper-thin pillows. Maybe it was time to leave it alone. Go back to Netflix and *S-Town* and leave the investigating until she had a degree.

Jonathan didn't seem fazed, though. He just shrugged and smiled at her. She smiled back, tentatively. It was silent in the white room but for a gentle summer rain pattering against the window. And it was warm. Natalie had expected that she'd feel uncomfortable lingering here, with Jonathan, but she just felt affection. Not the romantic kind—their kiss had been a mistake—but a companionable kind. She folded herself into the chair next to his bed and picked up the notebook on his nightstand.

"Hospital bingo, huh?" she asked, tapping the page. "You gotta add *Saw a butt* to this. I saw at least four on my way in here. People are seriously lax with their gowns."

Jonathan grinned and grabbed the notebook, penciling in a new square. "Okay, you got it. Let's play."

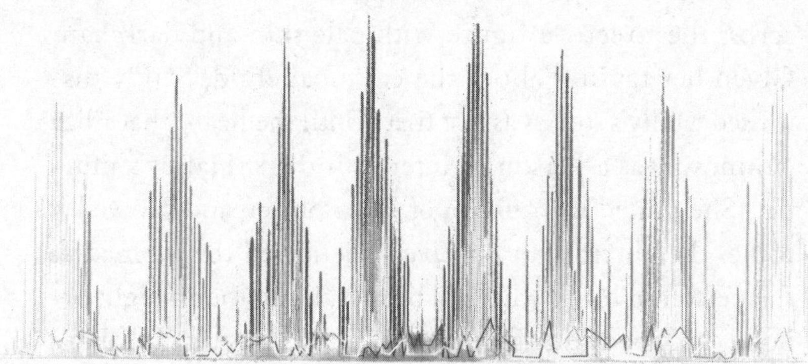

CHAPTER THIRTY-ONE

Ten-year-old Molly Tarver was Eliza Minnow's undoing, to hear Sandy Tarver tell it the next afternoon in the diner. Natalie had had to wipe down the table directly behind Sandy's for roughly twenty minutes in order to get it all. By the time she was done, it was sparkling. It had all started that spring, months before Mrs. Halsey's death. Molly's older sister, Sarah, had been driving her crazy with stories about Molly's closet, where Sarah claimed there lived a little girl who had died in the house many years ago. The little girl, Sarah said, did *not* like Molly and would come out and bite her toes off if she fell asleep. Terrified of the toe-eating ghost, Molly stayed up most nights, looking out the window until she passed out.

On several of these nightly vigils, she told her mother, she had seen a figure in black approach the Halsey house across the street—a figure with pale skin and dark hair. Given her ravings about the cannibal child, Sandy dismissed Molly's stories as just that. Until she heard that Eliza Minnow was a person of interest in Mrs. Halsey's murder. She pulled up a photo of Eliza online and showed it to her daughter, who positively identified the woman as the person in black who had been stalking their neighborhood. Natalie wasn't sure a ten-year-old was that reliable a witness, but the emails they'd retrieved after Mr. Halsey's death alone were pretty damning: all the cops needed was one more puzzle piece.

"They arrested her in front of everyone at that seedy bar she works at," Sandy was telling the Garden Club as Natalie finally finished wiping down the table. "And she's obviously guilty. They said she wrote threatening emails to Mrs. Halsey. It's open-and-shut, really. She's likely to fry."

Cheryl Masters, vice president of the Garden Club, gasped. "Do they have the death penalty in Connecticut?" she asked in a tone that was more salivating than scandalized.

"I don't know, but if not, we should write a letter to the paper," Sandy announced. "Molly is traumatized. Just think, she was *this close* to witnessing a murder." She sounded almost disappointed.

Natalie turned away from the gabbing of the Garden Club and tried to focus on refilling coffee cups, far too many thoughts jumbling around her head to sort through at that moment, chief among them Kurt. It wasn't that she wanted to be thinking about him—she really and truly didn't—but everyone was talking about him. And being Ferry's favorite eatery, the citizens congregated at Helen's to discuss the ruin of the Minnow family—or the Barracudas, as Sandy Tarver had dubbed them. Theories abounded about their plot to take down the good people of the town, especially when those incriminating emails were indeed found on Eliza's computer—and she didn't deny that she had written them.

And everyone wanted to get an eyeful of the Minnow boy's supposed girlfriend, which was easy, seeing as how she now worked in the diner from open to close, always within a ten-foot radius of her mother. Most had known her their whole lives, but that didn't stop the rumors from flying.

Natalie had put her headphones on in an effort to dampen their voices, but she could still hear the buzzing as she served up hamburgers and refilled coffee cups. *She was dating that monster Her poor mother I thought she was a smart girl No girls are smart when there are boys involved That's why I never married I wonder if she was involved in some way It was probably a love triangle and that poor Jonathan Pressman got the brunt of it Jonathan was too good for her She was always morbid Remember that Halloween she dressed as that morbid thing Which Halloween She was always morbid Do you think she's still in touch with him The cops should just follow her around She probably made him do it She probably knows something She definitely knows something She—*

"I forgot how much these people *suck*." The voice rose, unexpected, from the booth she was hovering near, a pot of coffee in hand. She jumped and slopped hot coffee on her hand, surprised at the directness of the address. Sure, everyone had been talking *about* her, but they hadn't been talking *to* her.

Natalie popped out her headphones, paused *Serial* season four, and took in the twentysomething woman in her smart black skirt and green silk tank. It took her a moment to place her, but when she did she inwardly groaned. Jessica Whitestone. From True Crime Club. The woman in front of her looked nothing like she remembered, though. Gone were the metal T-shirts. Gone was the stringy hair. Natalie was surprised to see that under all that grime, Jessica was actually normal-looking. Pretty, even. She instinctively reached toward her phone to text Katie and then remembered that they were no longer friends.

Jessica gestured around the diner. "They're all talking about you like you're not there. They're ghouls, don't you think?" She folded her hands on the sticky tabletop and leaned toward Natalie. Her dark hair was in a low bun; she looked like a substitute teacher that all the kids liked but gave a hard time. What had happened to her in college? Jessica had gone to Columbia. Despite her predilection for murder, she was smart, and the Whitestone family was rich. Her parents had both been hedge-fund managers in New York until they'd relocated to Ferry and opened an ice-cream shop downtown. Despite having access to endless free ice cream, though, their daughter was still deeply unpopular. Partly because she didn't earn her good grades: she was famous for finding ways to make other people do her work.

"Yeah, they suck." Natalie shrugged. She was unnerved by the way Jessica was staring at her. Like she wanted something. Like Jessica was a cat, and Natalie was a bowl of cream. "Are you back to visit your parents or something? Haven't seen you since graduation."

Natalie and Katie had had an unofficial party after Jessica graduated, elated that they now had the True Crime Club to themselves. It was a short-lived victory, since the official club dissolved, but they partied all the same.

Jessica shrugged. "I'm staying with them, yeah." Then she leaned forward even more. "Doesn't it bother you, though? The way they're talking about you? It would bother me." She drummed her manicured nails on the tabletop. They were painted a dark green to match her shirt. "People here have no lives. I forgot about that, too."

Natalie just wanted to put her headphones back in and continue ignoring the situation until college came, that was the truth, but she wasn't sure why Jessica deserved to know that. "I don't know," she replied. "Is this all you wanted?" She pointed toward the coffee.

"Actually, no." Jessica dug into her dark blue Kate Spade purse and pulled out a business card. It was thick and creamy white, and her name was printed in an elegant, looping font. Natalie thought immediately of Patrick Bateman.

"I work for a public radio station in the city," Jessica said, her voice prim and brimming with pride. "We were hoping to turn the Minnows' story into a podcast series. We thought maybe you'd like to be interviewed?"

Natalie froze, baffled. "Their story? I don't understand."

"You know, how his mom is a killer, and he's this violent, lost boy on the run. We're exploring if this kind of thing runs in the family." Jessica smiled. "They're making great strides in forensic genealogy. It's fascinating stuff."

"I'm sure it is," Natalie replied, filing that term away for a Google later. "But no one has been tried yet. Eliza Minnow hasn't had a hearing, and no one has even spoken to Kurt."

"Well," Jessica said smiling and taking a sip of coffee, "we wanted to jump in on this one early, while it progresses."

Natalie stared at Jessica, dumbfounded. This had been her story. She had been on it since the day Mrs. Halsey died. And now here was Jessica, marching in, once again, to claim ownership and credit for her work. Natalie had broken into a computer and her boss's office and, apparently, consorted with an alleged murderer's son. Natalie had lost her best friend and chipped away at her mother's trust.

"Here." Jessica shoved a pair of headphones at Natalie and stared at her until she put them on. "I want to play you the intro I'm thinking of using. I think you'll like it." One of her shiny fingernails pressed Play on her phone screen.

Shrieking heavy metal filled Natalie's ears, and she cringed, gesturing at Jessica to turn it down. The music faded, and then Jessica's voice intoned through the melee of guitars like a crypt keeper on some old horror show. "Ferry. A sleepy Connecticut town. A haven for families. Torn asunder by a mother and son with a thirst for blood. An insatiable need for violence that left one teacher dead, her husband hanged—and the town's golden boy bleeding. For WBTY, I'm Jessica Whitestone, and this is *Teacher Dead and Dearest*." The guitar sliced in again, and Natalie tugged out the headphones and threw them on the table, her breathing coming in ragged and hard.

"Pretty good, right?" Jessica said, winding up her headphone cord and popping it back into her purse.

"You're kidding me, right?" Natalie breathed. And Mrs. Halsey had thought *My Murder Obsession* was bad. This was some straight-to-the-dredges-of-streaming shit. "That... that's grotesque."

Jessica frowned. "What do you mean? This is a true-crime podcast. This is how true-crime podcasts sound, Natalie." Her voice was maddeningly pedantic.

"Yeah, but this is *Mrs. Halsey*," Natalie replied, searching Jessica's face for some iota of remorse. "She was our teacher, and we loved her, and now she's *dead*. Don't you care about that at all?"

Jessica's lips thinned, and her eyes darkened. "Of course I care, Natalie. Mrs. Halsey was the only one at that godforsaken school that gave a damn about me. That didn't treat me like a freak."

"Then, why are you doing this?" Natalie pleaded. "Why are you turning her into some kind of...sideshow?"

"Because this is what true-crime podcasts are, Nat," Jessica said, seething. "You, for one, should know that. You're just as much of a fan of this stuff as I am. In fact—" a bitter smile stole over her face "—weren't you doing your own research on the Halsey case? I heard you were there when they found Bill."

"That was different," Natalie protested. She would never have framed Mrs. Halsey's story that way—with the metal and salacious phrasing and spooky voice. She had wanted to honor her teacher. Sure, she had strayed along the way, but now, presented with Jessica's mockery of what a real story was, she started reconsidering her decision to drop the case. She couldn't let Mrs. Halsey's legacy be this—this titillating trinket meant to thrill bored housewives and people stuck in traffic.

"How?" Jessica pressed. "Just how are we different, Natalie? I really want to know."

A million answers cycled through Natalie's head, but she didn't want to argue with Jessica anymore. She didn't think anything she said would really get through, anyway. She had *learned* from her investigation thus far. She had learned humility. Empathy. Jessica wouldn't be able to understand until she plunged in herself, and Natalie swore to herself then that she would do everything in her power to stop the other girl from doing so.

"I don't want to be interviewed, thank you," she said tightly. "Did you want to order any pie? We have good pie."

Jessica shook her head, her nose wrinkled. "No, I don't do carbs anymore." That was a surprise. In high school she had lived on Doritos. "Frankly, I'm a little surprised. I thought this is what you wanted to do. I hear you're going to school to be a true-crime reporter. I could definitely give you some tips."

Natalie bristled and took a step back. "Sorry, the answer is *no*."

"That's too bad…" Jessica said, looking genuinely disappointed. "We could use someone like you at the station. We have a great internship program in the summers."

Natalie stilled, coffeepot in her hand forgotten. If Jessica had come just a month or so ago and offered her an internship of this caliber, she would have just about died from glee. But this was her story. Hers. Jessica with her macabre fascinations wouldn't be able to do it justice in the same way she could. Seaming together her lips, Natalie headed back to the counter to pick up another round of orders, giving Jessica's table to another waitress, Ashley Starker. Jessica never took her eyes off her, though—until she finally put her money on the table and gathered herself to go.

Ashley stopped Natalie at the end of her shift and handed her a business card. "That woman left a pretty good tip. Thanks for that. I think this is for you, though."

Jessica Whitestone, Executive Producer WBTY the card read in that looping print. The paper was thick, heavy in her hands. It felt expensive.

She walked it toward the trash, but instead of banishing it to the sea of coffee grounds and half-eaten fries, she shoved it into her jeans pocket. Just in case. In case of what, however, she didn't know.

That evening, Natalie collapsed onto her twin bed with her laptop, intent on escaping from real life for a few precious hours before the oblivion of sleep claimed her. There was a new season out of a zombie show she liked, and those shambling undead corpses were calling her name. She flipped open the laptop and hunched forward in bed to surf over to Amazon, but as she did so, the device erupted with a series of pop-ups. Her email.

Baffled, she navigated to her in-box, which was usually

a near wasteland except for emails from school. Now, it was full to bursting. Brow furrowed, she clicked on the first message.

Dear Ms. Temple, My name is Daniel Moss, and I'm a reporter for the Connecticut Current. I'm doing a story on the Minnow family of Ferry, CT, and I was hoping for a moment of your time.

She clicked out, her breath coming in ragged. It was understandable that the citizens of Ferry were talking about her—that was what they did—but the newspaper? Jessica was clearly a craven opportunist, always had been, but now Daniel Moss had appeared. How had news of her involvement spread so fast? Sandy Tarver came to mind, but this seemed extreme, even for that old gossip.

Heart thudding, she scanned the rest of her in-box.

Dear Ms. Temple, I'm a reporter from…

Dear Ms. Temple, I have a podcast on…

You should give that boy up. He's a menace.

You slut. How could you open your legs for that monster?

Killer. You're a killer, too.

Your poor mother must hate you.

Stay strong. My guy is in jail, too.

The emails avalanched on: missives from reporters, strangers calling her all manner of terrible names, and, perhaps most upsetting of all, an email from the editor of something called *Death Row Dreamboats*:

Hey there, Nat! I'm Gail from Death Row Dreamboats. I did some snooping on your dude, Kurt (SWOON!), and we would LOVE to feature him as this week's Dreamboat—even if he hasn't killed anyone (yet) (!). Can you fill out the below survey so our readers can get a better picture of this Killer Cutie?! Also, maybe send a few steamy snaps???

What followed was a list of questions that ranged from *What's Kurt's favorite color?* To *What does it feel like to make out with the son of a murderer? Be specific.*

Natalie's hands went numb. She was supposed to be the journalist, not the subject. She felt extremely exposed, like someone was watching her through her laptop's camera. Her mother was always trying to get her to cover that thing up with tape in case some perv hacked her computer to ogle her…watching true-crime docs? She was never clear on what the worry was there.

She kept scrolling through a seemingly endless deluge of emails, until she got to messages from UPenn and bulletins from Ferry High. Before the messages from strangers began in earnest, though, an email with no subject leaped out at her—dated the night before. She clicked on it, and a cold, numb feeling crept between her shoulder blades.

Nat, I need to talk to you. I messed up. I know I did. It was an accident, though. I need you. –Kurt

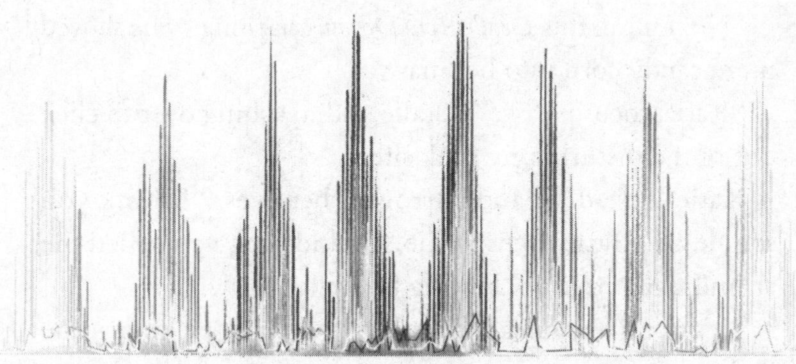

CHAPTER THIRTY-TWO

"This is so fucked." Katie shoveled a handful of candy corn into her mouth and leaned over Natalie's laptop. The origins of the unseasonable snack were unclear to Natalie, but she didn't care. Her friend was back.

Natalie flopped on the bed next to Katie, nearly vibrating with happiness. She had been freaked about Kurt's email and hadn't known who else to turn to. She had expected Katie to tell her to fuck off when she called, but instead, Katie had showed up at her doorstep fifteen minutes later, candy corn in hand. Apparently, Natalie wasn't the only one who missed her best friend.

"I *know* it's fucked," Natalie said, fear eddying through

her joy. "What does he want from me? What the hell is going on?"

"No, I mean this *Death Row Dreamboats* thing." She shoved more candy corn into her maw.

"Katie, focus please," Natalie said, reaching over to click out of the disturbingly pink site.

Katie looked up and narrowed her eyes. "I think you should be a little nicer to me. Considering you called me at midnight after not talking to me for *weeks*."

"It's not like you called me," Natalie said, picking at the bedspread.

"This isn't a contest, Nat. We had a fight. It happens. But it hurt that you didn't even try to fight for our friendship."

"You told me you wanted to take a break!"

"Oh, whatever. You were supposed to call my bluff. Clearly." Katie rolled her eyes. "You need to learn these things before you go to college and start dating non-sociopaths."

Natalie tried to fight the smile working its way across her lips but lost the battle. "I missed you at lot, Katie. Even if you are pain in the ass."

"Amazing apology! Four stars!" Katie grinned. "Let's try that again."

Natalie put her hands on her friend's shoulders. "I'm sorry, Katie. You're my best friend. One of the only good things left in this sham of a life. I missed you terribly."

Katie shrugged away. "Enough with the sarcasm."

"I'm not being sarcastic." Natalie seized her wrist. "Things are fucked up, Katie. Jonathan was in the hospital, and Kurt put him there. People I don't know are calling me a slut. And now Kurt's trying to get in touch with me so that he can tell me...what? That he beat up Jonathan by *accident*? What the hell does that even mean?"

Natalie opened the email from Kurt again and stared at the short missive. The thought of his lips on hers made her skin run cold. He lied about his name, his mother. He solved problems with his fists. Who knew what else he was capable of? But, on the other hand, who knew what else he *knew*? He had tipped her off about his mother's emails. Could he be the key to solving the case? To telling Mrs. Halsey's story correctly and completely? To getting justice for her teacher, at least? Eliza had been arrested, sure, but what if he knew something that would *prove* she was guilty?

"I dunno... I would turn this email over to the police so that they can trace it." Katie shrugged. "We're beyond playing detective here, Nat."

Natalie nodded. "Yeah, I know. You're right. It's just... fucking *Jessica Whitestone*. That awful podcast. If I give this to the cops, it'll just be one more thing she can use to make Mrs. Halsey's death into a twisted Lifetime special."

Katie rolled her eyes again. "Are you still on about that? Dude, I bet no one will even listen to that garbage. She's a loser. She'll always be a loser. Even if she somehow managed to graduate, like, a year early." Katie stared at Jessica's Facebook page. "And is this for real?" She pointed at Jessica's graduation date. "She's straight out of college and working at a radio station? How many people did Mommy and Daddy have to pay off to make *that* happen?"

"But this isn't her story! She'll ruin it," Natalie exploded, not all that interested in taking a tour of Jessica's ill-gotten achievements. "I know I'm supposed to drop it, and I know bad stuff happened, but I did all this work, and now fucking *Jessica Whitestone* is just gonna swoop in with her Columbia degree and stupid hair and steal it from me? Turn the Halseys and Eliza and Kurt into caricatures? Fuck no."

"Well, what do you propose we do?" Katie sat back, closing the tab where Jessica smirked in all her shiny ex–Aileen Wuornos glory.

Natalie picked at her coverlet again. She was making a sizable hole, and her mother would be pissed. "You're going to freak out."

"It's far too late for that, Nat." Katie gestured toward the massive cardboard cutout of Fox Mulder in the corner. "Don't even *try* to deny you used to practice kissing on that thing."

Natalie rolled her eyes and pushed her laptop closer to her friend, stabbing at the screen where Kurt's email loomed, Spartan and strange. "Can you find out where this email came from?"

"Well, yeah, of course I can. Any halfway computer-literate person could. You just have to track the IP address," Katie scoffed, then raised her eyebrows, her mouth forming an O. "Oh, fuck no, Natalie. You are not going to go talk to that maniac. Weren't we *just* saying he's fucked up? Weren't we *just* both very, very freaked out by this psychotically vague email?"

"I know he's a creep. But hear me out." Natalie raised a hand. If Katie started talking, she'd change her mind—and she couldn't let herself do that. She was too close. "Kurt likes me. I seriously doubt he'd hurt me."

"Oh, well, if you *seriously* doubt it," Katie muttered.

Natalie ignored her. "Imagine if I could get an interview with him. About his mom. About everything that happened. I bet he would talk to me. I could find out what happened to Mrs. Halsey. I could finally find out why. Why she died. Why someone killed her. Just…why…" Natalie said, tears edging their way into her voice.

Katie breathed out, long and hard. "Can we just…sleep on it tonight, Natalie, please? Can we just get a full eight hours under our belts before you go off and do something else that will piss me off? Maybe in the bright light of day, you'll finally realize that I'm right about everything and you're a total fucking idiot."

Natalie studied Mulder's face for a moment as she turned it over in her brain. Tomorrow it might be too late. Tomorrow, who knew where Kurt might be?

"Okay." She cleared her throat. "Here's the deal. Tonight, we figure out where that email came from. Tonight, I see if Kurt will talk."

Katie opened her mouth, but Natalie held up her hand again. "And *tomorrow*, I swear I'll turn the email over to the cops. Plus, anything else Kurt might tell me."

Katie groaned and tugged at her hair. "You're just going to do whatever you want anyway, aren't you?"

Natalie heard disappointment in her friend's voice, the anger and sadness. She had been steamrolling Katie. She had been unfair. She couldn't lose Katie again. Not so soon after getting her back. She swallowed, holding Katie's gaze. "No, I won't. I'll only go tonight if you say I can."

Katie huffed, a mingling of frustration and relief. "Okay,

fine. Let's just figure out where the hell this email came from before you go playing Nancy Drew."

She hunched over the computer, and Natalie watched as she tapped away, plugging in the IP address and pulling up a map of Ferry. "Huh," Katie said, sitting back on her heels. "I wasn't expecting that."

Natalie leaned forward, squinting at the screen. "What is it? Where did the email come from?"

Katie pointed at the screen and smirked. "Not quite the den of iniquity I would have expected. He's probably not even still there."

"Does that mean I can go?" Natalie breathed, staring at the screen.

"Only if you text me every five minutes to let me know you're still alive—and if you wear that weird mace necklace your mom got you. *And*..." Katie plucked Natalie's phone out of her hand and started tapping away "...I just installed a tracking program on your phone in case he kidnaps you and takes you to Mexico."

Natalie stuck out a hand for Katie to shake. "Done, Big Brother."

It didn't take long to get to the East Ferry Public Library; she didn't even need her bike. Looming next to the church, the building was usually a cheery, rusty red in the daytime, but now, at night, it cut a blacker silhouette against an already black sky. Opting not to attract attention with her phone flashlight, Natalie circumvented the building, trying to figure out how Kurt might have gotten in. The more she thought about it, the more she doubted that he had just walked in the front door. Also, she had double-checked the time stamp on the email and saw that it had been sent at eleven the previous night. The library closed at five. He had to have broken in somewhere.

Crouched against the side of the building, Natalie pulled herself behind hedges that reached out and raked her legs, her feet sinking into the loamy earth abutting the stone foundation. Every once in a while, the headlights of a passing car skittered across the lawn, and Natalie pressed herself into the foliage, but no one stopped and demanded to know what she was doing, so she assumed the drivers hadn't seen her. She had made it almost all the way around the building when she happened upon a basement skylight, opened just a crack. Firing up her phone to the lowest brightness setting, she examined the lock, which had been broken.

For a long moment, Natalie crouched by the window, staring down into the darkness of the cellar. As far as she could tell, nothing was moving down there, but that didn't mean Kurt wasn't there, sleeping in the corner surrounded by his meager belongings. Or, as some dark part of her brain told her, hunkered down in the pitchy black with a knife, brain fixed on mad revenge.

"You're being stupid," Natalie muttered to herself, squinting down into the gloom. And, like Katie had said, he probably wasn't still there at all. He had probably just sent the email and left. But maybe he had left something behind—some clue as to where he had gone.

Clenching her teeth, Natalie cracked the window open far enough for her slender body to pass through and started scooting through the opening on her belly, her feet reaching for an unseen floor. Every horror-movie heroine she had ever seen started cursing in her head simultaneously, but it was too late; she was hanging from her hands above a dank basement floor, alone in the darkness. The enormity of her stupidity hammered her brain as she dropped to the concrete floor and spun around to face the rest of the room. Her hands shaking, she finally flicked on the flashlight app and aimed it in jerky motions around the basement.

"Hello?" Her voice quavered. "Kurt? Are you here?"

The light jumped in her hands as she tried to survey the scene all at once, but as silence continued to reign in the underground space, Natalie's hands stopped shaking, and she was able to take in the dark shapes around her. They were empty card-catalog boxes—hundreds of them, piled into towers that reached toward the ceiling, creating their own jagged kingdom of obsolescence.

Satisfied that Kurt wasn't lurking somewhere in the corners, Natalie started picking her way through the piles of drawers, trying to see if there was any evidence that he had lingered here for a while. It was late, deeply late, and Natalie was alone in the guts of the library, looking for clues that likely weren't there. She sighed, sweeping her flashlight around the room. Clearly, Kurt had just snuck in and out.

Sighing, Natalie turned toward the window and freedom, but her light caught on something swinging from the pile of drawers before she could complete her rotation. It was a belt, pink and blue, covered in cavorting whales; a piece of paper was impaled on the teeth of the buckle. Natalie froze, eyes locked on the paper.

She paused for a few moments to slow her breathing before approaching the belt, reaching up to seize it and tug it from its resting place. She detached the paper with care and lifted her light to better see what was written there. Or typed, rather. At the bottom was a phone number Natalie didn't know.

> Natalie! You found me! Kind of. I have moved on. I knew you were smart. I knew you would know where to go. I need to talk to you. I need to see you and explain. About what happened with your friend. And with your teacher. Go to the place we played truth or dare and go soon. I'll be waiting. K.

When Natalie slid through her doorframe and back into her bedroom, Katie was reclining on her bed in her faded Snoopy pajamas, Natalie's laptop opened in front of her. She had helped herself to some of the instant coffee Natalie's mom inexplicably loved, despite owning a diner that brewed its own. "So was he still at the library?"

The note felt like a telltale heart in Natalie's pocket, but she shook her head. "No, he was gone. I think he got in through the basement window and booted up one of the computers when no one was there."

"He's a sneaky little shit," Katie scoffed. "So you're done now? Can we just go back to normal? At least until college starts and life as we know it changes?"

"Yeah, I think I'm done investigating," Natalie said, subtly crossing her fingers behind her back. It was a childish gesture, she knew, but it made it feel less like lying to her best friend somehow, less serious. It harked back to those days when the worst untruth one could tell the other was *I'll stop tickling you, I promise.*

Katie raised her eyebrows. "Does that mean you'll give the email to the cops?"

"Yeah, sure. I'll send it now, even. And to your dad and Mrs. Pressman." It's not like the email would help the police find Kurt. He wasn't at the library anymore, and Natalie had the belt and the note—and she was the only one who knew where he was now. It was unlikely anyone would check out Jolly Times on their hunt for the missing assault suspect. The place was nearly forgotten. It only mattered to two people in Ferry, and one of them was likely hiding out there, waiting for the other to come find him. The question was, should she?

As Natalie stretched out next to Katie in her warm, safe bed, she grappled with that very question—the same one she'd been asking herself since Jessica had shown up at the diner, threatening to take all her hard work away. And as her breath deepened into the kind that preceded sleep, the question hammered on.

CHAPTER THIRTY-THREE: THEN

Helen woke up dazed somewhere much softer than her dorm-room twin bed. She lifted her head slowly—it was pounding—and looked down at the blue plaid fleece blanket covering her in the dim of an unfamiliar bedroom. Heart vibrating against her chest, she lifted the covers and took in her sparkly top, the tight jeans. She was still dressed, which meant nothing had happened with…whoever's bed she was in.

Feeling dizzy, Helen flopped back on the woodsy-smelling pillow and studied the ceiling, which was spinning much less than it had last night. Last night. She had been sprawled on Matt's bathroom floor. Matt. Humiliation crashed in, and she dragged her hand over her face. How was she ever supposed to go to his class again? She scanned the room: no Matt. He had said he'd sleep on the floor, but maybe he'd crashed on the couch downstairs since she'd evicted him from his bed.

Shame flooded her chest, and she put her hands over her face again. She could just sit in the back row from now on, slumped over in a hoodie. At least then she'd blend in with the rest of the class. Now all she had to do was get out of his room without further confrontation. Sitting up slowly so as not to jostle her brain any more than necessary, Helen swung her feet to the floor, noticing—again, with a spike of shame—that she was still wearing her sneakers. Poor Matt. He seemed like such a clean guy, and here she was messing up his pristine bed. She would leave an apology note if she had a pen or paper—or could figure out how to possibly explain last night.

Now to find her purse and get out of there without anyone noticing her. After that, much Gatorade would be consumed. And perhaps a breakfast sandwich of some sort. Helen crawled across the bedroom floor to save all the bending and whatnot—and the remaining contents of her stomach—feeling around in the dark for the faux-leather bag. As expected, Matt's floor was also pristine—unlike the one in Helen's dorm room. Amanda was unsurprisingly not all that neat and tidy. Once Helen had found literally five dollars in change under her dormmate's bed while trying to conquer the thicket of trash covering the floor. She kept it—payment for the live-in maid service.

Having cleared the space around it, she reached under the bed, and her fingers brushed something small and hard flush with the wall. Maybe it was her phone, escaped from the confines of her purse. She could at least use its light to do a better sweep; she didn't want to turn on the light and let Matt or anyone else know she was awake. When she pulled out the device it was, indeed, a phone. But it wasn't hers. It was a newer model than the hand-me-down from her dad. Likely Matt's. She was about to put it back under the bed when it started ringing in her hand, classical tones blaring into the sleepy silence of the bedroom. She flipped it open with a little shriek, attempting to turn it off, but instead pushed the Answer button. "Damn it," she swore, fingers fumbling toward Hang Up. Before she could press the button, though, a voice issued from the speaker, frantic and hopeful, "Jenny! Jenny, oh my god, it's Mom! Please don't hang up."

Stunned, Helen did the opposite, staring at the screen as the call ended. For a second, she just blinked at the device in her hand, uncomprehending. Maybe it belonged to a different Jenny? Matt's girlfriend, perhaps? Something told her that despite how common the name Jennifer was, though, this belonged to Jenny Roberts. Plus, the voice on the phone sounded an awful lot like her mom. Hadn't Matt freaked out over her story? Maybe they had been dating. He *did* say Helen reminded him of Jenny before he kissed her. But why did he have her phone when she clearly was not there?

Helen clicked over to texts and into the first string, which was between the phone's owner and a contact labeled *Mama*. There were several recent messages from Mama begging Jenny to call her. To at least let her hear her voice. There were no responses. The thread of increasing, frantic messages from who Helen now knew was Mrs. Roberts soured her stomach—and this time it wasn't the booze.

"Aw, shit," a voice behind her said, again finding Helen where she wasn't supposed to be in a span of less than a few hours. "I knew I should have gotten rid of that... I just couldn't..."

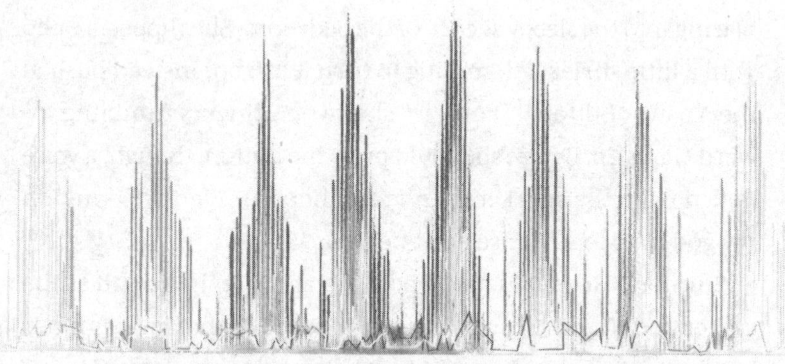

CHAPTER THIRTY-FOUR

Helen Temple pulled on Katie's ponytail as she set a heaping plate of pancakes in front of the girls at their usual booth. The top one had a massive smiley face painted on it with whipped cream and cherries, a visual representation of Helen's good mood.

Natalie wondered what her mother would have drawn if she'd known what her daughter was thinking at present—of trying to interview a wanted fugitive she had made out with a few times about his mother, a suspected murderer. She probably would have just stabbed the pancakes with a knife and let the cherry juice flow. Natalie had decided in the throes of sleep that she would do it. She would go to Jolly Times and see what Kurt had to say. He was the only one—aside from his mom—who knew why Eliza would have hurt Mrs. Halsey, and he could help Natalie finally lay her teacher to rest. But first she'd turn any relevant information over to the police and put Eliza in prison—where she belonged.

"We missed you around here, Katie," Helen said, pouring a generous helping of syrup over the pancake mess. "Hope you've been keeping Natalie out of trouble."

Katie shoved a bite of piping-hot carbohydrates into her mouth and snorted; Natalie kicked her friend under the table and picked up a fork. "Thanks for breakfast, Mom." She reveled in the civility of their conversation while she could, steeling herself for the torrent that would likely rain down on her head whenever her podcast saw the light of day.

Helen smiled and headed back to the kitchen, leaving Katie to snag the last pancake off the plate before Natalie could even finish chewing her first bite. "Your mom seems to have chilled out about the whole podcast thing, huh?" she asked around a swirling mass of pancake. "I can ask my dad not to tell her about that email from Kurt for a few days, if you want. Give her a break from worrying about you?"

Natalie poured another packet of sugar into her coffee and concentrated on getting the right coffee-to-cream ratio. The truth was she hadn't sent the email to Mr. Lugo or the cops, and she didn't intend to. Not right now, at least. Not until she talked to Kurt. She took a sip of coffee and winced. "Nah," she replied after her tongue cooled off. "I'll tell her myself. I'm done messing around."

A slim form slid into the booth, knocking Natalie inward, and she found the business end of a microphone shoved in her face, the phone it was attached to gripped in Jessica Whitestone's manicured hand. "Can you repeat that, please? But put it into context, like 'I'm done messing around with police business. I give up.' That would be perfect." Jessica smiled a red-lipsticked smile and flashed her white, white teeth.

Natalie stared at the little blinking light on the recording app, flummoxed, before regaining her cool. She leaned back in the booth and recited a well-trodden law that was both comforting and completely appropriate at this juncture. "It's illegal to tape someone in Connecticut without their consent."

At the same time, Katie asked, direct as ever, "When did you get hot?"

Jessica clicked off her recorder and leaned her chin on her hand. Natalie noticed that her nails were painted red this time to match her scarlet silk top. "Aw, you two are still friends? That's so sweet. I hardly ever talk to anyone from high school anymore. But, then, I'm just so busy at the station, you know?"

Katie scowled. "So you didn't try to text me the other day? And I didn't viciously ghost you?"

Natalie put down her fork and painted on a smile. "No offense, Jessica, but I already told you I don't want to be interviewed for your creepy podcast. I would suggest you stay and see who else might want to chat, but I'm guessing my mom wouldn't want you bothering people at her place of business."

A smug smile creeping over her face, Jessica made no

move to get up or collect her things. "I'm guessing she also wouldn't be all that pleased to hear that you snuck out after midnight to meet your little boyfriend."

Natalie slumped back down into the booth, her heartbeat increasing. "You've been spying on me?" She hadn't thought anyone had seen her casing the library, but it had been dark. She should have been more careful. She would have to be from now on.

"I can't help it if I like to take late-night walks." Jessica shrugged. "Not my fault that I happened to see you break into the East Ferry Public Library basement and call out Kurt Minnow's name."

"What do you want?" Natalie asked flatly, sweat soaking through her T-shirt despite the AC in the diner. If Jessica was lurking around, how could she ever finish the podcast? Tell Mrs. Halsey's story the way it was meant to be told? Her hands started to buzz with the feeling that precedes a panic attack, and she locked eyes with the woman next to her and grabbed her shoulder—hard. "Why can't you just leave me alone?"

"Because you are the key to this story," Jessica almost growled, removing Natalie's hand from her shoulder and squeezing. "Don't you see that?"

Natalie took a deep breath and shook her head. "I don't know what you mean," she lied. Jessica was just trying to use her like she used everyone else. And she couldn't let that happen. Not again. This was her life. This was so much more than just *her* life.

"Listen," Jessica said, leaning toward Natalie—so close that she could smell the woman's musky perfume. "I don't want to make you look bad or out you or anything. I just want all sides of the story. You know how often you get that with podcasts like this? Never. You get the killer's family or the victim's family, and it all ends up a biased mess. I just want to tell a story that's *true* for once. Something *real*."

Katie laughed loudly, breaking the spell that Jessica was weaving, and the reporter's head snapped up. "What could possibly be funny about anything I just said?" she cried, her fists clenching on the tabletop. She was losing her cool, finally, and Natalie could see a much younger woman through the cracks in her poised facade.

"What's funny," Katie replied, turning her phone around so that Jessica and Natalie could see the screen, "is your boner for the truth. *Executive producer*, my ass. You're an intern. Shouldn't you be making someone coffee somewhere? I'm guessing real-life reporting is not a part of your job description."

Jessica shrugged. "Ever hear of *dress for the job you want*?"

Katie ignored her, smirking at Natalie. "I told you her Facebook profile was sketchy. What's the first rule of journalism, Natty?"

Natalie rolled her eyes, and both she and Katie chorused at once, "If your mother says she loves you, check it out."

Jessica slammed a palm on the table so hard that the syrup jumped. Luckily, the Tarver crew wasn't in yet, or heads would be turning. "So what? I lied. A *little* bit," she hissed. "But this story could make my career. Don't you understand that?" Her hair was coming loose from its polished bun and sticking wetly to her damp forehead.

Natalie knew that being a true-crime writer would

be hard, unbearable at times, but there had to be better methods of reporting than threatening to tattle on confused eighteen-year-olds. Hopefully, this eighteen-year-old would make her career before she reached that level of mania. She thought she would. She couldn't imagine herself so blatantly trying to leech off others. She had to hope she was above that by now. After all that happened.

"I'm sorry," Natalie said. "I told you before that there is no story yet. The jury is still out on what happened." Plus, Jessica couldn't tell it the way she could. She wasn't invested enough: she hadn't been living it for weeks. "That's all I have to say," Natalie said, picking up her purse and shoving past Jessica out of the booth. "Except—" she turned toward the woman in her wilting silk shirt "—don't follow me around anymore, Jessica. Bad things tend to happen around me." Only half of that was bravado; the rest was a sincere warning. Kurt wouldn't hurt her, she didn't think, but Jessica...

"Can I quote you on that?" Jessica yelled at her back as Natalie made her way out of the diner, Katie at her side.

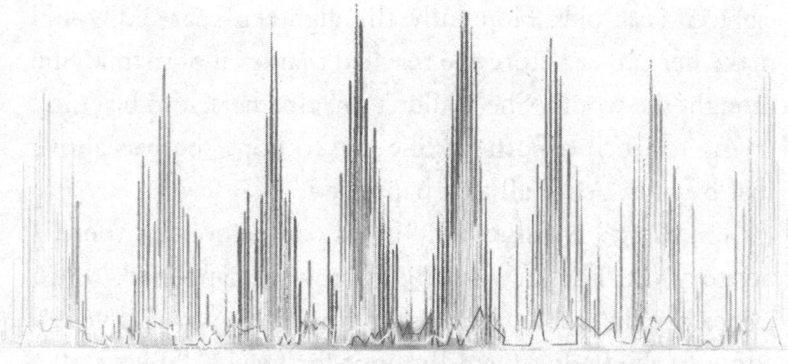

CHAPTER THIRTY-FIVE

Jessica Whitestone wasn't so easily thwarted. There was a small park across the street from the Temple house, complete with a bench facing Natalie's window, and when Natalie peeked through her curtains at around three in the afternoon, Jessica was perched on said bench, her hands folded on her lap. The woman caught her eye and fluttered her fingers, but Natalie just wrenched the curtains closed and collapsed on her bed.

It wouldn't be dark for a while, which is when she planned to sneak out to see Kurt—something that seemed all but impossible with Jessica out there, waiting like a starving buzzard. Stewing, thinking, she started shoving old school papers into the boxes her mother had brought her that morning to move along the cleanup process as college loomed ever nearer. In went crumpled math papers and old English assignments, bio labs, and French essays. She lingered over A papers with a mad nostalgia; it seemed so long ago that getting into school had been her only worry and good grades had been the custom-made key.

The days had crept up on Natalie. With everything that had been going on, she had almost forgotten about school—the classes she had salivated over in the online course catalog, and the intrigue of clubs dedicated to horror-movie viewing and true-crime TV. A cheerful girl named Valerie had sent her an email introducing herself as Natalie's future roommate, but she had yet to answer it. Valerie's message had been all about her summer trip to London with her parents and her love of Jane Austen. What was Natalie supposed to write back? *The Tower of London sounds cool! I was kind of dating the son of an alleged murderer!* Didn't seem smart.

Now, Natalie could only think about six hours into the future, and they seemed like torture. What she needed was a distraction—for her and Jessica both. Wringing her hands, she tried to think of what could possibly draw the would-be reporter away from her post. Jessica was fixated on getting a scoop, she knew, but what could she reasonably give her that wasn't her own head served up on a silver platter? Kurt's mom was still in custody, awaiting a hearing date, and the boy had no friends. But, maybe—the thought came to her, sending her lips curling into a smile—she could furnish one of Kurt's almost-friends as a welcome distraction.

It seemed late enough that Jack would be awake by now, but just in case, Natalie forced herself to rewatch the first episode of *Sharp Objects*, which had become a twisted comfort show for her. She liked the small town it was set in; it reminded her of her own. As she watched, she fumbled for last night's jeans, looking for Kurt's typed letter, but when she shoved her hands into each pocket, she came up empty. Panic gripped her windpipe and squeezed. Her hands shaking, she started tearing through her box of cast-off school papers, surmising that perhaps she had shoved it into the trash with all the rest. Still, after upending the box onto her bedroom carpet, the paper was nowhere to be found.

Surrounded by crumpled detritus, Natalie leaned against her bed, breathing hard, trying to think. Her mother hadn't found it; if she had, she would have been in here screaming her face off, not making her smiley pancakes. Katie wouldn't have been able to keep her mouth shut if she had happened upon a message from Natalie's…whatever Kurt was. Her ex? Was anything about that relationship real? Plus, even if someone did manage to find the paper, how would they know what Kurt was talking about? No one knew about their meetings at Jolly Times.

Natalie took a deep breath and stared at the wreckage around her. She had probably tossed it out with the last round of trash. It was the only answer. Luckily, she had already programmed Kurt's new number into her phone, so could reach him if she needed to. It could all be over tonight. She might finally find out the truth behind Mrs. Halsey's murder.

After throwing all the papers back into their box, Natalie paused her show and called Jack, unable to wait much longer. He picked up after far too many rings, but at least he didn't sound like he had been sleeping.

"Hey, Nat." He drawled. She could hear him take a drag off a cigarette, the noise of the TV blaring in the background.

"Hey, Jack. I gotta ask you for something..." She started, trying to figure out just how to phrase the question before he inevitably got bored and stopped paying attention.

"Yeah? What?" Apparently, that softness that he had shown the night of Jonathan's party had been short-lived.

It was a bad idea to call Jack in the first place. He had always been a creep, always would be. But who else was there? No one. She swallowed. "I want you to distract someone for me."

"Who, what, where, when, and how much?" Jack rattled off, taking another audible drag.

Natalie rolled her eyes. "She's a reporter. On my ass all day wanting to know about Kurt. Can you just come over here and talk to her so she'll leave me alone? She's sitting on a bench across the street. Tell her what it was like living with him or whatever. Maybe feed her a few extravagant lies?"

"I do like extravagant lies," Jack mused. "How much?"

"I dunno. Twenty dollars?"

"Make it thirty dollars, and we're in business," Jack shot back.

"Whatever, thirty. I'll Venmo you," Natalie replied. "But don't hit on her. We want her to actually *want* to talk to you. And this goes without saying, but don't tell Katie."

"Wouldn't dream of it," Jack said solemnly. "You know, Nat, I always liked you. I always felt like we could be best friends, you know? Why aren't we? What went wrong?"

Natalie swallowed a frustrated scream. "Just get here at, like, eight, Jack. Bye." She hung up, tossing her phone on the bed. There were still four hours to go until she was rid of Jessica, and a quick peek out the window confirmed that her vigil was still going strong.

The hours dragged by, but night came soon enough—and by the time it did, Natalie was starting to have second thoughts. Maybe it would be wiser to call the police, let them deal with it. But wasn't this what being a journalist was? Chasing down leads? Talking to unsavory characters? At least, in this case, she knew that the character in question wanted to talk, that he had relevant information.

She paced the room, trying on and discarding shirts as she went. She wasn't all that worried about what she looked like; it was just that nothing felt comfortable. She settled on a black tank top that scooped away from her neck—one that didn't feel like it was strangling her—and then she put on the mace-filled necklace her mom had given her. Just in case.

She flipped open the curtain to see that Jessica was no longer alone; Jack was perched on the bench next to her in his ripped-to-hell jeans and Metallica T-shirt, leaning forward to talk into her mic while not so subtly staring down her shirt. Jessica was listening raptly, nodding her head so hard her glossy hair had come loose from its bun. It was now or never. Pulling her curtains closed, she dashed to the other window, the one facing her own wild backyard, shimmied across the roof, and dropped to the soft grass below. (Luckily, her mom had made her practice this exit numerous times in case of an intruder.) The yard abutted a row of houses, but they were vacation homes, time-shares rented out by rich

New Yorkers who spent their weekends at Ferry's beaches. It was a weekday, though, so the houses were all dark; only the really rich New Yorkers stayed the whole summer, and those houses were in the classier part of Ferry. The streetlights illuminated the road somewhat, but there were more than enough shadows for someone to hide in.

Natalie's bike was in the garage, so she didn't risk grabbing it, instead opting to pass through a neighboring yard to skirt the woods that ringed the town—the same woods where teens partied and women disappeared. The living and the dead. It was a longer trip without her bike, but once she hit the road, making sure to stick to the shadows, it was easier going than whacking her way through brambles and vines. As she looked into the windows of homes she passed, she saw a TV glowing in each one, families tucked away in the bowels of the beast, luxuriating in AC and after-dinner beers and drama that stayed safely within a screen. She felt a bit out of time. Like she was a visitor from the past exploring an unfamiliar future. Then the Victorian came into view, and she crashed back into the present, growing chill in the summer night when she remembered Jonathan splayed on the basement floor. She clutched her mace necklace, suddenly feeling terribly bare, vulnerable and exposed. The blank eyes of the broken windows seemed to watch her as she passed by. She held her breath like she was six and driving by a graveyard.

Her sneakers slapped the pavement with a kind of lonely sound and, up ahead, Jolly Times swam into view, broken picture windows glinting in the streetlights and faded lettering hanging crooked. A surge of half-remembered carnival music swam into her brain, and she wondered, idly, why they even used that kind of music nowadays, when it seemed to be intrinsically tied to horror movies. Maybe because delight and horror are so closely melded when we're young. How else would you explain roller coasters and rides that replicated plunging to one's death?

Hiding in the shadows so as not to attract the attention of passing cars, Natalie slunk around to the front of Jolly Times, creeping across the cracked asphalt of the trailer park's parking lot. "He might not even be here," she muttered to herself, not entirely sure whether she wanted that to be true or not.

The main door to Jolly Times was closed, but when Natalie pulled on the handle it crunched forward on filthy hinges that protested with a sound like wailing cats in heat. She cringed at the din and paused a moment on the threshold. Inside, it was darker than dark. In the gloom, she could make out shapes she could only identify by memory: Big Bertha, the dunk tank, the fractured carousel. She hovered in the doorway, waiting for her eyes to adjust somewhat, then took a tentative step inside. It was sweltering, and a smell of decay pervaded the space, an odor she hadn't noticed during that lazy afternoon with Kurt.

"Hello…" she said softly, shuffling into the dilapidated fun center. "Kurt? Are you there?" Her eyes struggled to pick out anything in the darkness and failed, and a kind of wild terror rose in her throat. "Kurt," she croaked, but before she could say anything else, a chilly hand sealed her mouth, muffling a shriek.

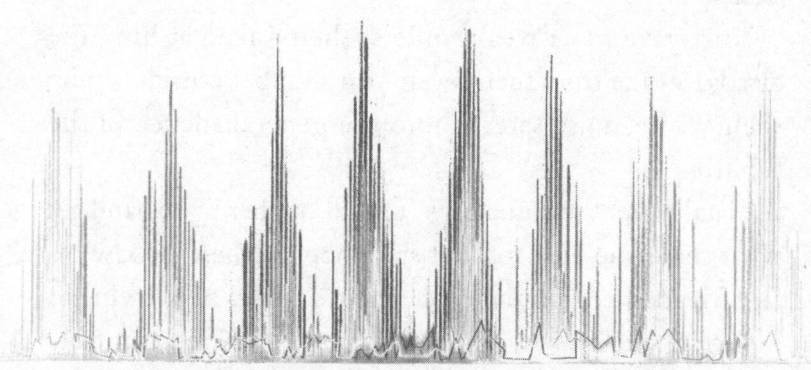

CHAPTER THIRTY-SIX

"Natalie, stop," a voice hissed close to her ear, and then cold lips brushed her cheek. "It's me. I just didn't want you to keep calling my name." She tasted grit on her lips from the hand that had clapped over her mouth and reached up to rub it away.

The black spots cleared from her eyes gradually, and she saw Kurt standing in front of her, his blond head cocked to the side. He was clutching a small penlight so that Natalie could make out his features, his eyes hollow in his white face. Even in the dark she could see that he was worn-out. And it didn't matter how little of him she could see, she could certainly *smell* him. The musk of boy had intensified to the stink of man—man that hadn't washed in quite a while. Natalie got to her feet, partly just to escape that stench.

Kurt gave her a weak smile as she blinked at him, the cicadas awake from their seven-year slumber outside, doing their white-noise scream into the general silence of the suburbs.

Natalie went to smile back, to pull out her phone and get what she came here for, but she stopped when she saw his face, the desperation there. She moved back a step, trying to put some steel in her voice. She'd never fully felt comfortable around Kurt, but now she felt straight-up itchy. "So…" She coughed. "I came. What did you want to tell me?"

"I'm so happy you did. I mean, I knew you would, but I'm just so glad," Kurt babbled, ignoring her words and putting a hand on her shoulder. He did smell, but there was something else. He vibrated with a cold mania—an intensity that she had noticed before and found herself drawn to, now distorted and full of sharp edges. His ragged nails cut into her bare shoulder, and she winced.

"I guess I could have called you or something, but I wasn't sure if the cops were tracking all that. Plus, I just really wanted to hear you say it in person." Kurt moved another step closer, his hand curling in her hair, his eyes unfocusing. His black jeans were covered in dirt, and he was wearing the old-man loafers again, but now one of the soles flopped away from the toe like it was screaming.

Natalie pulled away from him slightly, eyeing the door. Alarm bells were ringing in her head. Kurt was thinner, his smile tight and strange. He looked a little like Ted Bundy after he escaped from prison for the first time and hid in the mountains of Colorado: bone-thin, handsome, embarrassed, and affable—and not a little insane.

"What did you want to talk about, Kurt? You said you were going to tell me what happened. With Mrs. Halsey," Natalie pressed. Despite his appearance, despite his mania, she still wanted to know what he knew. She just had to make sure he remained calm enough to tell her. Still, she fingered the mace necklace around her neck as she asked, her voice tentative.

"I came to hear your apology." Kurt cocked his head to the side and wrinkled his brow. "Your apology for kissing that guy. I was mad for a minute there, sure, but I really missed you, Nat." In the dark, Kurt's voice came soft and low and full of need. His hand went toward hers, and she shifted away. He had hit Jonathan with those hands. She didn't want them on her if she could help it. He frowned. "Why won't you let me touch you?"

"Because you beat up my friend," Natalie said, folding her arms over her chest. She tried to keep her voice level, to grab control of the conversation. Apparently that worked, because Kurt groaned and dragged a hand through his hair.

"I told you, it was an accident. I didn't mean to do it. I just saw him with you and..." He groaned again, this time a deeper and more guttural sound, bordering on animal.

"And what? What happened?" Natalie asked, taking another step backward and curling her fingers tighter around the mace necklace. She hoped she wouldn't need to use it, but having it on hand was comforting.

"Look," Kurt said, hands fisted at his sides. "I know you were pissed because I wasn't returning your texts. That you were trying to make me jealous. But my dad had just *died*. I thought you would *understand*. Instead you went and hooked up with someone else."

Natalie stilled, goose pimples rising on her skin. "What are you talking about? I thought you didn't talk to your dad anymore…" she said in a voice just above a whisper.

"Not that loser. My *dad*. The real one." Spittle misted Natalie's face. "Don't pretend you don't know. You found him. Where she fell. All of Ferry knows that, even the bad side."

Natalie's legs froze like they do in those dreams where you don't remember how to walk correctly. Kurt looked even more like a stranger now than he had when she met him. Who was this boy? What had he done?

"What are you talking about, Kurt? You're scaring me…" She stared at his old-man shoes, the ones he said his father had given him, and a horrible idea started blooming in her mind like a corpse flower. "Are you saying Mr. Halsey was your father?" Natalie asked, eyes still trained on his shoes. Mr. Halsey's shoes. There had been one print at the scene of Mrs. Halsey's death. Mr. Halsey's. Or had there been? Had he given Kurt an old pair? They looked a lot like the ones Mr. Halsey was wearing in the gym that day at his wife's memorial. The kind he always wore. There had been a boy standing behind him that day, she remembered suddenly. A blond boy she didn't recognize—at least not yet.

"He could have been. Not by blood, sure, he could have been," Kurt said fuming, starting to pace. "He practically was. And then he went and did *that*. He left me alone. Just like everyone else."

Natalie's hand rose to her necklace again. She knew she should run. That would be the smart thing to do. But she had to know. "Kurt…did you have something to do with Mrs. Halsey's death?"

"It doesn't matter now. Nothing matters," Kurt said, turning his blue eyes on her, electric and pleading. "Leave town with me, Nat. Please. I have a car. We can just leave. You're the only one I trust, the only one I care about. Everyone else just…lies."

"Please tell me, Kurt," she asked, ignoring his insane plea. "Please."

Kurt's face crumpled. "It was an accident…" he almost whispered. "I just wanted to scare her… To show her how it feels." He was weeping now, which was more terrifying somehow. He looked at her, his eyes full, tears cutting tracks down his dirty face. "Please don't leave, too, Natalie… I need you."

Natalie's hands started shaking, and she felt sick. He had done it. This boy who she had laughed with, who she had kissed. He had killed her teacher, her friend. She felt like screaming, but she swallowed instead, trying to keep her voice steady. "What do you mean, an accident? What did you do, Kurt?" She backed away slowly, tensing to run, to start screaming for her mother—even though she knew Helen wouldn't be able to hear her across town.

Kurt slumped to the floor like his bones had leaked out of his body and leaned against the rotting wall. "I didn't mean for her to die. I just wanted to scare her. Grab her, tie her up, drive her around a little so she'd freak. But she was so scared…" Tears dripped down his face, mingling with snot. Natalie looked on aghast as the boy unraveled. "She fell," he said in a small voice. "She fell, and I ran away. I didn't know what else to do."

"Why?" The word wrenched itself from Natalie's mouth as she watched Kurt weep. "Why would you do that? What did she ever do to you?" Tears started pouring down Natalie's face, and her stomach churned at the thought of him touching her all those times before. "Why?" she asked again, her voice wretched. She'd never understood women who were in love with serial killers before, and now she understood them even less. Knowing Kurt had touched her made her want to tear her skin off.

"Revenge," Kurt said finally, softly, studying his linked hands, the tears starting to abate. The cicadas sounded almost human in the darkness, their screams more frantic than before.

Anger blazed in Natalie's chest as she stared at Kurt's profile in the dark. Anger and confusion and sorrow. "For what?" she choked out. "What did Mrs. Halsey ever do to you?" she repeated.

Kurt shook his head, looking up at her. In the half light he looked like a beast from the forest, shoulders broad and heaving, hair a mess of snarls. "No. Not her. Revenge against you."

Natalie stilled, even though her whole body told her to run. He wasn't making sense. She hadn't even met Kurt yet when Mrs. Halsey died. Was he insane? Was this boy truly unhinged? The cicada scream was a warning now, as if nature itself was telling her to flee.

"Then I realized—too late—that you didn't know. What

your family did to mine. Because she lied to you," Kurt said, getting up and walking toward her slowly, wearily, like a much older man. "And I realized how alike we are. That no one cares about us. Everyone always puts themselves first. Which is why you need to leave with me. Now." He extended a hand that Natalie shrank from, her fingers going again to the necklace around her neck. Her pointer finger hovered over the lid.

"I don't understand a word you're saying," she said, her voice shaking. Curiosity was the only thing keeping her from fleeing the room. Curiosity and fear that she was about to hear something that would change her life forever, that would ruin her.

"Your mom," Kurt said, his eyes blazing into hers. "She's lied to you your whole life. Never told you about why she really left college. Where her money came from. Who your *dad* is."

"I don't understand," Natalie nearly whispered. Helen left school to take care of her dad when his cancer got bad. Her money came after he died, an insurance payout. And her father—well, that was a mystery. And it was the only thing keeping her from macing Kurt right then and there.

"Your mom knew my aunt in college," Kurt said, his voice almost kind—as if he hated to break the news. "My aunt was killed, and your mom wrote a story about it for the school paper. Turned into national news. They even made a movie. Some piece of shit called *Teacher's Pet*," he spat. "My family fell apart, and your mom lived off our bones. Don't tell me she didn't sell her life rights for a hefty sum. Heather Baker—" he made air quotes "—was definitely the star of that movie." Kurt was almost spitting now, his eyes unfocused and manic. "Not that you knew anything about that," he added almost apologetically. "I started to realize how little you knew the first time I met you. How much she'd lied. You didn't even recognize the name I put on your ID."

Natalie's knees went all liquid. *Teacher's Pet.* A piece of pure early-thousands trash—and the movie her mom had flipped out at her for watching that night with Katie. The movie that led to her fallout with Mrs. Halsey. It was about a teen reporter who discovered that her classmate was killed by their TA—her body buried under a planter in his backyard. The girl's name was Heather Baker—the same last name Kurt had put on her fake ID.

"I need you to know," Kurt was saying, holding her limp hands in his. She hadn't even realized he was touching her. She was numb, too many thoughts swirling through her head. Her mom had solved a murder? Kurt's family was involved? "I didn't know you when what happened with Mrs. Halsey happened. Not like I do now. I was mad. I was mad for so many years that your mom's life flourished while my family decayed. I found your grandfather's obituary, saw your names. I had them set as a Google alert for years until there was some article in the paper about a contest you won...and there was this picture of you and Mrs. Halsey. You looked so happy. Proud. You had the life I should have had. The family, the future. I stalked you online, and when I found that podcast...it seemed like you were just like her, your mom. The same. A vulture. You called Mrs. Halsey your mentor in one episode, and I just...

I was so angry. Luckily, your best friend's cousin was looking for a roommate." He took a deep breath, his grip on her hands tightening. She was too frozen to wrest her fingers away. "So I wanted you to understand, okay? I wanted you to feel what it was like for someone you cared about to be hurt. When I met Bill I got distracted, though; I thought maybe he'd be enough—that I wouldn't need to hurt you. Then you and Mrs. Halsey had that falling out, and that's all they could talk about. Then your mom started coming around, asking how to connect with you, and I just…lost it. You had everything, and I had nothing, even then. So I decided it was time. Enough hanging out with Bill and forgetting why I came here in the first place. I had to do something to get your attention. I thought if I scared her a little, you would both learn your lesson and stop fucking around with people's lives…"

"My mom…what?" Natalie asked, the facts failing to resolve into something linear in her head. "My mom was there?"

Kurt snorted. "Yeah, she used to come by all the time after work, begging for Mrs. Halsey's help. It really pissed me off at the time, because I'd always have to turn around and go back to the trailer when I saw her coming. But I guess the kid across the street noticed and told the cops, which was just an added bonus for me, to be honest."

The woman in black with the dark hair who Mrs. Tarver's daughter kept seeing at the Halseys'. Her mom, not his. He had let his own mother get arrested to save his skin. A tremor started moving through Natalie's legs, unfreezing them and traveling through her limbs like fire. Anger. Yes, perhaps at times she had relished true crime a bit too much. And, yes, maybe the podcast idea had gotten out of hand. But Kurt wasn't a god. And he didn't get to mete out justice like one. "So you moved here to, what? Torture me?" she asked in a low voice simmering with rage.

Kurt didn't seem to notice the anger in her voice, the way her fingers had tightened in his like claws. "I moved here because I wanted to see who you were, yes. And because my future was such a fucking blank that I had to get out of Illinois. Mom came with me because she's fucking hopeless on her own. I've had to take care of her since I was a kid."

Natalie realized then that their one podcast listener from Mount Carroll, Illinois, did indeed exist. That he was standing right in front of her. "And Mr. Halsey? How did he fit into your plan?" Sarcasm laced Natalie's voice like acid. His blood was on Kurt's hands, too—even if he had killed himself.

Kurt dropped her hands as if agitated and dragged a hand through his hair, making it even wilder. "My mom did date Ron. He took us to that Halloween party at their house last year. I mostly went because I knew you were going to be there." Natalie shuddered. "I didn't know anyone, so I just kind of hung out in the living room, and I met Bill. He showed me some history books, talked to me. My mom never did anything with him. They got that wrong. But he did let me hang out. He helped me." Tears started coursing down his cheeks again. "He was a good guy, the only good guy I've known."

"So you killed his wife?" Natalie spat. "That's how you thanked him?"

"I told you that was an accident." Kurt wheeled on her, hands in fists now. Natalie took a big step back and pressed her back to the wall.

"Were you really so mad at a story, at a movie, that you allowed that to happen?" Natalie gasped. "Was it really that important to you?"

"Do you really not know who your father is?" Kurt countered, laughing humorlessly. "Even now? Don't you understand what he did to my family?"

Natalie started to shake her head, but a scene from *Teacher's Pet* flitted through her head then. Heather Baker. In bed with the TA. Right before she found the missing girl's phone. Her whole body went cold, and she watched as Kurt watched her, saw the realization kick in.

"Your dad is a murderer," Kurt said, trying for gentle and failing. He sounded gleeful, almost.

Just then, the door behind Natalie burst open, the flashing lights of a police cruiser framing a trio of cops, closely followed by Helen, bathrobe swirling around her feet like the cloak of an avenging angel. "That movie was bullshit," she snarled. "Now, put your hands where I can see them, and get on the floor."

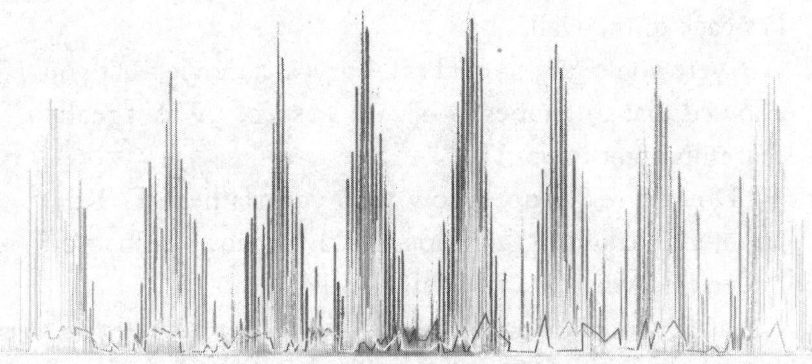

CHAPTER THIRTY-SEVEN

The sun was just beginning to paint the sky pink when the police finally left Natalie and Helen alone, wrung-out and wired at the kitchen table. Wordlessly, Helen poured one very big and one very, very small glass of whiskey and placed them on the glossy red lacquer. "You probably have a lot of questions," she said after taking a giant swig of her drink.

Natalie studied the glass of liquor in front of her and took a tiny, burning sip before twisting her face into a grimace of disgust and pushing it away. "I mean… I'm not sure where to start, but yeah." She was sure the shock of the evening would set in soon, but now she felt eerily calm, like she was seeing everything in greater detail, sharper relief. She saw the grief chiseled into the fine lines on her mother's face, the slight gray at her temples. The way she watched Natalie hungrily, as if checking that her limbs were all accounted for.

"The beginning is always a good place," Helen said, folding her hands on the table in front of her and taking a deep breath. And so she began, telling Natalie about sitting next to Jenny in class, about her joy over her sister's baby—who she now realized was Kurt. About how she interviewed Mrs. Roberts without her permission and got fired from the paper. About the party and finding Jenny's phone. How she realized that Jenny had never left the campus—never left Matt's yard.

"And he just let you call the cops?" Natalie asked, eyes wide. Helen had just reached the part about Matt discovering her with the phone, how he confessed to her that he hadn't meant to do it. That they had been fooling around and, drunk, Jenny had fallen and cracked her head against his nightstand. How he had buried her in the yard and had the planter installed the next day. Gave the cops a fake tip that Jenny was cheating with her brother-in-law to throw them off the trail.

Helen shrugged even as her daughter studied her, awe writ plain across her face. "He wasn't exactly in the clearest state of mind, but I tried to level with him. I told him that if he killed me and got away with it—if he put in a new planter—his whole life would be ruined, anyway. He would have to just live with this secret. Stay in the house so no one ever dug up the backyard. It would become his reason for existing."

Natalie nodded. That all made sense to her. There was a podcast she loved about a missing college student from California, Kristin Smart, whose disappearance was pretty similar. The case was still open, but the podcast put forward the theory that her classmate had killed her, perhaps accidentally, and his life had just become dedicated to making sure she stayed missing. Prison was bad, sure, but that seemed like its own kind of prison.

"And before you ask," Helen said, finishing her drink, "Matt Hunter is not your father. I didn't sleep with him. That stupid movie took a lot of liberties, and I really should have sued, but I didn't want my name in the papers again."

"Then, who is?" Natalie asked, trying to keep up with the many different versions of her mom kaleidoscoping in front of her. The woman who had wanted to be a writer, too. Who had given up that dream when she became the story. Who had changed her life to escape it.

Helen sighed. "That's a much less dramatic story, really. He was just a boy I dated who didn't want to date me anymore. When I found out about you, I also found out that he had started dating someone else, so I didn't really feel the need to bring him into our lives." She reached across the table and grabbed Natalie's hand. "I can give you his name if you want, though. I probably shouldn't have kept it from you for so long, but you never were his, really. You were always just my girl."

Natalie unexpectedly felt her eyes fill with tears. She'd never really understood why anyone would cry with happiness, and she wasn't exactly happy. She was mad at her mom for lying for so many years but also kind of impressed.

Helen had caught a murderer, had a child at nineteen on her own and saved her from a troubled boy. "I wish you had told me all this before, Mom," she said with a sigh.

Helen nodded. "I kept wanting to. Especially when you started getting into all that true-crime nonsense. It can be fun and interesting and thrilling and all that, true, but it can also be so dangerous." Her voice caught, and Natalie squeezed her mom's hand. "And I know what that boy said, but you have to know I never profited off any of this. I wouldn't have taken money if they had offered it to me. That's why I went home, why I quit school. To help Dad, but also to just figure myself out. What kind of person I wanted to be."

"Do you miss it?" Natalie asked, watching the sun slide above the horizon and cast the late-summer morning in red and gold. "Writing?"

Helen nodded. "Yeah, I do." She watched the sun for a moment with her daughter, then turned to Natalie with a tired smile. "I'll go back to it again one day, though. When I figure out what story I have to tell."

CHAPTER THIRTY-EIGHT: THEN

Helen trudged down the steep hill where her dad lived to the CVS near downtown, her boots growing icy and damp from the rapidly melting snow that had dumped on Connecticut a few days earlier. She'd been walking a lot lately, aimlessly—to the farm down the road with its bounty of tiny horses and chickens and donkeys, down to the water where the high-school crew team rowed, despite the face-freezing temperatures. When she was walking, it was easier not to think, blaring the Strokes on her headphones so loud it felt like she was in her own music video—a painfully normal, suburban one, but still. She'd been home for a week, and her dad had made it his number-one job to entertain her, serving up heavy breakfasts of eggs and bacon every morning, planning hikes at the nearby nature center, and queuing up bad superhero films every night. It felt like she was in middle school again, safe in the familial cocoon, and she intended to stay there for as long as possible: thinking too much about Matt and Jenny and the rest broke her brain. She hadn't looked at the news, and her dad studiously hid the paper from her. It was much easier to pretend the world outside had stopped on its axis. But this morning, her dad had woken up with a cough that racked his chest and roused her, even from down the hall.

He'd been coughing for a week now—maybe longer—and she'd been urging him to see a doctor, but he'd waved off her concerns. Why was it that doctors were also the most resistant to seek treatment themselves? When she insisted on at least getting him medicine, he'd protested mightily until he started coughing so hard he'd had to sit down, winded, in his well-worn leather recliner. She'd left him watching *Antiques Roadshow* in his pajamas, and her heart hurt a little to see her big, usually grinning father look so small.

Helen pulled her hoodie over her messy hair as the automatic doors to CVS whooshed open. A lot of kids from her high school worked at local businesses like this, and the last thing she needed was one of them asking why she was home. Also, she had something much more sensitive on her list than just cough syrup—something that had kept her from fully losing herself in her daily walks and family time. The store was already blaring Christmas music, even though it was way too early and the shelves burst with ribbons and fake trees and jolly dancing Santas that bleated tinny holiday songs seemingly on loop. She ducked down the medicine aisle and grabbed a bottle of the most expensive cough syrup—seemed like a safe bet—then approached an aisle ambiguously labeled *Family Planning*, looking over her shoulder as she went.

She'd always thought that was a weird designation for condoms and lube and whatnot, as if the only reason to have sex was to plan for a family. She wasn't here to buy any of that, though. Instead, she was stuck staring down shelves and shelves of pink and blue boxes with promises like *Instant Results!* and *The Most Accurate Choice!* Well, she did want accuracy—and she wanted it fast. She grabbed the one with the most accolades and hurried toward the front of the store, grabbing a few random items as she went, as if a bag of chocolates and some dental floss would obscure the fact that she was purchasing a pregnancy test. Her heart thumped hard in her chest, and her hands started to shake as she reached the checkout counter, then calmed slightly when she saw that the woman manning the register was older, maybe in her fifties, and not one of her former classmates. She really didn't need it getting around town that Helen Temple, top of her class and daughter of the illustrious Dr. Mark Temple, was quite possibly knocked up. She hadn't even managed to fully dissect the implications herself—it seemed too impossible.

She kept her eyes down as she dumped her purchases in front of the woman, Rhonda, according to her name tag. The register was flanked by the kind of tabloid magazines she'd usually ignore, but it seemed wiser to scan the headlines now than watch Rhonda's face as she rang up the test. It took her a second to register what, exactly, she was reading, and when the words finally resolved themselves in front of her eyes, she clutched the counter, weak. "Sexy Slain Co-Ed's Roommate Speaks!" "Matt the Hunter: The Killer TA," and finally, her face, an old high-school photo smiling from the front of a shiny, cheap paper with "Did This Student Sleuth Sleep with the Enemy?"

Her mouth fell open, her hands went cold. She had assumed

Jenny's murder would make the news—which is why she had been avoiding it—but *this*? And why was her face on the front of a magazine that usually bleated about pop stars cheating on their husbands? The words blurred before her eyes, but not before she saw something about Hollywood courting the editor of the college paper, a tiny headshot of Sam grinning in one of his stupid ties flanking the text. Most of the magazines, though, promised stories about Jenny and her "sexy college exploits," complete with photos of her looking sultry in tank tops and bathing suits—a.k.a. the kind of photo every teen girl alive had taken once or twice. It was horrible. It was worse than horrible. Helen's heart wrenched for Jenny's mom and sister as she spotted them in another tiny photo, hiding from the camera next to the text "Slaughtered Sorority Sister's Sis Stays Silent."

Shaking, she shoved some twenties at Rhonda and grabbed her bag, running out the door and up the hill as fast as she could in the ice and the snow. It was decided. She wasn't going back to that school. She couldn't. She would stay here, make sure her father took his medicine and try to atone the best she could for the damage she'd done to that family. She still hadn't figured out what she would do if the test in her bag came back positive, but she promised then and there that if it did, she would protect whoever was growing inside her fiercely, wholly, forever.

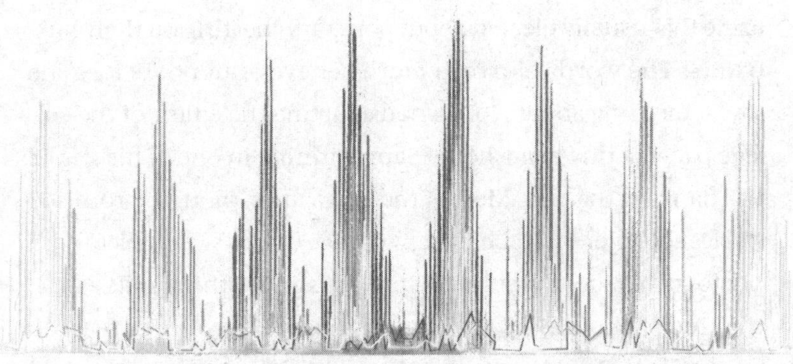

CHAPTER THIRTY-NINE

Natalie used to like graveyards—before she properly knew what they were for. They were quiet and well-manicured, and the tombstones boasted intricate carvings and pretty stone angels. Plus, the East Ferry cemetery was by the sea, so the waves added to the general serenity.

When she was around eight years old, she and her mom were walking around the perimeter when Natalie found a robin's egg, blue and hollow and perfect.

"An egg, Mom!" Natalie had proclaimed, holding the object up for inspection. "I'm going to bring it home and wait for it to hatch." She cradled the egg in her hands, trying to keep it safe from the cold ocean breeze.

Helen had looked down at her, a sad smile on her face

that Natalie could still remember to this day. She never could lie to her daughter. "That one's not going to hatch, honey. The bird inside is gone now. It died."

That was the first time that Natalie truly understood what death meant, and she cried all the way home—after insisting on holding a tiny funeral for the egg, which they buried under the pristine turf of the graveyard. After she and her mother had muddied their hands making the grave, they had stared out at the ocean and whispered goodbye.

More than ten years later, and Natalie was still grappling with the concept of death in that same cemetery: the whole town had gathered to say goodbye to the Halseys. The Ferry Fantasias turned out in force, but thankfully, they were not there to sing. Lucy Erickson stood in the middle of the sobbing throng of sopranos, eyes hollow and damp, lost in a cloud of hair and sweet perfume. Jonathan was beside her; all the grief and drama that had unfolded that summer had brought them back together in the end.

It brought all of Ferry together. Mr. Sprouse, and the yoga teacher, and all the ladies from the Garden Club. The other waitresses at the diner, and all the kids that had been at the party that night on Sycamore, strung out with the nervous energy that precedes leaving for college for the first time. Ron K. Stackman was even there, holding a bouquet of roses in his big hand, his hair slicked back, looking dapper in his black suit.

Mr. Halsey's fellow teachers stood at the front of the assembly, together placing roses on Bill's and Lynn's graves. Bill's, especially, was drowning in blooms, as if the citizens of Ferry thought they could repent for their cruelty during the remainder of his life by buying out the floral department of the ShopRite. Helen Temple stood beside the couple's remaining family, always the kind ambassador.

Despite her mother's presence at the front of the crowd, Natalie stood in the back with Katie, who was wearing a black dress for the second time that summer. This one was old and dated with puffed sleeves and a high neck—it likely belonged to her mom—but Natalie thought she looked older. Nice. She would never tell Katie that, though: she knew better. Still, as she stared at her mother, supporting the Halseys' only living kin, Natalie felt Katie's arm loop through hers and leaned her head on her friend's shoulder. Sandy Tarver and a few other ladies had been shooting Natalie dark looks over their shoulders, and she knew that they blamed her, at least partially, for all that had happened. It didn't matter to them that, in the end, she had actually helped crack the case.

Natalie blamed herself a bit, too, she supposed, but mostly she just blamed Kurt. Kurt, who had tried to call her so many times from prison that she had requested that her mother get her a new number.

"I'm not going to apologize, you know," Katie whispered into her friend's ear. "Never in a thousand years." Her voice was wreathed with a whiff of her old bravado, but mostly she just sounded tired and sad.

Natalie wrapped her hand around Katie's. "What would you have to apologize for?" she asked, watching.

"I found that creepy note Kurt sent you," she said, shuddering. "I wasn't sure I was going to tell your mom or anyone about it, but that tracker I put on your phone that night you went to the library? I set it to alert me if you went near the trailer park. I called your mom that night when you… when the cops arrested him," Katie finished, her voice thick with emotion. She grunted as if to dispel any heavy feelings. "Not that any sane person would be mad at me, given the outcome. But, you know, you get mad about dumb stuff, so I thought I'd put that out there."

Natalie was happy to hear that Katie was still Katie, even in the face of tragedy.

Sandy Tarver shot a poison look over her shoulder, all raised eyebrows and cat's-ass mouth. Katie flashed her an extremely unsubtle middle finger, and Natalie slapped in down. "You can't do that in a cemetery, Katie," Natalie protested through giggles.

"I can, and I will. She's a nosy bitch," Katie whispered. "Anyway, for real, are you mad? That I snooped?" She actually looked worried.

Natalie slung her arm around her friend. Anger was the last thing on her mind. She was too filled with love, with affection for her strange, protective friend. "No, I'm impressed, yet again, by your creepy techie skills."

"Good," Katie said. "Because it sucked when we weren't friends anymore."

"Yeah, it sucked," Natalie agreed, hugging her friend close as everyone started shuffling out of the cemetery to their cars. "You go ahead. I'll meet you at the diner with everyone else."

There was going to be a wake at her mom's place; she and Helen had been cooking all morning, periodically answering the door to usher in endless casseroles from well-meaning Ferry residents.

After Katie said her goodbyes, Natalie approached the Halseys' twin graves, near the towering marble angels and the mausoleums with their metal gates. The ocean crashed against the shore on the other side of the graveyard gate, and Natalie could smell salt in the air. It was a lovely day. A lovely, sad day.

In the shade of a particularly impressive tomb lay Mr. and Mrs. Halsey, side by side under a pair of simple granite markers. Natalie sat on the ground between the gravestones and listened to the silence of the churchyard, the calling of the gulls, and the buzz of the cicadas in the trees.

"I'm sorry I didn't come sooner," she said, feeling a little silly to be talking out loud to people who couldn't hear her. Still, she continued—she needed to. "I should have. I should have come and said thank you, Mrs. Halsey, for being a good teacher and a good person. I should have said I was sorry, Mr. Halsey. You were always nice to me." She paused, tears burning her eyes. "I'm sorry to you both. I should have remembered that you're people, real people. I should have remembered that."

Someone plopped next to Natalie in the grass and sighed, and the girl looked over at her new companion with a start. "That's nice," Eliza Minnow said, staring at the tombstones. "That's really nice." She sounded like she meant it.

Natalie blinked, wiping tears away with shaking hands. "What are you doing here?" she asked, not unkindly. Eliza had lost someone, too—more than one someone.

Eliza shrugged. "I came to pay my respects, but it didn't seem right to stand with the rest. I saw you in the back. Guess you felt the same?"

Natalie nodded. "Yeah, there are some people who aren't happy with me right now..."

"Because of my son," Eliza said, leveling her blue eyes with Natalie's. "It's okay. You can say it. I know what he did to them. To you."

Natalie looked down at her linked hands. "Yeah," she muttered. She picked up a daisy that had escaped from an arrangement on Mrs. Halsey's grave and spun it around in her fingers. It didn't seem right to speak poorly of someone to their mother. Even if they deserved it.

"My idiot son." Eliza smiled wryly. "He dragged you into his bullshit. You didn't deserve that. You're a nice girl."

"I don't know about that." Natalie laughed without humor. "I get too wrapped up sometimes. I make judgments."

"Sounds to me like you're a teenager." Eliza smiled. She gestured toward Mr. Halsey's grave, and her eyes took on a teary sheen. "Did you know Bill at all?"

Natalie thought of the man in the blue convertible and shook her head. She hadn't known him. Not really.

"He was a good man," Eliza said, staring at his name etched in stone. "He really helped Kurt a lot. As much as Kurt could be helped. I take some of the blame there, I guess. Since my sister died... I wasn't there. For a long time. And his dad, David, was just useless. Kurt didn't even want to share his name. Things were better for a while when we moved here. It was his idea. All that corn was driving us crazy, he said. We needed to see the ocean. I guess I was wrong, though." She paused, picking up her own daisy and tying the stem into a knot, considering, eyes distant. "Maybe I'll take most of the blame, then," she amended.

Natalie frowned, listening to the hum of cars leaving the cemetery, that night after the party filtering through her head. "I don't think it's your fault," she said softly. "I mean, I don't know the whole story or anything, but my mom told me something the other day that I keep thinking about… That what you do matters, not the excuses you have for doing it. Kurt may not have meant to hurt Mrs. Halsey, but he decided to lie. To let you and Mr. Halsey take the heat. And everything fell apart from there."

Eliza nodded. "I'd like to believe that. Maybe I could someday." She twisted the flower into a ring, staring at the graves for a few moments before abruptly digging in her purse. "You mentioned you mom, so I thought you might want to see this…" She pulled out a wrinkled piece of newsprint that looked well-read to Natalie's trained paper-scanning eye. Eliza smoothed it out carefully, then handed it to Natalie.

Natalie's fingers shook as she took in the byline, *Helen Temple*. It was the story her mother had written about Jenny's disappearance. All the memories Mrs. Roberts had unwittingly shared with her.

Eliza watched as Natalie read through the story, her eyes filling with tears even though she hadn't known Jenny. The words her mother had written made her feel like she did, though. "We were so mad at this story, because of how your mom tricked my mother, but I secretly always loved it. Every time I read it I could see Jenny again, kind of. It was the only story that was about *her* instead of *him*," Eliza said.

When Natalie looked back at the woman, tears were dripping down Eliza's face. "The only thing she got wrong in there is my name." She pointed to where *Constance* reportedly hadn't been available for comment. "That's my middle name. Thanks, Mom. And of course I changed my last after…everything." She gave a crooked smile that looked so much like Kurt's that Natalie's stomach lurched.

She looked back down at the story, the last words her mother had ever written. Kurt had been so convinced that everything that happened after Jenny's death was her mother's fault. But now, looking at the phrases that had buoyed Eliza during years of loss, she wanted to shake him. It was Matt who had ruined their lives—who made the choice to hide Jenny's death. Her mom may have messed up when it came to her reporting methods, but at least her intentions were right: to tell people about Jenny, to remind them that she had lived. As she read the story for a third time, an idea started taking shape in her mind.

"You can keep that," Eliza said, standing and dusting off her skirt. "I think I have it memorized by now." She turned to go but twisted back at the last second, her skirt swirling gently in the sea breeze. "Your mom should start writing again," she said as if the decision were already made. "She was really good."

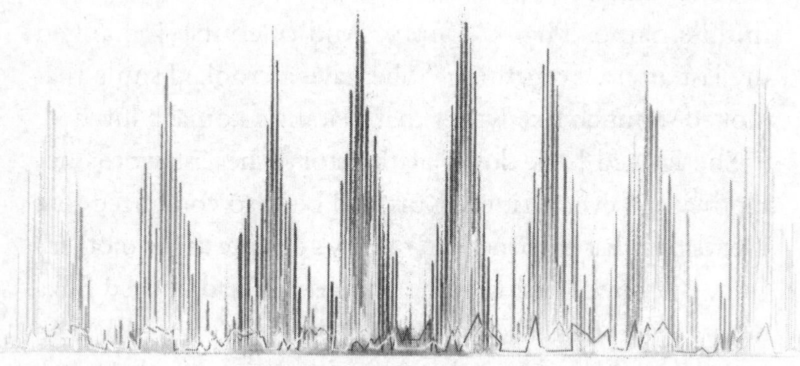

CHAPTER FORTY

When Natalie pushed through the door to the diner, her mother was waiting for her, arms crossed, cell phone clutched in her hand. "Where were you? I've been worried—"

Natalie cut Helen off with a hug that knocked her mother back on her heels, rocking back and forth with Helen in her arms, heedless of the convocation of mourners shoving pie and crudités into their mouths. "I love you, Mom," Natalie said into Helen's hair, which smelled like the grill and, underneath, her favorite bluebell-scented shampoo.

"What's all this for?" Helen asked, pulling away with her hands on Natalie's shoulders. She still had circles under her eyes, but she looked far more perky and awake than she had all summer. "I don't think I remember the last time you told me you loved me."

Natalie frowned, trying to remember herself. She was ashamed that the only instance she could clearly remember was when her mother grudgingly agreed that she could intern at the paper. She resolved then to fix that, to be more open with her mother even if it made her angry. The fact that her mom had been going to Mrs. Halsey for help had not only touched her but made her sad. They obviously needed to rebuild their bond, strengthen it, and the very least she could do was say three words.

"I'm sorry, Mom," she said finally, studying Helen's familiar face, ravaged only a bit by age and still distinctly *mom*. "I should tell you that more."

As Helen smiled, putting a soft hand to Natalie's cheek, the girl heard Sandy Tarver's distinctive bray from the booth on the left. Ordinarily, Natalie would have tuned her out, but she noticed that Sandy was studying her mom and her with performative bemusement.

"If that were my daughter, she'd be more than apologizing. She'd be groveling," she whispered loudly to Connie Fieldstone, who nodded wisely. "Too easy on her, always has been. And now look what happened."

Helen froze, her hand on Natalie's face. Her eyes grew flat and flinty, and from within sparked a crackling fire that Natalie had never seen before in her mother. Helen patted her daughter on the cheek, then whirled on Sandy, hands flying to her hips.

"Something you want to say to me, Sandy?" Helen said.

Sandy rocked back in her seat, curls bobbing around her

sharp face. They had an agreement: they allowed Helen to be part of the town, and Helen, in return, fed them and kept quiet. The other Garden Club ladies shot each other delighted looks, leaning forward in the booth, their eyes glazed with anticipation.

Sandy recovered quickly, folding her hands on her table. "I don't believe I was talking to you, Helen. Could you be a dear and get us all some more coffee? Oh! And some of that lovely apple pie." She smiled her poison smile and gestured with a dismissive hand. The other women stifled their nervous laughter with manicured fingers, all painted varying shades of soft pink. Only Sandy sported talons of red.

Helen crossed her arms in front of her chest and locked eyes with each Garden Club lady in turn, ending with Sandy's flat-blue ones. "Get out, Sandy," she said evenly, voice steady and firm. She opened the door, which jangled cheerfully, as if agreeing with Helen's command.

Sandy blinked, her pink mouth dropping open. "Excuse me?" she sputtered.

Helen jerked her head toward the entrance of the diner. "I said get out. I've had enough of you and your rumors. There's no place for that bullshit at my place, let alone at a memorial. You should be ashamed of yourself."

"Well, then, maybe there's no place for you in the Garden Club anymore," Sandy replied, her voice choked with tears and strained pride. Her lipstick was smudged, Natalie noticed, and her fake tan hid a tributary of fine lines around her mouth and eyes. Too much scowling, she supposed.

Helen laughed. "Some Garden Club. All you ladies do

is drink gin and gossip, anyway. You wouldn't know a perennial from your own skinny ass."

Natalie watched the proceedings with a gleeful smile on her face, an overwhelming feeling of respect for her mother blooming in her chest. For her writing, her strength. She also saw how much her mother had sacrificed for them to fit in, how much of her true self she had hidden away to appease the Sandy Tarvers of the world.

Sandy stood up, her black cocktail dress clinging to all her sharp curves, her hair vibrating with rage. "Fine. We'll go," she said stiffly, gesturing toward the rest of the ladies, who looked at each other with open dismay. They obviously didn't think they were included in the package when Helen had told Sandy to leave. Still, they stood en masse and exited the booth with their leader.

"We've been meaning to check out the new wine bar, anyway," Sandy crowed so that the rest of the diner could hear. "Your chardonnay tastes like cat piss." With that, they marched through the front door in a cloud of hair spray and expensive perfume.

The denizens of the diner stared after the women for a moment, and then someone—Natalie thought it might have been Katie—started a lone clap that grew into a thunder of applause.

Helen grinned at her daughter and shrugged. "That stuff comes out of a box, anyway. Who orders wine in a diner?"

"Fools, obviously," Natalie said gravely, then wrapped an arm around her mom. "Seems like everyone else agrees, too," she said, gesturing toward the mass of mourners, all applauding her mother, food momentarily forgotten.

Helen nodded, tears in her eyes, and bustled back toward the kitchen, her arm still around her daughter. "All you can do is what you think is right, Nat," she said, lifting a coffeepot.

A few of Natalie's former classmates had gathered in a booth, drinking endless cups of coffee and trading stories about Mrs. Halsey, but Natalie and Katie kept their distance. Not everyone was as direct with their ire toward Natalie as Sandy Tarver, but that didn't mean they wanted to hang out with a killer's ex. Even if they hadn't really dated.

Natalie was sitting with Katie, single-mindedly demolishing a giant plate of fries, when Jessica slid next to them, kitted out in a tight black dress. If she had been at the memorial Natalie hadn't seen her. Her hair bouncing and her face flawlessly made-up, Jessica looked far too perky to be in mourning.

"Hello, ladies," Jessica said, grinning. She pulled out her phone and placed it on the diner table, her black fingernails tapping at the screen. "Long time no see."

"We could keep that tradition going, you know. Indefinitely," Katie sneered, leaning back in the booth and crossing her arms like she was a very large man rather than a very small girl.

"You're hilarious," Jessica replied, not laughing. "But I think your friend here might be interested in what I'm about to propose."

"Me?" Natalie said with exaggerated confusion. "Nothing about you interests me, Jessica."

Katie tittered.

"Oh, I think you may be wrong about that," Jessica crowed. "It's about a job. And your ex, the murderer."

Natalie stilled. Sleep came hard these days, and when it did Kurt came back. Natalie was working hard to banish him, but she worried that he'd always be there when she closed her eyes, the thread that held together all the other nightmares. As if sensing what Natalie was thinking, Katie reached out and looped her hand through hers.

Jessica, seemingly unmoved by Natalie's gray face, pressed a button on her phone, and suddenly Kurt was there, at Jolly Times, accusing and crying and breaking down. Natalie clutched Katie's hand. "Turn it off," she choked out.

Jessica just smiled, letting the tape play, until Katie's hand shot across the table. Next thing Natalie knew, the phone was in pieces on the diner floor, and Katie was breathing hard. Jessica just blinked. "Come on, Katie. You know all about the cloud, honey. You're going to have to try harder than that."

"Where did you get that?" Natalie asked, practically whispering.

Jessica shrugged, eyeing the broken pieces of phone with an impassive face. Of course, money didn't matter to her. She'd just buy another. Meanwhile, Natalie had her mom's hand-me-down. "I followed you. Nice try with that Jack kid, though. Maybe next time hire someone to distract me who's not quite so obvious about it."

Natalie's mouth fell open, thinking of Jessica out in the darkness, listening to all the horrible things Kurt said. How could she think that was ethical journalism? How could she think that was right? "You just sat out there?" she spat, finally. "You didn't call the police or try to help or anything? What the fuck is *wrong* with you, Jessica?"

"Whatever." Jessica flapped a hand. "It's not like nature photographers fight off lions when they're about to chow down on a gazelle. And before you get too riled up, let me tell you what I want, and what *you'll* get out of it." Jessica apparently took Natalie's stymied silence—did she really just compare her to a *gazelle*?—as consent and soldiered forward. "The station is giving me my own podcast on Kurt, Jenny, the whole thing, *if* we can use this audio… Which is where you come in." She flashed some truly regrettable jazz hands.

"And why the ever-loving fuck would Natalie let you do that?" Katie asked, shoving fry after fry in her mouth. Natalie eyed her friend. This level of stress-eating seemed like a portent of more violence to come.

Jessica pushed the fries away in disgust. "Jesus Christ, you're going to throw up." Katie actually snarled. "Because," Jessica yelped, eyeing Natalie's nearly feral friend, "I'll give you a job at the station if you do," she said, speaking so quickly the words all ran together so as to be almost incomprehensible.

"You'll what?" Natalie asked. The diner was nearly empty now, and night had started to gather outside. It was getting cooler as the summer wore down; there were a few weeks to go until Katie and Natalie left for school. Soon autumn would come and bring its own rebirth through death and decay, and then winter would layer all the dark places, the haunted places, in pure ice and snow.

"It would be super entry-level and remote, obviously, but you would be working on real podcasts," Jessica said, calmer now. "I know that's your dream, Natalie. And all you'd have to do is let me use this tape. Maybe do an interview or two?"

Natalie sat for a moment, listening to the cicadas in the dark, her mom bustling around the back of the diner. She thought back to Jessica's horrible podcast introduction, the raging guitars, the ominous voice, then reached into her pocket and pulled out her mom's article. She had two choices here, and it was pretty obvious which one was right. Holding her mom's story, she looked up at Jessica, squaring her shoulders and meeting the other girl's eyes. "Sorry, Jessica. You can't use the tape, and you can't use me. Not anymore."

Jessica stared at Natalie, lip quivering and glossy hair trembling. "What the hell? This is a mistake, Natalie. And you're a goddamn idiot not to see that." She rose from her seat, her whole body vibrating.

Katie gave her a lazy little two finger wave. "Bye, now!" she trilled, gesturing toward the door.

Jessica gave the girls one last fiery look before she turned on her spiky heel—tripping just a little bit—and thundering out the door.

"Now that that's over with," Natalie said, turning toward Katie, her eyes glowing, "I have an actual good idea."

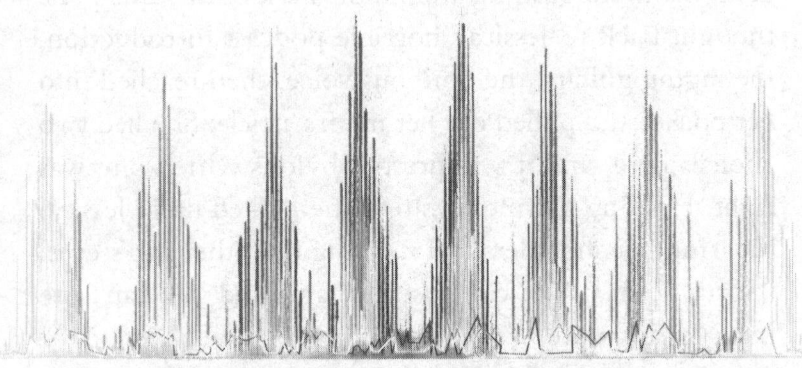

CHAPTER FORTY-ONE

Helen had agreed to shut down the diner for the first time in more than twenty years, but there was still a line around the block when Katie unlocked the door that morning. Ron K. Stackman stood at the threshold, dressed in a fine gray suit and a matching cap. He smiled nervously and peered into the diner, where Helen Temple was wiping the counters clean. The windows were open to let in the breeze, and he watched as a bumblebee drunkenly circled the ceiling.

Stackman took off his newsboy cap as he walked toward the table where Natalie was set up with a tape recorder and a pitcher of water and stood twisting it in his big hands before her. He smelled like woodsy aftershave, and although his hands were scrubbed clean, there was still earth rimmed under his fingernails, as if he had stopped to plant a rosebush on the way over.

"Hey, Ron, you can sit down if you want to," Natalie said, gesturing toward a folding chair. Her blond hair was cut to her chin: she had decided it was time to let go of its unruly length. To show her face instead of hiding. "Do you want some coffee?" she asked Stackman.

Ron nodded, and Katie went off to get the pot. She had taken to wearing the ridiculous neon-yellow fanny pack everywhere, and today it was brimming with sugar packets and individual creamers. She had dubbed herself Natalie's official Coffee Bitch/Engineer and requested that she be listed as such in the credits of her friend's as-yet-unnamed podcast.

"I don't know why I'm so nervous." Ron cleared his throat, taking a grateful sip of coffee as Katie settled herself next to Natalie and fiddled with the recorder and the mic in turn. "I guess I just never thought I'd be in a podcast, you know? And I'm up first, too! There's such a huge line out there." He jutted a thumb over his shoulder.

Through the plate-glass window, Natalie could see Jonathan waiting, a smile on his face. And behind him there were Lucy and Mr. Sprouse, and behind them a snaking line of citizens of both East and West Ferry.

Natalie smiled. "Don't worry, you'll be great. And I'm guessing you knew Mrs. Halsey better than most of those people, anyway." She gestured at the line. "That's why I wanted to make sure you got enough time to talk."

Ron smiled. "So this whole show, it's just going to be about her and Bill? Not what—" He broke off and dashed a tear from his cheek. "Not what happened?"

"Yes, it's just about them," Natalie said, picking up a pencil and jotting down Stackman's name. "So why don't you start off by telling me about the first time you saw Lynn Halsey."

Ron leaned forward toward the mic and started to talk, and Natalie listened close, letting his recollection of a young Lynn in her leather jacket and colorful shoes filter through her brain. The line grew longer outside as the day wore on, and Natalie scrawled name after name into her notebook. The whole town filled the streets that day in August, and as the day grew long and the fireflies blinked to brightness, on everyone's lips were memories—sweet, sad, and alive.

After the last Ferry citizen headed off into the evening, Katie settled herself behind the microphone, turning it, at last, toward Natalie. "Okay, Nat, you're up," she said, pressing the Record button for the last time that night.

Natalie stared at the red light, thinking back to that day, months ago, when she had painted the floor red with ketchup. When she had heard that her favorite teacher, her friend, had been taken from her. Tears threatened to spill down her cheeks, but instead, she took herself further back. To that day in the hallway when her life had changed. She parted her lips, let the words come without filter.

"My name is Natalie Temple, and I met Lynn Halsey when I needed her most. When I was sad and lost. When I didn't understand what a story was. She pulled me aside and showed me the way. And I'll always be grateful. I'll always remember the way she cared, the way she lived."

*****

ACKNOWLEDGMENTS

Writing a book is a maddening, lonely process, and you often feel like you're yelling into an ether no one cares to visit. As such, I need to thank all the people who made me feel like I wasn't doing so in vain.

Thanks, first, to my amazing agent, Dana Murphy, who, upon first meeting me, told me she only signed on to books she'd get in a bar fight over. Thank you for having my back. And thanks for putting up with my not-so-subtle *Just checking in!* emails. Thanks, too, to my editor, Rebecca Kuss, whose excitement over this book made *me* excited. Her edits have been invaluable, and her enthusiasm is contagious. Much gratitude to the entire Inkyard team, who took a chance on *Killing Time.*

My family is also owed a wealth of gratitude that I will never be able to fully express. To my mom (whose karate prowess definitely inspired Helen), thanks for telling me I could write a book someday. To my dad, thank you for your endless and steady support. Lara, my sister, thank you for our childhood and years of editorial notes. To my niece, Imogen, maybe someday you can read this? When you're eighteen, at least. Gratitude is also owed to my extended family—my brother-in-law, Doug, my mother-in-law,

Regina, and my aunt-in-law(?) Holly. Thanks as well to the Enos family, the Dakos family, and the Nedds family.

Thanks, as well, to the friends who have supported me over the years: Radhika Marya, Stephanie Feuer, Leah Konen, Ashley Halsey (Mrs. Halsey's namesake as a nod to our youth), Nimai Larson, Heather Hanselman, Hanady Kader, and the crew at *Rolling Stone*. And, of course, thank you to the true-crime writers and podcasters who have brought humanity to the genre.

Finally, endless thanks to Morgan, my best friend and biggest cheerleader. I'm eternally proud of you, and I love you more than the universe.